ONE BIG BED

ALSO BY JOHN KRICH

A Totally Free Man

Bump City

Chicago Is

Music in Every Room

JOHN KRICH

ONE BIG BED

McGRAW-HILL BOOK COMPANY
New York St. Louis San Francisco Hamburg
Mexico Toronto

Earlier versions of some passages contained in this book have appeared in *Commentary, City Miner, East Bay Express, Bump City* (City Miner Books), *Chicago Is* (Legatoria Piazzesi/Eureka Editions), *Sweet Little Sixteen* (Rowohlt Verlag).

1 2 3 4 5 6 7 8 9 DOC DOC 8 7 6

ISBN 0-07-035408-1

LIBRARY OF CONGRESS CATALOGING-IN-PUBLICATION DATA

Krich, John, 1951–
One big bed.
I. Title.
PS3561.R47505 1986 813′.54 86-7397
ISBN 0-07-035408-1

Book design by Kathryn Parise.

This one is for the sounding board:
Aron, Mike, A.M., Dad

ONE BIG BED

". . . love comes empty-handed; the eternal proletariat . . ."

—Norman O. Brown

COMING DETRACTIONS

9:27 p.m. Everyone's story begins and ends in the dark.

Pray for darkness. If I don't, I may never find my way back to the Pacific Rim Cinematheque. Consigned to the basement of a cubistic bunker, camouflaged by a sculpture garden, this museum screening room is a curatorial afterthought. Like hired help, the movies have been let in by the back door. Berkeley's cineastes, not unlike sodomites, are forced to get what they need via the rear entrance. Our magic lantern's muted in the aesthetic grayness of jutting wings weighty as art, suspect as a concrete house of cards. No swirl of marquee bulbs lures us toward the picture show. A sole cement stanchion bears the nightly schedule, hand-calligraphed on rice paper: René Clair—*Le Quatorze Juillet*. 7:30, 9:45.

"Is movie in American?"

"Subtitles. Can you read them?"

"Bad boy! Of course, I read. I ask because I do not like silent movie."

"Me neither."

"I like art be noisy. Rock 'n' roll. Twentieth century very noisy."

"No electric guitars in this one. Just a few scratchy renditions of *La Marseillaise.*"

"Does that mean it new wave?"

"I think you'd probably call it very, very old wave."

"Too many waves, no? More waves in art than in ocean!"

My escort's seen-it-all toughness is see-through enough to be touching, and possibly the only attribute we have in common. For I, too, wear more disillusionment on my sleeve than I've earned. I'd better seize this moment before my air of experience turns downright rank—exploit that delicate juncture where I can play the "older man" with women not all that much younger. How I'd like to sit this schoolgirl on my knee and instruct her in the ways of this world! So what if she's a printmaker who gushes over Christo's running fence and wears a vinyl jumpsuit instead of knee socks? That she claims fluency in two cultures? Or that her hair's shaved to the skull behind one ear and curls down her neck in one raven strand while mine's in auburn bunches less combed than made to heel?

Pray for darkness so we can't examine each other too closely. Him: with white linen jacket, the kind everyone buys on their first traipse through Italia, worn in homage to Cinecitta; tasteful checked shirt tastefully unbuttoned to mid-chest; pressed blue jeans, pointy canvas shoes. Her: in a one-piece sack that looks as if it's been sewn from a surplus parachute, with its single tantalizing zipper guarded ineffectually by a striped Guatemalan scarf, an outer wrap that's reversible felt, black on one side, saffron on the other, the high-fashion cloak of some Taoist monk; a self-conscious polyglot from straw planter's hat to translucent red plastic sandals, black toenail polish. Since this downstairs neighbor accepted my impromptu invitation, I've been trying to figure out whether her colors betoken some superstition, ideology, or an admiration for Kandinsky. Or does this artist mean to project a vision of man as the quick-change artist who's unaffected underneath? As for me—for a number of years now, I've been working on a face with character.

"What again we celebrate? Not your birthday maybe?"

Pray for darkness because I'm getting too old for first dates. After a day like this, I feel too old for first anythings.

"It's the start of the French Revolution."

"And how come you observing other country's holidays?"

"Movie reviewers need all the holidays they can get."

"Of course, tough work." She winks. "But you are not being French, no?"

"*Oui, oui.* My real name's Martin Poivre. They changed it on Ellis Island."

My date doesn't get the joke, since she herself is too soon off the boat. "I have two sets of names: Daphne Woo is American legal, other is Chinese top secret."

"I'll coax it out of you. I have my methods."

"When I choose, I tell. After I decide to come out of room."

"The ladies'?"

"Not nice! I show you room, in all my silkscreens. Sometimes a stair lead out of the room, sometimes window starting to open. I use art to climb out of room. Until then, I belong two places. I make myself whatever I like."

"An internationalist!"

"A big mix-up."

"Aren't we all?"

"Oh no, you total American. You complete, finished mix-up."

"Then that's why I got this day backwards. Instead of letting the prisoners out of jail, me and a few pals managed to let ourselves in . . ."

Pray for darkness because I can only see ghosts.

"Small world, Pepper man!" This one lurks at the sculpture patch portals, offering his customary siren song. "It's a small world."

In the years since we met at Steffens College, we've never agreed about anything, never argued, never actually been friends, and yet, in this small world, coincidence takes the place of affection. It's enough for Dan Herbst that both our parents were Communists in the thirties, that we both lived in the same dormitory, both favored the same strength of Italian coffee. Dissent isn't possible with him. His speech is subpoena: he expects full compliance.

"What brings you out on a Saturday night?" Not simply a movie, that would be too frivolous for Herbst. Ideologically unapproved. Poised in the night with his brow thrust ever upwards, his hair one bristling wave, Dan is the museum's unwitting watchdog, a doorman in denim. He carries no whistle, just a ream of fresh leaflets.

"Propaganda. Bombardin' the intelligentsia."

"A cushy assignment." They're all cushy in the Red League, a Trotskyist sect that's become Herbst's latest hobby horse—following close upon the hoofmarks of his aborted career as a "people's disc jockey." From prior Herbstian diatribes, I've learned that this group targets its efforts toward the partially converted and mostly affluent. They champion a program which sends agitators to film openings and benefit dances rather than coal mines. This strategic emphasis is justified in tomes of theory about the replacement of blue collar with silk collar and the historic role of the "new working class." I'm never certain if anyone I know is a member of this class, since so few of them seem to be working.

"Can't beat the hours," Herbst is willing to concede. "Just think! A month ago, I was bourgeois through and through. Today, I'm totally cool people."

I don't doubt him, though I've barely gone through a change of clothes since last month. Nor do I remind him of similar claims made at the crest of his Jewish black nationalist phase, preceded by his LSD visionary phase, which came on the heels of his back-to-nature phase, overlapping his I'm-not-really-a-student student phase.

Squinting through shard-thick lenses, the wire frames atilt, Herbst sidles up closer. "Pepper man, The League's analysis is infectious. Depression, fascism, war—we've got to stop the cycle. Everybody's doin' it."

Herbst makes his politics sound like a dance craze: "The Mashed Potatoes" or "The Locomotion." The League's latest "line" is a ditty to be spun, a favorite r. 'n' b. tune from his forty-five collection. "The organization saved me from my bad self, like it could save you."

"But what can a film critic do for the cause? Organize the usherettes?"

"He can quit bein' a critic and become a comrade." Herbst can leaflet and castigate at the same time. "You know it better than anyone. There are no individual solutions."

With that, Herbst admits to his own. "Anyway, I'm on the move, son. Party promotion, you know. Headed for the Big Three."

"Big Three?"

"Yeah. That's Chitown, the Apple, or El Lay. Where the industrial proletariat does its industrial-strength thing. This town's too soft. No militancy."

"But you've never lived anywhere else."

"I heard that. I think it's my Oedipus complex."

"Is The League good for that, too?"

"You bet, bro'. Time to get out of the womb. Pretty soon, this red baby will throw away his diapers! You should try it sometime!"

"Red diaper babies never grow up. They just lose their colic. . . ."

"Not me. I'll be cruisin' the funky streets of the Big Three, hangin' out in blues bars, rappin' on war and fascism, helpin' to build the labor party. I'll be so totally cool, it'll be cold . . ."

Pausing in his rhapsody, Herbst finally notices Daphne. "Who's this, Pepper man?" He tucks the leaflets under an arm, pats down his curly mop and preens. "Not your latest recruit?"

"No, I volunteer." Bless her heart. "But for what?"

"For the cause of vacillation and latent careerist hustlerism. The hallmarks of the Pepperist life-style."

"Thanks, Herbst. It always helps to have old friends."

"Old friends are just another politburo. Remember all, forgive nothing. Like you an' that squeaker . . . what was her name?"

"Missy."

"Yeah, you an' squeaky parted company first, then me an' Janet —did you know she came out?—then Annie, the bovine one, an' that hopeless individualist Ayer. The higher the consciousness, the quicker the split." I'm not sure if I want to accept this competitive model or the backhanded kudos that go with it. "Speaking of which, what happened to you an' Annie?"

"We're all through reassessing."

"As in baby, won't you reassess me all night long?"

"As in the long breakup method."

"Ah, yes! The fabled quicksand of heterosexuality! You know Berkeley's version of a hot date? Six months of telephone networking and you get to go to lunch. I went gay just in time."

For what, I want to ask like Daphne, but Herbst shoos us away with copies of his handout. "Move along now, children. I'm neglecting my duties. Time to pester some more dilettantes, some moronic old hippies. . . . Seein' the same flicks year after year, sitting in the same Cafe Depressos, combin' the same shelves of the same bookstores. Do you think they'll ever find what they're after?"

I have no answer, except that I keep running into Herbst at those flicks and cafes.

"Come on, volunteer," I urge Daphne. "It's getting late."

"Later than you think, my man!" Since Herbst never laughs, it's hard to tell when he's giving up on a gag. "Watch out for this longtime symp!"

"I watch," Daphne promises. "But what is symp?"

"A cat who hoards contradictions the way some people hoard pennies. Much too highly evolved for happiness!"

Pray for darkness because happiness is the trick I keep coming here to perfect: a matter of allowing the segments of brightness to bleed over the black, believing each radiant frame can obliterate the emptiness that follows.

In line for my pair of comp tickets, Daphne and I pass Herbst's leaflet back and forth. It's an unpunctuated rant, swamping both sides of the page in six-point type.

"How we can read this in a movie?"

"You're supposed to decide the movie can wait."

"Until when?" The handout does not answer, but addresses itself to several stirring imbroglios into which The League has belly flopped in an attempt to make an immediate splash. Just to provoke Berkeley's ire, they've come out in *favor* of nuclear power and against ahistorical "eco freaks"; for good measure, they offer strident support for the Red Army's incursion into Afghanistan, branding it a long overdue, if somewhat drastic, means of removing the veil from Afghan women. Surprisingly, there's nothing on the sheet that refers to this day's revolutionary significance. No attempt whatsoever by The League to take credit for the Bastille's storming.

"Maybe none of their members were there."

"Very good," I compliment Daphne, dropping the leaflet in the first museum can. "You're getting the hang of it."

"Very bad! I wanted that!"

"Sorry, I should have given you a longer crack at it."

"No to read. For collage."

"The Drowning of Berkeley in a Tidal Wave of Words."

"Oh, no. I title everything 'Untitled.' I am not liking labels. Already enough things in the world have names."

I want to tell her that I'm quite prepared to save her a lifetime supply of scraps and ticket stubs. Instead, I ask, "Don't you want to know more about the film?" Or me?

"Oh no! Please don't give away! I love surprise end!"

"I've never caught this one, believe it or not. The calendar calls it 'the most Parisian film ever made.' "

"That mean it come with baguette, and maybe rasperry jelly jam? Can be nice for starving artist."

"Everyone gets a bottle of *vin ordinaire* . . ."

Pray for darkness because the only thing that the movies cannot do for me is eat. The lobby outside the screening room reeks of *boeuf bourgignon*. The museum cafe, known as "Eat Your Art Out," has set aside its usual, humble fare: fettuccini Fellini, quiche Renoir, raw tuna Ozu, carrot cake Costa-Gavras. In honor of the date, the restaurant puts out a full-course *Guide Michelin* spread.

"Shouldn't they be serving prison gruel?"

"Bad boy! I think you like very much to dislike."

"I'm allowed to dislike that place. I used to work there."

"You, work? I thought never."

"It was convenient for my reviewing, and only six hours a week. At four dollars an hour—plus all the day-old bagels I could carry. I was one of the people who tried to organize a union."

"You *organize*?"

"It died when they gave us a dental plan. But we did get rid of the microwave oven."

"Very good. Microwave bad!"

"The employees didn't want to risk their gonads heating blueberry muffins. It was the most memorable political victory of my life."

"You *political*?"

Pray for darkness because there's no better training ground for a moviegoer than politics, that supreme form of putting other people's illusions ahead of one's own. What have mine earned me? Lifetime java privileges at the cafe—gained by threading my way through the tables, which are decked out tonight in candelabras and tricolor tablecloths. Behind the counter, a newly hired scullion with purple-streaked hair looks up from the tureen of *soupe à l'oignon* (vegetarian broth) and recognizes me as an honored alumnus of the minimum-wage demimonde. She lets me pour out a couple of Viennese blends to go, swipe a macadamia blondie and some chocolate chip rugelach. In the days when I manned the steam tables, I'd hear patrons admiring my latest piece on *film noir* as American confessional, while barking at me to fetch another round of Chablis. The first ten times, this scene was amusing—after all, not everyone gets to play the Invisible Man! Later, it only increased my sense of personal discongruity, of what Herbst might call my "combined and uneven development." There were moments at the cafe when my legs seemed to be sliding out from under me—as if the chasm between my two lives was widening. Still, I never let any of the customers in on my identity. Eat your art out, loyal readership!

Have I really grown up in order to advise Berkeley on its leisure dollar's worth in escapism? But Mommy, I wanted to be a fireman! Or an arsonist! Not the resident interpreter of wide-screen iconography for the free newspaper that dares to call itself *The Last Word*, which provides just that on the wares of croissant makers and starving bluesmen, Cajun chefs and low-budget *auteurs*. In cinephile circles, my name's probably influential as any of the diners, including most of the university film department and their brood of tweedy kids. One of them complains about being "quiched-out." I overhear a genuine Frenchman at a corner table speaking the *gastronome*'s tongue. What's the difference between a gourmet and a gourmand anyway? A gaffer and a go-fer? I tiptoe out like a busboy with my styrofoam freebies. Pray for darkness before some unleashed editor blows my cover.

I'm relieved to get back to Daphne, who's saving our place in line for the second show. We file down the hospital sterile galleries past a row of classic promo posters. The best Hollywood had to offer: *God Is My Co-Pilot, The Return of the Cat People, I Married a Ghost, One Evening in Rio.* And what about *One Evening in Berkeley*? Does so much happen in American movies because so little happens to Americans? At what exact moment in the twentieth century did real life become more trite than the imagination? I'm aching to ask Daphne any of the above, but refrain from exposing her so soon to this continuous internal soundtrack of mine. Better to dam up my stream of "Pepperisms."

"Mmm. Nice colors." Daphne examines the posters. "Blue-black, green-blue, red-orange."

"I guess I'm old-fashioned. I read the words. And I want the people in the posters to be us."

"You wanting too much! You my first pure white boy."

Oh no! I never thought I'd have to uphold the honor of the race —at least not that race.

"And what are you?"

"Nothing yet. I just a machine. For model clothes. For seeing maybe."

"Come on, my machine. Time to adjust to the dark."

"I adjust. I go with all colors." Then she asks, "What do critics like to do in the dark?"

Pray for darkness so I can show her what critics *really* like to do there. Too bad necking's been banned in this hall—along with popcorn. In the name of high art, the museum enforces a purity that's almost as stark as real life. My new escort and I can't tiptoe in through some formerly opulent lobby, then slink down threadbare auditorium slopes, treading stealthily on a trail of strewn Crackerjacks, clutching our survivalist supply of Good and Plenty, feeling our way toward anonymity. No matinee matrons patrol here, seeking truants with their flashlights; overhead, glaring spots instead of chandeliers. The aisles are wide for wheelchair access; the seats are rigid and Danish, tasteful as they are uncomfortable; their upholstery moves from self-righteous red to cosmic purple in subtle gradiants, suggesting we make a statement by where we plop. The screen itself is a matte forehead, unprettified by tasseled bangs. No fantasy figures dot the draping, which is cortege black from ceiling to floor. All the illicitness has been taken out of our pilgrimage.

And how about some coming attractions? I can do without melted lard residue on my fingers, forgo Jujyfruits or *amaretti*—but I can't bear getting transported cold, without stages, from my own main event into the selected feature. Actually, I prefer those blustering come-ons, those absurd reductions of theme, to almost anything full-length that follows. We should all have our own trailers: where the future's been trimmed to a single frame of passion, followed by one tableau of anguish, the only embrace that braces and the only snips of dialogue that tell. Yes, compression can do wonders for the dreariest of narratives! See! Sharon Smith lose her cherry! Never before on the silver screen! Jimmy Jones ask for a raise! Gasp in amazement! Pete Peters barfs up his lunch! Cringe in horror! Bring the whole family! Brought to you by the world reigning master of suspense/chuckles/melodrama. No one will be admitted during the surprise ending! Thrill! Gawk! Amaze! What is plot but a grinder? And all of us, meat. So shove us right through those obvious beginnings, middles and ends. Every life, like every film, must have at least ten or twenty good seconds.

Instead, we're the ones who're on view. That's the trouble with these aisles raked for optimal lines of vision, these bleachers scrupulously maintained through endowment funding, this trove of celluloid lit indiscreetly as any bank vault. Entering the cinematheque at screen level, Daphne and I have to run a carpeted gauntlet. Is this what it's like to take a new steady into the nickelodeon in some Bible Belt town? Scaling the rafters, I wonder if anyone is commenting on my brightly bedecked consort. "Finally landed hisself a young 'un!" The lowest seats are claimed by an informal *kaffeeklatsch* of retirees. These old folks show up at practically every program, whether it's the Kuchar Brothers' rambles in obscenity or a retrospective of early Bulgarian epics. There's a few bald gents in suspenders, dapper if lame, accompanied by several intellectual bag ladies indigenous to this area, who let their white locks grow out in long squaw waves, wear peasant skirts, carry Nepalese handbags. Yet there's a certain logic, even nobility, to spending the "golden years" traveling the globe via movies. Not so when matinees extinguish one's youth.

Having paid their good money to go into the dark, everyone's forced to spend these few minutes examining faces that look more etched with disappointment at every show. Though I can't help sneaking one brief pan of seats, I dare not linger over the reclining riot of bearded faces or beaded torsos, lest I recognize too many from the first Black Studies Strike picket line, the antidraft mobilizations, the Panther Defense Committee, the *Barb* or the *Tribe*, from the Weather Collectives, the Free Speech Movement and the Lesbian Mothers and the Death-to-the-Shah Association and the Sexual Freedom League and the Insane Liberation Front. Most of what's left of the prematurely retired New Left has come out on this nostalgic date, roused as ever by symbolism. These days, they're outnumbered by a single fraternity down the block and kick up far less of a ruckus. And what's worse about seeing all of them is that they see me and will continue to see me, because I share their need to enter a world where only movies have to move, talkies talk, and everyone else is spared further effort.

Faced with a dull screen that mirrors our own listlessness, there's nothing left to do but supplicate on behalf of a quick and merciful fade. Pray for darkness so I can turn this herding together into a most private act. If I'd made it to Commissar of Culture, I'd have instituted a law banning all chatting, tittering, coughing, squirming, sneezing, whining once a film's under way. The death penalty for feckless laughter and the unwarranted unwrapping of silver foil. If the head in front's obstructive, off with it! That's justice in the tradition of the Bastille.

"You coming here always?"

"I live here." And what kind of life is that for anyone to join?

"Like me, in my studio."

"Except that I don't make anything." Just whip out my battery-lit pen and steno notebook. Pray for darkness because, like some desert creature, confined to an aridity of my own making, I've learned to thrive where others grope. Alerted by an artificial change in atmosphere, I forage and find sustenance. And just when no one else can see, I'm at my best; when they're of the least use, I stumble upon my convictions.

"You make understanding for everyone. You well known in this room!"

Which is why I must insist upon imminent darkness. Wouldn't you, if the only two women with whom you'd had carnal relations within recent memory were making their way up the aisle?

"Friends?" This artiste is too all-seeing for her own good.

"No such thing in Berkeley. Only former coconspirators, temporary allies."

"I see. Too many principles. That make room very stuffy."

Pray for darkness so that the two of us can remain here, insulated from the aphrodisiac effects of summer nights in this university town where the eucalyptus go on smelling sweetly, waiting to be turned into coughdrops.

"But you looking maybe for woman-type friends?"

What makes her think there are any of those in these parts? It is only this critic's educated guess that, among certain backward sectors, courtship and mating have proceeded unabated. I'd have never encountered the two providers of random verification now entering the screening room had all of us not been in disguise. What am I supposed to make of the fact that my only recent successes have come while wearing a mask? The only time men and women exchange phone numbers in this town is at Halloween. Climbing into gorilla outfits, how we wish to be noticed for "our true selves"! There's Little Bo Peep now, who turned out to be an aspiring actress and accomplished hysteric, living in one perpetual hot flash, desperate for a protector and apparently babies, since she perfected a method for tearing condoms with her innermost pincers; and bow before Madame Butterfly, actually a *zaftig* folk singer with Medusa curls, who strummed paeans to sisterhood and silk-spinners before clutching me to her heaving chest and confessing an irresistible desire for men who wore starched shirts like her father's.

Oh, the claim to love women! But I also love cheesecake, samba, Ozu, nights in the streets of foreign cities. And I do not do without them. Somehow I get my fill. But where the challenge was once learning to respect females by letting go, the challenge is finding a female whom I can respect enough to grab. Have they left me too well schooled in a politically justified heartlessness? I know just how these two must feel. I'm nodding toward each of them in turn, trying to vary the intensity of my contrition. I don't want either to think they've played the same cameo role. I've got to distribute recognition for meritorious service where I cannot offer the constancy they'd have preferred. I feel obliged to let them know that I haven't erased the memory of our few nights' explorations, while hoping they don't recall too much. Let's have darkness so this pair won't have time to compare bedroom data, their limited Kinsey survey, concerning favored positions, lobe-nibbling propensities, or the speeches I fed both about my preoccupation with the starving masses of Namibia as an excuse for my undisguisable detachment from the physical act. Bring the darkness before their whispers reach the next potential victim beside me, willing and probably multi-orgasmic.

Pray for darkness because going to the movies is no different from going to bed. Next to you, in the dark, it could be anyone. But it never is just anyone. I've got to steal a last peek at Daphne. Her profile is magnificently uncomplicated: pert nose, earnest chin, high cheekbones rounded enough to make turrets for the eyes. An altogether noble package, oozing good health despite her best efforts at degeneracy. She faces forward with an unaffected greed for experience and can't seem to help being exactly who she is. Why can't I just leave her as I've found her? By the time I'm through, she'll be scratching her head and clutching her gut. She may even learn to doubt herself. Now she turns in time to catch me inspecting her charcoal suggestions of eyebrows, that arch and rise with unverbalized epiphanies. Daphne gets her first full frontal view of my wonder, along with accompanying trepidations, and, reacting quick as a cornerback, pats me on the nose with a single finger.

I shudder at her touch. Too soon, so soon, she's hit a nerve that I felt confident was no longer exposed. Luckily, Daphne returns her gaze filmward—ever expectant, ever rapturous. She does her impression of Donna Reed's cuddly adulation for Jimmy Stewart in *It's a Wonderful Life*. I wish someone would give me that wonderful look. Perhaps the silver screen is the beneficiary of such attentions because it cannot flinch or respond. That's the secret: refrain from sneaking a gaze back, keep your fans from knowing how much more you need them than they need you. Want something too much and you'll never get it—that's well known. But there's nothing yet known to stop the wanting.

Like a moth, fluttering toward the light of some idealized object—that's the other aspect of this mole who burrows into the darkness. My deepest urge, born of emotional and ideological conditioning, is to play the victim. No wonder I've stopped playing this courtship game altogether! Whether it's a matter of emotions or principles, I'm only willing to volunteer when the cause will make me feel more worthy. And what cause is worth anything unless it requires self-denial, or better yet, martyrdom?

There was a night when I actually hoped the darkness could be forever forestalled—while waiting for Missy to meet me at that late showing of *Umberto D.* What made me think that she would always show up in the seat next to mine? Why did I insist upon the attendance of that one, anointed coviewer? And how come I couldn't sense that she'd found other entertainment? How could that self-appointed expert on the world's injustice have assumed that he was somehow exempt?

I don't know what was wrong with me then, but whatever it was, it's not the same thing that's wrong with me now. At twenty, I enlisted devotedly in impossible causes. There was Missy and there was "the revolution." I loved both of them slavishly, uncritically. How else can it be with first loves? Past thirty, most everything has become possible, while little seems worthy of sustained devotion. Where I was once the guaranteed sold seat on the ride to any protest, now I've got a free pass to ride this favored aisle seat—on the left side (always to the left!), at the back of the theater (the nearest I ever got to the back of the bus). Where I strode toward a realm of perpetual light, blinded by the glare of uncontested truths, I now trust only in the revelations that come between flickerings. At the end of a day that marks the end of a decade since the decade I thought would never end, I'm as much in the dark as when I began.

9:46 p.m. At last, the black draping pulled tight, the welcome dissolve under way. My prayers answered! That's easy when your God is only as far away as the nearest projectionist's booth. So twist your dimmers, align teeth to sprockets, All-Illumining One! Rescue us, quick-stepping movies! Sweep us away, disciplined blur! Deliver us unto the blindness that makes us open our eyes.

I'm disappointed before the credits are through. I don't want this version, or any version, of *le quatorze* to carry a seal of approval from some French board of censors. My Fourteenth wasn't grainy, on low contrast stock, but sun-washed in California cinemascope. Shot entirely on location, under a cloudless scenarist's sky. Without script, just plenty of hand-held vérité. The prisoners in my movie wore orange monkey suits that read "Fort Co. Jail," but I'll settle now for a view of that thinking man's penitentiary, that jail among jails, that Sing Sing à la 1789. Whither Le Marais, the Jacobins and the *sans-culottes*?

Like the anniversary I've just been through, there are plenty of twists in plot up ahead—but harmless, so fatally right. The men in flat caps are too jaunty, the women in gingham aprons too sturdily picturesque. The forces of evil are a snap to spot with their five o'clock shadows—evil is ever unshaven—while the tipsy, slumming millionaires are conspicuous in their top hats. A cabbie serves as one-man Greek chorus, spouting street philosophy and emitting Gallic grunts. Guileless ingenue and faultless beau try to pull themselves up by the bootstraps when it's obvious that nobody in this film can afford boots. Is there anything for my use in these brisk montages of the eternally buoyant *peuple*? How can a studio approximate the City of Light? I don't know how to stroll around this *arrondissement*. In these establishing shots of dimpled burgher's daughters hanging out tricolors in place of laundry across the facades of Parisian walk-ups, I glimpse not a blush of self-consciousness, no confusion of roles. The cobblestones are freshly washed, the *boulangeries* well stocked, the storm clouds painted, the production values suffused with prewar innocence.

What can I make of a work of art that harkens back to a time when the quotidian was still worthy of being sentimentalized? When we thought we knew what a work of art was for, when we thought we knew what daily life was for. When men were men, when women were women, when *amour* was *amour*, when proletarians were proletarians, when cops were cops, when croissants were croissants, when Paris was Paris, when holidays were holidays, when a gavotte was a gavotte and a rondelay a rondelay, when poverty was poverty (only more jolly), when injustice was injustice, when crime was crime, when wars were wars, vendettas vendettas, when blood was blood, when grief was grief, when censors were censors, when movies were movies, when black-and-white was black-and-white (not a loss of print quality), when a happy ending was a happy ending, when laughter was laughter, when pathos wasn't pathetic, when lust was lusty, when purity was pure, when pals were pals, when wine was wine, when neighborhoods were neighborhoods, when dirty laundry was dirty laundry, when dusk was dusk, when bed was bed, when Holy Communion was Holy Communion, when marriage was marriage, when music was music, when stars were stars, when time was time, when all was right with the world was all right with the world. This Bastille Day is not my Bastille Day.

BEGINNINGS

6:56 a.m. History is the loudest alarm clock.

Bastille Day again and we're all still in jail. Or should I say we're in bed? The one I'm in now is much too big. California King, they call it, but I don't feel like one. My entire court is this Japanese cushion, covered with a print of cranes that soar like my longings. Made of all-natural fiber, it absorbs my secretions, becomes naturally dampened and hardened like me, and like me, must occasionally be left to dry out in the sun. My fold-up mattress is popular because it's primitive, spine-stiffening and a clever space-saver, one more means of lowering expectations. Lately, I've been attempting to lower mine to the point where nothing can possibly disappoint. To the point where I positively yearn to feel cramped, not to mention entwined. Luckily, this bed's portable as a street vendor's stock, transferable at the first decent offer. In the daytime, it folds into a kneeling cotton Buddha. At night, it feels vast and underpopulated as the Mongol steppes.

The explanation for mornings like this can be found in the night before and the night before that. It takes time to travel from surfeit to scarcity, from free love to no love! Having once had so many bodies beside me, it seems that one just won't do. So come on, Big Mac! Shake out the communal cobwebs! Rip the sheets off our solitude! Abandon pillow perches all! In a few hours, at my insistence, we'll try to climb back into our purposeful slumber. Once again, and at my insistence, I'll have to face that one peer group which forms the murky mirror wherein I see my true face. No wonder I'd like some more greedy shut-eye, an hour more of beauty rest to smooth over the years.

The Big Q. In dawn of a more hopeful day, there was always some noble excuse to get out of bed. Those last vigils began with the romance of waking early—perhaps as early as the prisoners themselves! And what better replacement for missed sleep was there than the conspiratorial exhilaration of sneaking toward a demonstration's assembly point while the powers-that-be drowsed? It didn't seem to matter that Martin's premature rising this time was merely for the sake of standing witness. Or that each week, as the trials dragged on, there were fewer and fewer cars making the trip.

It had become a rule of thumb in the Movement: a hundred promises, a dozen drivers. That last time, Martin hopped into a beat-up Volvo wagon, with its stacks of leaflets hogging the cargo space. Several large mutts shared the pilgrimage, along with the obligatory medic. Once, everyone had sang, had known the same songs: from "Bandiera Rossa" to "The Revolution Is For The Young," with its inexplicable second line, "That's why we dig Kim Il Sung." Now the trip was made in silence. Where they were going, you kept your peace—assuming you had any peace left to keep.

And there it was, this purposely inconvenient destination, at the end of a long bridge over the Bay's sublime blue. Furry tips of island, too small to have been built upon, interrupted the water. The surrounding hills were the foreheads of drowned men. Flat tankers passed under the bridge, its silver span self-cleaning as a cat. Martin always noticed how clean San Quentin looked, stationed on its sea promontory, how sand-blasted the khaki turrets! Once, quiet beaches must have graced this point, now capped with a condom of asphalt held tight by barbed wire.

They formed a line outside the main gate, waited in an orderly fashion for the chance to be disorderly. A revolution, they'd learned, involved lots of waiting. Also frisking, by the warden's boys, as they were ushered through the narrow guardhouse and onto golf carts that took them to what had once been the prisoners' recreation hall. Pistol-laden officers herded them into a penitentiary mock-up of a Perry Mason set: four rows of collapsible chairs, several tables and a podium. Just one look and those in attendance felt they'd made their point. This kind of justice clearly had something to hide. Too bad they made the point only to themselves.

Too bad they had to rise for the stern judge. But that meant they soon got to see their prisoner-for-a-day. The last morning, Martin was very lucky, if you could use the word lucky in here. The plaintiff was a Movement "name," who still bore the wounds of his heralded deed. It didn't matter that he was such a small man, almost a miniature, being carried in by two immense guards. His bandages, wrapped haphazardly around his chest under the faded prison shirt, seemed constraint enough. Over them, a more formidable layer of link chain wound around his torso and arms, binding him to his captors. Unable to walk, tied in gauze and laws and steel, this man was still dangerous. A fire had entered the room, and the audience rose as one to warm themselves. They shook their fists, and the prisoner, chest heaving and swollen with encumbrances, managed somehow to shake his in reply.

There were pleas, counter-pleas, more swift denials from the judge, deliberations that granted only delay after delay. Everyone needed more time to figure out how to handle—and punish—a man who not only refused to be found guilty, but refused to be judged. As the prisoner was being carried out, the audience stood for him, waved their little paws again. Through a wince of pain, the prisoner gave them a wicked smile that was well worth the price of admission. At the back door, he screamed toward the judge. "Nazi!" There was no hysteria in his delivery, no whine. "You can't lynch me so easy! I won't be tried by no Nazi court!"

No doubt, the guards paid him back for his outburst, but waited until they were out of view. That was the fatal weakness of this witness stuff—they could only see one outrage at a time, they couldn't keep up. The truth was that they wished to continue watching what they hoped to stop as much as the state wished to stop them from watching.

The prisoner, too, had shown his weakness. For all his courage, he had chosen the wrong epithet to hurl. No doubt this court was an operation which insured that the boldest of black men lost their freedom for good, but if the man in charge was SS, then there had been something very wrong with all those World War Two movies. And this wasn't a movie. This was the Big Q.

They were only a hallway from the gas chamber where a lot of cats had passed, had taken their place in the galaxy! You couldn't afford to be inaccurate here, since the next word you spoke might be the last before you were gagged. And the Nazi equation, instead of stirring them, made these witnesses doubt all they'd seen. Nobody seemed to care about getting the words right, but if a revolution meant lifting the veil off things, then the right words were needed to do the lifting. You couldn't just throw down a blanket of rhetoric and smooth it all out. History was like a proof—there had to be intermediate words, just as there had to be intermediate steps. If the words were correct, if the equation was balanced, there would be action. Action would transform their need for the old, inaccurate words and help create new ones. But if the words were wrong from the start, then they remained leaden—and leadership turned to beratement.

It was just like all that talk about how "we were all prisoners." That was what finally kept Martin and the others away. It made for too generous a scale of social relativity. If they were all prisoners of this system or that, then they could be lulled into thinking that they were all equally miserable. Since many of them were actually not very miserable at all, it followed that those actual inmates probably weren't so bad off, either. Everyone was in the same cage, weren't they? People could know all they needed to know about social injustice without leaving their living rooms, couldn't they? There was no reason for going to the trouble of seeing the real prisoners anymore.

7:02 a.m. The mud below, the landlord above.

This morning's reveille is for the sake of a renovation. These keepers of mine are pitiless men. Now I'll never get back to sleep. Too bad this infernal pounding isn't the work of some riotous mob banging down the gates, trying to spring me from my high-rent cell! Come out of hiding, *monsieur*! This day, if any, is the one for an escape! But there's nothing commemorative about the clatter overhead. These speculators and their handymen henchmen are more spiteful than chain-gang bosses: ripping out the nails of one cage, they reinforce the confines of another. Meant to demolish sheet rock, their wake-up call works just as well on domestic tranquility. But why so early, and with such vandalistic gusto? Are they really shot-putting cinderblocks? Bookcases and U-joints and all manner of household shrapnel shower down past my window and into a waiting dumpster.

Of course, I could get ear plugs. I have considered soundproofing, also *hara-kiri*. The only thing I haven't tried is shouting out. Or banging back with a broom handle: yes, noise is the only language that doesn't need any translation. The last resort, or in my case, the first, is that one's enemies will simply exhaust themselves. There is this single advantage to premature retirement from the fray: doing nothing just may enable me to out-endure the foot soldiers of profit. If only doing so little of what one really wants to do didn't turn out to be so tiring!

These fellows upstairs, for instance, don't really have to go through all that scraping of two-by-fours overhead, their shuffleboard game played with chunks of old plaster, accompanied by the day's first lung-clearing obscenities. With me, a whisper would have the same result. Right, gang? Wasn't I the one whose role was the light sleeper? He who is so easily roused, yet never quite fully awakened. Once again, I'm poised to chart my former bedmates' nightmares so my own won't come to pass. I am, remember, scorekeeper, judge; the self-appointed keeper of this group's Book of Changes, which means that I don't have to change in the least. Call me the vigilant one, ever on watch. Waking first just gives me the chance to catch the others with their libidos down.

Starting with my sidekick Dana Pearl, who pumps out stale Marlboro exhaust in adenoid trills, waterfalls of catarrh, who won't have any trouble in the grave because he goes there nightly, his sodden sleep uninterrupted by a fantasy life he saves for the daylight. Or Annie

Wyman: no one should be allowed to drift off that conclusively, her dormancy a kind of tidying up, her reveries but buoys on a still sea, whose locations and pitch she'll dutifully note in a flowered Chinese notebook, toting up her omens in columns like an accountant, watching always for the holy Zuni squaw who wraps her in robes warmer than any man. And Ayer Wilcox, her double ex: who rests most securely in anonymous motels with the twenty-five-cent vibrator going, swathed in Americana, his rapid eye movement bouncing him from dream to dream like hustle to hustle, his visions like bad wallpaper. Don't forget darlin' Darlinda Swen, who prefers a waterbed because it's a life raft on which she can float unrescued, though even her sleep's a persistent form of self-improvement. Last but not least, my Missy Monroe, who's been known to cry out, "That's great!" or "Gee, this is terrif!" in the middle of the night, our somnambulist cheerleader, able to get exclamatory about any creature or gender she finds herself lying beside.

"Where are they now?" becomes the simplest of questions when posed at an hour like this. In fact, it's the only time of day when I've no moral qualms about their current behavior. How can I object to either of the activities most commonly practiced in bed, though I seem to have lost the knack for either? The truth is that we always knew each other better when asleep than after rising. We approved of our dreams so much more than we approved of each other.

7:08 a.m. Friendship: the return to the scene of the crime.

The Big Bed. They found it easy to institute their unusual form of housekeeping. It was done without a vote, through direct and popular action, on the day they moved into their three-bedroom headquarters. Little did their landlord know that three bedrooms were not so prized as one! Missy led the charge, when she "accidentally" dropped the thrift store mattress that she and Martin shared in the back room where Dana and Darlinda's foam pad, tied like an oversized scroll, already stood in one corner. After all, this was the largest, sunniest bedroom and each couple considered it the height of bourgeois selfishness to grab it for themselves. So why not split the sunshine? Darlinda, depositing a milk crate full of sweatbands, discovered Missy's error and institutionalized it by laying the bedding edge-to-edge. There was just enough room for Annie and Ayer's, too.

"A room that's all bed!" sang Darlinda, skipping down the stairs. "A bed with lots of room!"

The rest followed, crowding the doorway to see what they'd wrought.

"Whoopee!" Ayer proclaimed. "Now we're living like Puerto Ricans!"

"Is this going too fast?"

"Not for me, Missy-poo," answered Ayer, always one to take up a dare. "I wanna be the vanguard in my pajamas. . . . Except how do we get fitted sheets for this?"

"In bolts," volunteered Annie. "Or I can stitch all of ours together."

And Dana immediately dubbed the effort "Socialism in one room!"

This wasn't so sweeping as socialism in one country, but they had to start somewhere, didn't they? Hence, share everything: communalize down to the snores, expropriate the groans and the sighs and the shivers, turn their rapid eye twitches into a hydroelectric project, nationalize their nocturnal industries and let them mingle.

"And what if I want to read my Zap comics?" asked Ayer.

"Oh pooh! Bed's not for that!" But what would it be for? Since they were committed to a regimen of cooking beans by schedule, swabbing the toilet in strict rotation—so the men couldn't get out of it—they could easily doze by timetable, nap in order, and make love according to the dictates of a new sort of rhythm method. If the women didn't get out of that!

Watching Missy tugging at the mattresses' too-pliant corners to align them perfectly, laying six pillows case-to-case, Martin couldn't help but lend a chivalrous hand. He tried to share his girlfriend's delight in the completion of the padded chamber, their wall-to-wall romper. He didn't dare speak his fears about how little romping would take place in the absence of some bourgeois privacy. Missy's charm was all in the fact that she was so magnificently unaware of her motives, and once again Martin let himself be charmed. Ever since they'd met, he had been trying to make his ward conscious at every turn, but now he restrained himself from making her conscious that she might be using this ploy to get away from him. Martin didn't want to lose Missy, so he let her and the other women "take the lead." In obeying their newfound assertiveness, he could further the dictates of his love and his politics. Yet the first time Martin luxuriated with his Miss on the unmade big bed, he was aware that the lover who lives by politics must die by politics.

The Light Sleeper. In the beginning, there was politics. And even before the beginning—which may explain why Martin was so eager to come into the world. Six weeks premature, he announced his entry on the Number One Broadway Local, somewhere in that horizontal chimney between Fiftieth and Fifty-Ninth. His mother was on her way to retrieve the papers and personal effects of an early trade-unionist leader who was dying in Martin's grandmother's Miami Beach boarding house. Gallant trooper, Mrs. Pepper did not hesitate to take this long and wearing ride to some *yiddisher* newspaper office on the Lower East Side. She'd tried so awfully hard to have this child, as she tried to be loyal to her ideals. Still in service to the Old Left, Martin's mother abruptly bore the New.

Through his umbilical fluids, Martin ingested the CP along with the DDT. From his womb listening post, he got his first sampling of sectarian debate: Mom and Dad still going over the pros and cons of the Hitler-Stalin Pact. Before he could say Mickey Mantle, he knew all about that slugger, Senator Joe McCarthy. He would people his only child's play universe with mythic figures like the Scottsboro Boys (did they wear kilts?), the Rosenbergs (but wasn't that the name of Mom and Dad's jewelers?), Sacco and Vanzetti (an obscure juggling act?). Since his parents had been thwarted in doing the job, he would come to America's rescue. Prenatally, he practiced a clenched fist. Unarmored, Martin geared up for his historic task.

Already precocious, not merely premature but prematurely anti-Fascist, Martin was summoned forth by the abrasive clatter, the pounding of steel upon steel, the aortic flow of the great city. All that lurching in a dark cave not unlike his own! Why wasn't he lulled back to sleep by the rockabye shudder of the Rockaway line? Why couldn't he have been swayed to stay put by the precipitous swaying of the train on those overused tracks? Disorder and disrepair were just what he was after. Through the uterus, he glimpsed a reason to be born, some injustice to squawk about as soon as his lungs were cleared of fluid. Peeping out of his fallopian periscope, he caught a view of grizzled, mumbling winos, mustachioed Puerto Rican cleaning ladies, delivery boys cracking farts and wads of gum, leering construction workers thrashing through their morning *Daily News*, hurrying through blood and scandal toward the racing forms, perhaps momentarily cheered by stories about our boys beating up on those reds over in Korea. How he wanted to rewrite those headlines! Breathless, factless, he nonetheless strived to inform the misinformed. To warn the overpainted secretaries on their way through the underground furnace to job interviews, "You'll never get that job! You'll never please them!" Martin knew all about "them" and "us" before he knew about himself.

Right from the amniotic start, he wanted to rub his pug nose in the ugliness. His place was here: right where more prudent creatures would never dare go. His time had come: the worst possible time. One sniff of dried bubble gum crud, the vortex of industrial grime whipping through the tunnels, of cheap port seeping from burst paper bags, of desiccated vomit, deodorants, garlic breath, police leather, the unsweetened exhalations of despair, and this kid said to himself, "Kid, let's relocate! This must be living! This is it!"

The fetal bag burst just below Fifty-Second Street, where Charlie Parker was raising his people's raucous birth cry. Mrs. Pepper was alarmed by so much muck and seepage, though nobody else in the subway car even noticed. They were used to a little blood. It was red, the workers' color, but Mrs. Pepper had the sense to terminate her act of solidarity and make for a phone. On the other end of the line, while more trains roared past, everybody's left-wing obstetrician was shouting, "Get to the hospital, *bubbaleh*! You're in labor, and I'm not talking *Das Kapital*!" But for Martin, his mother's pain and his own were so much surplus value. Already he focused on external traumas, and this tragic distraction proved a powerful anesthetic. From the start, as he squeezed forward and struggled for air, Martin had come to the conclusion that his own struggle did not count; somehow the shock and exertion weren't authentic. His own birth was not real enough.

Saving the world became such a habit that he didn't notice how little he was learning about saving himself. Besides, Mommy and Daddy would always be there to take care of their one-man cadre, best pal and fellow aesthete. No wonder they doted on him! He was more intellectual at six that he would ever be again. He was the cameraman needed to record the family's summer jaunts through Provence and the Uffizi. "Summer camp," said his parents, "is for children who aren't loved." Not only did his parents love him, they were his playmates. The main peer pressure in Martin's childhood was figuring out which kind of "ist" he was going to be. Mommy was a Stalinist, who taught that blind loyalty was better than none. Daddy was a Dadaist, who taught that art was long, life vastly overrated. Mrs. Pepper was a failed actress who became a theatrical publicist, Doctor Pepper a failed poet who found a late shortcut to respectability through the dubious profession of sexologist. They were both of a postimmigrant generation that couldn't help succeeding. "Nothing too good for the working class" was their battle cry. Martin shouted it whenever he could, though they sent him to schools where the only workers' kids were on scholarship.

At ten, he campaigned for J.F.K. by putting a signboard on the family Scottish terrier, because his mom told him the dog would remind people of F.D.R. When Kennedy's rhetoric got too anti-Russian, he threw his support to Alfred E. Newman. At twelve, he tutored Harlem kids and dreamed of joining the Peace Corps. At thirteen, he wrapped sandwiches for Reverend King's civil rights army, slipping inspirational homilies in beside the potato chips. While taking a hundred lashes from wet locker room towels snapped at his behind, he was advocating "people's war" in the junior high school debating club. As the crusading high school paper editor, he lambasted dress codes and the draft, linking the two as only a tie-throttled adolescent could. His parents backed him up all the way—even when he became the first kid suspended for growing his hair, the first member of the boys' swim team made to wear a bathing cap. Every year, they took him to the Weavers' concerts at

Carnegie Hall, where Martin sang along to the leftist battle hymns. It didn't matter to him that most of those battles had been lost. History, it seemed, was one big hootenanny and Martin was eager to get on the right side and in the right key.

Doctor and Mrs. Pepper shouldn't have been mystified when a college counselor told them that their son would never go to Harvard because he wasn't competitive enough. Martin's parents, in making him too much like them, still strove to protect him from the results. The summer before Martin entered tiny Steffens College, the only liberal arts college liberal enough to accept a certified troublemaker like him, his parents would not allow him to demonstrate outside the Chicago Democratic Convention. Trying to convince them that it would be safe for him to go, he'd written to see if he might stay with a kid named Dana Pearl who'd been assigned his roommate for the fall. Dana wrote back that he was a camp counselor and wouldn't be in the city that hot, fabled August. Besides, Dana confessed, his dad was an arch-Republican judge who'd never let him put up anyone who was coming to town for a riot. Such an objection had never occurred to Martin. He thought everyone's folks had politics like his.

7:12 a.m. Contrary to popular belief, politics has nothing to do with constructing the future, everything to do with explaining the past. Hiroshima to Selma, the Fourth International to your third girlfriend, politics means assigning responsibility and blame. What went wrong? Why did we listen to this guy and what was he really saying? Who's gonna clean up this mess? These are the questions that prompt us to action, and more often to that ultimate form of politics, inaction.

Encouraged to dream big, I'm willing to settle for such small victories. Like a moratorium on pounding. Or a limited test-ban on renovators. I mustn't blame the sheet rock rockers—always blame the "system"—since they're just an advance goon squad of devotees, loyal to my latest warden. Somehow, I expected greater sensitivity from the pony-tailed EST graduate who goes by the name of Lorenzo Sunshine. Having just purchased this subdivided Victorian and my solitude with it, he's apparently turning the floor above into his meditative center—until he can sell it for thrice what he paid. "Don't conceptualize me as an owner," his first rent increase read. "Conceptualize me as an individual whose energies are focused on actualizing the common good. . . ." Actualizing before he's moved in, lord Sunshine reorders his domain without regarding to prior occupants, bent on improving our lifestyles whether we like it or not.

Perhaps some postescrow day, he'll get around to enlarging his tenants' confines. Entered through an overwrought facade, its trim accented in ocher tones, this studio at the back of the second floor must have been this mansion house's maid quarters. It doesn't take me long to roam this one room sectioned off into approximation of hall, kitchen, bath and sleep chamber. With no room for living. My exorbitant rent does give me crawl rights to a sunporch, where Lorenzo cools his excess Zinfandel, along with custodianship over an indoor ant colony, supervised by my cat Jean-Luc. There's just one wall surface large enough to handle my original first-run poster of Bertolucci's *Il Conformista*. My desk and *Cahiers du Cinéma* back issues fit under a window which affords me a view toward the hills where others make up for my lack of participation in "the good life." I don't do all that badly: in my refrigerator, there are seven brands of hot sauce. A general assembly of chilis. The kitchen stove's shoved into an alcove that can't quite accommodate it, so that each burner slants toward the pull of separate celestial bodies and everything I fry comes out half-burnt, half-greased. Despite a dozen appeals to Massa Sunshine, the toilet tank runs like an eternal spring, my built-in Jacuzzi spa.

It came as no surprise when I learned that the occupant prior to me had been driven to spray-paint the walls a flat black, string up sailors' hammocks and scrawl across his front door, "Welcome to the Pit." There's a notch in the molding around the door for each human who's dared to enter this Pit. Three notches in two years, and one was for a newsboy collecting on a subscription. I don't count the burglars who came calling in quest of my Olivetti—in Berkeley, all the second-story men write short stories—or the neighborly old ladies who drop off pamphlets about "Christ, Your Only Fallout Shelter" or Jean-Luc, who's more continually on the hunt than I. No trophies today, I see: no crumpled field mice, placed paws-up on my pillow, no truncated garden lizard parts (the ones he kills seem to be one unbroken headless vegetal segment). Returning once, I found that he'd chased inside, tossed about and chewed through a young jay. The Bluebird of Happiness was disassembled in gossamer bits. I worked furiously to eradicate all traces of the carnage. With each clump of pale velour coaxed toward my dustpan, I grew more proud of my thoroughness—until I filled my tub and a soggy quilt of bird confetti rose to the top.

In my closet, neatly folded, I keep my prized Rajasthani throw rug—a token effort at interior decoration that needn't get needlessly soiled. Reserved for special occasions, its striated bands throb brightly, like the recessed levels of want in my gut. I've been told that the tiniest atom, properly photographed, emits just such colors. But how did the ancient weavers know? I am going to ask that question of the first woman who gets to see my rug.

7:16 a.m. The "new celibacy" is very much like the old celibacy.

Occasionally, there's muffled evidence of this subdivided mansion's other inhabitants: rumors spread by strained pipes, whimpering washers, the uproar of a bath. When there is flushing, it is me that is flushed away. The thumping of stereo bass, the last moments of a spat: what comes through walls is the worst of humanity.

The most dire moments come when I'm given some fleeting glimpse of all that I miss—like the time I caught my downstairs neighbors sunbathing in the yard. Even with their clothes off, they look like art students—or, better yet, figure-drawing models. Such nicely oiled canvases stretched taut on bony frames! On their front door, these elfin roommates have painted a red cardiac blob, then stenciled in white,

"Art Ache." I've been meaning to ask them if it's the name of their *atelier* or their ska band. By the time I bump into any of them, they'll probably have formed a string quartet—though I did almost speak to the Asian imp who slinks about in neon socks and a curious reversible cape. Just after they'd moved in, during a walloping rainstorm, I looked on from my parked car while she fiddled with a faulty copy of the front door key. I watched her get drenched, immobilized, unable to come to her rescue. The perfect opportunities always strike me as hokey. My neighbor got in at last, leaving me to pound my dashboard.

7:18 a.m. Even the great earthquake, when it comes, will be welcomed as a social opportunity.

With a Crash. She came into Martin's life with a bang, or, to be more exact, a hit-and-run. He and Ayer Wilcox had just skittered across the darkened billiard table of the Steffens College campus, two furry eight balls seeking any warm pocket, sinking into the functional dorm room that belonged to Annie Wyman, a miniskirted Texas girl who'd been claimed by Ayer. Annie was about to serve them up another joint and some home-popped popcorn when in rushed the second half of the cheery roommate tandem they'd dubbed "The Smiley Sisters." Only this one wasn't quite smiling now. Sweeping black bangs frantically from her forehead, she bit down hard on her lower lip, suppressing a half-grin born of terror. She seemed to be reveling in the crisis, delighted that shock could make her so sensate. From the start, she looked good in shock.

"You won't believe it, guys! I almost killed someone! I'm not kiddeen!"

Her curious Imogene Coca inflection stretched endings into squeals. Everything became a pinched, joyous whine. The girl was wearing the same hooded coat she'd hid beneath all freshman year. Was that why Martin had barely noticed this lanky Miss Red Riding Hood? They followed the gleefully shaken roommate back across the main quadrangle lawn, beckoned by ambulance lights and police car flashers that beamed like lighthouses through the Oregon fog. A real emergency! With Annie comforting her, the second Smiley Sister returned to the scene of her crime and confessed. In the dense mist, stoned out of her gourd (she didn't tell this to the police), she'd turned the corner toward the dorm parking lot and struck the jaywalker. "She *was* jaywalking, huh?"

But the victim was hardly dead. She'd already gathered her skirts and gotten up, unscathed, from her sprawl on the asphalt. Luckily, amazingly, this madcap cruiser had steered her spanking new Barracuda into the fattest girl at Steffens College. Two sets of bumpers had met; Annie's roommate was off scot-free. From then on, though, the gang called her "Crash"—not Melissa Sue Monroe, daughter of Moose Monroe, the lower California Valley's most renowned Dodge Boy. Soon to become Martin's very own moving violation! The fog cleared for spring, and Missy knew the quickest shortcuts toward the best roadside stands where Martin sampled his first taste of fresh boysenberries and asparagus and love. Martin couldn't imagine ever tiring of his newfound navigator's untutored charms and moonlit ways, of a face crowded with dimples, scarred with contentment. The car dealer's daughter became his favorite chauffeur and pretty soon he didn't care where she drove him. Smooching in the front seat, while she steered. Bop-shoo-bop. A vision of trust, while they veered. Bop-shoo-boop.

They tried to make their initial pairing discreet, but the rest of the gang knew that Missy and Martin were a couple before they did. They had to kick Annie out and into the next cubicle, where she popped a batch of popcorn and tried not to listen. Just two weeks before semester's end, Martin found his first good reason for attending Steffens College. He found it in the upper bunk of Missy's dorm room. They certainly took full advantage of this first mattress, even though it was college-owned! In her so-bad-it's-good manner, the walls to Missy's cubicles were wallpapered with hand-me-down psychedelia, Hell's Angels rolling joints and day-glo deco posters for concerts of the Quicksilver Messenger Service, the satanic flotsam of Haight-Ashbury that no one ever admitted to buying but which turned up everywhere. From the ceiling, John, Paul, George, and Ringo in a set of standard glossies supervised all.

Those cutesy Beatle faces beamed down on Martin and Missy, permissive cupids.

In the pole lamp stuck between floor and ceiling, Martin discovered that Missy had placed colored bulbs to enhance her first marijuana experimentations. With each alternating current of their affections, they could switch on nightclub red, undersea blue, goof-off yellow. The whitest blue was their favorite tint for staring across pillows with icy concentration à la Alain Resnais. Murky greens and throbbing pinks went with the positions of a how-to book they went through without referring to any text. In a closet mirror, they spent hours gawking at the mere physical evidence of their couplehood. Awash in their very own light-show burlesque, they struck Jim and Jean album cover poses, Sonny and Cher in the buff.

Between stagelight variants of their choosing they would give one another review quizzes on Martin's ABC's of protest, punctuated by more dog-love. Or give air time to Crash's tales of country childhood, short but never over. Not just playing male to female, city slicker to country lass, Martin offered ideas (of which Missy was in awe) and she returned an encyclopedia's worth of feelings (of which he was in greater awe). Or maybe they prattled on about how "theoretically" everyone ought to love everyone—while resting on each other's sighing parts.

"You taste Jewish," Missy whispered once.

"Is that bad?" Her answer was a kiss that made their pleasure so brazen that the whole campus had to know. Until, finally, a patch of wax blue daylight seeping through the dorm told them they had to sleep, not get up. Then Missy hummed a Girl Scout lullaby, all energy transmitted to feet that twitched against Martin in the dungeon light.

"Sing for me if you want." On Missy's shoulders, he could fall asleep without wondering if he was going to wake up. And she would comply in a high whisper, through the full-teethed embarrassment of a Dinah Shore delivery:

"Desert silv'ry moon a-shinin' pale moonlight,
Coyotes lappin' lazy on the hi-ill,
Sleepy winks of light across the far skyline,
Time for millin' cattle to be sti-ill.

Hey-ho, the lightnin's far away,
The coyote's nothing scary,
Just singin' to his deary.
Hey-ho, tommora holiday,
So settle down yer cattle 'til the mornin' . . ."

7:27 a.m. Is it possible to retain one's love of mankind without getting a sample from a singular member of the species?

Help! A shattering's got me sitting up, with a start. The handymen's lullaby has one bang-up finish. My morning drowse is shot to hell with a definitive crack. Some piece of shrapnel from upstairs has tumbled off its trajectory and caromed into the window just over my head. The sound of a new world being born, that's what we used to call window-smashing. Apparently, there's no place for me in Lorenzo's brave new one.

I see that the pane's been slit in three even sections, with the smallest one landed like a nice, flat skipping stone on my pillow. Another few inches closer, and I would have a lawsuit. This must be my cue to get up and at 'em. But what can I do? Stage a one-man rally? Standing with the layers of blanket gathered around my shoulders like a battle robe, protecting myself from hitherto unknown breezes, I must look like some dispossessed Indian chief. This is no longer some noble last stand, it has become self-defense. The time has come to fight back, or at least, wash my face.

7:35 a.m. And the meek shall inherit what the un-meek leave behind.

The Sound of a New World Being Born. Rending glass was breaking on through to the other side! Going giddy with a logic taken to the street! It was doing everything the Man said was bad! Beneath the leaflet hyperbole, shattering soft storefront windows with any hard projectile at hand was actually a way of getting maximum chaos out of minimum effort—the lazy man's shortcut to insurrection. But picking on the social order's most fragile facade was good enough for Martin, that conscientious objector since the sandbox. Property damage wasn't rough like roughhouse, especially a midnight raid against the flimsy, defenseless wooden booths of the Steffens College annual "Renaissance Faire." Wielding baseball bats, he and Dana hacked away at the underpinnings of this exercise in lily-white delusion, this prissy symbol of ivory towerism. What did dressing in doubloons and tooting on fifes have to do with Third World oppression or academic complicity with the military-industrial complex? The next day, the Steffens student newspaper branded the culprits as "barbarians." Genghis Khans with Louisville Sluggers!

Or water pistols—like the one he held at the back of a Dow Chemical recruiter being escorted off campus. Or a shovel, handed to him by some agent provocateur—which he wielded against the display window of a Berkeley art supply store that was unlucky enough to be located around the corner from People's Park. Or Central Park quarry rocks—on the night in New York when Missy and he had been among those avenging the police killing of Black Panther Chairman Fred Hampton. After an hour or two of tame picketing a Nixon speech at the Waldorf, their adventurist band roamed from Park over to Fifth until they'd reached hated Rockefeller Center. In the alcove graced by the statue of Atlas holding up the world's banking infrastructure, all of New York's mounted finest were waiting. With horses bearing down on him, Martin reached for his pocket-sized retaliation. He paused just long enough to fling, but not to see where he got in his licks. On all sides, everything that was solid was coming apart, amplified in the skyscraper echo chamber. This may not have been the sound of a new world being born, but it was certainly the sound of an old one in need of repair. Escaping down a convenient subway entrance, where those ahead hurdled the turnstiles, he made the mistake of looking back. What would Chairman Fred have said? He had struck a blow upon Saks Fifth Avenue, where his own father had lovingly dragged him, year upon year, to outfit Martin in camel's hair jackets and tattersall vests; where, just a few weeks earlier, the generous Doctor had bought Missy a designer peasant dress that, despite the price tag, she couldn't resist. Martin vowed to aim better next time.

7:44 a.m. The tests one imagines, the challenges to which we'll rise! The test is always in progress. The time to rise is now.

I am emerging from The Pit. Streamlining my transition from *futon* to foyer and hopefully back again, I reach across the floor to where yesterday's jeans landed. My T-shirt is a conversation piece that reads, "Free Chol Soo Lee!" Unfortunately, nobody's yet bothered to ask me who that is. Maybe they rightfully surmise that this is just another case of retail compassion (available in small, medium, large or extra-large). According to the *ad hoc* committee that peddled it, Mister Lee is a Korean immigrant sent to San Quentin for a series of murders he wasn't fluent enough to deny. Another man in another pit—except that I leave mine unlocked, in case I can't hack it on "the outside."

The door across the landing is open, leading to the landlord's new digs. I can hear someone up there, hammering while they whistle a Doobie Brothers tune. Probably not Lorenzo exerting himself, but in any case, I dare not ascend to meet the enemy in his lair. I scurry back into my kitchen and grab the recycled grocery bag from under the sink so I can pretend to be emptying what little garbage is in it. Outside, following the pavement laid between the hydrangea bushes and the oft-buttressed foundation, I turn the corner and find a row of six cans—the only items in this house that haven't been subdivided beyond utility. I also find one of the workmen, shoving origami shapes of plasterboard into a receptacle. He's a rangy, tranquilized rocker with red hair parted down the middle and falling to his shoulder blades. One brass hoop of earring swings back and forth while he labors at a pace reminiscent of a giraffe doing *tai chi.* A paisley bandana protects his freckled neck; below, he's encased in a white painter's suit that's so stiff with dried splotches and studded with spikes of plaster that he looks like a NASA drone foraging for moon rocks.

"Howdy, commander. Gotcha goin' early today?"

"Oh, no. I was meditating." Don't give him any satisfaction. "Until you busted one of my windows."

"How do you mean 'you,' commander?" Every handyman in Berkeley is a moonlighting metaphysician.

"Your crew, then. Some of that shrapnel they were heaving out over the side must have struck the glass."

"Coulda just as soon been some kids in the yard, commander. Vandals throwin' rocks."

That's it: blame it on vandals, terrorists, spontaneous combustion. Stonewall it, private.

"I'll just have to take this up with your boss."

"You do that, commander. . . ."

Coming back through the front door, I run smack into her. At least, I think this harried woman is Penny, described in our rental increase as Lorenzo's "significant other." She's rumbling down the stairs and into the lobby wearing one of those Marimekko maternity aprons —a print of giant coffee beans, or are they beetles?—plus Birkenstock sandals, those flapjacks for the feet. She carries a Navajo black pottery vase big as a beer keg.

"Please, could you either go in or out?" Though I'm holding the door for her, she's taken my aid for obstruction. I don't bother to introduce myself because I figure she must know I'm not some passerby. But she neither acknowledges me nor pauses en route to her van in the driveway. Strands of mousy hair flop across Penny's broad forehead; her nostrils are permanently flared, as though held open with sutures; and not even the most sparkly eye shadow can hide the advanced drooping of her lids, prematurely weighed down with the tasks of affluence. The eyes themselves are dull as old coins. They don't study life so much as speed read it. In those eyes, I see months of rent receipts, years of trouble.

The critical moment approaches. How do I speak up when she

won't even acknowledge that I'm there? When I know that, no matter how incensed I get, she'll just thank me for sharing my insights? Or suggest holistically that I possess free choice to move out? How dare I interrupt her installation of skylights and terrarium with talk of mere glass and running toilets? My landlady's through the front door and I've said nothing. I vow to get bolder on her next pass, then I hear her ignition and realize there won't be a second opportunity. I'm a bubble that bursts at the prick of other people.

7:52 a.m. In the end, complaint has very little to do with protest.

I Took the Limo to the Demo. Entering the grounds of the army base, there had been a front and back to this demonstration. The Steffens College Women for Peace had insisted on leading the way. Since this was their first action together, Martin and the Big Mac affinity group were pleased to remain at the rear. They entered an open, sloped field on the only side without barbed wire. Everyone was strident and confident: thinking they were going to make an easy symbolic conquest of the barracks, presuming they had the army outflanked. Now the front of the march met an obstacle Martin couldn't see. The line was fanned out across the field, flattening like a snake with its head chopped off.

They were facing infantrymen, one on one. If Martin had not seen the gas masks, camouflage boots and ready bayonets, he would have thought that everyone was about to begin a Virginia Reel. He looked behind him, expecting new orders from the rear. There was no rear. No generals. And the army across the way had so many privates, standing their ground, one every five yards. They awaited orders from sergeants further removed who kept looking back for a signal from the officers' jeeps parked far up the hill. The demonstrators seemed to be doing little but waiting, too. The signal was invisible to Martin. The riflemen bent their weapons for a moment, as though they might lunge. All Martin could remember from his hours of training was that he should pull out his handkerchief. He did that just in time.

Cannisters went in with staggered clacking. Then out, with a nearly silent white discharge. Popf! Popf! Handkerchiefs came out in a courtly flourish; the march bowing to the smoke's curtsy. Martin unfolded his handkerchief and began breathing through it as instructed. The handkerchief was working. He thought that the army might be bluffing and took one dos-à-dos forward. After that, he couldn't see anything. It hurt too much to see. It hurt to breathe. That frightened him.

The others circled away from him. He could judge their distance from their brutish coughing. In between the wheezes he hoped still qualified as breathing, his lungs worked with great concentration. It hurt so much that he thought he was having the dry heaves. In the field's changing terrain, he could no longer tell how far he was from the ground. He missed a step at the bottom of a grassy staircase and fell. When he opened his eyes, it felt like matches were being put to them and they burned shut. He tried to put out the fire with tears but the tears ran out his nose and his eyes were all snot.

He pushed himself off the ground with the hand that wasn't holding the handkerchief. He ran and fell and got up. Something unbearable was happening in his chest. With each breath, he was taking in boiling acid and letting out equal parts of water. He couldn't see, hear, or sense anyone near him anymore. He tried to concentrate on Missy. And the affinity group. Its password was "Double Cheese." He could not utter it. He fell again and got up again. Just before his eyes had to shut again he saw a gully with a little stream and he fell into it.

Perhaps he was running the wrong way, across no-man's-land and to the wrong trenches. Perhaps he was already behind enemy lines. This must be some other battlefield, he thought. Antietam or the Marne, not green Oregon. He got up again. It was getting easier to see. The meadow was trembling, translucent, a hundred colors through the tears. The handkerchief, he realized, had outlived its purpose. There was probably more gas trapped in it than anything else. Besides, it was embarrassing. It was heavy with drool and hardly came unstuck from his inflamed mouth. He let it go.

Martin could open his eyes long enough now to see that he had left the open countryside. He bumped through a grove of trees and burst onto a paved road. He fell down hard. A hand picked him up by the elbow. He began to make out a long trail of bowed and weeping marchers. The stronger ones were picking up the chant. "Brass lives high while GIs die. Turn the guns around!" It grew louder, sung through phlegm by a thousand voices. Martin didn't feel like chanting yet, but he found that he could call, "Double Cheese!" No one answered. Another battalion of soldiers watched the demonstrators' disorderly retreat, guarding their Quonset huts with angled bayonets. They were as mute as the protestors were clamorous. Martin could breathe again. The pain in his chest was going away too quickly. It made him feel cowardly. It made him feel he'd been tricked. He did not know that CS gas was meant to hit hard but leave no scars.

"Double Cheese! Double Cheese!"

They were calling for him. Martin ran blindly toward his affinity group and dove into their pocket of sound. There were arms around him. There was encouragement to shout, "Brass lives high . . ." A hand propped up his head. Martin felt water being poured down his face. He opened his eyes and his mouth to sop up all the water that he could. His eyes needed it most. They knew how to drink. He liked the hand at the back of his head. He hoped for more pouring. It reminded Martin of how his mother soaped and rinsed his baby hair. And he felt good.

7:56 a.m. What if we ever got just what we demanded?

Now I've asked for it. On how many runs to the trash have I been angling for this moment? The door to the downstairs apartment is clicking open, one dead bolt at a time, but fast enough that I can't flee the lobby. I don't give a hoot about my window anymore, only that my hair looks like it's been vandalized. Better not get too close. I haven't brushed my teeth, either. Hope it isn't her, but one of her less exotic roommates. It's not.

"Good morning, mister!" How can someone look so good in a chenille bathrobe? "Why you wait there? Selling something?"

"I wish. I'm your neighbor, Martin."

"Of course, movie man. Famous all around. I see name in paper! I hear typing all the time."

"That's for a book."

"Writing book, too? Busy guy."

"It's not a book yet. I mean, I'm still waiting to hear from the publisher."

"I sure they publish."

"Do you have psychic powers?"

"Just average fortune cookie."

"I divined your name from the mailbox."

"Oh boy! Neighbors can hide nothing. But I no big name. Only half-Chinese girl, come from Taiwan to go college. Never planning return . . . but don't tell family, please!"

"And what are *you* doing out in the hall?"

"Just checking." From her cowboy shirts and basketball sneakers, I'd presumed that Daphne possessed a native twang. But she hasn't learned English so much as twisted it into a means of retaining her playfulness. I feel confirmed in my many months' hunch: this artist's spunk isn't entirely storebought. "I wake up, too, from noises."

"They broke one of my windows."

"Too much disturbance. Maybe good for art, but not good for artist. . . . I artist."

"I know. I've seen you sketching in the backyard."

"You can see backyard? You seeing too much then."

"Nothing I didn't like."

"Bad boy! I think I don't say hello to you. . . . We do that after roommates and me taking champagne too often. You like champagne now?"

"For breakfast?"

"Maybe instead Blue Mountain Jamaican?"

"No, thanks, I don't smoke that stuff anymore."

"Not smoking! Is coffee! You come in from hallway?"

"I don't want to disturb you." And I'm not wearing any underpants.

"Stop worry. Too early for making art. And you don't disturb worse than landlord."

"Have you met Princess Penny?"

"Hard not to meet." We're giggling now, though Daphne stifles hers and rolls her eyes toward the penthouse. Then she whispers, "Me and roommates, we make plan for her. You follow Daphne now, please. There is something I am having to tell."

8:17 a.m. The fear of women: anyone who doesn't admit apprehension at a form of life unlike their own is lying or isn't looking.

"Look out please for my men!" Daphne warns.

I imagine that I'm about to get acquainted with three or four rivals. "Be nice, or my men attack you!"

To illustrate, she reaches down into the base of a potted palm in her cramped entranceway, and comes up with a miniature play soldier gripping a bayonet. While she jabs the thing toward me, I look down to follow the trail of an entire division of a rubber army, green GI Joes crawling on their bellies across the floor, seeking a foxhole or camouflage.

"Is this your hallway or the battle of Corregidor?"

"This Daphne's army. Every house must have own army."

"Oh. I don't think I could land one in the Pit." From what I can glimpse, this staging area is bigger and brighter. In the hall, Daphne and her roommates have hung their various hats, straw and felt and slicker on a grid of nails so that they form a kind of Vasarely pattern. Or is it Frank Stella? Beyond, I see a checkerboard linoleum in the kitchen: perfect fifties dinette. In the other direction, a hissing fluorescent coil casts the living room in pinkness, echoed by a poster of Christo's pink-swathed Biscayne islands. It's all too artistic to be true, chaotic but pulsing with good taste. Just the kind of cosy ferment I'd like to come home to—but Daphne's run off to grind coffee without inviting me further inside.

"What this pit?"

"My place upstairs."

"It very small. I know."

"How?"

"We checking. At city hall, deed to property. Roommates and me find out how much house is selling. Just in case. We find out lots of things."

"What for?"

"Here, I may speak," Daphne says. "Roommates go to Berkeley Tenants Union. You know, what new landlord do is not proper legal. Called 'constructive eviction.' Great name! It happen all the time. Drive out people with noise, then raising rents. But we can refuse leaving. Not give rent. Can be fighting back . . . except maybe for you."

"Thanks."

"No, your apartment too teeny-tiny. Not proper legal. So maybe you cannot do nothing. Like you do not exist."

"Then I should be paying the non-person rate."

"None of us pay, that be perfect. Begin rent strike. Make big noise back on them."

8:05 a.m. The first time—so much easier when you've no hopes for a next time.

Always a First Time. Martin's first house in Berkeley was on rent strike: the archetypal crash pad with one room painted purple, one glossy black with strobe light, failing flea market couch draped with paisley yardage, a pack of Labradors who regularly besmirched the worn rugs, an icebox crammed with thirty-seven paper bags, each bearing a name in crayon. The house had been rent-free for so long that it became a clearing station for draft evaders. The F.B.I. had come calling twice—a favorite brag in those days. But no one ever planned for the possibility of the strike being settled. Martin got stuck with the job of figuring out how to pay all the back rent. 'Round the cable spool dining table, he determined that there had been fifty-five housemates over the duration of the strike—fifty-five he could remember and name, most gone on to cheaper pastures. He was left to break down the debt into fractions of fractions, calculating who owed what for a month, a week, a night on the couch, a moment's enlightenment in the garage, a slurp of soup, two tokes, an orgasm.

8:06 a.m. Throwing our lot in with others: we do it so we can have steps to retrace, witnesses, alibis.

"Hey! Famous critic! Where you go away to? What you thinking?"

"I was in a rent strike once, when I first came to Berkeley."

"You win?"

"I don't remember, but I doubt it. We never won anything."

"Easy to become critic when you losing. Easy to get depress."

"What makes you think I'm depressed?"

"From colors. You always wearing white jacket outdoors, burgundy sweatshirt inside. Either too loud or too quiet only."

So now I know she's been looking at me. "And which are good colors?"

"Blue best. Like my car."

"What kind of car do you have?"

"Blue." That tells me a lot. "You get feeling better against landlord. You do this with us?"

"I'll think it over . . ."

"Thinking too much get me scared. You too?"

I don't answer, because I'm terrified of so much more than I'm willing to tell. When Daphne gets around to asking if I'd like to share a cup in her kitchen, I hear myself answer, "Another time, maybe. I can't have coffee yet. Not before my run."

"Where you run?"

"Three miles every morning, to the high school and back."

"Running nowhere then." Running away is more like it.

"Except past the plum trees, the jasmine and acacia . . ."

"On certain summer morning, Berkeley is Shalimar." So Daphne proclaims, as if she's the first person who ever noticed.

"But the first Shalimar was a lovers' rendezvous," I remind, trying to sound both scholarly and flirtatious.

"Too bad," she says. "Love obsolete."

Scene One (The Study Group). DARLINDA: "Love . . . is . . . a . . . reaction . . . formation. . . . a cycle of envy, hostility, and possessiveness."

She was having trouble reading the paperback way down in her lap. Such tiny print, and so many big words. Darlinda went on trying to maintain good posture while sitting cross-legged on the floor. This attempt made her look like a prim schoolmarm and she was reading slowly enough, enunciating carefully enough, to be entertaining a kindergarten class at nap time. "It is preceded by dissatisfaction with oneself . . . a yearning for something better . . . created by the discrepancy between the ego and the ego-ideal . . . the bliss that love produces is due to the resolution of this tension . . . by the substitution in place of one's own ego-ideal . . . of the other. . . . This love is the height of selfishness. . . . And this is the love process today. . . . But why must it be this way?"

Why indeed, teach? The collective was dumbfounded at first, scattered on torn foam pillows in a bare room lit by a single dangling bulb. Over Darlinda's head, on the collective's very own bulletin board, Missy had pinned a torn strip of newsprint with a single word on it. "Dependency." This was the first night's topic, chosen by the women. Their first assigned reading was a chapter from Shulamith Firestone's *The Dialectic of Sex*.

The only other item posted in their newly designated study room was a popular cartoon of the day that sought to depict the state of affairs between the sexes through variations in circles. "Sometimes I feel like this," said one caption, and above it the female circle was a tiny orb swallowed by the distended male; "Sometimes like this," the circles barely touching or floating free; "I want to feel like this," many small circles interlocking to form a big one. The collective's geometry on the floor was less spherical.

DARLINDA: "Shall Darlinda continue?"

ANNIE: "That's an earful for now."

MISSY: "It's all so horrific, and so *true*."

MARTIN: "But where do we go from here? What does it have to do with the topic?"

MISSY: "Everything, Pep. Seeing all the things you lack in somebody else is what breeds the dependency, no? It's believing all that matters in life is some Top Forty song."

MARTIN: "But there's a reason everyone listens to those songs."

DANA: "What does *that* have to do with the topic, son? Unless it's more proof that romantic love has got to be the enemy."

MARTIN: "I thought the ruling class was the enemy."

AYER: "You can be awfully naive when you want to be. Selectively naive."

MARTIN: "Let's not get personal."

DANA: "We're gonna have to get personal. That's what the collective is for."

MARTIN: "I thought it was for sustaining us so that we could go out and transform the world."

DANA: "That, too. But the women haven't been feeling sustained."

MARTIN: "I don't feel that sustained, either."

ANNIE: "That's what we're working on, Pep."

MARTIN: "All right. I agree with everything in the passage under review, but the question at the end is dangling. How are people gonna do without all that transference? Without having one most-important other out there?"

MISSY: "But we have to try and create alternatives, no?"

MARTIN: "Not too many alternatives at a time, please."

DARLINDA: (flustered, in the same babyish tone with which she was reading): "I think, Darlinda thinks, that Marty is defending. He's frightened. He doesn't want to be an equal. To share is scary. But he's the one who wrote the program. Didn't you write down that we should study, Martin?"

MARTIN: "I'm not against studying."

AYER: "Just putting into practice what you find out."

DANA: "Praxis makes perfect, dude."

MARTIN: "Yeah, yeah. I just think there are some curious implications floating about. Anti-socialist implications."

MISSY: "How so?"

MARTIN: "Socialism is all about dependency. The highest form of dependency. Alone, we're just potentialities. Groping. Feeble. Instead of man against man, the new order is man leaning upon man."

DARLINDA: "And woman leaning upon woman."

MARTIN: "But don't forget woman upon man, man upon woman."

MISSY: "I'm sorry, Pep. I don't want to be feeble anymore."

DARLINDA (leaning over to kiss Missy on the cheek, fumbling to retrieve her place in the book): " 'Men can't love. We have seen why it is that men have difficulty loving and that while men may love, they usually "fall in love"—with their own projected image. Most often they are pounding down a woman's door one day, and thoroughly disillusioned with her the next; but it is rare for women to leave men, and then it is usually for more than ample reason. . . .' "

Martin's Trick. Sweating under a bum-size overcoat he'd chosen for the occasion, he circled Times Square. Mapping out the girls' migratory trail, testing sets of eyes under sets of mascara and cotton candy wigs, he barely knew what he was after, knowing only that she would be the first. Tiring, he claimed a strategic spot outside the Muffin Treat, a luncheonette obscene as its name. He spied through steamed-over windows at the counter where the ladies nursed cups of coffee—guessing which would emerge next onto the street, fearing he'd be the first male on the planet to get rejected by an Eighth Avenue hooker.

"You wanna go out, honey?" one called at last.

That meant in. He nodded.

"I'm glad you chose me, lover. I flip for that sexy long hair."

"Where do we go?" His answer was an arm yanking him toward the Hotel Chez Paree.

"What's your name, darlin'?" Why did she have to ask? Or talk?

"Martin." He wanted to say Ricardo, Miles, Hoss—anything that would make him feel as tall and resplendent as she looked in her bouffant.

"I'll be calling you my lover man real soon. Come on, baby, let's get warm. It's killing out here!"

At the front desk, a pair of dead eyes looked over the familiar odd couple. But there was a ritual to be performed.

"It's five for the room, lover." He didn't see why but he paid up. She led him into a pink elevator, up to the third floor, down a hall where all the lights had blown. This wasn't the airy boudoir he'd been expecting. It wasn't even all too private—since the door to her room looked too small for the frame it was on and was locked only with a loop of string on a nail. The next surprise was that she didn't open it, but knocked.

"We have to wait just a second, lover. I got my big brother stayin' with me." Through the gaps in the doorway, he could see a tan, resplendently hugh character asleep in boxer shorts on the bed. "I gotta customer, boy! Get your lazy ass outta there!"

"I don't know about this—"

"Hold on, lover. He'll be out in no time and we'll have that bed to ourselves . . . Get a move on in there! I gotta john!"

A Martin, who no longer knew what he was doing in this grim hallway. To make sure he stayed, she began rubbing his crotch.

"Just a minute more, lover. . . . Move it, sucker! He's slow, poor child. With no place else to go. . . . There we are, baby. The premises is vacated."

The string had been untied from the inside. The overgrown child had disappeared through a second door to another part of this suite.

"Now jus' relax yourself. He won't bother us none. He barely knows where he is, poor thing."

She might have been talking about Martin. He watched her throw a tasseled, army green spread over where the man had been lying.

"Well, then, what's it gonna be?" Martin did not know what to tell her. He was standing over the dresser and staring down at a collage of yellowed snapshots that had been shoved under the glass top. There was a graduation picture, from junior high perhaps, a black girl in pigtails. There was the family fishing trip, there was Mom bearing her peach cobbler.

"How's about my 'round-the-world, you sexy thing?" He wished she would cut out all the cooing. Her tone was sweet enough to kill. "All the boys go for that. Or you after somethin' special?"

"Like what?"

"You gotta tell me, baby, I can't guess. . . . Maybe you'd like to try on some o' my rags."

No, she wasn't dealing with a transvestite, but with a trans-classite. Was there such a category in his father's sexology books, amidst the Krafft-Ebing case histories on coprophiliacs and princes of onan by which Martin had first masturbated?

"Make up your mind, lover. We only got a half hour."

That seemed a shame, considering all the time he'd taken to work up to this. He couldn't concentrate on negotiations, only on those snapshots. He no longer saw what any of this had to do with sex.

"I'd like a long time. No hurrying. I want to come twice."

"That'll cost ten extra, lover man."

He pulled the bills out of his thick wallet so quickly that she was stunned. Martin was stunned to see that whores actually did tuck the money in their brassieres, and worried that she'd caught a glimpse of the secret compartment where his parents made him carry an "emergency dollar." He had finally found a room where his parents could not enter. He had invented an emergency they could not help him meet.

"Shuck those rags now, honey."

Martin followed orders. He let his clothes fall in a heap at the foot of the bed. He could see the Fifth Avenue label in his rags. He wore no underwear, a newly acquired bohemian touch.

"Gee, lover, you're all prepared, ain't you?"

So prepared that the object he'd sought no longer seemed worth having. It came out of baggy polyester bell-bottoms and lace panties, revealing hairs that were not dyed blond, his first view of black on black. The whore's legs had dark craters on them, blotches like something had been spilled and left permanent stains. She did not remove her top, just hoisted up her blouse and bra halfway, letting the rounded bottoms of her breasts flop out for inspection. Martin was unsure of what came next. He felt like an explorer, mapping some unseen coastline. He would write an article for the *National Geographic* on this body. His hand went down between her legs, but the whore jumped back.

"Enough of that now, lover." She led him to the bed. "Gee, you got a righteously big one. You jus' lie back an' I'll take care o' business."

He did as he was told, mainly so that she would quit all her lies. He expected her to curl up beside him. He wanted to see black against white. Instead, the prostitute sat facing the organ of immediate concern and drooled a big wad of spit down on its cap. She began working the saliva in, talking more than she rubbed.

"Ooh, baby, ain't that the finest? Don't my hands know how to do you right?" Was this all? It may have been worth the money, but it wasn't worth the guilt. She kept wetting him up, only occasionally leaning over to plug up her mouth. When Martin didn't spasm at once, she reached up and scratched at his nipples.

"You're too far away," Martin finally got up the nerve to tell her. "I can't make it, unless we—"

He did not have to finish the sentence. The whore groaned and lay down beside him. Martin was just beginning to enjoy straddling her when he heard the "brother" pacing and whimpering oddly in the next room.

"Don't stop, lover! Don't pay him no mind!"

"I wish he wasn't in there—"

"Now, that's not very sportin'."

"If this is some kind of trick—"

"Ain't no trick. I told you, he's simple an' he don't know how to entertain hisself so good. . . . Let's go now, sexy boy. We got plenty o' lovin' to do."

She was grabbing at Martin, trying to milk him. This was not what Martin had bargained for. A bargain was not what he was after. There was nothing to do but bury his face in the whore's elastic neck. He smelt Ivory soap. He could hear her grunting, trying to disguise stabs of pain as pleasure. Something was wrong down there. For her sake and his own, he tried to get done as fast as he could. He imagined the retarded fellow peeping in, learning to count to ten from following the bobbing of Martin's buttocks. Screw, honky, screw!

"That was so sweet now, wasn't it, lover?" She pushed him off and went to get a towel. Martin could hear the whore turning faucets and whistling. He couldn't recall why he was waiting for her. He got into his pants more quickly than he ever had—especially when he heard the handle turning and the door to the next room opening. Martin froze at the foot of the bed, with one sock on, one off. The whore's brother came out in the full uniform of a security guard—complete with hat, epaulets, polished boots and a shoulder holster. In the uniform, the guy looked hulking and there was something in that holster. Something black and metallic, not just a prop. But all he did was lean against the useless radiator and give Martin a smile that was neither kind nor accusing.

The whore came back in a flannel nightie that made her look like she could be somebody's sister. She carried a thin, sopping rag. Martin saw that the towel bore a drawing of a bowler aiming at ten pins and the inscription, "For Your Balls!"

"Look at you, lover man! All put back together! He's such a shy one, this one! Such a gentleman!" Why didn't she just come out and hate him? With every forced compliment, he was more sure that she did. "Was it special for you, baby? What happened to that second go 'round?"

He'd forgotten all about it. "I can't—not with him here."

"Well, that's too bad now, ain't it, honey?" The whore kept on with her prattle, combed Martin's hair for him and flashed a smile that included one gold front tooth. "You know, I like to leave all my boys satisfied. How's about if I give you a little extry credit, lover boy. I'll treat you to something extra special next time."

The prostitute got back in her working disguise, straightened her wig, then kissed the hulking relative on the cheek, not quite sisterly. The three of them went down the hall and crammed into the elevator. Martin was more trapped now than he'd been with his pants down. They could have stopped on any floor and done anything to Martin that they wanted.

"Isn't he just the sweetest? You are a honey, you know that. I'll bet you got lots of girlfriends. No? I can't believe it. Isn't he just the sexiest?"

At that question, the goon could not help giggling, then covering his mouth, like he'd heard his first dirty joke. Going through the lobby, the whore let go of Martin's arm, patting the square bulge in his overcoat pocket.

"What you got in there, honey? A book? You wanna make me a present of it, lover?" At the moment, Martin couldn't remember the book's name or why he might be carrying it. He restrained her. The whore pretended a pout.

"Okay, you be that way. But if I know you like I do, then it's some hot book, something really sexy, ain't it?"

Soon as he ditched them, Martin grabbed for his wallet. His emergency dollar was still there. Then he checked the title of his book. It was *The Autobiography of Malcolm* X.

Out into the fog: a nasty sky-sealant that shrouds summer mornings. A reminder, courtesy of the Pacific, that malaise can be a year-'round affair. In its climate, and in this way only, Berkeley and I are alike. Perhaps I should give up and do as the Berkeleyites do—enroll in a workshop, join a support group, take a refresher course. "Being human, a six-week introduction." In this town, there's a fierce faith in social engineering that's less Marxist and more American in its origins than the residents are willing to admit. Correct answers thrive along with the flora. This garden's too lush, a laboratory experiment in overhabitability: where any new seed, given an ounce of ocean mist, can take hold and send up great shoots; where nature seems to be saying, "Don't blame me if you can't prosper"; where even the zen hoboes, the ultra-high-frequency schizophrenics, the battery-operated paraplegics, live well. And the only challenge is living right.

One thing I can do right is stretch. Though I'd never be caught in a yoga *ashram*, I've cribbed the "archer's pose" from other runners. One knee bent, arms stretched with eyes following the target out past your fingertips, one long exhalation while I ease lower and lower. This may not be all that great for the hamstrings, but it's terrific for getting stares from passing motorists. Is Daphne peeking out at me? To her, I probably look ludicrous, but at least my ludicrousness takes an erudite form. Can she guess that I'm loyal to this regimen only so I can stay trim enough to meet someone like her?

If my industriousness doesn't recommend me, I hope she's impressed by the coordination of my one-man team colors. I'm quite the dazzling high priest of fitness in blue satin shorts, striped ghettoesque knee-high socks. My tank top reads "CUBA SI!", which makes me as progressive as anyone can get in athletic togs. A wristband attests to the fact that I'm a sweaty guy. The truth is that I wouldn't be able to run if it didn't involve dressing up. I missed my chance at the high school varsities, collegiate letters, and now, at least, I want to look the part. Besides, for a film critic, I've got good legs.

But who ever notices? And would they sprint after me? I'd only give them the back of my thigh, as opposed to the back of my hand. I catch no sultry eyes except for shepherd watchdogs, hyperadrenal Dobermans. There are certain streets that I've learned not to go down. Still,

I'm tempted to test the canine patrol where the pavement's lined with stunted fruit trees, their block-long arcades of blossom turning from their spring burst, white as flashcubes, to a deep rust.

Trotting past those brown shingle cabins where dissertations are bred, I'm on course for the high school track, just three and a half digital minutes away. It's hardly where the chic meet to reek. At this hour, the other legs grinding the cinder belong to the girls' relay team, the Yellowjackets, who, according to a pennant that flies above the splintery grandstand, were runners-up for the state championship. Their coach, a fat bumblebee in bright yellow warm-up suit, blows his whistle to regulate the team's sado-maso paces. The girls wear braces but their growth hormones have turned them prematurely lissome. They've all twisted their hair into cornrows, the braids held tight with wooden beads that click with their strides. Gossiping while they gallop, the team shouts from the corners of the four-forty their one-of-a-kind surnames: Shawndra, Aleuthra, Deeandra, Debron. All I need to know about their reason for being here is in one easy pass of the baton. All they need to know about mine is the goofy grin that comes with exhaustion.

8:37 a.m. The hardest work in America is to get exhausted.

On the periphery, at the edge of the track, I spot another dedicated ne'er-do-well. You would think he could do most anything with that body: compact in black muscle shirt and stretch pants, with hamstrings and pectorals giving width to his well-defined breadth. Before he discovered weights, he was stocky, instead of beefcake—bowlegged, too, while he's now "centered low to gravity." No exercise, though, could improve that curly mane, those earnestly thick and quizzical eyebrows, the charming ease of that smile. Jack Giacomo, the happy-go-lucky kid who got a scholarship to Steffens College and was supposed to become its resident physics genius, now spends much of his time working his way around the high school's eight-station fitness course.

Somewhere along the line, Jack lost his mind, and found his body—with a vengeance. He would be a fixture at the nearest body-builders' salon, if he could afford it. After some years of driving a cab, picking grapes at some pals' winery, doing construction work for one or another of his more stable siblings, Jack earns his rent money snapping photographs of runners at the end of marathons—then persuading them to order a glossy or two of themselves breaking the tape or hitting "the wall." Not exactly an occupation essential to the world economy. When our SDS chapter occupied the college president's office, we found amongst his files a sincere letter from Jack the high school senior proposing a four-point plan to get tiny, liberal Steffens out of debt. Now he can't get himself out of debt, since he prefers the payment of myriad pals' admiration. Soon as he's finished a hundred leg-lifts on a slanted pine board, I know he'll be over to collect from me.

"Still buddies?"

His greeting, meant to resolder old fraternal bonds, always makes me wonder what treachery he's pulled in the interim.

"Still truckin'." But not quick enough, with Jack the wonder physicist breathing down my neck. "Doing my bit to fight arteriosclerosis."

"Sounds mighty revisionist, boy." I'd been the one who first introduced Jack to that word and he delighted in reminding me of the days when I trotted out that bit of vocabulary with much gravity. "Putting in your revisionist mileage on the revisionist track."

"Revisionist feet, don't fail me now!"

"Hey, Pep, you should let me do some eight-by-tens of you on the track." Asking for a photo session was Jack's way of asking for money. "Portrait of the artist as young revisionist."

"You already took some." And I'd paid for them, in advance, a year back.

"I know, I know. I just haven't had the funds for developing fluid. But the negatives were gangbusters, I swear. . . . Still buddies?"

As much as we ever were: huffing our way toward the revisionism of middle age.

"Hey, Pep. 'Time is the biggest hassle.' Remember? 'If you like the Living Theater, how come you don't like the way I eat?' Remember that one? Remember? 'I've set my mind back to zero!' "

8:40 a.m. We were the envy of everyone, even ourselves.

Mind Zero. A Steffens College broadside. Edited by Free, alias Martin Pepper. Date: Third week, Black Studies Strike. Cost: Free!

TO: a faculty that hires and fires by cocktail party,
that dishes out elitist shit to isolate us from reality,
that obfuscates the class struggle,
that generally requires people to be unFREE!

NOW: let's start with a 50/50 student-faculty share of power on every committee in the school, leading eventually to a state of NOOO-ONE having any power over anyone—people should hire and fire themselves on the basis of how well they think they've done at what they do. You want to isolate us, faculty, okay isolate us from the competitive capitalist rat-race that fucks us all. No more structures over anyone. DESTROY PROPERTY AND CREATE ART!

AND: burn down all the buildings and start all over again (leave the trees). Move the library to a working class district so that every student has to walk through it every day and study that! End college requirements, more independent study, less shit food, no more bans on mattresses on the floor (WHAT IS THIS?), admit all Third World applicants, end closed meetings and closed minds.

ESPECIALLY: corporate recruiters off campus, weapons research out of the labs (if Steffens has gotta produce scholarly cripples, at least it shouldn't help make cripples in Vietnam), Western civ. out of our heads.

STUDENTS: weaken institutions, increase FREEdom, begin naked every day, study life, act out modern drama in the streets, change history, pass joints in lectures, don't learn how the bullshit committees work, learn how the heating plant works so you can shut it OFF.

Play-dough not Plato!
Delirium by any means necessary!
The streets belong to the manholes!

(Softball wars: Aristotelian reactionaries watch out for SDS fuckoff cell, Sunday!)

8:41 a.m. Society: nature's boot camp.

The track team is lapping us for the ninth time.

"I'd like to drop a half pound of cottage cheese between *her* legs!" says Jack about one of the sprinters.

"Small or large curd?"

"That reminds me, I finally got my count . . . at the sperm bank."

For some months, Jack has been obsessed with obtaining this ultimate measurement of physical prowess. A reading on the biological stopwatch.

"You made a donation?"

"Tax-deductible, sport. That was the easy part, compared to sweating out the test results. But I'm cool. My genetic cup runneth over, as they say. Even when it's frozen into a popsicle. Buying into fatherhood here, power."

"But who's the lucky bearer?"

"Whoever applies. Probably some specialist on Sapphic poetics. I don't wanna know. I just want the Giacomo line to continue. Take my best shot at immortality."

"You can be anything this time around . . ." I remind him of our favorite Timothy Leary dirge.

"You can be Lord Krishna this time around."

"You can be a janitor this time around." Jack has a gorgeous, husky laugh—but it rings hollow as anything that becomes an end in itself.

"You can be the Peter Pan of socialism this time around! Remember when the Young Republicans called you that? . . . Speaking of which, what's your view of this Peter Pan complex?"

"I'm not grown up enough to comment."

"You know what they're doing? They're changing the terms on us. Last year, or last decade, we were demi-apes who had to put down our clubs. Now we're a bunch of sissies fleeing our ordained role. Make up your minds, ladies! I don't know what women would do if they couldn't complain about men. The terminology changes, but the activity's age-old."

"I think they just want to sell magazines."

"Awfully materialist of you, sport. I say, fuck 'em. High or low consciousness, they all want the same package. Grim realism plus hearts and flowers, utter fidelity plus that indefinable aloofness, someone to lean on plus someone to push over. Plus your left ball in a trophy case." These are the sorts of things that men talk about in the fog in the morning in Berkeley. "Tapping out here, power. Thanks to liquid nitrogen, we can still be patriarchs. Right, sport? The penisless ones want to exert influence—man, they've already got half the planet drooling after them and they don't even know it. They don't deign to see it anymore, right? I guess beauty is just too big a responsibility. They want equal rights—okay, they can have the right to grovel, the right to be ignored, the right to get blamed for most every calamity. Is that it, Pep? You're the answer man. A leading revisionist commentator. You tell me, buddy. What more do they want?"

But I'm out of breath, on my last straightaway home.

8:48 a.m. California's latest health craze: aerobic weeping.

Daphne's fled. No blue car on the block. And the mail has yet to arrive. No letter from the adventurous press where I've submitted my book. In either case, the suspense is preferable to any likely outcome. Whether in my box or my bed, I've grown content with deferred deliveries.

Valentines addressed to occupant. In this town, the mail's sluggish movement seems purposely aimed at putting us a day behind the rest of the world's unclean enterprise. It doesn't help that most of Berkeley's letter carriers are American Sikhs who meander about, vacant-eyed, sporting white turbans that transcend the gray woolen uniform of their second calling. Around here, the main task of the working class seems to be the avoidance of work. But I did no better during my voluntary stint as an "infiltrator" among these postal shirkers. I am no one to criticize.

Go Amongst the Workers and Peasants. Four Attempts:

1. They took anyone at the post office. It was a college of hard knocks with an open admissions policy, and that was the only sort of school Martin was willing to attend. To get in, the enrollees had to drag a fifty-pound sack stuffed with sand some twenty feet or so. Martin also had to swear that he'd never conspired to overthrow the government, and how could they doubt him based on the results thus far? If you got a decent score on the civil service test, they had to let you in. Junkie or kleptomaniac or Ph.D. The PO, like a grim reaper, called your name when your number came up.

In Martin's group of hirelings, there were a couple of palsied Korean War vets, a gang of black truants, plus a bona fide delusionary bag lady, who showed up for her orientation in an Easter bonnet, fishnet stockings with gaping holes. She kept interrupting with inquiries about possessed spirits lodged in the Christmas cards—but that didn't disqualify her. And then there was Martin, a novice in the back row, for whom the concept of wage labor was dazzlingly foreign. He was the most eager student of all, who'd signed on in order to be oppressed.

In this regard, the PO did not disappoint. It was so much like the army. The drill sergeants were paunchy supervisors in boat shoes with beady eyes and clipboards and a hundred honeyed ways to make Martin and cohorts feel like errand boys. They liked to hear themselves boss, explaining the simplest regulations again and again, ignoring flagrant inefficiencies and exposed conveyor belt hazards. Each new batch of privates quickly learned that there was only one untransgressable rule: Act dumb and go along. Martin discovered that he possessed a natural aptitude for this first survival tactic of the working class. He showed hidden talents for going vapid; took to scratching his head at the simplest commands. And they were commands, since a postal worker could be fired for refusing to obey. All this for six bucks an hour and lifetime security! Even dogs required more incentive to come when their masters called.

Dog work, as the old-timers called it, was reserved for newcomers like Martin. Unprotected by seniority, he and the other "temporary indefinites" were dispatched to single-handedly unload fifty-foot trailers crammed with mildewed number three sacks. The gray bundles looked and felt like proverbial bodies sent to the bottom of the East River. Every night, on the swing shift, Martin had to dredge them up, with drawstrings whipping, metal labels cutting, burlap roughness grating. Sometimes, he was rewarded for his efforts with the bonus of a Coke. This was presented to him with great fanfare by that living sarcophagus of a supervisor known as "Whistlin' George." Martin did everything Whistlin' George wanted, except pretend that he was content. Martin had no prior experience at that. "Give us a smile, won't you?" Whistlin' George needled. But Martin never obliged. He gave the PO his time, nothing more.

In the fluorescent-bathed universe of the work floor, where every hamper, hand truck, container, dolly, desk, chair, water cooler, locker, toilet, railing, lunch tray was stickered, "Property of U.S. Gov't.," time itself was a commodity that could be purchased and leased. Martin's time never passed because he'd rarely known any that wasn't his own. He knew few methods for getting around regimentation. From his fellows, he copied and perfected the science of being there without being there.

Martin completed his apprenticeship in insolence under an old rum-nose named Mac, who'd accumulated so many hours on his time card that he could blow smoke rings in Whistlin' George's mug. In the No Smoking zone! It was Mac who caught his latest adjutant blithely tossing a case of metal screws atop a hamper full of gift boxes marked "fragile" and "agricultural." Such labels were routinely ignored and Martin was just picking up the routine. This time, the packages at the bottom exploded in gushes of rotten avocado. He had to spend the rest of that day wiping green slime off all the brown wrappings. He stamped "Damaged in Postal Handling" on everything down to the pits. From then on, Mac called him "Guacamole Man." Martin had won his place in postal mythology.

But belonging is hardly the same as proselytizing. And how could he deliver his pitch at this working class when they weren't just workers, but black? How to become fluent in black speak when he'd hardly begun to stutter in the language of resignation? Such questions faded once he was assigned to a permanent work station. Elevated from loading trailers to "throwin' flats" into his own set of slots, he found that no turning of the head was allowed here, and no chatter. That must have been why it took Martin several weeks to realize that something was peculiar about this section of clerks. In order to try his hand at organizing, it seemed that he would have to learn sign language. The workers around him were vocational trainees from a local school for the sensorially impaired. They were deaf. So the PO did take everyone! If no one could hear the Guacamole Man, maybe that wasn't so bad. Martin would have plenty of time to figure out what he was burning to say.

8:52 a.m. Words never fail, except in the larger sense.

My manuscript contains four hundred thousand of them. That's another reason why I don't blame the publishers if they're a little slow in responding. Since I've waited nine months, I suppose I can hold on for another weekend. Maybe I'm being given all this time so I might ascertain why I'm so anxious to see my name on a dust cover, as the esteemed author of the essays I've audaciously titled "Films Against Their Audience." How many mornings have I stood here, shivering in my shorts while composing the back jacket blurbs? "Where has Martin

Pepper been? Nobody west of the Mississippi speaks more eloquently about how the movies speak to us. . . . More than a critic, Martin Pepper is someone who's actually fearless in the face of ideas. . . . Indispensable for anyone who lives for the movies—or wants to quit." If only I could write some blurbs about my personality and pin them to my lapel—or distribute to nubile passersby! I must want this book so badly because I went to progressive schools that never gave out report cards. Finally, I'll have something to run home with and prove that I have actually been paying attention. I can almost hold this one, bound and ink-scented, in my hands.

8:53 a.m. Programmed to succeed, programmed just as surely not to savor that success.

9:03 a.m. What's death but the ultimate rejection slip?

9:06 a.m. The reason for living alone: in this locker room, no one's got a bigger one.

9:11 a.m. No wonder I can't get clean, when each time I step in the shower, I think of *Psycho*.

9:12 a.m. What do my thoughts have to do with my ankles?

9:15 a.m. Pampering myself with drugstore extravagances: Cocoa Butter, Aloe, Oils of Spearmint and Jojoba. Has anyone ever seen a Jojoba?

9:17 a.m. Crow's-feet around my eyes don't bother me. I take them as proof that, on occasion, I have actually laughed.

9:18 a.m. In the fogged mirror, Peter Pan notices his first strand of gray.

9:19 a.m. Desperation: getting aroused by the prospect of a haircut.

9:24 a.m. No skeletons in my closet, just love beads.

9:26 a.m. The first time you let some Oriental do our laundry—a tacit endorsement of the injustice of the world.

9:28 a.m. On every hanger, a shirt I bought to impress a girl I never met, buttons missing.

I've got outdoor wear that's never seen the light of day. My hair shirts have lost their itch from too many tumble dries. Burgundy briefs: I'd like to think that I've started wearing them because my masculinity is no longer threatened, not because they hide the come stains. Go for a T-shirt to highlight my hard-earned trim and eternal youthfulness. But which message will I promote on my chest? On my closet floor, I can find a silkscreened flyer for each sports team in these parts, each Third World support group, each *taqueria*. I reach into the pile, hoping to draw a blank.

Contact lenses in place, monkey cheek whiskers scraped off, beard trimmed down to a neat suburban hedge. This must be the "new Martin" that I wish to unveil before those few experts on the old, still-extant. But what to wear to the prom? We set the dress code this time. So it's come as you are. But how am I, anyhow? And if I came as that, would I be asked to leave?

9:31 a.m. Reconstructing the solidity of ourselves every day: to do it, we must have access to familiar materials, however trivial. The particular typeface of our hometown newspaper, the sketch of a cat on our favorite glass.

9:33 a.m. God's not dead, he's just been replaced by Vitamin C.

9:34 a.m. In the objects around your own kitchen sink, enough mystery for a lifetime.

9:35 a.m. Why is it always so much easier to make someone else's bed?

Get my stovetop espresso machine going, heat up the milk gradually. I know how to take care of my breakfast with style and *mit schlag. Sans* Daphne. I'm the new male who knows how to iron and sew, sort his socks, hang pictures straight, stir-fry with the best of them, can take care of myself very well, thank you. So what do I need women for and vice versa?

Almost out the door, I nearly forget my contribution to the pot luck. It's a potato salad tickled up according to Julia Child, French-style for the occasion. Then I remember to turn on my answering machine. Lord knows why I've got one. If there's a message, it's either my editor with a screening date or a wrong number. Little black girls asking me to fetch "Tina." I wish I had Tina's tips on popularity! I ought to learn not to replay the tape or pick up the receiver. But relatives must have their fair opportunity to be the bearers of bad news. Coronaries aside, they phone every Christmas, good Jews that they are. In a rickety, immigrant English that's so much more evocative than my smoother kind, they assure me, "You are mature now. You know how to smell the air of responsibility." And I always thought it was the garbage!

My callers are greeted with a message that's a reversal of Godard's postulation about the film he wanted secretly to live. "This is the life we secretly wanted to be a film," says the prerecorded critic. "Please contribute your voice-over." But why does this soundtrack suggest that my life is a silent? Wait, the red light is blinking. Warning: human groping for contact in the vicinity. I didn't realize that I already had the damn thing turned on, and that someone's paged me during my run. I rewind back to hear, in a half-speed slur meant to disguise, "People! Yippies! You the Lumpen! . . . Touch me on the can during the dance!"

There's only one person who could leave this message. So Ayer Wilcox has finally stooped to check in on his past! I'm touched to think that he has the same nostalgia for this date—though I doubt whether he'd admit it in person. I don't want the chance to find out. I play the message over, trying to hear if there's long-distance static. The last I heard, Ayer was roaming Nevada on some state grant for a job title he'd improvised on the spot. They say he's an "artist-in-residence," whose residence is probably a shiny new pickup, whose art is whatever hops in the cab. I don't know why I should care anymore, but I hope he's out sketching on some atomic testing range.

9:39 a.m. Overrun by the past—but why do without landmarks, memorials, debts, when France can't, Mongolia can't?

Leaflet.

People! Organizations! Groups! Yippies! Political Parties! Workers! Students! Peasant-Farmers! You the Lumpen! Poor People! Black People, Mexican-Americans, Puerto Ricans, Chinese, etc., etc. WE MUST DEVELOP A UNITED FRONT AGAINST FASCISM!

WHYS!!!FOR A NAT'L CONFERENCE:

- Primary: Community Control of Police
- Freedom of Political Prisoners
- How to Deal with Law and Order Politicians
- The Right to Self-Defense Against Fascist Tactics
- Huey P. Newton Incarcerated Without Bail Because of His Leadership to Establish the Right of Self-Determination
- James Rector Murdered by Fascist Alameda County Sheriff Who Placed Private Property of Finance Capital Above Human Life So-called Trespassing With Respect to People's Park

National Conference for a UNITED FRONT AGAINST FASCISM. Oakland, California—July 18, 19 and 20, 1969. Conference Headquarters—Black Panther Party, 3106 Shattuck Ave., Berkeley, Calif. 94705.

The fog's lifted, thought it's never defrosted inside Federico, my comic Fiat. Like any good Italian, Federico frequently goes on strike. I didn't buy him for reliability, but for his tasteful lines—since marred by an encounter with a West Oakland junkie in a Fleetwood Brougham. Though it would have been an easy job for a body shop, I had the work done by some wandering gypsies who promised that my one crumpled door would end up looking just like the rest. It might have, if they hadn't tried to sand it by hand, smear on putty with spoons and spray it with the only paint they had ready—which happened to be black. Now it looks like one side of my white car got in the path of volcanic lava. Some people have egg on their face, but mine's on my chassis. At least, this morning, the thing starts. It gets good mileage for a cereal box with room for six. In fact, I could cart a little league team. As I toodle about, I mostly converse with the passenger I call The Thing in the Back of the Car!

9:43 a.m. An only child always drives a station wagon.

Rogue Island. On a lot at the edge of their school on the edge of the city, they were poised before a fleet of cruisers ready to take them away. Missy and Martin were already circling impatiently in her Barracuda. Tonight, a surprise party was in the works for Ayer's birthday, and almost any excuse was good enough to take them away from this trimmed lawns and trimmed minds.

"DON'T MAKE YOUR SUMMER A BUMMER—DON'T TAKE DRUGS!"

Turned up full, the radio in Crash's four-by-four rocked the gang while they waited, but the only part of its AM warning they heard was about the summer. It was almost here—final exams just a week away. They could hardly wait for the moment, or for the birthday boy. Annie and Crash had organized his party, working themselves into a playful hysteria.

"Quick, you-all! Hide the food!" Placing three bags of groceries in the Dodge's trunk, Martin could see that Annie had purchased Tillamook wedges and loaves of French bread, perhaps in homage to Ayer's upbringing in a Parisian boarding school.

Striding down the concrete walk from the dormitories, in desert boots with fat mismatched laces, torn khakis, paper belt, cowboy shirt bulging open European-style, wispy hair to the waist and chubby, unshaven face was their unofficial ringleader and high priest, Ayer Wilcox. The scion of Philadelphia blue bloods, he'd come back to America from his French schooling a precocious acid-eater and *anarchiste*. Martin thought of him as a deejay rather than a guru, speaking to them through musical selections or a Don Rickles punch line transformed into a quotation from Chairman Wow. He was grinning, sheepish, as he shook their hands formally one by one—his trademark. He could see that the little birthday spin Annie had suggested was going to be more than that.

"Kiss my bongo drums! Where to, Mac's?"

"You get the great outdoors on a sesame seed bun!"

"With two all-beef patties?"

"Hint o' onion?"

"Our own special sauce!"

"Let's race!" suggested Missy. In a moment, they'd all leaped into their vehicles, like the drivers at the start of the Indy 500. Dana took the wheel of the Barracuda, so that Martin got to have Missy on his lap, slide his arms around the waist of her orange sundress, feel black female hair brushing into his forehead. All he could see of the road were snatches of water towers and blocks of shacks where the thirties had never ended. Then suburban green. The city beyond their campus was but an encampment, a frontier outpost. Nature surrounded it. Around a turn, civilization stopped dead. It did not dare violate the enemy's earth-space, and the enemy was an ambush of trees, and water breaking all the laws, a conspiracy of dispossessed snow under cover of fog banks that hung in the gorges.

"Run, you thirsty mother!" Martin cheered on Dana, as they caught sight of the birthday boy and his moll in their Austin-Healey, Ebenezer their favorite mutt taking up the backseat with ecstatic quiet and car alertness. The Dodge went into the lead just as they entered Rogue River National Park, coasting down an unpaved slope into a parking place made of fallen pine needles. After Ayer arrived, he was blindfolded like a kidnap victim. Then he was led to a reserved niche in the state-sanctioned wilderness beside the coursing river. A picnic table was laden with Ayer's favorite items of bad taste: a pair of mauve socks with peace signs knitted in, a Don Rickles album, one British blues forty-five and one Elvis, four packages of baseball cards, doubles of Juan Marichal, a monstrous bag of Gaines Burgers for the dog, hyperthyroid size.

"Mondo absurdo! I only wish all this wasn't, how you say, transitory." They all knew that the birthday boy was talking about more than their freshman year. "It's shame for us to get separated now."

"But you haven't opened your most special present!" Missy came forward with her own flimsy brown package. While Ayer grappled with the wrappings, all of them gathered 'round—the full charter membership of Big Mac, the name they'd recently given to their collegiate clique trying to be a street gang, in homage to the franchise they'd begun frequenting on all-night, marijuana-dizzed flights from their student ghetto. But there were no proper names yet for what they were. Love circle, action committee, rock band without instruments—these last months, they'd spurred each other into considering a permanent detour from the futures planned for them. They could leave this school that had brought them together now that they'd established their own curriculum: Introductory Reality, Advanced Cruising, Friendship Seminar, the Aesthetics of Graveyard Shift, Unknown America, Discoveries In Class Consciousness, Hash Brown Potatoes 101.

At first, Ayer's present looked just like another kiddie coloring book, *The Thief of Baghdad*, filled in with hallucinatory colors, green hands with black fingernails, with all their names crayoned above the thief and his gang riding a magic carpet. Below, the message, "Reunion in Moose Meadow."

"*Qu'est-ce que c'est?*"

"We only have to be apart for a month," said Missy. "My folks are in the mountains all of July! I can donate our house for group use."

Shazam! The one-armed bandit of decision clicked behind their bloodshot eyes. Together, in the California valley, they'd bask in the dropout sun, then agitate among the heathens. (Which ones? They'd figure that out later.) For now, all that mattered was "Let's keep this group thing alive . . ."

The compact was sealed with a joint, that handy aid for simulating emotional unanimity. Then they gobbled the Tillamook and brownies and digested cross-legged, while watching the sun fall into the tan, sprinting river. Beyond were endless Douglas firs and they had to venture into them and away from flannel-wrapped Oregon families encircled by ice chests and Blitz stubbies. They formed a caravan down a path through a tunnel of twig along the riverbank. Dana took the lead, while Martin lagged behind, tailing Crash.

"Why do you stare at me all the time, huh?"

"I can't help it," Martin confessed.

"What do you see?"

"I see someone who's going to meet me this summer."

The path led to a clearing of mud by the river. Across from this opening was an islet, just a glorified sandbar sprouting with trees Martin could not name. The trees grew straight in a grove of wiry, leafless poles. The sandbar appeared to grow from their trunks, not the other way around.

"What an incredible island, huh?"

"Can we wade across?"

Ayer plopped his Hush Puppies into the mud. "Let's get this cock-sucker on its ass!"

They formed a chain against the current's tug. The channel deepened just before they got to the islet, the Rogue pressing jeans to their thighs. Martin waited to hoist out Missy, her dress stained to just below her breasts. The sun was almost down, taking the pigment out of everything. On the island, they scattered, sopping wet, without a plan. They played tag, pushing aside the puny stalks of no-name trees. They lost each other in this leafless layered grove of vertical bark, calling, "Crash!" . . . "Ayer!" . . . "Martin!" . . . "Annie!" . . . "Dana!" Their need for each other was earnest, even if they were only pretending to be lost.

9:55 a.m. This is the story of two families: the one we could not quite leave and the one we could not quite find.

First trial of the day, time to pick up the first ghost. Why couldn't Annie have met me for coffee—no, her anima's decaffeinated—instead of making me return to the setting of my last involvement? Why hasn't she moved already, instead of continuing to nest as she does? Annie's the happy hen, without rooster or hatchings. Though we've been nominally separated going on five years, each visit here reminds me of a hundred after-supper promenades when the two of us rated the flower arrangements in more prosperous front yards and the color combinations of painted trim, gave one another a good case of house envy, of couple envy, waxing on about how we wanted a yard like that someday, a house like that someday, when we were settled. Dreaming the same dreams, we wanted to share them with someone else.

Yet the connection between us is too sturdy for simple demolition. So's this preearthquake brown shingle that's three solid floors of redwood, with white eaves that droop like junkies' eyelids. The front porch is in need of repainting, but that doesn't matter because no one sits out on it anymore, not in this neighborhood. Not even Annie. She's carried on courageously with her front yard garden despite the rampaging German shepherd pups and ghetto gangs who regularly trample her seedlings. Once, the local *comité sanitaire* had raised their guillotines to decapitate a row of aristocratic sunflowers. Poor somber swollen heads of seed! Annie merely planted again. That was her idea of politics: modest goals, quiet example. Around here, such saintliness has put her under siege.

Along the side of the house, down the uneven stairs crowded with pots of the succulents Annie calls "chickens 'n' hens," I fumble for my key *comme d'habitude*. I know all too well why I insist on retaining a key, though I'm less sure why Annie lets me keep it. I don't think I've abused my right to free access. I use my house privileges only in an emergency, though my definition of one may differ from hers. I consider it urgent when I haven't been supplied my fortifying rations of Annie's chili and jambalaya, her authentic buttermilk biscuits and peppery corn pudding and upside-down cake, her red beans complete with "pot likker." Her confederate legacy is drawn from alphabetized index cards passed down from a great-aunt who ran a cafeteria in Port Arthur. Annie's food is the sort that can get you across the most searing deserts, the most vapid plains, the dust bowls of depression.

There've been times, I'll admit, when I've dropped by hoping for another sort of handout—something Annie can't retrieve from her recipe box. Her sweet recipe box! Before testing the front door, I try to make certain that she isn't occupied with some "back door" man. I don't bother pretending it's me any more, though there would be no harm in that: Annie and I were always pretending to be a couple, right up until the day we pretended to break up. It shouldn't come as a surprise that the key to a house left so obligingly turns out to be a key without value. Annie's still attempting to live her life unlocked, pretending that Oakland's just like the Panhandle town where she grew up. She skips barefoot through the shrapnel of empty lots; invites local sociopaths in for lemonade.

"Hey, hey!" I feel the need to let her know which sociopath this is.

"Hold your horses, hon! Keep away from here! I want my dish to be a surprise."

Is it because she grew up among so many frisky siblings that Annie constructs and relishes these ritual unveilings?

"What is it?" I'm already hungry. "Texas Toast? Baked Alaska?"

"Hah-hah."

"Don't worry. I can't even smell it."

What I smell is the mildew bred in this always darkened lair. Not even Annie can scrub it all out. I stand in the long, redwood-planked living room, letting my eyes adjust to this realm of the windowless. In the corner that once housed my desk and Zavattini scripts, Annie's stationed her loom, a baby-lock sewing machine, shelves of yardage and patterns of butcher paper shaped like flattened cuts of beef. The tools of her trade. Though she once had ambitions to become a therapist, Annie's designing toddler clothes for a trendy firm called Cupcakes.

Over the fireplace, she's left the garage-sale moose head that I always found morbid. I suppose she views her stuffed mascot as a back-handed tribute to her backwoods ancestry, or some Buddhistic reminder of death's proximity. Her place is part hunting lodge, part Shinto shrine.

I pass into our old bedroom, the apartment's one sunny perch, jutting over a neighbor's yard. I inspect the three masks that Annie made for herself in a mask-making class and hung in a row over the bed. All sides of Annie, I presume: the moon goddess in white plaster of Paris, the death mask of ancestors in black, the fount of fertility in painted floral. A bulletin board bears drawings of Jungian archetypes and inspirational clippings. "Life is a journey and I want to make clothes like the wind, suited for the wanderer"—Yamamoto. On the nightstand, I see the school notebook in which she dutifully records the appearances of her spiritual Dear Abby. Beside it is her "dream stone": some dense pebble she clutches because a rock is an area of calm—though I suspect she places the thing in her cervix for organic contraception. In the far corner, above several rubber plants, she's placed the dress form (size ten) which she uses for tailoring her customized kimonos. Headless, but nude, it's Annie unveiled. I try not to look at the bed or I'll get ideas. At least it's made. How can someone get a Moroccan donkey blanket to lie so smooth? I glance about for incipient signs of a man. No way. Annie's bookshelf: behind the Simone de Beauvoir and Judy Chicago, a complete series of Harlequin romances. Annie's bedroom: so clean it's sad.

10:03 a.m. Sex on the brain—never concede that it might be in lieu of something better.

She joins me, wiping her hands on a dish towel. Now we go through our to-kiss-or-not-to-kiss tussle. I never can decide whether it's best to initiate or wait. I can't figure out exactly where to kiss, when she's giving her best broad grin, which makes her lips dissolve into her gums and her chubby cheeks crease into dimples. She's shoeless, showing feet that are soft, arched, bunionless. Tight jeans highlight an accepting pelvis. On top, a Japanese housecoat is one loosening of the belt from showing cleavage. And though I'm not about to reach for that belt, I'm relieved when Annie offers a sisterly hug and whispers, "Good on ya!"

It's an Aussie greeting passed on by her pa, who did some oil drilling there. I don't know the proper Aussie reply.

"Did you have any good dreams last night?" This is Annie's version of good morning.

"Just my top ten nightmares."

"Are you sure? It's an important day, you know. A day that makes us seek a guide."

"If I took my dreams as guidance, I'd head for the nearest cliff."

"Go ahead, then. . . . Just do me a favor, wait 'til this evening. I need a ride out to Missy's."

Annie doesn't put up with my bad moods, which is strange, since she's the only person around whom I reveal them. Often, I don't even know that I'm in one until she's there to get infuriated by it.

"You're getting grayer." Garlands of the dread color run through Annie's thin mane, her locks parted down the middle as they were when she was four, and will be when she's sixty.

"I know. Isn't it wonderful?"

"Just terrific. Now you can mainline Grecian Formula."

"Come on! Every one of these hairs is a lesson learned."

"Or a lesson flunked."

"You are chipper this morning, buttercup!"

"Maybe it's because I just got a prerecorded handshake from an old beau of yours."

"Ayer?" she intuits. "I told you! It's a day for banishing demons."

"Gee, I'm glad I brought my suntan lotion . . ."

"What's eatin' at you, Mister Grump?"

"Nothing. . . . Nothing a month's sensual massage wouldn't cure." Annie's the only one I keep apprised of my sensual deprivation. The two of us, who agreed to part so that we could play the field, have been brought closer by these years of finding that field barren.

"You haven't been having any 'adventures,' have you?" That's Annie's inaccurate euphemism for my flights into whoring. "I hate to think of you in some raunchy hotel. That's not the true Pep."

"How do you know?"

"Because I remember you from before. Before what you let Missy do to you, really. You're the last romantic. Your heart pumps chocolate pudding. . . ."

"So how come no one wants a taste?" I continue to bait Annie.

"The group does."

"What group?"

"Shoot." I've pushed Annie's Southern hospitality to its precipitous limit. "You're getting me furious, real fast. Cross as two sticks. You're the one who organized this event, and you're already trying to spoil it. You push us all to mark the anniversary, and we're grateful that you do. But you aren't. You just can't be content with the fact that we've all been friends half our lives."

"We've drifted so far apart. We should have done better."

"Should, should, should—" Annie turns her head sharply, so that all I see is a blur of hair, still more chestnut than gray. Inexplicably, she senses that someone else has followed me through her open door.

10:09 a.m. There are one or two things that cannot be explained by childhood. There are one or two things that cannot be explained at all.

American Heritage. Annie's great-great-granddaddy shot Sitting Bull. The rumor followed her wherever she went, passed along each Thanksgiving over biscuits, corn bread dressing and candied yams at Aunt Connie's cafeteria. It was such an all-American meal, all-American rumor, all-American family: scattered, restless, admitting to their interdependence only when they were apart. There were whispers, too, that another daddy among granddaddies killed a runaway slave in the last days of the Confederacy—but items like that tended to accrue when you were American for too long, with a family tree planted in a muddy Tennessee hollow called Hickihola Bottom. Most of Annie's ancestors were dirt farmers who wandered to West Texas in search of something honest to do with their hands. There they discovered that what was good for Phillips Petroleum was good for them. They never forgot about those honorable hands. They were hands that delighted in keeping the machinery going, and didn't care to know about the machinery's purpose. They were hands put there by the Lord so every fix-it man could pull his own weight. With each batch of corn pudding, Annie built her adherence to this ancestral ethic. With each sift of baking powder, she proclaimed her self-sufficiency. A Christian love for acts simply achieved was passed down to Annie by her barefooted mom, whose love-thy-neighbor mysticism only fed Annie's faith in that prairie creed which teaches that good is eventually rewarded, somewhere in the universe, maybe in some heaven where there are trees. Never mind that it drove her many brothers to guns and long Bowie knives, to hunting and brawling and dope-smoking insolence, especially Jed, the favorite, whose birthday was celebrated as Jedmas. Annie's tool-pusher father was never around to be anything but a goad to the boys, left Annie nothing but a love of good hardware—and a constant, chunky-toothed grin which hid everything, chubby cheeks and wary Asiatic squint so that at first the others figured she might be an Eskimo. In the freshman funnies, after all, it said she was from Alaska, where Daddy had gone, following the oil. Annie followed for the last years of high school where she took a deep breath before joining the sixties, backpacking over the Chilkoot Trail in search of Sitting Bull's spirit.

Gone Fish-In. Everyone knew they'd reached the reservation when all the roads, all the arable land, turned to mud. At a checkpoint, the Steffens contingent had to leave Missy's Barracuda behind. Wheelless members of the tribe, they sauntered past road's end into a swampy clearing that was serving as an informal mobilization center. At the one log cabin, squaws in overalls ladled out canned corn and chunks of gummy bread. There was also free dope everywhere, judging by the smell. More red eyes than red men, everyone sloshing about in the sewer earth. The swamp was graced with a few genuine tepees, rigid and unadorned. Also a few Indians, whittling as they ambled about in the muck. There were other concerned students, too, friends of the Red Man, an admiration society of quietude and the land and barter beads and revenge. They all seemed remarkably at home—waiting their turn to try out the tepees. "Hey, bro', where's the Fish-In at?" Dana asked.

"Down at Frank's Landing. Volunteers needed."

There was a general groan, but the new arrivals were ready recruits. Hopping into an old Chevy that spun through back roads to the landing, which was more mud, with a coffeepot on an open fire and a few fir branches stuck in the riverbank to ground the tribal rowboat. The river roared past, looking like it wanted to be left alone. From this torrent, the Nisqually Indians coaxed a few slippery salmon daily. Nets were strung across. One half-flooded rowboat was used to set and take up the netting. This leaky boat was illegal, the torn nets a threat to the state.

The volunteers were supposed to make sure the fishing went on by offering themselves to the police, who'd already taken in practically half the tribe, and by keeping guard against hostile whites or roaming firewatered Indians. This time, all they found were a couple of young braves around the fire, singing, "You can get anything you want at Alice's Restaurant . . ." If they'd had a television, they might have been watching reruns of the Lone Ranger.

Grudgingly, they offered the next shift their Disneyland ride across the river. Somehow, the Nisqually navigated with one splintered oar. They let Missy hoist the nets and she was thrilled to find a single flopping silver prize. Back at the shore, Martin and Missy wandered over to a Ford wagon caked with mud up to the middle of the door. An old Indian sat at the wheel.

"You kids from the colleges?"

"Yeah. From Oregon."

"Oregon? We are from Oregon, too. We are Yakima. Much of the Willamette Valley once belonged to us."

What could we say? "Sorry to hear that."

"There has been a fishing law in effect in Oregon for years, you college kids should know. One young man of our tribe—can this be told?—came home from the service, on leave from Vietnam, when he went out fishing in the normal way. He was arrested that very night—just for fishing in the normal way on the rivers of his people who knew no other skills. For this he had won medals? There was little food. So that he grew angry. To avoid the county sheriffs, he went out late one night, without a flashlight, in turbulent water. He was drowned a few days before he was to return to Vietnam. He was one of the last of our sons on the reservation. So, you see, there are many things you should know about and also study, you must study up on all this very well."

He started his car and took off, a sad old delivery man for sad stories. The five of them stood guard 'til dark, drawing up closer to the fire, coffeepot and the young braves listening to their favorite top forty. They remained very quiet, out of respect for the Indians' radio-listening rite and because they knew that their conversation would lead them to wonder who was giving direction to all this muddle. That was the thing about genocide: given an initial push, it worked on its own momentum.

The next morning, they were still waiting for some bold strategy, levitation, Pocahonduras! After peppermint tea and banana bread, the camp formed a caravan in VW's and headed for Olympia and a climactic demonstration at the state capitol. Three hundred or so of them tramped through silent park grounds, with fountains shut off.

"Where's Chief Knock-a-Homa?" asked Missy.

"Will you settle for Dick Gregory?"

"I hear he has a great act," said Ayer. "Ninety days without food or water."

"Man is limitless!" cried Dana, under the influence of Nietzsche. "Where's the action?"

"Trust in the Great Father," answered Annie.

The demonstrators spread out across the wide sculpted steps of the legislature's fake Parthenon. At the top, between Doric columns, an Indian addressed them through a bullhorn. "Brothers and sisters, our purpose here today is to bring our message to the lawmakers of this great state . . ."

Something was very wrong. There was nobody here but the protestors. No legislators, secretaries, camera crews, no one. No state business to block, no civil authority to disobey. It was Sunday: for six days, the

White Man created genocide, but on the seventh day He rested. So Chief Frank auctioned off a nine-pounder instead—the salmon passed back to the highest winner through upraised arms, its lofted silver side glinting in a momentary display of sun.

Before heading back to their dormitories, they could not resist trying out a tepee. A Manhattanite in moccasins supervised at the flap. "Go ahead in, man. It's far under!"

Crouching, Big Mac took their places in the sacred mud. A small fire was dying out in the center. A young kid, leaning against the canvas, strummed a guitar. Beside him, an even younger one in a headband was working away on a joint.

"I had to leave home. Just couldn't hack it. Now I drift."

"Bet you never thought you'd end up in here."

"I don't know where to go next . . ."

"Just pass the joint, friend. . . . You know what Tim Leary tells us about a tepee? It's the best place to get high, because the beams, everything, carries you up, up, and out to the sky! Makes you feel part of the cycle, man. Everything's a cycle. The Indians, they know that. Winter and spring, pigs 'n' brothers, gettin' busted 'n' gettin' sprung. I'd rather just trace the smoke, follow the beams of this tepee up . . ."

"Stare not too long into the abyss," Dana intoned, "Lest the abyss stare into thee!"

10:12 a.m. Self-determination: what the poor want, what the rich don't need, what only lunatics have.

A prowler is entering Annie's house, but this one's familiar as a face on a most-wanted poster. He carries no tools of the criminal trade, just a backpack so permanent a part of his figure that it seems to function as a brace. His burden is what holds him up and he sets it down only when he's well indoors. The clanging of camping utensils, so like Tibetan wind chimes, announces this burglar. He works with the deftness of an abominable snowman; his hiking boots clomp straight toward us. He doesn't give a hoot about witnesses.

"Hey there, mister!" He plods right by us without a nod, his radar set on the kitchen. "Where are your Texas manners?"

No answer. There are weeks, even months, when this gluttonous visionary doesn't utter a sound. Still, he's no fledgling Meher Baba; his silence is often the result of his mouth being full.

"Where've you been this time?" his hostess asks.

The intruder's preoccupied with unpeeling the foil cover from half of a fresh-baked pecan pie that sits atop Annie's refrigerator. He breaks his concentration to answer, "I been looking for the place where the earth's crust is thinnest."

"How come, hon?"

"Cause that's where the space messengers are bound to land."

"Which messengers?"

"The ones hitchin' a ride on the Lord's rocket ship. The ones comin' to set it all straight."

Such prophesies would carry more impact if the bearer didn't grin like a good ol' boy while commencing to work his way through his favorite eats. Disdaining a plate, this messenger cradles the half pie like a big pizza slice. His fingernails are black. Highway dust falls off him like flea powder. One hopes, above all, that he will not remove his boots. His hair is about the same length as Annie's, parted just as naturally down the middle. He wears considerably more jewelry: barter beads, fragments of abalone shell, motorcycle pirate's earring hoops, holy amulets, charms, and a surgeon's suture clamp that lies against his unsterile chest. Atop his head, he models a colorful skullcap that he's crocheted himself, implanted with a blank silver button that serves as an unbatting third eye. Nearly swamped by all the holy-man garb is a long, mournful face; eyes that are beginning to disappear from too much squinting after rides and hallucinations; thin lips held tight by an imposed piety; a jaw so resolute that it nearly impedes his swallows.

"You'll want some milk to wash that down, won't you?" He puts it away with the ease that Annie puts it out. "How long's it been this time?"

She means since he's last eaten.

"Four weeks in the desert. I been too long out in the wind."

"Well, come on inside." Annie always knows what this prophet signifies. Sometimes, so does he. "Did someone hurt you?"

"No nails this time." He stops eating to inspect himself for stigmata, since he's a serious Christian, so serious that he's occasionally overtaken with the conviction that he's become the god he's worshipping. "I been gathering testimony for the Lord's trial. I been all the way out to where the evil ends."

"Big Sur?"

"Maybe Death Valley."

"Why so much death this time, hon?"

"Because I'm working to save everyone from it. Direct orders from the Son of Man."

"I think it's time to quit working so hard, hon."

"Time to get shelter from the wind."

Which means he's come home, to one of his many homes, for a refueling in starch and dope. If this hobo has any title, then he's the divine mooch, Haj Maalik Al Mooch. The path of his righteousness is also the path of dependence—and both have a way of wearing thin. Shunted about by a rotating pool of devotees, this self-appointed saint's best known for performing the routine miracle of emptying fridges and smoking up stashes. In a dozen Berkeley households, he's tolerated by former colleagues in street scrounging who've made their transition to adulthood. Lawyers, French chefs and systems analysts keep him as a pet so that he can remind them of their former, uncorrupted selves. He's the last hippie on earth—an oracle in overalls, who reappears to gobble a little of the temple dwellers' bounty, then leave behind his blessing or curse.

Annie has her own reason to be attentive. This prowler is her younger brother, Jed. Since his exile from the land of Edwards, Billys and Chucks, he's called himself Fire. Renamed, rebaptized, rekindled.

"We're all gonna need protection from His wrath!" Fire proclaims, with a belch. He moves on to Annie's leftover corn pudding. "From the maker of the cleansing rocket wind that propels holy astronauts!"

The term schizophrenic does not do Fire justice. But I know that his fire often goes out. It's only in brief conditions of religious exaltation that he's motivated enough to get threatening. And the worst deed he's perpetrated so far is a Satanic ceremony in someone's garage where he burned coded messages to Jimi Hendrix. Once he's fed, Fire usually turns mellow and self-effacing.

"He sure likes your cooking, don't he?" I ask Annie.

"So do you." Fire flashes me his best country wink, the first hint that he knows I'm here. "I see that you keep comin' back for seconds."

Fire's holiness often enables him to be brutally lucid.

"I'm mighty pleased you're around, Martin," he adds. "You're like a rock. But remember, men can't compete with she-wolves in my family. They've got to keep movin' or they can't survive."

"You'll survive," I assure him.

"Only because I can be on both sides of the mirror. That's the only way to keep the doom off my head." There's such a pointed slowness to Fire's drawl that his words come out with a wince. "I been busted for the crime of looking into the eyes of a highway patrolman. Robbery of his soul, second degree. Also for takin' a picked wiss without a permit. Also for living too near the sky."

"There's no doom in that. You've committed no crimes."

"Thank ya, kindly," Fire replies with all the sarcasm his sanctified self can muster. "Thank ya, judge."

"Do you know what day it is?" Annie's still jogging to and from the refrigerator, or, in her parlance, the ice-chest.

"It's a day to get out of prison."

She pinches me.

"That's right. It's Bastille Day. The anniversary of Big Mac's bust. And we're having a party out at Missy's house."

I wish she hadn't said that. But Annie never excludes Fire from the flow of her life. She takes his comings and goings more seriously than her dream omens. How can he say that the men in this family cannot survive? This sister puts the utmost significance on the timing of her brother's starvation.

"I love Missy," he states flatly. "I'm comin' with."

10:19 a.m. Madness: it has to be quantifiable, like the exact point where the amount of brain cells given over to the present are outnumbered by those given over to the past.

Crash's Letter

June 2, 1969
"WHEELS AND DEALS SINCE 1915"
Moose Monroe Motors
Moose Meadow, California

Dear Marty-poo:

Life is a total bummer to which your letter was a shot of thorazine. I miss you incredibly. I can't believe you've only been gone three days. I came back here Wednesday, got cheezed-out and had a good cry. Ayer and yes, Ebenezer, came that night. Ayer was even more incredulous over Moose Meadow and this household than you. He kept mumbling, "You can't stay here." We went to Berkeley Thursday. Had a few to kill, so we took half a tab of mescaline each. (I've got to watch myself—getting into that heavy Swiss Cheese bag.) It was totally insane, because we were trying to figure what was going on at the People's Park march, what the general mood was, but couldn't comprehend.

I don't think these type demos mean anything anymore, with people chanting "We love you" to the National Guard and Oakland Tac Squad blue meanies! There was this tremendous opportunity to mobilize people, but the march just ended, people drifted away sunburned and liberal and co-opted. Now it's Saturday in the Meadow, being bored with myself, so selfish, so uncertain of the future, getting back into that hateful drug-crime scene. Even had my first run-in with the M.M. pigs. They turned out not to be mean, or even scary, just dumb. I was driving very fast down this subdivision honking the horn (super cute, I know). They found some aspirin in the car and wanted to have it tested. But then they just let me go because I was a Monroe. I WANT TO DESTROY THIS TOWN!

The sky is full of crazy, eerie flashes of lightning and the air is sticky hot. I felt sort of half-depressed, half-giddy waiting for you to call. I'm scared by two things: your image of me and the radicalization of Missy Monroe. They're interlocking, I guess. You wrote that you thought of me as a goddess. Even the most flattering interpretation of that word frightens me—wait, just the image you have of me frightens me—because I'm afraid that when we're together again I won't be what you've built me up into. Okay, that's natural, but I think you're really relying on me to develop politically, and I want to, but I have no confidence in my ability to develop any "meaningful consciousness." All my "revolutionary" thoughts seem totally basic, uncreative.

I can't write any more about this. I'm scared—you're so far away. I can't wait 'til the folks skip town and you can move in! With Dana, too? It would be great to know when you're gonna be back—bridging the gap between theory and practice, huh? I have to see you. No more idle dreams and crossed fingers. It's ten to five and the post office is closing. The lady who works there hates my guts, I don't know why. She's worked there for about a hundred years. I'll take Ebenezer to protect me. Eba's been an all-around groove. Eba drinks out of the swimming pool. Eba wants to hold you (subtle projection). Remember the Rogue island? Does it still sound special when I say I love you? I want it to.

Crash

10:20 a.m. All this search for perfection, in a mate or a calling, is but an attempt to narrow the choices.

Number One. On the way to California, there was Chicago. Before Martin could join Missy, he had to get his main man, sidekick and communal first adjutant. In fact, it had only taken a week of being roommates for Dana Pearl to pull Martin into a dim corner near his bunk bed, turn down the volume on Creedence Clearwater, look him dead in the eyes and swear, "You're my number one for life."

Martin dismissed the pledge as hastily as it was given. He'd already noted that this judge's kid, trying to act so gangster reckless, was prone to extreme pronouncements. How could this scrawny, high-waisted brat, sporting wraparound shades and a peace medallion, breeze into an eternal commitment like that? And what qualified Martin as the recipient of his fealty? Was it that Martin was the sort of Jew his parents had kept him from being—the kind that didn't play football, drink milk by the gallon, study for the bar? Or was it that Martin had been given a head start in speaking for the revolution and that Dana was primed to take orders on behalf of same?

On the night they'd taken over the college president's office, Martin first recognized how much his roomie needed to take orders. Occupying the administration building in support of a Black Studies program for Steffens's nine or ten blacks, Martin and Dana were on patrol duty in the empty hallway. Impulsively, Dana raced to the nearest pay phone and put in a collect call to the Pearl residence.

"Sir," he'd begun, "there've been these disturbances here at school . . ." Martin had never heard Dana use this falsetto tone, let alone call anyone sir. ". . . I'm sure you've heard something about them. First, there were strikes an' we couldn't go to class. Now some people—even some friends I've made, my roommate—are sitting in the president's office. They've got all these demands. I don't know what to think, sir. . . . Yes. . . . What's that? Buckle down. . . . Get back in class. . . . What's that? Communists, sir? Are you sure?" It was a remarkable performance, and hardly Dana's last. Though Dana walked away from the phone call with a wink, then did a sassy two-step back to the occupation's command post, he must have known that his nonchalance wasn't entirely convincing. He was a little too good at playing both sides in the conversation.

As a bad influence, Martin didn't have much to do. After all, it was Dana who'd hung the red flag emblazoned with Che Guevara on the balcony of their ivy-covered imitation Oxford Tudor dorm; swaggered about the country club campus like the ghetto bully he'd always aspired to be, always carrying at his side any blunt stick or tree limb he could find; lip-synched into a swiveling study lamp and did ecstatic solos on an all-air guitar; pranced about naked whenever he was given the chance, laying his prick across the nonfunctional TV; chain-smoked Marlboros and marijuana, sucking balefully at either like some hard-boiled detective, until he strewed the butts on the floor and sniffed after them on all fours; flunked Russian and most everything else, but introduced himself at parties as "My name eet ees Alexander Poosh-kin," and masterminded a heist of the complete poems of Mayakovsky from the Steffens bookstore, enlisting Martin as "cover man"; sprung up at SDS meeting, unprompted by Martin, to rant incoherently in support of most any wantonly illegal act. It was Dana who'd packed up his duffel and left before final exams.

Dana proposed that Martin come through Chicago so they could attend that summer's SDS convention. Unfortunately, he could not guarantee Martin a place to stay. Since he'd dropped out, Dana himself had been disinvited from the Pearl crib, that sterile and dehumidified full-floor tomb some twenty stories above Lake Michigan. At the convention, the two of them were better appreciated, even fought over. Though neither would be returning for another term, they comprised the entire Steffens delegation. Entering a sweatshirt-colored auditorium that was normally reserved for roller derby, scanning the seats filled with earnest, work-shirted comrades, Dana declared, "This is it, dude! We finally made it to the big leagues!" How they wanted to join in the ideological group grope which marked this fabled organization. Instead, they filed past table after table bearing the verbiage of the Left's most ancient and least known sects, anarcho-syndicalists selling their wares like pitchmen of dice-and-chop gizmos at the county fair. They watched carefully synchronized cheering sections, rising as one and brandishing the Quotations of Chairman Mao at a speaker who did not meet their approval, using "the red book against red book." Courted by feuding factions, they were made to choose sides before they realized the organization was about to come apart.

While everyone else was being driven to extremes, Dana and Martin were just extremely young. Just as they swelled the ranks of the Movement, it stopped moving. Now that they were ready to assume their rightful duties—to start cranking up the mimeo machines, to issue demands, to boycott, confront, support, petition, occupy—they found that too many had already gone before them and been frustrated by these tactics. Robbed of a context in which to act, they could never quite be idealists, never quite terrorists, never quite Marxists, never quite be proponents of the youth culture, never quite be back-to-the-country purists or academics or organizers. They left their number one convention without realizing that it would be the last for SDS—and that Big Mac had been cut adrift, born too late, fated to play both ends of the line.

10:27 a.m. Correct so early that we could only confound ourselves.

The only consolation left in my friendship with Dana is that I get to see that there's someone more confused than I am. Hurry up, my man! I need you this morning. A honk's usually enough to rouse him from his book-lined lair. This time, we wait long enough for Fire to slump into a backseat stupor. Unless he's blasting out Albert Ayler's "Universal Indians"—music to dematerialize by—my erstwhile brokerage clerk and pal should be able to hear us. His second-floor apartment is flush with one of the barest and baldest streets of a city which specializes in bareness and baldness. Though the facade is textured eggshell stucco instead of chipped fire-engine brick, this is the closest replica he's found to the sturdy Chicago walk-ups he adores. Chicago and Oakland: those are the only settings unpleasant enough to satisfy Dana's insatiable demands for "the real." He's spent his adult years yo-yoing between the two towns, yanked back and forth between friends in one and family in the other. His most permanent abode and voting residence is Lakeshore Towers, Chicago. Everywhere else is mere sublet.

Two more honks, and we've got to go get him. The hall smells of cat piss and motorcycle transmission fluid stored there by the dyke-on-a-bike who lives downstairs. Dana's front door is the one that's festooned with off-center French posters: a gruesome reproduction of a World War One warning about poison gas, an original *Leon Blum Pour Président*, and that classic May '68 pasteup about being realistic by demanding the impossible. He has always been impossible by demanding the realistic. Impossible as the scrawny good Jewish boy playing the shit-kicking crazy; impossible as the scion of a wealthy political family working as in print factories; impossible as a "returning student" who became the star of a doctoral program in French history, coasting on charm and a collector's eye for obscure tomes, and now, not so much impossible as improbable, working as a low-level "service rep" for Richard Rimbaud Discount Brokers. Not exactly real, but pointless enough.

Seeing him now at the door, I realize that I've respected Dana only so long as he's championed impossibility, however impatient that's made me.

"Good morning, little schoolgirl." My impatience this morning is twofold: Dana's still in his terry robe. "What's up?"

Not Dana, who lets us in with a terrible deliberateness. The owlish circles around his big eyes have gone purple.

"What does not kill me makes me stronger." He manages to mutter a Nietzche aphorism much cited in olden days, but fails to punctuate it with his sarcastic happy-face smile.

It's been some time since I've seen him so subdued. Ordinarily, Dana's garrulous on command, almost frantic to show signs of former ebullience. Now he moves stiffly, steps prudently. He's like a shipper trying not to rattle the fragile contents of body and mind. He slumps into the flea market rocker jammed up against the grill of a gas heater in his tiny sitting room. The heat's up and all the windows are shut, though this is turning out to be one of the hottest days of the year. California is never "hot 'n' nasty" enough for Dana. And he doesn't look like he's ready to handle fresh air.

"You don't want to cancel out?"

"Nah, man. I got my front-row seat for this production. . . . Just hold on until I can see straight."

There's not much to see in Dana's apartment, except for books. Eschewing the solution of shelves, Dana's got his anarchist classics, historians' theses and Anglophile thrillers stacked against every wall: Dana's flock of ugly ducklings that follow their protector, via box loads of parcel post.

"Got some news from back home?" I guess. "A juicy political scandal brewing?"

"I wish. Then I could breeze back into town as the crusading reformer."

"Is everything all right with Polly?" Annie tries, inquiring of the Chicago lady to whom Dana's just as inordinately loyal.

"Couldn't be better."

"A hard day at the office then?"

"Harder than your six inches, dude." Dana must be feeling better already, since he's returning to a familiar theme. "But that ain't all."

Then the problem must be the one he gets each time he confronts his past.

"Headache?"

"Drop dead and rotate," Dana confirms.

10:34 a.m. A brief history of the headache. It is most modern, one of those maladies invented to be cured, the flip side of aspirin. A capitulation of the capillaries, often hereditary. For additional information see: a brief history of the Israelites.

The Judgment. Every evening, at the dinner table, the children prepared for it. They sat up straight in their chairs, trembling, waiting to see if the head of their table would come to the table with his head in an ache. Would he enter with gavel in hand? With bald brow majestically crowned in laurel wreath of Ben-Gay? Or worse, with towel wrapped in a turban that only emphasized Judge Isidor Pearl's status as sheik of this diaspora clan? Too bad no bailiff could appear to cry, "Clear the court! The Judge's gone blotto!" That's what they did in the Loop, where the patriarch of the tribe was as famous for his migraines as for his indeterminate sentences. Nothing could spare Dana or his siblings from this terrifying ritual—or the wrath that followed the maids serving pot roast and Le Sueur peas. When Daddy had a headache, he could not get through his "*Baruch atah adonai . . .*" without peering up toward his God, the only appellate whose jurisdiction he recognized, and imploring, "Lord, why did you curse me with such children?"

This was before the children did anything, other than be children. Before average report cards, gangs, long hair, or rebellion, the court was displeased. On the record. Those nights, it was woe to the boy or girl who let a single pea slip off his plate, a single sliver of well-doneness hit the tablecloth. Woe to the child who lost a grip on the avenging butter knife! They would be written out of the Judge's will. To be in or out of the will, crammed with family real estate holdings and defense contractor stocks, was to be in and out of favor. But Dana and the other children could not help it. By not living up to his unbending Pearlian standards, the Judge's children gave him headaches, his meddling brothers gave him headaches, his sycophantic cousins gave him headaches, Chicago's Puerto Rican gangs gave him headaches (no wonder the Mayo Clinic had been unable to effect a cure), the world gave him headaches. But this judge was not a bad man, just affronted by anything in the universe which he could not gavel down.

"You know what I live by?" Dana asks. "Market volume. Every time the volume goes over eight hundred million traded, us suckers have to jump. The less stake you've got in the system, the more you're tied to it. The big boys can always transfer their paper losses, but the little boys have got to sweep up."

I feel closest to Dana when his talk turns to tales of workaday woe, and farthest away when that talk gives way to behavior.

"Actually, I almost got canned yesterday. They took me off the lobby, indefinitely. Which is pure Zola, or maybe Balzac, since I always figured I'd shine out there. I had this notion the place could use a superstar. Only it's a fuckin' one-track betting parlor. That's all playin' the market is, an' I'm the one who takes the rap if some investor's best horse, some hobo's portfolio, doesn't come in. Screw it. I can't handle all these Oriental cats, gambling away their tip money, or the cagey rednecks with their million shares of Exxon stuffed into their fishin' boots, or the dudes in Mexican serapes who'd sell Betty Crocker into white slavery. All the lonely old bastards with money on their breath. *Merde!* 'When you know where you're headed.' That's how the corporate rasp reads over the entrance to the lobby. An' everybody in that lobby seems to know but me.

"Which is how this helpless mutt of a senior got on my case. The emotions get bureaucratized real fast, but the point is this half-lame dude's wife had just kicked, the love of his life according to unconfirmed reports, an' he was starvin' in some waterfront dive, so he said, an' what was worse, he'd fucked up the paperwork so that he couldn't get at his wife's municipal bonds to cash 'em. So how did he expect me to get around the rules for him? I'm just a peasant in the lobby, right? Only he hung in there good as an Uptown wino an' worked me over until I got sick of saying no. Got cornered into impersonating a human. Big trouble in the lobby any time you try that.

"I jus' cracked. I mean, suddenly I was this old man's main man an' coconspirator. I was gonna shove his fuckin' request right down the system's gullet. It was like one of my old power trips. Like the torching of the South Side. I was the Emperor of Chicago, or at least the first Jewish president. I was slidin' in with the winning run an' it didn't matter if both my knees got scraped. In fact, the more blood, the better. So I told them to just approve it. Push it through. On my okay, like I got the power to okay jackshit. Which was when they came down on me, real gentle. They said they understood about the lobby. Told me how they'd started out there themselves, a phase we all go through, an' that crap. Said they were movin' me over to quotes. Stick me on a terminal where I can't do no harm. An' I took it. I let them demote me to the back bench. I wasn't no ninth-inning hero. No judge's son."

He stands now, all six-foot-four uncurling, hands to pulsing temples. I know that he doesn't want to hear any critique but his own. Heading off to get dressed, he offers his own moral, "I know. It's too late for my *éducation sentimentale.*"

On that Bastille Day long ago, Dana wore patched bell-bottoms, hobnailed boots, a black tank top in homage to Bakunin and his trusty red bandana around his neck, matching Mao's Little Red Book in his back pocket. His hair was matted and biblical, rigid in two masses down to his collarbone. His untrimmed beard shot out in unequal billy goat curls. Now the chin's clean, the upper lip sprouts a droopy Fu Manchu, the hair's nicely shagged, disco-length. Dana's even taken to wearing oversized executive glasses, though he doesn't need them all that badly. They're the final touch in his disguise, which he dons to appear competent, but which is so forced it makes him look goofy. His whole face, including the severe Judge's nose and those Sephardim eyes, is in retreat.

While he's changing, Annie calls out, "Did you make a covered dish for the pot luck?"

"Yeah. Check the fridge."

"Bring your swimming trunks, too."

"Righto, sport."

"It's balmy out beyond the space heater, you know. And you don't need your downtown outfit. You're among friends."

Despite my admonition, he emerges in the school president tweed sport coat, a pink Oxford shirt and repp tie. Maybe Dana's forgotten who his friends are, or knows something that I can't admit.

"That's it, gang. Let's hit the wind!"

Voice-Over (Dana): Señor Brother Gypsy. That's what they called him. Warrior Chief Numero Uno, the boys whispered in the back alleys. By day, all of them worked together on the loading dock of one bruiser of a factory in one bruiser of a city. At night, they were the tightest gang on the South Side. Their program was simple: the more the pigs made them sweat during the a.m., the more they made the pigs sweat during the p.m. And Gypsy was their leader.

It hadn't always been so, he recalled, teasing his mangy black hair (on his rescinded license it still said brown) in a full-length mirror at his main squaw's apartment. It was a riches-to-rags story, the best direction to travel. He'd been raised the seventh son of a well-known South Side pig politician. From the beginning, Gypsy was convinced that it was all a mistake. When it was lights-out time in his parents' plush crib, he'd strain to hear the sounds of the streets below over the hum of dehumidifiers. He was beckoned by the call of conga drums on the Point. He got this fantasy going that he wasn't really the vengeful patriarch's flesh and blood. That explained why he didn't want to do his homework or go to temple on the High Holy Days. Why he didn't run in fear from the little black dudes, from the Peace Stone Nation or even the Catholics. Why he flunked out of school because he couldn't understand all that teacher chatter. On the streets, they talked his language. Every gang in the 'hood wanted him, in Woodlawn too, but they were all afraid to initiate him. Until his old man revealed publicly that Gypsy was really the orphaned offspring of the family's black maid and a half-Seminole, half-Aztec janitor who worked in the building. Disowned, Gypsy was free.

As soon as he could, Gypsy ran wild and free. He paid his dues and took his beatings. He rented the body electric. He came to know the South Side streets, especially the sin corners, the way an Indian knew the forest. No more Hebrew school! No college prep or campaign appearances! Armed with a knowledge of martial arts, incendiary devices, larceny, drug reactions, brotherhood, lookin' slick, and, of course, people's culture all the way down to the murals of Diego Rivera, Gypsy lived naked. All he needed were his gloves for working, his boots for fighting, his free lifetime pass to all the Greek coffee shops south of the Loop. The coffee was weak, the people strong! Strongest of all was the gang that would follow him to the end. That was where Gypsy was taking them.

If tonight wasn't the end, Gypsy thought, running his ringed fingers through his unshorn warrior's locks, then at least it was the Big One. The battle that he'd been mapping out since birth. The Paris Commune comes to the Midwest; the siege of Stalingrad brought out of mothballs. Gypsy's main women prepared his battle garments: the loincloth, single coral earring, sparkly shadow for his ultraviolent eyes. When Gypsy went to the window, he could see Stoney Island Boulevard going on with its bad business. The black world, congaland, was stirring, waking up the better part of him. Another whole big part of him slept, coolly through the ages, but that was okay. Sleep was the ultimate form of resistance, it was permanent revolution. And it did wonders for his nerves. Gypsy was ready. His main lady was dressed for her shift of waiting tables down the block. Gypsy wanted her to keep pouring that java, like nothing was going on. Like nothing would ever change. In her linen supply outfit, she looked so fucking pure—little did her regulars know. He wanted to quote the Great Helmsman to her, about how the workers and peasants are the cleanest persons though their feet are smeared in cow dung. Still, he was glad his lady didn't smell of that. It wouldn't have gone over too big in the 'hood. She had to leave for work and he wanted to give her a million-dollar tip. He would give her the city instead. He wanted to kiss her squaw feet. Instead, she kissed Gypsy farewell.

Downstairs, on the stoop, the rest of the gang was poised. There was Ivory Root, the original I-Don't-Give-A-Fuck guy; the Big Z., a Polish demolitions expert; Roscoe Derr the defrocked preacher, Rocky Rachman the point guard; Cigar Man, Tarzan Waters, Li'l Negrito, poet laureates of the displaced, itinerant lecturers on the Spanish Civil War, and all-around cannon fodder. All of them knew their assignments. All of them knew what they were fighting for.

"One final item, brothers," Gypsy told them, before they headed out across the glass-strewn lots of Woodlawn that they knew so well. "It's time we gave ourselves a name. Not for the Man's sake, but for the people to remember us by. . . . Any suggestions, comrade warriors?"

They held a quick criticism/self-criticism session in the charred alley, crouching and passing a hookah. They were the most highly evolved gang on the planet. They knew dialectics and alchemy. They were handy at acupuncture, meditation and stomping on labor scabs. They played bass, rhythm and lead all at once. They could recite by heart the final speeches of the Haymarket Anarchists. To them, Black Flag wasn't just an insecticide. How could the gang come up with a handle for all that? The Red Ramblers was what Rocky offered. Utopian Riders, the Big Z proposed. Marat's Marauders. The Chicago Durutti Column. The Anarcho-Syndicalist Home Boys. The Al Fatah of the El. Then Root came up with The Midnight Socialists. They all liked the ring of that and went for it, unanimous.

Before they dispersed, the gang got in a football huddle, each of them grasping a handwritten scroll that bore their nineteen-point program for a society of mutual aid with the heading "Power to the Future!" They held it towards Chicago's apocalyptic sky. Always a nasty gray-yellow, always about to storm. Let it storm already. They would be the storm. That damn frowning sky was the only one they'd ever known, but that made it a good sky to die under.

Gypsy took up his post on a secured rooftop where they'd placed an army surplus bazooka. The barrel was aimed at the Rockefeller Chapel. Gypsy wanted that target. He imagined The Midnight Socialists fanning out to their battle stations, set to detonate all their devices once he raised the gleaming fist. Big Stan would quiver. Big John would buckle at the knees. The Wrigley Building would double up like doublemint. Then the Civic Center, police headquarters in all precincts, every ward. The Field Museum, dioramas and all. The Emerald City, underpinning of the Drive. The Stockyards, too, once the cattle were liberated. All the viaducts leading in and out of the thirsty grid. Yeah, they'd have to scramble the grid. Blast the Dan Ryan and the Done Runnin'. The Paddy McGillicuddy Center for the Study of Graft. The Conrad Hilton and the steel mills. The killer factory where they toiled for Christmas bonuses. Only Haymarket would be spared. Maxwell Street and a few of the blues bars. The Taylor Homes and the rest of the projects, to be turned into exhibits of the dilapidated old days. The Picasso sculpture was a goner. Frank Lloyd Wright could beg for mercy. The Loop was in for a jolt.

People's art would make the city its canvas and paint it in red smears with grenades for brushes!

Gypsy dedicated this action to Chernashefsky and Mother Jones and to his old man's black maid, his true mother. He tore a thousand speeding tickets from his back pocket and spread them to the Windy City's wind. They were little pieces taken out of his Gypsy soul. They didn't go far; the Windy City was never windy enough. Gypsy hummed a final, favorite song. It was a dumb, shitty song, actually, but he'd heard it so many times on so many Chicago-made jukeboxes that it became his favorite. He took a last drag on a Marlboro laced with hash, then his bazooka kicked. He saw the spire of the chapel crumble. He leaned forward to enjoy the light show. Bonfires were breaking out across the city. Six stories below him, there was a symphony of sirens. He went into a trance. He did a fire dance on the rooftop. He must have danced and tranced for too long. Climbing down the fire escape, he was spotted. He knew he'd been spotted, down to his Indian acrobat's spine.

By the time he got to the ground floor, dropping to the turf that he ruled, benevolently, where his subjects paid him respect in cartons of Marlboros, just as soon as his sprinter's legs could be set in motion, the area was cordoned off with checkered pig cars. They gave Gypsy no warning, no tip-off except the pig scent, their pink eyes in the night. But that was cool, since he'd done the same. Those were the rules in Chicago. Shoot to maim, make excuses later. They didn't bother to read him his constitutional rights. Nobody in Chicago went through with that farce, even though his old man stood by as the legal adviser to the pig captain with his electric bullhorn. Even the pigs weren't stupid enough to ask Gypsy to surrender. That word was too big for his vocabulary.

Then Gypsy heard the order to shoot. The best fade-out to his favorite song. The ultimate Chicago compliment. As he fell onto the pavement of the South Side, just before he lost track of why it wasn't the North Side, Gypsy reminded himself that Chicago is two signs in the window. The first says, HELP WANTED. The second says, WE NEVER CLOSE.

Going down for the last time, Gypsy had time to think two thoughts.

The first was, "They really wanted me. They wanted me really bad."

The second was, "Ain't no big thing. Fifty more years o' this an' I woulda been bored to tears."

10:50 a.m. Youth: what to do until the Apocalypse.

It takes a long time to leave Oakland. Where there is no center, all is outskirt. The nondescript incorporates the indistinct. Is a city only as splendid as its number of freeway off-ramps? "Rome, Next 18 Exits. . . . Timbuctoo, Scenic Viewpoint . . . Ur and Chalcydes, Business Loop . . .

Atlantis, Gas and Lodging Ahead . . ." If so, Oakland must be judged one of the best. It floods out in waves of damp stucco. As the redwood rim of San Francisco Bay crumbles, so do the distinctions between country club hills and flatland ghetto. The suburbs beckon with their baffling, cut-rate equality; our adopted hometown's farthest boundary isn't marked by the usual discreet state placard but by an immense American flag, permanently unfurled and chemically stiffened, over the first of many cornucopian shopping malls.

"Salute, chillun!" Dana orders. "This here's Checkpoint Charlie. Are your papers in order?" Blunting out everything beneath the freeway as it unfurls, the flag shields a realm we've often tried to subvert yet have never entered.

"Welcome to the free world, *meine Herren und Damen*!"

Only Missy is a fully naturalized citizen; the rest of us, just resident aliens.

"Do you think she actually likes it here?" Annie and Dana know which she I mean, what it is.

"It's not such a long way from Moose Meadow."

"But there was a time when Missy would have killed to get out of there. She was quite a rebel. The leader of the pack."

"Before you ever got your hands on her, dude."

"And long after, Pep!"

"But now she's come home . . ."

"And just think of the detours she took!"

The Cowboy Liberation Front. "Bale of hay, bale of hay, make a wish and look away . . ."

The cows in the field were looking straight at them across the checkerboard of wheat. With a set of joyous twitches reserved exclusively for her hometown, Missy was bringing Dana and Martin back from the L. A. airport, through Bakersfield and finally down the one-lane rural route. Every grin and involuntary squeal attested to her ceaseless amazement that such an unabashedly normal place continued to exist and that she belonged to it.

"On the left, please note the Rotary Sign, 'Welcome to Moose Meadow. Within These Boundaries Roam a Contented and Progressive Herd.' . . . On the other side, there used to be a sign that said, 'No Filipinos After Dark' . . . Real progressive, huh? . . . There's the Mormon Church, and Vern's Tavern . . . and the Lutheran Church, and the elementary school I went to . . . And here's the four-way stop, the center of town. And there's Monroe Motors . . . and the Monroe Savings and Loan (owned by you-know-who!) . . . Andy Boy's Tacos, the B. of A., the Shell Station (tough hangout, it closes at nine!) . . . the saddle store, Western variety . . . Everything you could want, huh?"

"Except for an industrial proletariat." Dana grumbled. But we had to start somewhere, didn't we?

"Look! That used to be an Orange Julius. It's up for rent, huh?"

"Just the right size for an alternative coffeehouse and Movement bookshop," Dana mused.

"I'll bet this town is aching for one."

"Hey, we could do draft resistance counseling, hand out drug information, shelter runaways, send busloads to demos, organize communal farms, land reform . . ."

"These aren't Mexican peasants, they're rednecks—"

"I know, an' we ain't no Zapatas."

"Oh, pooh! Cowboys are just paper tigers!"

To prove she knew from which she spoke, Missy continued her travelogue. "There's the old train station, they don't use it anymore. . . . Once, the train stopped just for my grandma. . . . And there's her old house, my dad still keeps up the garden. . . . And now we're on the other side of the tracks. . . . The good side, you guys! . . . The lumber company, the Portuguese farmers' hall, and there's where Mrs. Bateman kept her retarded daughter locked up for thirty years! . . . And the sheriff lives there . . . Roy once burned a swastika on his lawn with chlorine! . . . And right around the corner . . ." We could read, "Monroe Avenue—County of Tulare."

They were mightily impressed, even if this avenue was but a block-long dead-ender with houses on one side, walnut groves on the other. Down a driveway longer than most of the neighboring lots was the ancestral nest of the Monroes, shrouded in eucalyptus and scandal. In the parking lot, there had to be at least a dozen sets of wheels, ranging from Model Ts to metal-flaked El Caminos. Beyond was a flat-roofed, all-redwood split-level, so contemporary amidst the farmhands' shack-town. The Monroe estate included a gaming room, music room (with baby grand), changing room, sauna and pantry. This wasn't a house, it was one giant refrigerator to raid (stocked with a lifetime supply of valley tomato juice). It was hardly the most appropriate setting for their commune's first headquarters, but with the Monroes having fled the summer heat to their cabin in the Sierras, how could they resist?

About two hundred feet down the main hall, sharing the premises of Missy's younger and wilder brother Roy, was Ayer Wilcox. As always, he looked in his element. This wing had been transformed into a demonic clubhouse, the redwood paneling papered over with day-glo posters, the curtains finger-painted to allow for maximum hallucinations per second. Over the couch where he sprawled was an old-timey Gold Rush town calendar, on which some souvenir shop had printed, "Welcome to the Saloon. Featuring Crazylegs Miss!" Ignoring the beet-ripening heat and all challenges beyond, our leader was playing with one of the numerous nineteen-inch tubes, watching a patriotic special for the coming Fourth of July. He'd adjusted the colors so the stars 'n' stripes waffled in a sizzling lavender and green, the purple mountains' majesty was a clown yellow, the precision flyers blazed in red formation against an orange sky, the bombs burst in air brown as shitcakes.

"Welcome to the Cowboy Liberation Front!" Ayer grinned.

It was an idea that would last exactly ten tomorrows.

Tomorrowland. Moose Monroe met Mina outside its portals. On a man-made Treasure Island, at the General Motors pavilion for the 1939 San Francisco World's Fair, they found one another. Moose was in his naval ensign whites, had a square jaw, crew cut, slanted lips and a shy way of pawing at his eyebrows while explaining to the U.S.O. girls about the innards of the Plexiglas "Car of the Future." After the service, he intended to take over his old man's Dodge dealership in the valley town where he came up, but Moose didn't act like the devious businessman. He was too optimistic for deviousness. Mina, too, exuded a cheery faith in the future that could only belong to a wide-eyed schoolmarm. Once they got away from the crowd, Mina appreciated the way Moose listened intently to her crackpot, if horribly approved notions about family planning and the importance of the arts in a well-rounded education. She saw at once that Moose wasn't as hokey as he appeared, but took joy from his hokiness anyhow, including the boast that he sang in a barbershop quartet, trying to sound like Tex Beneke. Before the massive diorama that showed General Motors' bone-clean idea of the city of the future, served by eight-lane freeways—oh Lordy!—filled with models that he would sell, Moose tried out his motto: "Yes, siree, there's plenty of room in California!" But he agreed when Mina said that she wanted a vegetable garden and decent values that didn't have a thing to do with engineering.

At the World's Fair, the optimists sealed their futures with an exchange of dimples. Moose Monroe Motors rode the postwar boom, the dealer's affability working well on late-night TV ads. Mina became the high school's assistant principal. Favorite hobby: collecting owl figurines, owls representing wisdom. This wise couple soon owned most of the town of Moose Meadow, which was too tiny and creeky to do anything with but disown. It was their fond little joke, and they never took themselves too seriously, even when they created the redwood Shangri-La on Monroe Avenue. And Moose and Mina begat Melissa Sue, the Polara princess. She was born with her bare foot on the accelerator, and, after a cautionary wink, handed the keys to Tomorrowland.

10:57 a.m. Optimism, too, is a foreign tongue, learned early or not at all.

"I know it's hard to believe, Pep, but Missy's content where she is. Spyros may be just a short-order cook, but . . ."

". . . a tall order husband, right?"

"And now their restaurant gives her a stage to perform on."

"What did they end up calling it anyway? 'Chez Crash'? 'A Taste of Fresno'?"

" 'A Girl and a Greek'!"

"Oh, lordy!"

"Missy's made a place for herself and her baby. . . . Did you hear? She's joined La Leche League."

"What the fuck?"

"The charter member of Women for Armed Revolt is out to promote breastfeeding!"

"There are worse causes, you-all. And you know Missy's nature. She's the kind that makes the planet hum. An enthusiast."

"Right. She's been an enthusiastic Girl Scout, enthusiastic hippie, enthusiastic feminist, an enthusiastic terrorist, an enthusiastic waitress . . ."

"Enough, son."

"He left out the 4-H Club . . ."

"Maybe it's his mantra." Fire hasn't yet dozed off entirely in the backseat.

"The chameleon changes its spots because it's got something to hide. Something of value." Annie can't help defending her old roommate. "You know she's just been Missy throughout."

"That's what gives me the willies. All the mannerisms are there, all the spark, and yet . . ."

"Not this again! Hit the radio!"

"You aren't a sparkly seventeen yourself, Dan'."

"Who wants to be?"

"I do, just for a day. I only wish we weren't staging this celebration out in nowheresville . . ."

"We're heading straight toward the maws o' the monster, right where you always said we should go . . ."

"I was hoping we could dream up some event as spectacular as the original."

"I couldn't live through that one twice!"

"Maybe not. But we could have at least flown to Paris. Seen the real Bastille."

"What the fuck for?" Dana grouses. "I ain't no *sans-culotte*."

"I'm sure your old man would have been willing to subsidize the trip."

"Subsidize yo' mamma!"

"We could have tried getting our hands on some more bad acid . . ."

"*Merci, non*. I had enough regressions for one lifetime. Like that time at the War Council, all of us trippin' to Coltrane's 'Om'. I was bawlin' like a baby, thought I'd reentered the cosmic womb, until this kindly Weatherwoman led me off to her sleeping bag . . ."

"A memory!" I nudge Annie. "He actually has them!"

Even his gruff protestations, his refusal to be swept into any touristic euphoria, harken back to the old cruises when I steered us toward Utopia and Dana rode a surly shotgun.

"Relax, dude," he has to add. "It's only a page torn off a calendar."

July 14-21, 1969. Richard Nixon called it "the greatest week in the history of the world since the Creation." It began with a Bastille Day and ended with a Moon Day. In between, Teddy Kennedy drove off the bridge at Chappaquiddick, Eldridge Cleaver surfaced in Algiers, Secretary of Defense Melvin Laird announced that "the corner has been turned toward peace in Vietnam," while three astronauts landed on the lunar surface and came home—just as the sixties, in the high summer recess that followed People's Park and preceded Woodstock, reached their spaced-out zenith.

So did they, thanks to Dana. Flipping on the afternoon news, he'd seen revived attempts, in honor of Bastille Day, to tear down the university's fencing around Berkeley's disputed piece of green. Eager for street action, Dana convinced the others to head north at once. It made some sense to be proceeding straight toward the latest civil disturbance—since they'd enrolled as the Big Mac delegation to the Black Panthers' United Front Against Fascism conference beginning in

Oakland a few days later—but with what logic did they gulp down four of Ayer's mescaline capsules? Was it really to keep them humming on their nightlong shimmy up the coast? Missy picked out their transport vehicle, the gem of Moose's antique fleet: a yellow 1936 La Salle phaeton, complete with whitewalls, running boards and salacious fender curves. The car lasted longer than they did.

Just after they'd reached the coast and hoisted the convertible top, the big mescalito hit, with devastating effect. Ayer went into a trance, mumbling, "We took this to stay awake?" Dana's answer was to take charge and try to get them back home. But the road had turned into one seething hallucinatory mess and not even Martin's favorite chauffeur could hold the wheel much longer. On a slanted grade, the La Salle seemed to capsize, swerving bumpily onto a gravel rest area. Staggering out, they reeled beneath Bastille fireworks of their own invention, a planetarium out of its straitjacket, the last light show. Convinced they were poisoned, dying, turned to straw, they whimpered for a sanitarium hospitolium. Get a shot, feel better. Only Captain Dana was capable of flagging down a pickup and forming the words "drug reaction." Clutching the truck siding, the four of them traveled through tunnels of interminable spoking and gratings, until they were dumped before some satellite community's abandoned gray windowless civic center monolith. Crawling about on all fours, they turned a street corner into a disaster area.

Some black-suited citizens helped Dana phone for help. It arrived in the form of sirens getting nearer, red lights gyrating in formation, bubble-top squad cars screeching to a stop, helmeted officers storming out on the double, yanking them up by the shoulders and spewing: YOUAREHEREBYBEINGPLACEDUNDERARRESTFORVIOLATION SECTIONONEHUNDREDFORTYFOURCALIFORNIAPENAL CODETHISISTOADVISEYOUOFYOURRIGHTTOCOUNSELOF YOURCHOICEANDTHATANYTHINGYOUSAYFROMTHISMOMENT ONMAYBEUSEDASEVIDENCEAGAINSTYOU . . ." All in a round, sung to defiant Dana, goofy Pep, vacated Ayer, crazylegs Miss. But wait, they weren't criminals. To prove it, they told all: People's Park, mescaline, stay awake, feel better. "We got you, animals!" was the response from these creatures who strutted like flamingoes, with epaulets for wings, visors for beaks, their black knee boots making spindly legs and claws. These were birds, not pigs—the word Dana snarled in last-minute heroics while Missy clutched at their villainous bootstraps. "Punks, delinquents, pill poppers, look what you done to this poor, helpless girl!"

That was the last they would see of her. The boys were slammed against car sides, patted down, limbs spread, followed by the sounds of slicing, clipping, clamping down on their arms. Wrists wrung with metal, they were pushed into waiting backseats. They weren't going to the hospital, were they? A megasecond later, they were back on the freeway, skittering up a boiling liquid center lane in an imaginary chase, while Ayer awakened to plead his case before a gnome who grew in a piece from the rubberized steering console. "Excuse me, sir, but could you kindly take us home? I'm a student at Steffens College. Do you want to see my registration card? I have a French passport. I speak four languages. An' I think you'd better just pull over now, because I have to go to the bathroom!"

Dana and Martin slumped back in disbelief, their spines arched to avoid the faraway tingling annoyance of handcuffs, their eyes squeegeed against the same window while they weaved past game board gingerbread houses, animated loops of cartoon blocks in lulling duplication.

"This is it, dude," Dana finally dared. "How you say? Ze ultimate voyage."

Now that he knew they weren't going to die, Martin began to delight in this roller coaster through the social system. He leaned over and kissed Dana on the crown of his forehead, felt the warmth of his kiss trickle into Dana's sad eyes. He had a vision of the two of them as Semite nomads wandering in a kwikie-mart wilderness.

The ride ended long before it should have. Their flying saucer coasted up a ramp beside some whitewashed underbelly, the robots shoving them into a blinding white holding tank, crisscrossed with patterns of wire fencing. Cages within cages was what they were in, or maybe an aviary. A few crew-cut creatures in baggy orange outfits leaned against a bolted hatch at the back, hoses and pails at their feet, sizing up the new arrivals. Martin sensed that he was heading toward that last doorway, but in the meantime, he and his pals could keep on slipping and sliding across the linoleum, playful pups brought to the pound.

Before them, a wearied Chicano sat on a bench sanded smooth by anxious pants seats, trying to crouch into invisibility amidst the bright finality of consequence. His eyes came up slowly toward theirs, telling them all there was to know, showing a solidarity that touched hands with all the unfortunates ever stuck in dungeons, summing up this sad night when they all got caught in the act and hauled in, locked down, sent to the box, the can, the pokey, the shithole, to go through more shit, boring shitty ritual of retribution.

"You guys is pretty blasted, no?"

"Yeah, yeah . . ."

"You guys live in Fortuna?"

"Where?"

"I guess you don'. . . . Pretty blasted."

They were glad to be laughing so loudly in this place, but soon it was their turn to get called up to the screen. To yield up belts and personal effects. Into plastic tubs came a flow from linted pockets that included Martin's fat wallet, stuffed with family photos and his SDS card, Dana's Little Red Book and his suspicious allergy pills, Ayer's baseball cards and registration form for the Panther conference, "WE MUST DEVELOP A UNITED FRONT AGAINST FASCISM!"

The automaton on the other side of the cage went on typing as Ayer gave his name: "A-R-T-A-U-D, A-N-T-O-N-I-N." And Dana kept parroting, "Hello, I'm on acid. Hello, I'm on acid." Martin stood dumb, stupefied by monumental concepts like date of birth and mailing address. He couldn't even answer when his gawking finally won a "What you got to be grinning about, boy?"

He was getting a white plastic bracelet snapped around his wrist. He could see his name there, misspelled, and a long ID number. No more house keys, laundry stubs, identity. By the time he finished reading out all the numbers that stood for him, Dana and Ayer were gone. Shoved through separate doors. They couldn't do that, could they? They were going to end up in the same dorm room sooner or later, weren't they? There would be a decent stereo there, wouldn't there? Reading matter, of course. Night-lights. Radiators. Midnight snacks. A few of the natives in coveralls were clearing the way for him, making obscene popping noises. The bolted door loomed.

He was shoved out of the white cage and into a submarine landscape, dark green, mossy, lugubrious. All around were clammy aquarium tremblings, the gurgling and plopping of some swampy ooze, the pings and squeaks of water falling far and landing on metal rocks in hard drops that formed instant rust, bubbles popping beneath bubbles, undersea demons sucking the air right out of his ears. He wasn't inside a whale, but a courtyard with doors on all sides. Locked tight. In their power. A guard led him out of the briny yard. In a rundown office, two paunchy officers chewed their cud behind another barbed-wire desk. "Yer bail has bin set at six hunnert and twenty yer allowed one phone call wanna make it?"

Call who? Pizza Man, He Deliver?

"C'mere, kid, time to trade in your civvies . . . you're gonna get your farmer John suit, the one you've always dreamed about . . . we do custom tailoring . . ."

A pallid attendant emerged with a towel, bare hanger, and day-glo coveralls, stamped on the back, FORT. CO. JAIL. Martin figured he was supposed to get undressed, but kept shaking in crazy spasms, wobbling around and wondering whether the office boys were peeping.

"Man, you're a dumb one! Get in the shower, over there, kid!" Inside a corrugated plastic stall, curtains crawling with fungus, Martin made an instinctive reach for corroded faucets. The spray flayed his skin, which had lost all awareness of cold or hot. The water was penetrating him, making his insides gray as the surroundings.

"Spread 'em, monkey!" His armpits and pubes were shot with a stinging aerosol vapor. Eliminating all parasites on the social parasite. Still sopping, Martin slipped into the orange coverall with one zip from crotch to neck. For a moment, he felt pampered, in his soft baby cloth, Sunkist diapers. A metal cup and plastic spoon his, too. Then a bedroll tucked under his arm. All set for the pajama party.

"Come on, ya dumb animal! We gonna put you away for good!"

While the guard fiddled with the vault combination, Martin was entranced by the concrete seams, the patterns of rust turning on the machined plane, like microscopic lowlife in waves of useless migration.

A shiny wheel spun, turning the submarine controls, and a space was opening in the dark sea of bars, the digestive juices waters parting.

"Get movin, kid! . . . jus' keep walkin' 'til the door opens, then grab a bunk. You see? You gotta choice in this here hotel. Nitey-nite, monkey!"

He could hear pockets of groaning to his left. A section of pipe opened and Martin leaned into a gap. An empty slab hung from the wall at his knees. His mattress, of its own mind, flopped open there. The bars snapped closed, flavor-tight. There were four more bunks in his compartment, and at the far end, a throbbing metal commode. He kept wondering: Where were all these pipes dripping? Were these secret grottoes into which flowed the county's procreative juices? A Disney waterfall? Or the Okefenokee brew? The occupants mumbled and turned. But what to fear from men in orange p.j.'s like his, sleeping off their overdose of bad breaks? Sleep was guiltless.

There was none for Martin with this powdered pinch of amphetamine or Drano sloshing in his veins. Turning in his bunk, the metal cup in his coveralls pressed into his doughy gut like a cookie cutter. When Martin hid in his pillow, he was dizzied by imaginative extravaganzas, ten thousand cowboys tap dancing on rotating stages of sparkling ice, a million tinseled prelates tooting on bass saxophones, his own "Eyeball Playhouse Presents . . ." He kept checking his wristband to observe the odd name printed there, aware that he bore some faint connection to it. Okay, he was arrested—in space and time, perhaps, but mostly incarcerated by fascination. He was aware, intermittently, of being "in jail," though the exact ramifications of the term had conveniently slipped away. But what offense had he committed? He couldn't recall any except that he had some friends named Missy, Dana and Ayer, now flung amidst the galaxy. Why hadn't his upbringing prepared him for this? Or a Steffens lecture? His answer was the overworked word "relevancy." But nothing he'd done in the name of that word had prepared him for this.

The light came, filtered through so many levels of bar and lock and frosted opaqueness that it appeared as a sub-species of dust. Martin saw the first signs of an imminent day through three sets of striped shadow, an unnatural day without apparent source. Compared to this chemical's wearying grip, the jailhouse dawning was a contemplative processional. He began to hear consumptive coughs. On bunks suspended in the gray ammonia-laden dust, men were turning, anticipating the predictable jolts of their routine. Loudspeakers switched on, blaring a scratchy army reveille, first little dig of the day, concluded with a queenie-voiced rascal DeSade rasping, "Good morning, gang." The entrances to all the cells along the narrow corridor flung back in succession. The surreal was waking up real. Voices grumbled in the tongue of conspiracy. Or maybe Spanish. Martin heard brethren, brethren all around.

But would they be able to recognize him as such? The black kid in the upper bunk barely nodded Martin's way as he lumbered down to sit on the crapper, letting his dick dangle. Mexicans strolled the open gangway singing cantos of woe—until one paused by Martin's bunk to whisper, "Inspection." Somehow, Martin managed to smooth his blanket and clutch his tin cup while the guards sauntered through, banging the posts with their billies. In the mess room, eunuch trusties slapped colorless meat chips in sauce from poorhouse cauldrons onto metal trays. Martin gave his away to whoever was hovering closest. For three days, he had the stomach only for tepid coffee swill, didn't bother to wash, couldn't sleep—indeed, this chemical was keeping him awake. Its overdosage plagued him all those nights—along with the black kid above, who emerged from sullenness once they were all tucked in, to rave about lady friends he'd strangled and TV consoles he'd kicked in and how he was liable to do anything, ravage any motherfucker in sight, if the feeling came over him, especially in the dark.

More or less intact by day, Martin kept flopping back onto his bed to quell afterimages while half listening for the echoing clangs that signaled a summons from the tank. "All right, you mutt!" the guards would call grudgingly, beckoning him to go for mug shots and psychiatric appraisal. All he told the doctor on the other side of the glass booth was that he was eighteen years old and liked cheeseburgers. He couldn't remember much more.

This was his time to do time, be nothing but time. The blanks were filled in by a single television, mounted on the ceiling, its dial out of reach. The prisoners got "Sunrise Semester," "Captain Kangaroo," and fifteen minutes of exercise instructions. The inmates crowded close to the screen for this show—though there wasn't room to do a push-up. They looked hard as they could at the teacher lady in her leotard, hoping to catch their only pinup in an inadvertent breast bounce. Curiously, the evening programming was all cops and robbers. Martin cheered with the others when the bad guys outsmarted their pursuers, booed when the boys in blue made their inevitable kill. Every plot was set on its ear; happy endings in here were unhappy.

Martin was the only one who bothered to watch the news. There was so much of it those days! Especially those three days. Grainy clips gave Martin a glimpse of their former destination: such a puny piece of ground, that People's Park, never his park nor his people, surrounded by a flimsy fence and mobs of taunting students who looked earnest and horn-rimmed despite their battle gear. Martin saw none of the riotous ecstasy that Dana had envisioned. The Alameda Tactical Squad had called in reinforcements and the demonstrators had sulked away. Yet the next headline was an F.B.I. scoresheet on the past academic year: three million in property damage, sixty-one arsons or bombings, four thousand arrests, two hundred twenty-five colleges disrupted. J. Edgar Hoover had concluded his annual report on subversives by branding the Black Panthers as "the greatest threat to the internal security of the United States." And a mule team from the Poor People's March on Washington was heading down to Cape Kennedy to make its presence felt at the Apollo launch. "We're going to the moon," beamed the commentators, but that "we" excluded Martin and his playmates more decisively than it ever had. They got to watch the astronauts burst free of gravity from their cramped tank. In here, it was all systems stop.

The television did not tell the prisoners that the United Front Against Fascism conference had begun. They did not hear Eldridge Cleaver raving at the delegates from his Algiers hideout, "We don't need a space program, we need an earth program. We need rockets fired on Washington, South Africa, Mozambique. We need to send Richard Nixon and J. Edgar Hoover to Mars in a spaceship without enough fuel." They were not advised that Chairman Bobby Seale called for "fifty to a hundred committees to educate people about fascism and the Fascist demagogues, Rockefeller and Reagan." They were not informed of Huey P. Newton's statement from his own prison cell, "Our dummy civil government will soon be pushed aside by the Pentagon!" Or attorney Charles Garry raising funds to aid in the defense of some two hundred Panthers already facing felony charges. They could not join the chants of "Power to the People!" or get a glimpse of the five thousand conference participants and rally-goers, of whom eighty percent were white. But Martin could hardly complain that he wasn't one of them. He was getting a firsthand experience of fascism—or the next best thing.

His biggest thrill was having his arms and ankles weighed down with rusted link chains and marched off to court. That was because he was reunited with Dana and Ayer. The guards made sure they couldn't converse, call out, conspire—just shuffle in step with the rest of the condemned. It was inspiration enough for Martin to see Dana's gaunt face shining out, unbelievably, among the orange legions, his beard scruffier than ever, his Jesus locks stiff as stale cake, offering a get-through-it nod and his coolest, all-suffering grimace. Ayer, too, was bristling with defiance, his great guns of defensiveness cocked, but also studied and dignified, though his puffy cheeks and forehead dome were brighter than his coveralls, the skin stretched taut with shock, pink as a boiled lobster.

They even got to go outside, where California tantalized, cloudless as ever. Best of all, the tight security that accompanied their march down a back stairway, through a parking lot and into a prefab courthouse made Martin feel downright dangerous. With a twist of manacled limbs, he could see Dana and Ayer at the head of the orange line—diligent masters of a freaky scouting troop. In a mock-up for Perry Mason, real men and women in leisure suits, with leatherette valises, awaited, amazing Martin with their lack of reaction. Didn't he rate a gasp? Not even a chortle? These people were accustomed to the sight of these men in clown suits, too much accustomed. Once in the docket, the three inmates were unchained and given front-row seats.

"Murder in my heart for da judge . . ." whispered Dana.

"Sing the song, bro'," answered Martin.

"After ze revolution, nobody laughs when someone slips on a banana peel."

"Rant on . . ."

"Where's Miss Crash?" Ayer asked, back on earth. "We plead not guilty, right?"

What was a plea? What was guilt? Or a lawyer? After their names were read off, they were swarmed with public defenders. For some reason, Ayer refused all offers. Martin and Dana followed his lead. It wasn't until the next trip that they finally figured out that they were being arraigned and heard the exact nature of their transgression: "Being publicly under the influence of a dangerous narcotic." That didn't seem so bad, did it? And what proof did anyone have other than their own street corner confessions?

But an attaché toter in pinstripes popped up to explain that this charge carried a mandatory ninety-day sentence. He was a swank Santa Barbara lawyer retained at the request of Ayer's family, who'd been alerted by Missy from her hospital room. So someone had finally placed a phone call! If we wanted, he could handle all our cases—and did, getting the trial scheduled at summer's end, the bail reduced. And the last morning, Missy's little brother Roy appeared in the spectators' gallery, looking under the influence of something himself but gleefully waving the necessary cash.

Waiting for release on his bunk, Martin noticed that the dripping in his ears had finally stopped. Those were only aural figments of his delirium. This tank was not underwater, this place no apparition—these metal beds and orange men were sanctioned by the country of which he was a citizen. And even though he knew that his stay here had only been the product of a romantic fling, he vowed to think of himself always, proudly, as one more "animal." He never wanted to forget that so long as some men had the power to do this to other men, they had the power to do anything.

Even as the guards handed over his belt, shoes, wallet bulky with family photos, they kept reminding Martin of that power.

"You may be gettin' uncaged this time, animal, but you'll be back. We got our eyes on you an' your gang. We seen you hangin' around downtown . . ."

"But I'm not from here—"

"Oh yes you are, animal. We been keepin' tabs on you. We know just where you come from. Next time, we're gonna get you for a couple hundred years!"

The guards had him to the point where he almost believed it. But they were the ones sentenced to remain. A second later, reconstituted, Martin skittered down a polished marble hallway lined with the busts of founding fathers. No more exposed bolts, no ammonia smell—just the acceptable grandiose Greco-Roman facade that concealed tiger cages everywhere.

"Am I the first?" Roy told him that Missy had spent only one night in the hospital, one in jail. As a native Californian, she'd been treated only as a juvenile. By now, she was back in Moose Meadow and Martin had to call.

"Miss? Are you back in one piece?"

"Are you kiddeen? That was some super cheese, huh?" Her voice came through all new and untamed and his.

"They never gave you a shot?"

"Of course not! The nurses made me their guinea pig. First, they thought I was a runaway. I had no ID. After I told them about the drug, they kept on asking, 'Is it fun? What do you see?' They were ready to sample some themselves, Pep!"

"Poor Miss!"

"But, listen! This is too much! The La Salle was right where we left it, with the keys in the ignition! There was just this note on the windshield from someone offering to buy it. At any price."

"You're kiddeen!" Martin mimicked.

"The worst of it was this notice about my arrest in the *Moose Meadow Monitor*! What a scandal! I don't know how they found out, those snoops. Since my folks' cabin doesn't have a phone, they sent a forest ranger out to tell them I'd overdosed and was near death!"

"How did they take it?"

"Oh, you know them! Lots of tongue-wagging, but I think it gave them a kick. They're coming back, though. They should be here any minute. The collective's over, Marty-poo—and before it ever began!"

"Not over, just homeless."

"We really goofed, huh? Put ourselves right in the hands of the enemy!"

"We won't make it so easy next time. So long as you still love me."

"A silly bust can't change that! Go on, my hero! Go liberate the boys!"

Ayer didn't need liberation. He'd jetted off without a word to make sure he wasn't going to get cut out of any of his forebears' wills. Martin had no such worries, but had to place another call. Doctor Pepper and the Missus accepted his love, collect. If he had to apologize for getting in trouble, it was only because the reasons were not noble enough, the trouble not injurious enough to the status quo. Martin's mother had even made an appeal to Dana's father in Chicago, presuming Judge Isidor Pearl could use his connections to set them free. The Judge had told her that he hoped his boy would rot in jail forever.

But here he was, and all paid for: Dana reassembled in shit-kicker boots and red bandana, walking stick and histrionics.

"My name eet ees Alexander Pushkeen . . ."

"He's brainwashed!"

"Right, dude. It's lucky you sprung me. Another week an' I woulda been elected head trusty."

"I have no doubt. Hey, I just heard that my mamma had to call your daddy a bastard."

"Yeah, well my daddy can still beat up yo' mamma!"

"Yo' mamma, she can!"

"Celebration city!"

They had to wait a bit for the coast to clear in Moose Meadow—returning on "Moon Day," as declared by a beaming President Nixon. On that day, the California State Assembly voted 58–4 to expel trouble-making students from the state college system. Asked at a press conference if he saw any parallel between the original Bastille Day revolutionaries and the People's Park protestors, Governor Ronald Reagan replied, "No, I just see some people who haven't outworn or outgrown their pink booties." On the other side of the continent, Teddy Kennedy was still making excuses for his first brush with the law. He'd get away with his crime just like the four of them. He, too, was a first offender, from a good family.

At the same time, the fascism conference came to an end. The reports that filtered down from Berkeley were less than inspirational.

The Black Panthers' security had been unnecessarily strict, their bodyguards brutal, their rhetoric sexist, their manner too stern. Their "united front" was all talk: this group and that group had been turned away, some delegations walked out on other delegations' speeches, there had been scuffles in the aisles. The Left was fighting amongst itself, an old story. Why, their informants asked, didn't everyone know that the Communist Party was privately bankrolling the whole show? Didn't they see that the Panthers were all seeking persecution, were bent on martyrdom? Perhaps Martin and the others were not yet ready to see, because they had sought just such martyrdom with their arrest. What that arrest had made them see was the awesome power of the state, and the obvious weakness of the opposition.

In the meantime, Dana and Martin got one night to savor their freedom. They feted themselves with a coffee shop banquet—clinking beer bottles and offering a toast to consequences! Only consequences, however dire, let them know that they'd finally made a mark on the world. Afterwards, they strolled—perhaps in pink booties—down the honky-tonk sidewalks of a town they could inhabit solely as outlaws. They slinked about, bent-kneed, fugitive Groucho Marxes, puffing on Marxian dime-store cigars, feeling quite mature, handling all ironies. Then they holed up in a motel, proper desperados, and kept a lookout on the sleepy harbor which would forever serve as their high-water mark. The Spanish padres had christened this landing "Buenafortuna."

11:06 a.m. The rest is history we didn't make.

I can hear Dana rustling his paper. I should be offended, on behalf of the Bastille Commemoration Committee and its membership of one, except that he always brings something on newsprint along everywhere, taking hours each day to ingest the whole contents, from Ann Landers to the classifieds. This time, a glance over my headrest tells me he's not reading just any local rag, but *The Wall Street Journal*.

"Since when did you start subscribing to that?"

"Since I gotta deal with this shit every day."

"Found any growth opportunities? Read any good mergers lately?"

"Hey, it's a tool. You gotta use, if you know how . . . History's made on the business page, as any hard core materialist could tell you. Screw all those State Department briefings. The price of Japanese steel, Rhodesian chrome—that's how to gauge which way the *realpolitik*'s tiltin'."

"So you can get in on the ground floor?"

Dana hides in his paper, while Annie shoots me a you-go-too-far look. But I know he doesn't justify his latest form of employment in such lofty terms when talking to anyone else but his resident conscience. Dana's rationales are as wearying to follow as they must be to dream up; no wonder our friendship makes us feel tired.

Fire, who's been snoring away, wakes too alert. In the rearview mirror, I catch him scanning the environs of San Lorenzo as though he were getting his first buggy ride through the Plain of Jars. His reddened eyes are darting and greedy with alertness; he licks his lips like a hunting dog.

"Did we pass heaven yet?"

When Fire doesn't get a reply, he turns abruptly to Dana.

"Where's your old lady?"

"Back in Chicago, goin' to draftin' school."

"I thought she was a farmer's daughter."

"Nope. No way."

But Annie understands. "He means Darlinda."

"Yeah. The chick with the long braids, who walked like a duck . . ."

"She was my first old lady, only I don't think you can be an old lady when you're nineteen."

"It don't matter what you call her," Fire answers, in a tone remarkably engaged and earnest. "I think you better find her. I think she's in darkness."

"No, she's coming," Annie informs all of us. "Missy phoned her. She wanted to make a surprise appearance."

"That's all I need," Dana moans.

Fire gives us a belly laugh, forgetting his dime-store prophecy. "Had enough of her home cooking?"

"She was a shitty cook. Whole wheat, sardine with soy casseroles. Right, Pep?"

"What pond d'you fish her out of, anyhow?" Fire needs to know.

"Not a pond, a creek. The Kickapoo Creek Rock Festival. It started to pour an' she ran inside my tent."

"No shit?"

"It was fate, sixties-style. It wasn't a couple o' weeks before she moved to where I was crashin' in Uptown. That's hillbilly land in Chicago, seat of the white trash revolution. We did a summer with the winos there, then I brought her out here to join the collective. Shoulda been arrested for transporting hypochondria across state lines. I was so grateful at that stage to find a live body—the gratitude lasted two years."

"That's not the whole story," I correct.

"What is, storyteller?"

11:10 a.m. After how many tellings does a story become a story?

Darlinda's Farm. Darlinda's farm looked like a thousand others in the corn belt of western Iowa: slow waves of furrowed earth given order with the scattering of wood stakes that bore seed company packets, a willow tree near the house, lonesome concession to the scenic. The soil dictated anonymity. Darlinda's farmer pop was an anonymously stolid Swede with thick neck freckled up from too much sun, spread thumbs scarred but supple, beer belly, bald dome, wary eyes under the bill of his Davey Jones engineer's cap. Darlinda's pop was different in that he never seemed at ease with his dourness, was not just stoic, but downright self-effacing, liked to experiment with natural fertilizers, but took his differentness as an affliction. Maybe that's why he drank—not flamboyantly, since he didn't know how to do anything flamboyantly—but just enough so the redness was always on his face, a ruddiness from within. It was two beers before breakfast, another while tractoring, couple more after lunch, more with Darlinda's ma's Jell-o mold, bringing a hangover to supper each night and a quizzical sadness. Darlinda tried hard to battle her quizzical sadness, trying just as hard not to be brainy. She pined for dates, but spent the Saturday nights of adolescence with her pop's red face, the drab hook rugs in the television room, reading in the frightful quiet. It had been once broken by a brother. Darlinda was away on a field trip in Wisconsin the summer her brother came home to Darlinda's farm and killed himself inside the silo with Darlinda's pop's shotgun. Her brother had a kind smile, she remembered, and after he left, she could never get Pop to smile that way. Darlinda felt sure her brother was like her and wondered if she could have saved him.

"There's a lot of peace out here," says Fire.

At the wheel of Federico, Annie's having trouble distinguishing between the peace on our left and the peace on our right: the same single story spreads, same jumble of roof antennae, basketball hoops mounted on the same garages, chain fences around same malnourished lawns, same cul-de-sacs rounded like test tubes. "Do you-all remember where we turn off?"

"You can't have forgotten! It's Easy Street."

Of course! Our Missy resides just a hard left off Prosperity Court, down the block from Paycheck Avenue, across the second stoplight on Slumbering Masses Boulevard.

Maybe Fire isn't reading the signs. Soon as we've parked, he slinks down and warns, "We mustn't go in!"

The world's leading authority on empty houses can tell instantly that Missy's is one. His sister, not so easily spooked, leads the way across Easy Street, which is a sloped asphalt finger less than a block long. On the side where we've parked, there's an empty meadow, grass waist-deep and crisped brown with high summer. Across from it, there's an ascending row of smudged pastel bungalows. They're permanently strung with Christmas decorations, the miniscule front yard cactus patches dotted with flywheels and wagon wheels, so that this dead end's got a vaguely Mexican air, both festive and forlorn.

Climbing the stairs that zigzag through her plot of unkempt hedges, I realize that my memory's enlarged Missy's holdings. Her place on Easy Street is about as small a place as you can get. It's one of those stucco postwar quickies, and L-shaped cabana with combined living room and kitchen, two bedroom boxes tacked on the side, low textured ceilings, a peaked roof too small for an attic. Like the other Band-Aid-colored cottages on this outskirt block of an unincorporated subdivision, the Casa Spanakopita looks as if it never earned a proper return for its developer. This is just another mortgaged outpost, surveying a hollow where suburb meets foothill, making both appear ragged and senseless.

Fortunately, Missy's garage is bigger than her house. You can be sure there are a couple of shiny new Polaras in it, and another parked outside, with Moose Monroe Motors plates. But Fire is right; the front door is locked.

Along the side of the house, past garbage cans, we pass through a token gate into the back. This yard, too, is subcompact, cut-rate. Missy and her hubby Spyros have not wasted an inch of it. They've crammed in terraced plots of zucchini, tomatoes and fig trees against a retaining wall that marks the end of their lot. A raised redwood boardwalk takes up much of the rest of Missy's yard, complete with picnic table, swinging love seat, sandbox and spit for charcoaling baby goats à la Grecque. The effect is Mediterranean, except for the centerpiece. How could Missy do without a pool? This one's hardly as grand as that fantasia with tiled coves and islets around which she lolled away much of her youth—and a portion of mine. Rounded like an avocado pit, crudely lined with black rubber sheeting, it spills, untucked, over the water line.

The back screen door has been left open. Rattles and stuffed toys litter the kitchen linoleum. In a breakfast nook papered with fields of daisies, the morning's dishes are still uncleared from the veneer table. Dominated by beige pile carpeting, the living room is only half filled by one of those seven-piece sets, low couches and armchairs and ottomans and coffee tables in knotty pine with cushions covered in a broad tartan plaid. Bookshelves hold more miniature Greek soldiers than books. The fireplace is fake, but the mantel exhibits framed portraits of an honest-to-goodness nuclear family. A third wall, toward the bedrooms, is crammed with electronics. A monumental TV plays soap opera with the sound down.

The Empty Rooms (1). There was something downright wasteful about them. The bareness that cheered the others troubled Martin. The overflow of unused space in their apartment betokened the extravagance of white skin privilege, the excesses of imperialism, brought home to their very floor plan. Why had they bothered to rent such a large flat? Several peasant clans, or welfare broods down the block, might have been able to squat in the two front bedrooms that they'd so whimsically disoccupied. Was this their idea of an accomplishment?

The plan was for ex-bedroom A to serve as the study room, ex-bedroom B as the game room. "One room for attaining knowledge," proclaimed Darlinda, "the other for celebratin' it." Dana backed her up, always eager to form a united front: "This may reinforce the dominant culture's false distinctions between mind and body but we can't tear down imaginary walls unless we tear down real ones. I don't think we're ready for that." And Ayer added, "Revolution as renovation. Tasty! . . . In the interim, where's the poker game?"

Study was straightforward, but who would define play? As it turned out, any sort of Danskin gropings or sing-alongs met the qualifications—but not more structured male leisure pursuits, such as stereo sparring over whose favorite electric guitarist performed the best solos, an all-night round of monopoly, a triple-header in the dice baseball league which Ayer, Martin and Dana had organized at Steffens. A series of complaints from Darlinda soon banished rock and blues and all such sexist moaning to headphones. One day, the Monopoly board and its pieces—delicate thimble, frisky Scotty dog, stylish top hat—were sold off by Missy at a block garage sale. A week later, the tabletop baseball charts disappeared from their assigned spot on the shelf beside a couple of unisex catchers' mitts. This confiscation was the work of some self-appointed legion of decency, a tribunal that condemned by night.

Only Ayer was willing to denounce the terror. All Martin dared point out was that the playroom was turning into more work than it was worth. Like all new solutions, their nocturnal pooling had merely established a new set of problems. From the start, he felt that they'd be goaded on by the emptiness. What worried Martin most about their new sleeping arrangement wasn't what might happen in the room they all shared, but what was bound to happen in the ones they'd abandoned.

11:17 a.m. When visiting the homes of my intimates, always pee on the side of the bowl.

On the table is this note:

> *"Kids. Irena got this weird rash this morning and I was so lucky to get an emergency appointment with the only doctor that baby lets touch her. Cool your jets, Big Mac and have a few beers. Cheeze-out, please, in the yard provided. I'll be back soon, so soon. I promise. Has it really been so many years since we said good-bye to our minds?*
>
> *Melissa*
> *Have a swim. Really."*

"Baby comes first."

"Damn right," says Annie.

"You know how long 'soon' means to Missy?" Dana reminds us of her perennial beat-the-clock scramble.

"Since when has the fairy princess turned back into Melissa?"

"That's what her Greek family calls her. It sounds more distinguished, I guess. More foreign."

Missy is the least foreign person I've ever met. Despite the Balkan touches, her house is very much like one she grew up in: loud, Western, hospitable. A trusty saddle on which to ride through an indoor version of the wide-open spaces—but without enough surfaces to hold all the bowls of corn nuts and Cheetos, all the doodads and collectibles, the clay cowbells painted like hens, the photo albums of baby. It's very much lived in, clean and a wreck at the same time. Otherwise, Missy's living room might be a model on display at Montgomery Ward's.

"I don't wanna hang around," Dana speaks my thoughts. "Without the hostess, it's like a diorama of some post-scarcity habitat."

"Anyone hungry?"

Annie grimaces. She knows why I've asked, and Dana does too.

"Mac's?"

"It would be, how you say, apt?"

"Double-cheese, here we come." Dana's starting to lose that headache.

"But what about our nice pot luck around the pool?" Annie asks.

"Save that for dinner. Come on, it's the tradition. Give us this day our daily grease. Our prepackaged karma. . . . Even Fire favors McDonald's, I'll bet."

"All of America does," Dana echoes. "The whole globe, the known universe!"

11:30 a.m. A rebellion of aliens perceives that rebellion in alienated terms.

We do not have to find it because it knows how to find us. Within cruising radius, in the time one radio tune needs to spin, there has to be a McDonald's—there always is, at your service, the kitchen that does not feed people but gets fed by them. A few downhill curves get us within range. In Missy's satellite town, where residential and commercial are of one prefab piece, it's hard to tell if the strip grew up around the houses or the houses around the strip. A haze of monoxide, tule fog and barbecue exhaust has settled permanently over this eight-block, six-lane chasm. Missy's lunch counter may be somewhere along here, but it's hard to spot amidst the garish line of franchises. We run a gauntlet of swirling plastic—past Thriftimart, Taco Tango, Pronto Pup and Der Wienerschnitzel—scanning for the glint of those mammary arches.

There they are, forming their curvaceous "M," rising above the Hispano model, complete with tiled roof and dark overhangs in place of former bright awnings and peppermint stripes. Prime early seventies Mac's—a design meant to emphasize that this ain't no pit stop no more, but a safe and respectable family dive. This one's even got a playground for kiddies alongside the outdoor tables, a fiberglass chutes 'n' ladders. The climbable figurines spring from some instant Hamburglar mythology: advertising disguised as child care. The small print on the toned-down neon boasts of a bottom line in billions sold. Which means how many per day, per each human on earth, since which Pleistocene age? And how many head of cattle chewed? How much kilowattage generated in sluggish peristalsis to process how many patties?

"I'll take ten thousand french fry futures," says Dana, scanning the big board for today's prices. "Buy at seven, sell at nine."

"You'll take a double-cheese, fries, large Coke, pie." Some things never change.

"I'll take thirty-seven," says Fire to the Vietnamese order girl.

"Whoa! You can't save 'em up for the winter, you know. How about starting with two?"

"Five."

"No one can eat five Big Macs—and live."

"I'll do it an' get resurrected."

"Bet you can't." But how do you wager with a man who has nothing to lose?

"What you gonna put up?"

"What do you want?"

"Your sinnin' heart."

"No deal. . . . How 'bout my key chain?" It's a useless souvenir that says "Welcome to Universal Studios." I figure he can add it to the collection around his neck.

"Lemme scope the goods. . . . Okay, you're on."

He won't have to wait long. Dana takes possession of our bagful. Before we're back in the car, he's reached in to deftly unwrap much of the paper within paper, dumping a ton of instant, virgin garbage. Most of what's left goes to Fire.

"Now this takes me back!" Back up the hill, with burgers in tow, we're almost a gang—and the car's become a patent leather cosmos, which doesn't run on ethyl, just drumbeats and hope. Let the radio waft, engine spark, traffic surge! California is still our playpen.

"Yup. The double-cheese are fresh."

"If your needs are McDonald's," Dana declares, "they shall be met."

"I can't believe you remember the litany."

"I haven't forgot one thrilling moment, dude. Like after we got sprung from the bust. We hit Mac's near closing, right? A black-and-white console sat on the aluminum counter, matchin' the hardware, and we could make out the blurred figure of some blimp of a man poking at a dusty sandlot with his pogo stick. So what if he'd landed on the moon? We'd landed in the pokey! Who was that joker to think he could compete with Big Mac?"

Over Eight Zillion Sold. What was Mac's if not our temple? And Hot Apple Pie our sacramental wafer? More than a ceremonial meeting ground, McDonald's served as our oracle as well, its auguries read in the ancient manner, from the innards of fossilized pickle on cheese. Its strict uniformity guaranteed us the chance to unwrap identical truths wherever we pulled in. Not just satisfying our student craving to teethe on concepts, our burger fill-ups gave us a chance to play at being a gang, like the white lumpen greasers we'd been taught to put down as failures and delinquents. And even as Mac's addicted us to its additives, there were self-destruct buttons ground into the patties. A poison that begged for antidote. In every sungleam off those golden arches, the consumers' dialectic winked back, reminding, "What goes in, must come out!"

In the meantime, there's all that automated abundance to ogle. This plant, unlike some others, always runs at full capacity. The fish fryer, pie fryer, french fryer are all frying, industrial hammocks submerged in coffin plots that bubble grease and future heart attacks; helpless spuds are scrubbed and washed with flexible, Frankensteinian faucet attachments, a guillotine splits the veggies before they're enhanced, sugared, emulsified on their way to the big sizzle, the oily fritz; lighted instrumentation blinks everywhere, monitoring crispness and doneness; the bread-warming shelf slides like a morgue drawer into the stainless wall; the pie case rotates, exhibiting its crusty diadems; the Coke pumps dispense regular and ethyl; the shake man weighs synthetic shake formula onto a white scale, before the glop is frozen and shook; thawing patties are ripped from their paper backing and dealt like a bad poker hand onto the grill; the *saucier* finishes the job with his rotating-action dispenser of measured catsup dollops, baptizes in dill before the packaged premies are swaddled in cardboard, set in their shining silver incubator.

This was the sort of force feeding that had to lead to massive civil regurgitation. Eventually, as with religion, the plastic temples would lie abandoned. The mouths of the people would be open with speech, not stuffed with aerated buns. A Mac's might become a health clinic, a commune, a nursery, a pop art museum, a sex information post, a rehabilitation center for diehard carnivores. Cows and trees by the trillions would escape the chopper. Nothing would be more delectable, than our ravenous bite into that deep-fried Hot Apple Pie of unexpressed oneness, which carried the standard Mac's taboo, "Caution: The Filling Is Hot!"

11:42 a.m. Ideas to live for perhaps. But to die for?

We're all dying for Missy to get home. Sodden with burgers, we droop into the garden furniture around the pool. But Fire's got a victory to savor—and a new key chain. All praise to the Burgerhead and Baby Jeeze!

"Caution! My filling is full!" Needing to cool it off, he settles on the obvious way to enliven our wait. Never mind the rule about no swimming after gluttony. There aren't any lifeguards on his planet.

He starts by kicking off his road boots, which he's worn for some eons without socks.

"Kindly move the offending objects down the primrose path," says his sister. "I don't want to catch the disease."

That's Annie's long-standing name for the odor that's one of her brother's few enduring accomplishments.

"Kinda pungent, ain't they?" Fire stares down at toes that are black to the bottom of the nail. "Too organic for ya?"

"Move yourself downwind while you're at it."

"Hold your horses, sis. I'm gonna take a cure in a jiffy. Get cleansed all over. I'm goin' for a baptism."

Missy's pool hardly looks like a fount, and the water's more filtered than holy, but it's evident that's where he's headed when he stands by the edge and "drops trou." The old jeans, stiff with dirt, fall heavily as a Galilean ball. His belt buckle, in the shape of a marijuana leaf, must weigh a pound. The assortment of pendants and prisms come off slow as a harness, freeing up his sweat-stained hitchhiking toga. Naked in suburbia, Fire indicates that a life of scrounging for seconds isn't always dietetic. Saddlebags of fat flop against his broad back, beneath apostolic locks, above drooping buttocks. With a leap and a forty-niner's holler, this overgrown child of God is in. But parched Fire doesn't sizzle or swim. He waddles to the level where his feet touch and contemplates the water at eye level, making gurgling sounds and bouncing up to grin like a chlorinated Boddhisatva. Wet down, Fire's hair looks like sphagnum moss. Slicked to proper proportions, his growth's actually receding, and reveals a visage more purse-lipped than hang-dogged, a prairie evangelist's face all right, bordering on a Savanarola scourge, and not that young a one, either.

"Reborn in His image!" he gurgles.

Just like this lost preacher's made himself into a likely candidate for Christhood through much self-inflicted suffering: hitchhiking about for decades, gathering a rambling "oral history of the world" on a tape recorder that's often without batteries, sleeping in igloo-like hedges of public parks or sometimes backyards, eating, when he's not within reach of folks like Annie, out of dumpsters behind supermarkets and Kentucky Fried Chickens, spied on and shooed off by hordes of village cops, turned aside by his very appearance from the solace of sex. Faced with such a stubborn unwillingness to take up what others call an ordinary life, it seems natural to reconceive his vagrancy as a holy quest.

"Gather 'round me and be saved! Splish, splash, everyone needs a bath!"

Taking the Plunge. Dangerous felons awaiting trial, they spent the rest of the summer poolside. Sworn enemies of the state, Martin and Missy and Dana did most of their plotting from lounge chairs. Day after day, they worked on their breaststrokes and tans, dried themselves out like the local valley raisins, while crunching the sunflower seeds that were their parole rations. Nothing could keep them from lying low on the tiles: not the swimsuit competition for the first annual Moose Meadow pageant, staged by demented brother Roy with prepubescent belles recruited from the junior high; the continual trafficking of Roy's dope clientele, bearing shoplifted pieces of department store crystal to go inside the cabin of Moose's finest limousine so they could turn it into a rolling, tinkling, psychodelightful chandelier; or Papa Moose's "There's plenty of room in California!" which occasionally sent them scurrying for any old car, then up back roads through bare mounds of parched foothill and beyond to the Sierra. How could they get into any mischief up there?

Above the color-by-number contours of timber, beyond electricity, double-cheeseburgers, public defenders or even straying forest rangers, they paused on a hike to dip where a frigid mountain stream broke into flat pools. It turned into quite a long pause, since, for all their chatter about the communal cleansing ahead, this was the first time they were trying it without suits. This was a far more significant breaking of rules than their Bastille Day transgression—and a far more potent intoxicant. Martin started things off, the common nude in this triad. Dana followed eagerly, his gangling body white as the snow falling on Lake Michigan, squatting on a boulder just like the White Rock girl, except for his spindly rubber band penis. Then Missy took the plunge, strong breasts and forbidden hair tufts exposed in the raw mountain light, her grin a mixture of pride and pain at having to go through the inevitable "sizing up" before she hid her attributes underwater, squeezed against both men into the pool, that was too icy for them to feel one another.

They got back just in time to find their warmer swimming hole transformed into the site of the Monroes' annual charity luau. A boom-boom banner day at the Big M ranchero! Roast a pig for muscular dystrophy! Moose dug a pit, then filled it with hot coals and a foil-swaddled carcass, like he'd learned to do on one of his Dodge-sponsored junkets to Waikiki. By midafternoon, the outdoor banquet tables were heaped with *poi* and cuttlefish, *lomi lomi* salmon—after which, the local ladies' auxiliary returned home for their husbands and last year's *leis*. At sunset, kerosene torches were lit all around the pool; Big Mac's rehabilitation ward was invaded by the most prosperous and worldly Four-H'ers in the valley. Their Hawaiian shirts clashed with garish belt buckles and sta-prest slacks, crew cuts and pointy boots. In this town, it was "No Filipinos After Dark," but anyone could be a Polynesian.

The affair was an excuse to put down too many mai tais. Missy and some of her old girlfriends got the festivities going with a rendition of the old school cheer, "Groovy, groovy, groovy, crank, crank, crank, Moose Meadow High is rank, rank, rank!" When Martin had to support Missy on her way to the toilet for an equally ceremonial barfing, she managed to ask, "We've reached a new stage of intimacy, huh?" The drinks took Dana to a new stage of daring. He challenged the publishers of the patriotic *Meadow Monitor* to a round of eight ball in the Monroes' game room, during which he proceeded to tell all about the recent arrest and degraded life-style of that local girl-makes-bad, Melissa Sue. Read all about it in the morning! "The revolution ain't no tea party! Or no luau! Check it out!" By then, the two of them had attracted quite an audience. Butt planted on the pool table, shit-kicker boots dangling, Dana elected to give them a show. He did his best to convince the county's assistant district attorney that mescaline shouldn't really be classified as a dangerous narcotic. "Hey, dude, the Indians have been using the shit for thousands of years. It produces a feeling of oneness, an enlightenment that ain't no harm to nobody—except the repressive state apparatus!" The state replied, "W-W-Two! The Big One! I was there! I fought for my country, not like you kids."

Martin couldn't bear to stick around for the finale. He was drawn back into the yard by what sounded like dead weight thudding into the East River. The more drunken landed gentry had begun teetering on the edge of the pool, then practically lining up to get tossed in. The party flared out like the voodoo torches. In went the *leis*, the Stetson and the bifocals. In went the editor, the attorney, and finally Moose, who beached himself, beaming as ever, on one of the cement islets. Out across the lawn, most of this contented herd shook themselves down like wet dogs howling and hooting. The ladies dropped into the churning water last, white pumps in the air, print dresses shriveled and sticking to constrained midriffs. "You see!" shouted Mrs. Monroe when she caught Martin gaping. "This is how we country people take out our aggressions!"

We are farther than ever from a mood resembling celebration—especially Dana, who rocks in Missy's love seat with such an air of Byronial brooding that I dare not cross him. He has yielded to California by removing the clerk's duds, including shirt. His chest is so pale that it looks like a rice paper kite, stretched across balsa wood ribs.

Wisely, Annie has brought along a book. This one's a ninth volume in buckram of some extended pamphlet by some architectural guru who's gone back to the ancient mud skyscrapers of the Yemenites to find inspiration for the rehumanizing of twenty-first-century spatial use. Annie's reading matter never surprises me: she's interested in almost any topic on earth, from African mythology to Peruvian crop rotation to the latest biofeedback techniques, as long as they're presented in a manner that's vague and reverent enough to dovetail with her increasing spiritualism. I'm more intrigued by where she digs up these tomes: on the back shelves of herbalist apothecaries, in the library section marked Crackpot Studies.

"What's your book called again? *The Zen of Adobe*?"

"Inner Design for Eternity."

"That's what they need out here. Some way to keep the houses from looking like used mufflers."

"Or to somehow connect the people with the earth. With this good land!"

I see what she means, since I've gotten up to poke around in Missy's garden. Either she's got a country girl's touch or California's benevolent conditions forgive hasty planning, forgive everything.

"If the people who live in this place could just come to themselves as one more expression of the local fertility"—Annie pauses in her book—"it would be enough to make them happy."

"That and six hundred thousand shares of Data General," Dana adds.

In the meantime, I'm trying to keep from trampling on some tender fava bean shoots. Or are they limas? I'm unused to seeing a plant among others of its kind. A tomato, to me, is a common household item. Comes wrapped, and in three sizes: round, squeezed, squashed. Zucchini in triplicate, against black mulch, look as odd to me as vines of can openers. Snow peas droop, begging for stir-fry. The jalapenos look so harmless amidst their white glade, the peppers are only red nightlight bulbs. Baby eggplants inch along in the dirt, sun-sponges expanding before my eyes. I can discern no obvious seedling rows, no plan—yet Missy's everywhere in this leafy profusion. Her scattershot enthusiasm has found its best use.

But where the hell is Miss Green Thumb and Goodwrench, Miss Better Homes and Godheads, formerly Miss Child Care-on-Demand? And what can I possibly say to her should she ever deign to arrive? I try to rehearse the reply I'll give when she gets around to her obligatory "And how are you, Pep?" Missy speaks only in the present tense and there isn't much pep in my present. I can't tell her that I'm the AT & T of afterthoughts. I can't tell her that I've learned to smell the air of responsibility. I can't tell her that I like to spend plenty of quality time with my penis. I can't tell her that I'm the envy of everyone, especially myself. Instead, I'll answer, "Per usual. At the movies."

11:52 a.m. See! Martin Pepper devoured by the dragon of disillusionment! Amaze! Missy Monroe, feminist warrior, transmuted before your very eyes into a contented housewife! Follow! The high-speed disintegration of the New Left! (No trick photography necessary. No Disney time-lapse.) Cringe in horror at the invasion of the Feminoids! Don't miss a single vivid moment! The division of the species according to genital equipment! Human beings become stockbrokers! The battle of the beatific cats and the running dogs! Experience! The curse of the empty rooms! Gawk! At parties that no one would join and parties where nobody had a good time! The amazing Sapphic whirling chip 'n' dip dervish! Disputed egg rolls! A book disguised as a sandwich! The perils of bad posture! Amazing special effects: Peter Pans come in for crash landings! Self-doubt depicted with uncanny realism! A leg of lamb charred beyond identification! A brain sautéed beyond lobotomy! Oodles of shattering glass! The case of the disappearing diaphragm! The case of the vanishing monogamous relationship! An unforgettable portrayal of self-bombers! Confessed chauvinists! The romance of a girl and her rubber hose! Proletarian muteness! Emergency room mum! In Dolby stereo! With a cast of thousands, including the Fortuna County Sheriff's Department, the countless unshaven legions of Manpower! Five-finger discount! Coffee urns! Shocking deception! Cops posing as landlords! Ph.D.'s posing as paper boys! Wishes posing as the truth! With uncanny realism! Affinity groups! Assigned reading! Vietnamese lunch! No expense spared! The world's largest mattress! Nothing left to the imagination! (Maybe that was the trouble.) The greatest story never told! Explicit lessons in love, performed before fire escape pupils. Passion over a steaming plate of fries. A girl and a Greek! A boarder who came to stay! Caught between two men and two Trotskyist tendencies! Marriage by any other name! Adultery by nearly any other! Language corrupted! Morals defiled! Free love with a price tag! Nude comrades! Nude nudes! Wall-to-wall nudes! Hordes of the oversexed and the underemployed! Whores of delirium! Tenured whores! Conceptual whores! The stampede of a contented herd! Mai tais! Over forty trillion sold! Mistaken matings, dread offspring! Turkey basters! Heroic attempts to fuck like certain heroic parties! To organize the disorganized! Contortionists of self-justification! Ladies out of the kitchen and onto their backs! Sweeping across the screen and into your *après ski* conversation! A man called Fire and an innocent put to the torch! Innocence unabetted! Narcissism unchecked! La Leche League! Hurry to your neighborhood theater! Purges in nightgowns, bedroom *pogroms*! Rebels with a cause! Follow! Illegitimate afterthoughts! Witness! The horrors of acceptance! Gawk! The tribunals of negritude! *Hubris* in blue jeans! Watch! Women for Armed Revolution! Exposed! What waitresses do with hot tips! Complex complexes! A word or two of semiotics! For the first time time on screen! Materialists without material! Softball wars! Scale! New heights of ambivalence! Desire! The Girl at the End of the Shopping List! Thrill! To generational redemption! Gasp! At the dancer's despoiling! Cringe! At the dread blind date! Worship! Anything in skirts! Exorcize! White skin privilege! Communicate! With Jungian archetypes! Sitting Bull stands! The lonely unite! Be prepared! For anything but what actually happens! Gasp in amazement at what ought to have happened! Rise up angry! (But not before the last reel!) Swell up! Tote up! Collectives of one! Don't be shocked! Don't drool! Don't look! Leap! Into the big bed!

It's Missy who's the master of suspense. Unwittingly, she's got all of us right where she wants us. Once again, I'm killing time in her garden, swiping at butterflies without a net.

Scene Two (Butterfly Road). It was one of her most magnificent entrances. TRACKING SHOT, HAND-HELD. After the arraignment, Missy came skipping down the steps of the Hall of Justice, in a polka-dot dress with pleats, a white ribbon sailor's tie above grown-up nylons and shiny party pumps.

MISSY: "We're free, you guys! Back on the streets, huh?" She held Martin close, wrapping him in the smell of sunlight that she stored somehow for his personal use. TIGHT SHOT, too intimate for courthouse steps, of MISSY (speaking in the pinched, rewinding speed reserved for her well-established favorites): "You wouldn't have believed it! They made me plead guilty to 'being in danger of leading an idle life'!"

MARTIN: "Is that a crime?"

MISSY: "I'm not kiddeen! That's what goes on my record. Then the old coot made my whole family stand while he gave me this speech . . ." (arms flailing to illustrate outraged authority) " 'You're such an intelligent girl, attending such a fine college, why ruin your mind with chemicals?' "

MARTIN (kissing her on a central wrinkle): "Chemicals like a hint o' onions and our own special sauce."

MEDIUM LOW-ANGLE SHOT, from the knees, John Wayne sheriff-style, of MOOSE MONROE (moving into the frame, his craggy face one mass of honest wrinkles): "Are you pardners off the hook?"

DANA: "Yup."

OVERHEAD. Descending from the romanesque heights where the fair burg of Fortuna did its official business, Martin recounted for Missy the highlights of his and Dana's brief legal stardom: the thrill of hearing some legal minion spit it straight out, "The people of California versus Pepper and Pearl . . . ," their lawyer kneeling before the bench as though about to be knighted, the porcupine of a D.A. informing all concerned that the arresting officer was on vacation in Florida, his admission in legalese that there was no real case, duly confirmed by the judge's declaration that all charges against these two ruthless criminals had been dismissed.

MISSY (her arms were around both of them): "This must be the life that we secretly wanted to be a film!"

STATIONARY SIDE-VIEW LONG SHOT takes in the empty curbside that the three of them were approaching. Curb and composition were soon hogged by a turtle-waxed wagon, into which they piled.

MOOSE AND MINA: "Real good, real good, real good . . ."

MUSIC UP AND UNDER: Lilting violins, inquisitive woodwinds. Dmitri Tiomkin meets the frontier.

CUT TO: station wagon interior.

MOOSE: "And are you going back to Steffens in the fall, Martin?"

MARTIN: "No, I'm transferring to N.Y.U. Film School."

MOOSE: "Field school? Is that some newfangled experiment?"

MARTIN: "Not field school, film school. You know, the movies."

MOOSE: "Real good. That's dandy. Then you can come back to Hollywood an' get a proper job. If they let you across the state line . . ."

MARTIN: "But we're innocent!"

MINA (clucking): "You sure are!"

MOOSE: "Nobody seems to stay very long at Steffens, that's for sure."

MISSY (kneeing Martin next to her in the driver's seat): "If I go back there, I'll just get hooked on drugs!"

MOOSE: "Then you won't go, Melissa Sue!"

MISSY: "I want to go to New York . . ."

MINA: "Not unless you work and pay your own way." CLOSE-UP of Martin, amazed at the easy terms the Monroes had attached to permitting their friskiest offspring to live in sin with a Jewish longhair jailbird. Such twists took place only on the silver screen.

WIDE-ANGLE FRONTAL SHOT FROM CAMERA MOUNTED ON HOOD. While Moose and Mina dozed in back, the lovers in the front seat were going in high gear. Passion on the freeway: carburetors and arteries pumping.

MARTIN: "It's in the bag! Your father would hardly notice if we eloped!"

MISSY: "Look, if you think he's a hick . . ."

MARTIN: "The only thing that counts is what he thinks of me!"

MISSY: "Especially if I'm coming to New York."

MARTIN: "You'll need some kind of excuse."

MISSY: "I can write to some drama schools for applications. You said I'm a natural actress, huh?"

MARTIN: "My budding ingenue. That's perfect."

MISSY: "Living in the big city. Hold me!"

EXTREME EMBRACEABLE CLOSE-UP, steering column in the way. While Missy and Martin sparked, Dana's hand slipped up Martin's pants leg. It was just a tease, betokening a friendship that pushed on despite gravely unequal consummation, a reminder that he wanted some of the action, too. Dana was all set to leave for Chicago, the next day if he could. Chicago held sway over its native son, offering all the attractions of a sure fight.

DANA: "While you're studyin' off your debts at school, dude, I'll be workin' mine off with my tail." It was time for factory regimentation. Jail had merely been a sweet foretaste. MUSIC OVER. "Brown shoes don't make it. Quit school, why fake it?" The dashboard radio pulled in a San Francisco station's nonstop history of rock, the top hundred gut-wrenchers of all time. Rolling along, turning off the eight-laner and taking a shortcut back to tomato juiceville, the three of them cherished these manufactured notch marks along their lengthening trail, singing along to each payola swoon. "In the year twenty-five, twenty-five, if man is still alive . . ." The rhythms catapulted them out of the present. None of them cared where they might be headed so long as they continued, resolutely, to lead their version of an idle life. All that mattered was to stick together and comb the neon streets, prospecting for the meanings that others had left behind.

And Missy would be the driver. TILT SHOT of Martin's Lady of the Turnpikes, growing more placid as she tested speed limits.

CUT TO: Overview of the connecting road, which suddenly flattened out into an uninhabited valley disturbed only by California's aqueduct trough. From high up, the road could be seen stretching flat, a nicely ruled number two pencil line through the bumpy sheet of pastureland. The blacktop had been so recently laid through the fields of wild and blossoming mustard that it confused swarms of resident butterflies. They flew across the travelers' path as though there was no interruption in the yellow meadow. The car was ambushed with specks, just as yellow. CLOSE-UP. All at once, the windshield was clouded, then pelted, then pasted over with mottled wings flattened against the senseless onrushing. Missy had to turn on the wipers. The sheets of painted carcasses were barely swept away.

TIGHT SHOT. Missy bit her lip, glanced at the boys, then couldn't help crying. There was no other road to take but this butterfly highway.

CUT TO: Pale wing smears.

CRANE SHOT. Camera on aerial boom follows car from above at ever-decreasing speed.

CONTINUE CRANE SHOT. Expanded frame shows solitary wagon, a light blip tottering on black tightrope crease in topographic freefall of yellow.

SLOW PAN RIGHT. Reveals road that leads toward man-made, untainted blue lake of discovery.

STABILIZE FINAL SHOT. Full aerial view, glints of refracted sun spotting the lens. A Technicolor moment to seize with recognition and somehow make their own.

SLOW DISSOLVE.

MUSIC UP AND OVER: Chorale in the distance, no words.

MIDDLES

"Oh, Lordy!"

Lights, camera, Missy! Her kind of entrance, made blindside but with fanfare, *en retard* but *toujours gaie*, punctuated by flutterings and excuses and a screeched "Who's that helping himself to my chlorine?"

"The amphibious trespasser."

"In his birthday suit, too!"

"Well! This is a family neighborhood! And I don't think my husband would understand!" Like a deft vaudevillian, she turns her back on Fire to mouth in a stage whisper, "Who invited *him*?"

Missy's loyal following rewards her with a standing ovation. She acknowledges each of us with pecks on both cheeks. Her black hair is shorter than I've ever seen, neat on top and flared out in layers over the ears for that functional yet fem look favored by those in the "helping professions." Otherwise, she could be Melissa Sue Monroe, juvenile offender. Major identifying marks: dimples at the upper rise of both cheeks, button nose, square chin, winningly slanted smile. Her bundle of mannerisms are still loosely in place, from the constant flinging back of her head to the involuntary tapping of sandaled feet to the fidgeting with gangling fingers that suggests a continual tearing of invisible paper into confetti strips. The voice, too, is a thin and throbbing squeal that's so distinctive it makes an aural fingerprint. The main change is that, like a load of dishes in the crook of her arm, she holds her one-year-old.

"Are you going to say hello, Irenka? *Kali mera*? Do you remember Uncle Dana?"

"I ain't no uncle. I'm a corruptin' influence."

"Come on, Dan'! Be a sport! . . . See how baby's lookeen! See how baby wants to know."

"She'll soon learn all about her mom's sordid past."

"That's 'cause you're dying to spill it, huh Pep?"

"My lips are sealed."

"Hah! His lips are poison." There is some special reason why Dana does not like me today.

"Was anything wrong?" Annie asks.

"Of course not. I was just bein' supermamma. Huh, my Irenka? Huh, boo-boo?" This continual prodding and prompting suggests that Missy is pumping her daughter full of her own irrepressibility. "But I had to wait for hours. I must have read ten *Cosmos*. With fifty ways to excite your mate while baking a casserole, etceterah-rah-rah. An' who can say what I'll have to pay for our little chat? These doctors are such *pigs*, no?"

Only Missy, amongst us all, would still think to use such a word and only from her would it seem so incongruous. She hasn't forgotten the sixties, just frozen them in a Tupperware tray.

"Did you help yourself to lunch?"

"Helped ourselves to Mac's," Dana boasts.

"You didn't! Ugh! Boys will be boys!"

"It goes with, how you say, *l'anniversaire*."

"My, my! But we're still going to have our picnic together, no? I've got to grab a leg of lamb from Spyros' pantry."

"From 'A Girl and a Greek'?" That logo could hang over their marriage, if Pepsi would print one up.

"Natch. Owners' privileges, you know. Only the owners happen to be the staff. Why did we ever think it would be easier to open our own place? We should have at least made it a dinner house. Lordy, I need this day off. My first in a *month*. And isn't this weather dreamy?"

Dreamy enough that I can allow all passions, past and present, to get bleached away. In Missy's presence, I've already begun to operate on automatic pilot. I can so easily disappear into the role of observer incarnate. Better yet, I'll be the stagehand, let Missy be the star. This backyard sun is her spotlight, and I'm relieved as always to get out of the glare.

11:57 a.m. Fate is a jump cut, destiny a bad edit.

Martin Pepper Productions Presents. In cooperation with New York University Film School. "Living in the Big City!" Four silents in out-of-focus sixteen millimeter! Completing the requirements for Beginning Production, 101. Starring the budding ingenue, Missy Monroe. Costarring Missy Monroe. With Missy Monroe. Cameo appearance by Dana Pearl. Screenplay by Martin Pepper. Directed and produced by Martin Pepper.

Reel one: "The Bombing of the Empire State," a low-budget experiment in special effects. Missy appears in black terrorist raincoat, clutching a postcard of her target. She phones in her joke bomb threat, giggling all the way. CUT TO: the actual skyscraper wobbling on its foundations, swaying and storm-tossed, thanks to a few hand-held cocktail shakes from the director.

Reel two: "Yo-yo," an homage to Andy Warhol. Missy plays with a yo-yo, sauntering with country girl innocence through the most devastated locales New York City can provide. A Bowery idyll, entirely on location. With a cast of ten thousand derelicts.

Reel three: "Girls Will Be Girls," based on a suggestion, a hot breath, by Missy Monroe. A saga of sexual role reversal. Only Missy could have recruited her cast from the SDS women's caucus and gotten them to dress up in full makeup, false eyelashes, Frederick's of Hollywood wigs. None of the ladies admitted enjoying their masquerade, except the leading lady, who led them out onto the street to act macho, make lewd remarks and ogle the boys.

Reel four and finale: "The Revolution Is Not a Tea Party," a Godard-inspired melange of Maoist dictums scrawled on a blackboard and action shots of the visiting Dana Pearl attempting to destroy various branches of the Chase Manhattan Bank with his walking stick. No shooting permit required, no damage inflicted. Climaxing in a Bu-nuelian coda that took full advantage of the itinerant costar's exhibitionist tendencies. An impassive and buck-naked Dana stepping in and out of their apartment building's elevator, then disappearing through the lobby with the aid of a fancy edit.

World premiere! Screened at semester's end. After his classmates' boy-meets-girl in Washington Square Park sagas, jeers greeted his yo-yo epic and crude Vertovian montage. Poor Missy! The only acting she would ever do was in Martin's film. A star is not born, but a critic may be. This one-and-only matinee would be Martin's last college class. Not boffo box office! His fellow students were so outraged that many of them walked out. But Martin had beat them to it.

12:02 p.m. Know too much for our own good. Otherwise, gotta lot to learn.

"Here! Have yourself an educational experience!"

With that, Missy hands me little Irenka. She and Dana and Annie are heading inside to change. But I've got my trunks underneath—and get penalized for my preparedness. "Guess who's got to watch baby! You're a good watcher, Pep! Here. Gentle now. . . . I've got to swim right this sec!"

Suddenly I'm left with Fire making bubbles in the pool and Irenka dribbling spittle in my lap. Can she really be the only baby I've ever held? I've no experience estimating where the folds of blanket leave off and her Downy-fresh folds begin. I hope there's nothing breakable beneath the wrappings. Wondering how I'm supposed to monitor all functions, I give her a stare that would frighten off a grizzly cub. When she even hints at a frown, I wiggle one doll's toe. Try my hand at several nonabusive tweaks. That's quite enough in the way of introduction, plenty of mutual contamination.

Why be so cautious when Irenka's already been exposed to tartan upholstery, textured ceilings, dehydrated milk and juice in concentrate, plastic teething rings and robot toys, the television drone and the more numbing silence of this suburban mausoleum? As far as I can see, everything in sight is eroding her head start on perfection. Surprise, kid, you've got flaws! You're halfway socialized! Not only that, but upon closer inspection, she looks distressingly like her granddad. Framed in size zero overalls, I find Moose Monroe's twinkling blue salesman eyes and his goofy huckster smile, permanently askew like Missy's. Pencil in some hair and maybe a mustachio and you've got the face that launched a thousand used-car lots—a face that extracts its commission from life every time, gets its ten percent of the action.

Is there a gene for unwarranted enthusiasm? Just like there's a gene for self-pity? Snuggling close to me is another straight-ahead California optimist; an earnest, square-jawed mover in the land of wheels and deals. What a legacy for poor Irenka! What twists in our mutual course have brought forth this Greco-Waspo wisp! How unlikely a bearer of the Big Mac torch! For a moment, she nearly becomes interesting.

12:08 p.m. Have a child? Maybe, just maybe, I'll get another cat.

His One and Only Baby. If Martin hadn't been careful, this one could have been his. The withdrawal method was all Missy ever used during the Bastille summer's sustained screw or afterwards in their West Village studio. Their only chance to play house! They didn't mind if the house was a single overpriced room with more fire escape than floor space. On that steamy September night when they'd moved in, the two of them downed a bottle of champagne and did it, carelessly, on the bare floor.

Later, there would be lingering lays with the Sunday *Times* spread around. They grew to relish that ritual of buying the paper on Saturday nights, just like the natives did. Martin could teach Missy how to be a New Yorker without fear that she'd actually become one. Bundled now in a sheepskin coat, her tanned curves were ever more his private treasure. Incongruity enlarged her cheery contentment into something miraculous. She did take a few acting classes, the teachers did praise her as a natural, but Missy had no ambition to be anything but Missy. Being Missy was quite enough, thank you!

Though she grumbled having to take a part-time job, she was more comfortable once she became a cashier in their neighborhood supermarket. No one ever looked so good in a name tag! That comedienne's squeal was perfect for turning the drone of prices rung up into an absurdist monologue. Each evening, Martin would pass through her line and she'd pretend not to recognize him. She was a natural at this sort of acting, too. She'd charge him nineteen cents for nineteen dollars' worth—and come home to find it all cooked up for her.

Home to their cockroach gazebo where they made love happily, without considering the future or resorting to the pill. How did the chant go? "L.B.J., pull out like your father should have!" Daring the worst to befall them, it never did. Martin always had too much control, or luck. He seemed immune to those necessary calamities that drag people toward life.

12:12 p.m. The baby boom: one mass movement that doesn't require membership cards.

The Last Chapter. Why hadn't they left well enough alone? As soon as the two of them arrived in New York, Martin dragged Missy into the fray. All he had to do was give her his rendition of that standard soft-shoe, "You wanna be political, don'tcha?" Political meant SDS, which meant following the N.Y.U. chapter's latest "line," as formulated by a couple of male ideologues known as "heavies." These fellows laid the law down and preferred not to be interrupted. Martin found that out when he asked for a clarification as to why the chapter was supporting the counterdemonstration to the Weatherman faction's "White Riot." His answer was an hour-long harangue, spoken so confidently that it seemed to have been previously composed in longhand, by a paternal-looking teaching assistant named Irv Gunther—a/k/a Champion Heavyweight Irv. It was an accepted fact: their germ of a strifeless future was best depicted with a terminology borrowed from the gladiatorial past. It was divided into heavier and lighter rankings. Martin knew which one he was, and preferred to be. He never asked questions at meetings again.

Yet he and Missy remained knee-jerk loyal to the chapter, which rewarded them with unlimited travel: beginning with a defiant ramble through the Polish neighborhoods of Chicago where Panther leader Fred Hampton told all two hundred of their "Revolutionary Youth Movement Two" exactly what was wrong with "Revolutionary Youth Movement One" or Weatherman. Those folks were "opportunistic, militaristic, provocateuristic, Custeristic, crazyistic!" Right on, Chairman Cheerleader Fred! Never mind that Weatherman got all the publicity. Their side was "too proletarianally intoxicated to ever be astronomically intimidated!" Just like the Puerto Rican Young Lords in purple berets and fatigues who strode off the charter buses in formation at each Howard Johnson's rest stop and loaded up their khaki pockets with confiscated postcards and HoJo bars. Around Washington's Dupont Circle, they remained intoxicated, with the aid of pepper gas fogging machines. The troopers' life was a hard one. There was a run on gas masks and helmets in the Army-Navy stores of Canal Street that year. At the Justice Department, Martin and Missy helped "bring the war home"—retreating into a White Castle burger joint until their eyes stopped misting. A marshall in Ivy League blazer came through to warn, "Stay away from Justice. It's just a few adventurists mixing it up with the cops!" But Missy and Martin were satisfied just to be in on the adventure.

Not so with most students. Irv Gunther convinced the chapter to take their dwindling support as a badge of honor. "The beneficiaries of imperialism are no longer capable of attacking imperialism." Then who were the members of the chapter? Irv Gunther was speaking eloquently to himself. He kept laying out all the answers, except the right ones. On December fourth, Fred Hampton was murdered by crazyistic cops and the chapter retaliated crazyistically. The "line" had changed; the heavies had to prove they could be street-fuckers, too. They also changed the chapter's name to the December Fourth Movement, or DEFORM, a telling acronym.

With spring break came a fatal error. Most of the leadership landed themselves plum vacations cutting cane in Cuba. In their absence, the lightweights surged forward to displace them. Among those rising in class, there were even some women daring to step into the ring. Only they wanted to know: was this politics or sports? The women were beginning to ask a lot of questions, including "What makes you men think you've got all the answers? Why do you expect us to support a movement that's undemocratic? When are you going to give us our chapter back? And how are you going to fight male chauvinism? . . . We're serious. Wipe away those smirks!"

For the first time, the heavies had no pat replies. Their bludgeoning rhetoric ceased to keep the ladies in line; their verbal clubs suddenly became handicaps. And Missy and Martin watched the whole spectacle as if through a keyhole. After all, both of them were among the lightest of the light. Neither had a stake in the pecking order. Missy did go off to the first separate women's caucuses, but Martin wasn't threatened. Attending the equivalent male breast-beating sessions, he felt like a spy. The reasoned, articulate moaning on all sides sounded to him like "When do we get our women back?" But Martin still had his, and couldn't see how he might be affected. As always, he jumped to the conclusion that he was different from the rest. He was practically an honorary woman.

12:16 p.m. What feminism tended to discount, right from the beginning, was the number of men with "feminine" psychologies, though these were the men the first feminists relied on to stick around and bear the brunt of their initial critique—men who are malleable, loyal to a fault, identified with their oppressor.

"Is Pep a good daddy?" Missy calls from the house. "Huh, boo-boo? Is he?"

No answer is forthcoming. But the swimming party returns just in time. Irenka is beginning to whimper continuously, no doubt due to the anxiety I've transmitted through nervous pats and halfhearted pokes. I hand her over to the dimpled prototype.

"There now, boo-boo. Big Mamma's back in town." Missy soothes the child fast as a Valium, then plops her into the certified safe-for-groveling sandbox.

"Do you want to change now?"

"No need," I tell her, letting down my pants to reveal Speedos beneath. "I'm always ready for action."

"I remember."

"Yeah," adds Dana, "he last saw action around 'seventy-one."

"Don't be cruel to the one you love!" Missy croons.

I'm being coaxed into my familiar group role. Welcome, bumbling but lovable Pep—the fierce militant who can't take a tease. Do these people really know me better than I know myself? I doubt that just as relentlessly as I offer myself up for their assessment.

From the start, the others are bound together by inquiries about each others' jobs. This sense of exclusion is disconcertingly familiar, too. It never occurs to anyone that going to the movies can be a gig—or that it's possible to put in overtime with the *auteur* theory. What I think of Brian De Palma's latest isn't as juicy as Dana's jousts with management, Annie's gossip about Chinese sewing ladies, or Missy's new enterprise amidst the Greeks.

"It's terrific when they hear you're starting out on your own. I never knew my Spyros had so many cousins! One is in meats, another in linen supply, another rents the kitchen equipment, or sells insurance . . . an' they've got advice about how to stretch the sauces! Water the ketchup! It's a real community, huh? Every Greek in town has been by for a cup of coffee, at least. An' you wouldn't believe how many of them there are! From Macedonia, Thraki! Amazeen! Afterwards, they leave these fifty-dollar tips! A Ben Franklin on the counter! Lucky money, they call it. Just to get their countrymen going."

While the proprietress is describing the subtle variants on luncheonette fare which she plans to introduce, I find myself studying what Missy once called her "California bod." Unlike Missy's hot cars, this chassis hasn't been dented. This model was made to fit in a bikini. The frame's nicely stretched, as if offering itself for proper viewing, the hips break just right, the navel's sculpted. Her legs do look a trifle veinier, the knees knobbier, the toes more blunted and gnarled. They haven't changed so much as I have. There's no plastic surgeon more efficient than adoration. Bodies formerly loved: someone should invent a telescope that helps us glimpse them as we once did.

Still, there's something wonderfully fixed about Missy lounging in the beneficent California light. Her appeal's timeless and guileless as that of a Victorian postcard bathing beauty. Better yet, this grinning *maja* could be one of those spray-painted Great American Nudes: the very pop image of someone who doesn't have to bother about becoming an image. Seeing her poolside, it's hard to imagine that Missy was ever anywhere else.

Gelati Cioccolata. *Praenomen*, *cognomen*, *nomen*, their Roman holiday, Missy and Martin grabbing a taxi ride to the Forum and escaping the *parenti* Pepper who'd treated them to his spring fling. An afternoon hot as dishonored blood made them stop for *gelati*, *cioccolata* or *ananas*, any flavor so long as Missy got one each half hour to go with the pumpkin seeds she bought from the souvenir stands that grew like toadstools in the shadow of the true church. Missy said *grazie* again to the gelati man, trying not to tourist pronounce, so that word came out so humble it really did mean thanks in some swallowed language. But she didn't have to worry about behaving like an ugly imperialist in this spot where the term was perfected.

For the first moment since Martin's family had offered this paid vacation bribe to their prodigal and unofficial prodigal-in-law, Missy was really in Italy, the way Martin imagined she might be. Until now, they'd spent half the time squabbling over feminism with Doctor Pepper, the sexology expert threatened by a wave of unverified female assertions, so that, while speeding down the *autostrada*, they'd almost come to blows over Latin *machismo*—to Martin's Dad, it was a sign of good-natured mental salubriousness; to Missy a symptom of warped neurotic immaturity. Martin didn't dare admit that he, too, wanted to ogle and whistle at the sight of Missy playing archeologist in her hiked-up crepe-paper limeade minidress.

Up the cobbled fast lane of the Via Sacra, sacred freeway for Missy's recycled tire-tread sandals, Martin showed off his knowledge of the friezes on the Arch of Titus. Never mind that they weren't supposed to look at the marble legions sacking the temple in Jerusalem. Despite the sun, the Forum proved more sheltering than a convent. Here, there were no open-shirted Rossano Brazzis to pester Missy. She and Martin played hide-and-seek through vestal temples, near the *Rape of the Sabines*. Martin found mostly deranged hairless cats frozen in fear of something moving, before glimpsing that fruit-green tunic against brown tablet shards. He caught up with her in a stairway leading to the garage end of an excavated Vespasian wine cellar, next to the Senate steps where Julius the Porker met Lee Harvey that time. Martin scampered around her like a *paparazzo*, clicking before she had time to self-compose, but quit soon as he realized she was sinking into the ruins quietly. Missy paused to point at one Doric stump defaced with, "As Rome's ventures failed, so shall those of the U.S.A.!" A little high-handed, but who could doubt the writing on the S.P.Q.R.?

It was the only reminder not chiseled CAES IMPER DOMIT QUINTUS MLLXVIII like the round-the-coin writing of a dupondius of Augustus, "Ow-goo-steen-o" as the antiquities dealer in the Piazza di Spagna corrected Martin, then just a kid scrounging through the two-dollar *denari*. Martin had once collected such funny money, which was uncharacteristically pecuniary of him (from *pecus*, meaning cattle). His coins helped in him getting an "A" in ancient history. Martin came to know the emperors from their minted portraits the way his classmates knew TV personalities: Jackie Gleason Nero ("forced to commit suicide at age 31"), Phil Silvers Domitian ("slain by his own guard to obvious relief to all concerned"), Jimmy Durante Nerva ("one of the sane ones, despite his nose"), or the child stars like Mickey Rooney Caracalla ("murdered his brother and twenty thousand more"). What made 'em so evil? Maybe these calicos knew.

On the Palatine Hill, first suburban vomitorium playland, cattown now, they kissed with the Colloseum behind and Big Maximus ahead ("successfully plotted the death, by poisoning, of Drusus"). What were the two of them doing here? Any need to find an answer receded as they smooched to the ovulating cats' reproductive serenade better than any gondolier's aria, a sound which told them why their moms and dads had met and why the world might have to endure another Mussolini or two and why time turned so cruel on young love ("thrown unceremoniously into the Tiber") but they were decidedly there—the Forum was there, Martin's childhood coins were there through they'd changed venal hands a billion times—as they fell off the sacked slope, advancing arm in arm on next *gelati*.

12:22 p.m. The feminist message had to be true because it was two things at once: the last hope for a revolution, the institutionalizing of that revolution's defeat.

Bombing Out. By the end of that fertile spring, everyone knew: this "women's movement" was no bra burning, no salon event. Now there was an explanation for why the chapter's membership diminished as their positions grew more popular. Even Missy threw in the towel, "You can keep going but I can't take it anymore. It's the whole style, the arrogance, the jargon, the men!"

Then came the Kent State killings. Now SDS was trampled by a stampede of the same students they'd been trying to budge. Where had they all been six months previous? Ignored, the chapter's self-anointed leadership planned a final tantrum. They led the takeover of the Atomic Energy Commission building on campus and held its headquarters as ransom to pay the persecuted New York Black Panthers' bail. When the university wouldn't cough up the dough, a thousand squatters marched out, jubilant, believing that the six-million-dollar computer inside was about to be blown up. But the fuse on this last *macho* orgasm fizzled.

At least, Irv Gunther got indicted for extortion, made it into the big-time legal arena. Saved by the bell of semester's end, the heavies avoided technical knockout. Rid of their Marxist punching gloves, yesterday's contenders looked mighty puny. Without their women trainers, they went into premature retirement. Nothing could stave off the extinction of the heavy, not even the label "revolutionary." Their gentlemanly stepping aside only damned them further. Apparently, participatory democracy was no fun anymore now that the men couldn't boss it. To a chorus of weeping Trojan women, and one throwing up in a dormitory toilet, the chapter officially split in two. One per sex. Just look between their legs to find their membership cards.

At year's end, Union Square was full for the first time in decades as a new contingent celebrated International Women's Day. Martin "escorted" Missy. His new quandary: to chant or not to chant. During the rally, right on schedule, there was an eclipse of the paternalist sun. The symbolism was dazzling, even with infrared filters. So was the news phoned to the dormitory where the men were holding a last-ditch confessional. The caller asked for Irv Gunther, and when Martin caught a slight tremor of emotion beneath the Papa Marx beard, he knew something dreadful had happened.

"Teddy Gold and some Weatherman pals have gone and blown themselves up on Eleventh Street," Irv announced. "I'd say the meeting's adjourned."

And what had been, just six months before, the N.Y.U. Chapter of Students for a Democratic Society went off to mourn. They mourned a brother, a chapter, a movement nitro'd by its own unsteady hands. The New Left had proved a bomb with a very short fuse. It had exploded into fragments: P.L., Y.S.A., R.Y.M. Numbers One and Two, Weatherpeople, Third Worlders and Out-of-This-Worlders, heavies and lights and, finally, into blues and pinks. Irv Gunther and the others were left with a constituency that was more gaping than the missing front tooth in Eleventh Street's brownstone smile. For Martin and Missy, itching for California, ready to try Big Mac once and for all, the arms factory had popped like a champagne magnum. This self-bombing was their "Bon Voyage!"

12:30 p.m. Thinking about Missy is like trying to describe the taste of water.

The four of us are in it up to our necks.

"It's like taking a dip in the washing machine, no?" There's barely room for our hostess, still a landlubber and tending to baby.

"Get your butt in gear, Mom. We're already on the rinse cycle." That's Dana's way of saying that he and I remain in the shallow end, making like frogs on pogo sticks. We could hardly do laps in Missy's inverted water balloon, especially since none of us want to navigate anywhere near Fire. If there's a thing as breaststroking lice, he's got 'em. Sister Annie gets the closest. Bangs wet and ethnic garb shed, she's a bobbing smiley doll—ever oblivious to hazards. She also lingers in the depths to submerge a chunky pioneer's torso that's not angular enough to simulate Missy's poster girl look.

"Now sit tight, boo-boo. Mamma's gotta cool down, okay?" Missy's toes grip the chlorinated cusp, her arms forming a shield above her. She wavers coyly, holding her maidenly pose like a Busby Berkeley extra. She finds a lane between all of us for her dive's long afterglide.

"Mmmmm," she surfaces speaking. "The water's psychodelightful!"

"Yeah, dee-lightful. Getting our butts slammed in jail."

"It was a dreamy time, huh?"

"How we spent our summer vacation."

"I wish baby would give me a vacation!" Missy submerges, arching back ever so listlessly, then spouting a chemical mouthful—not in homage to the humpbacked whale but to some water nymph from a Bernini fountain. "Come on now, before Irenka wants me back. Let's all do water ballet!"

To illustrate, Missy pushes off from the bottom, then bounds weightlessly forward with a mock flapping of swan wings. Her eyes are firmly shut, for once off the baby, focusing on ecstasy with all their might. She pirouettes, pointy toes and all. A wounded creature of the glade, she dies elegantly in one slow, floating swoon. She doesn't seem the least bit worried about the rest of her ballet *corps*. Dana and I waddle forward through the pool, volunteers for a *pas de deux*, or *trois*. I'm amazed at how quickly I take up my part. I remember the days when I was the only lead allowed to turn, upraise and cradle this slippery nymph. Missy goes on sinking gracefully, perfecting her swooning. She knows that someone will be there to catch her. Someone always has.

Live Like Them. On certain summer nights, Berkeley was Shalimar. The grid of flatlands housing was set in a garden, choked with plum trees and acacia, oozing ramshackle bliss. The atmosphere was cloying, soaked in laurel and whiffs of wisteria, the natural atomizer of night jasmine on the puff, with patchouli oil, incense and sexual musk, also the logs of dog turd left by packs of tribal mascots; the heady fragrance of indignation. There were bins on every corner, offering recycled denim ponchos, sofas with a leg or two amputated, unraveled God's eyes, thrice-read volumes of Gibran and Marcuse. The brown shingle houses bore sashes, cut across their slanty-eyed eaves at a diagonal, as on swimsuit contestants. But these didn't read "Miss Vallejo" or "Miss Congeniality." They said, "Smash the State!" and "Power to the Imagination!"

Hurtling through the tunnels of university town green were three couples huddled close with the urgency of a plenary session taken to the sidewalks. These six didn't stop to sniff front yard flora, barely inhaled the jasmine, nearly forgot to step around the dogshit, took the strung banners as self-indulgence, didn't care to admire the earth mammas' seed packet cornucopia, couldn't wait to leap hedges and escape the garden.

They reached the uneven, spotlit tabletop of Ho Chi Minh Park and fanned out, spinning giddily and doing cartwheels.

"Big Mac, live like them!"

"A social upheaval disguised as a sandwich!"

"Go amongst the workers and peasants!"

"Arm one another against the monster!"

"Burrow into the belly of same!"

"Start our study group!"

"Criticize, self-criticize. Awright!"

"Share our cash, huh?"

"Fuck that. Pool our souls!"

Speech was amplified into slogan. And they didn't mind at all. At last, they were proclaiming the formation of their perilously small collective—the easier to collectivize, or so they hoped. Big Mac would be their unaffiliated utopian sect based on an unnamed tendency of a purposely ill-defined ideology in service of an amorphous crusade. Since they could hardly live up to all that, it was out of the question that they should notice what they actually were: three young couples falling gradually and inevitably out of love. Already, on the summer night when they joined forces, Martin stumbled, lost his footing, could no longer keep Missy in sight.

12:35 p.m. On this we could agree, no nests built for two. Yet the twigs we gathered were meant for one pair only.

Laboratory of the Real. They might have saved themselves a lot of house-hunting if they'd known they were going to sleep in one bed. Who was going to rent three bedrooms to six unrelated adults? A moonlighting Oakland cop, it turned out. He turned out to be color-blind. The place they found was dubbed The Big Pumpkin because of its fresh coat of orange paint. On the upper floor of this Victorian monstrosity, their three bedrooms, kitchen and living room with built-in hutch were all laid with a pulsating blue shag carpet. Otherwise, the site was perfect. Their neighbors were all on welfare, their corner market sold as fresh what Berkeley sold as day-old. The landlord even came for the rent in his squad car. They knew it was him—and not a raid—by the familiar four numerals on the hood. Everything in this town was marvelously streamlined: collector and enforcer were one. Authority was out in plain view for all who bothered to look.

Did the cop ever suspect that they were anything but some struggling young couples who had to pool their housing while they started down the road of life? No doubt, he envisioned that road without potholes, cemented over for "easy maintenance" like their backyard, like the whole neighborhood. In pragmatic Oakland, trees had been replaced by utility poles throughout. Luckily, they were within walking distance of one of the few square-block interruptions in the stucco squalor. Here, they found netless hoops and a sunken ball diamond dusted with broken bottles. The outfield got its main recreational use from pipsqueak gangs who set up their portable consoles and put on impromptu reviews by lip-synching along to the latest rhythmic plaints. "*Makes me wanna holler, the way they do my life. Makes me wanna holler* . . ." At sunset, with the grunted choruses crisscrossing, the glass chips retaining each pastel tone, this park of the people looked more splendid than a Watteau landscape. It was all the collective had sought: their very own playing fields of blight.

This city seemed ready-made to serve as a giant laboratory of the real. And there was even such a thing as the Oakland Liberation Front! They soon discovered that it was little more than a research project, but that was appropriate. After all, the prospective membership had to know exactly what and who they were going to liberate. This was perfect for Dana, who threw himself into gathering the World Book basics (population 340,000, elevation 80 feet), the thumbnail history of this squatters' town, the financial profile of this outpost at the end of the railway line, the scant attractions of San Francisco's ugly sister city. Thus far, the Front's only assault on the power structure had been the creation of an alternative food distribution network. Every Thursday night, Martin and Dana and Ayer joined in weighing out sacks of pinto beans and slicing up damp rounds of Raw Milk Jack.

The women didn't need any more practice at food preparation. From a leaflet posted at the neighborhood laundromat, Missy was alerted to the first organizational meeting of Oakland Womens' Liberation. They had found O.W.L.—and Oakland was sure to make them wise.

12:38 p.m. She does not have to operate under that greatest of handicaps, memory.

No wonder Missy can bound with such vigor from one activity to the next.

"Okay, boo-boo. Mamma's comeen. Just let me dry off a sec! . . . There. Hush now. Don't you like our anniversary? What do you say about all your uncles and aunts?"

"Not exactly all."

"That's right. What's become of Darlinda?"

"Who says we wanna know?"

"Oh, pooh! Let communal bygones be bygones, huh?" Only Missy can put verve into such a stale line. She's a living version of those adages found on bumper stickers, over cash registers or public johns. ("I owe, I owe, so off to work I go!") Missy's just as sensible, just as banal. "Come on, Irenka. Let's go inside now. Let's call Auntie Darlinda! That's lesson number one for you, daughter. It's no good unless everyone's here."

Swinging back and forth on Missy's fringed love seat, Dana's only comment is to sing, "He who rides with the Klan is a devil and not a man!" With his towel wrapped around his skull, it looks like the Coppertone girl has joined Al Fatah.

Revolution and Dance. In the midst of the revolution, Darlinda kept trying to relax. Each morning, when the light through the bay windows made the carpeting shimmer like a lagoon, she stripped and crawled out in the middle of the playroom's blue unfurnitured expanse, and began her "bridgies." These were stretching exercises, done on all fours, as prescribed by Leila Layne, a local dance instructor favored by all those Movement women who were drawn to the other sort of movement. Ms. Layne guaranteed to bring out the Isodora latent in every feminist, for not only did she run a salon over a Chinese restaurant in an obscure corner of Oakland, but she was also an inveterate left-winger. More than a typical backwater *artiste*, she might have been the bastard offspring of Martha Graham and Gus Hall. Her dance technique was modestly described as dialectical materialism in leotards. Her regimen, so devoutly followed by darlin' Darlinda, was aimed at taking a student through all the phases of natural evolution so that she—or he, in a few cases—could rediscover the natural fluidity and erectness that had disappeared with the division of labor and the development of property relations. According to Leila Layne, via Engels or maybe Margaret Mead, the cause of bad posture was capitalism, and the cause of capitalism was most certainly bad posture.

So Darlinda strained to perfect her "turnout," a way of opening the pelvis and taking weight off the spine that tended to keep her in a permanent waddle. Once on her knees, the disciple turned vermicular, a sluglike segment of ontogeny trying not so much to recapitulate as to reform her phylogeny. Darlinda made like a nude scrubwoman, scouring the floor to uncover her lost ancestry. She turned amphibian, became a tadpole emerging for the first time onto dry land. But she wasn't. She was just your average radical feminist impersonating a pterodactyl.

Martin was the one who got to watch. He had a perfect view from where he packed his lunch kit for the post office, and Darlinda was forthrightly opposed to shutting doors. He saw her naked more often than he was getting to see Missy. He could have sketched, from memory, her spread labia. Out of boredom rather than curiosity, he would check off each vertebra poking out of her pasteurized backside, each ripple in her waxen skin. She didn't seem to mind exhibiting all sorts of curious moles, fleshy pincushions stuck with a needle or two of hair, the many warts that couldn't be removed with rubbings of garlic. She did possess long, firm legs and a perceptibly grippable saddle of hips—but Martin wasn't intrigued. Was it his duty to be? Despite Darlinda's more than tacit endorsement of the polymorphous perverse, Martin presumed that his indifference was the response she sought to provoke with her continual show. No doubt exhibitionism was in the eyes of the beholder. But Darlinda did seem to prefer positions that made the sun shine where it shouldn't. The vulva, divulged, was devalued. Darlinda's sexuality, ever flaunted, was ever denied. If she wanted to remain unappealing to Martin, she was succeeding. Darlinda became just what she did not wish to be in his eyes: a limber anatomy lesson, a body remaindered, a quivering flank of meat.

Her body. This was Darlinda's pet project and all-consuming hobby. It was out there somewhere, down below, if only she could find it! If only she could stop looking for it! When she first arrived in California, Martin made the mistake of asking her what she thought of her "place," and she'd asked back, "Do you mean my house or my body?" Her unhealthy obsession with health was formidable, a worldview. She was an innocent wandering in awe through the sparkling chambers of her *corpus*. When she cut her little finger with a cucumber peeler, she studied the wound's condition assiduously, gave hourly reports to her comrades. She wasn't particularly fearful of infection. She just loved to watch her body, that do-it-yourselfer, do its healing thing.

It did not look quite so bad to Martin under dim blue light, on a wooden loft floor, wrapped tight as a supermarket ham in a beige swimsuit, about to perform. On the first Thursday of every month, the collective dutifully attended the latest installment in Leila Layne's "Explorations in Evolutionary Motion." These featured interminable gropings on toughened knees, executed by the grab-bag ensemble, into which Darlinda won quick acceptance through her perseverance and hours of volunteer office work.

But why should women be the only ones allowed to stretch limbs, worm about, take flight, exult? Behind Martin's back, a recruitment campaign was being waged. One evening, as Darlinda was about to leave for her class, Dana traipsed through the living room sporting a black leotard. He was plainly chagrined, but determined to enlist in the latest group mission. "Don't say nothin', dude!" he warned Martin. "Jus' watch this fuckin' *plié*!" Dana pranced to center stage, chest sucked up as if he were taking a deep drag of hashish, shoulders tight and haughty. His step was deliberately halting, outrageously self-assured. This imitation jive made for the perfect "turnout"—though a snapping of fingers and his sauntering up to an imaginary microphone made it clear he wasn't Nureyev but Smokey Robinson. In the skintight suit Dana looked Auschwitz-scrawny, showing off oilcan knees and rib cage symmetry. His bare feet stuck out like a clown's cardboard shoes. Against the evening gown black, his urban complexion was the color of permanent shock. His chest hairs coiled with irrelevance, and his untrimmed wastrel's beard hung low enough to be tucked inside the low-cut body shirt. Spinning on his heel, like he used to do on the playgrounds when he drove to the basket, Dana did his best to impersonate some sort of Bolshoi defector, but he looked more like a scarecrow doing flamenco. Straining and leaping to feminize, Dana only showed how hard he customarily worked at looking street-tough. Despite protestations to the contrary, Dana's stab at relaxation only led to discomfort. He went to Leila Layne's salon only once. Afterwards, the leotard got stuffed into his dresser, buried under tube socks and a jock.

12:40 p.m. Can a naked body have convictions?

"No reply!" Missy calls through the screen door. "Maybe Darlin's on her way."

Her trip indoors has served other purposes. She's put baby to bed and now cradles a tray loaded with snacks.

"Chip 'n' dip, anyone?"

"You shouldn't have!"

"I couldn't help it!"

Missy beckons us to sample the *Woman's Day* perfect hostess buffet that's always at the ready in her fridge: celery sticks stuffed with Cheez Whiz, tuna and pimiento on wheat thins, a guacamole with feta, Hellenic-style, an onion mousse made from soup mix. Setting it all out on the picnic table in the direct sun, she seems determined to run a test of spoilage retardants. Nothing organic for her—Missy's the de Kooning of junk food and her palette is the popularly available. The feast is like her: a whirl of side dishes in search of a main course.

As a garnish, Missy reaches into the pockets of her candy-striped *après swim* robe and brings forth packets of the sunflower seeds she cracks by the hour. She flings each of us our own supply. "Remember, gang. There's always room to plant a few seeds!"

Bird food suits her flitting about. Eating is merely another of Missy's tics, best done on the fly. She never gets hungry, just nervous.

"Dig in, guys! Wake it an' shake it!" We cannot resist joining Missy in her nibbling rite.

12:48 p.m. Why the boardinghouse reach when none of us ever lived in a boardinghouse?

Too Many Cooks. They were disagreeing over everything, spoiling the broth. In the two months that Big Mac broke bread together, there were clashes over what towels to use, which pictures to hang, even which supermarket to patronize. The only course of action upon which they ever agreed was that each of them should cook one meal per week.

This was hardest on Dana, whose association with food was the Judge's suppertime terror. One way to stay thin. He preferred his catering by coffee shop, but he was also painfully conscientious. He did not prepare dinner, he plotted it. Like a general, he copied out his cookbook orders in triplicate. He could turn a minute steak into a whole-day steak. Annie, the rugged individualist, was best prepared for the communal task. Having long watched her mother prepare brood-sized portions of a chuck wagon cuisine, she could whip out enough beans for any long march. Martin, too, was a born chef, duplicating the culinary triumphs of his European trips. His only problem was expanding the portions. *Vitello tonnato* for nine? Bearnaise sauce with sixteen egg yolks? Missy usually improvised something at the last moment, raiding Fannie Farmer for casseroles that crisped over when she wasn't looking. No one complained about her many accidents. Darlinda's devised concoctions were dreaded. She mixed banana and onion, poured tahini over soyed *bok choy*, tried to turn out thousand-year-old eggs in a day, substituted wheat germ for salt. Her only success was a pizza: she made the whole-wheat crust and let everyone add one topping. Participatory cuisine!

Ayer topped everyone when it came to theme meals. He went through cases of food coloring, staring with Dr. Seuss's green eggs and ham—on to purple pastas, blue fondue, Pink Floyd rice. He loved an excuse to buy his supplies in industrial quantities. Cans of peas wide as bass drums, ketchup in vats—if the collective ever worked their way through them, they got exhibited around the apartment and signed by the artist under the lids. He urged a mysterious boycott of cheese, advancing the slogan "*Queso es muerte!*" He took a rich kid's reverse chic to new depths with casseroles fashioned entirely of soup mixes, potato flakes, chipped meats, Rice Krispies, the dehydrated and the defoliated. Warning: flavors and colors are not previously found in nature. His greatest triumph was an all-American breakfast, starting with toaster Pop Tarts and ending with individual servings of Fruit Loops, slit open cesarean-style in their boxes. The gag displayed Ayer's talent and his penchant. He'd so dazzled his fellow cooks that no one noticed he'd managed his meal without having to do a moment's cooking or cleaning up.

12:51 p.m. Our unquestioned assumption: that we had to change ourselves and the world at the same time—the world because it was corrupt, ourselves because we were innocent, or maybe the other way 'round.

The last one lapping up Missy's goodies is a crook-tailed Siamese who's sauntered over from the vicinity of the garage.

"Who invited you, Martha? Go on, shoo!"

"Is that yours?"

"Lord, no! Spyros hates cats. I think he's a teensy allergic. I'm just keeping this one for a neighbor, her and a bunch of others. . . . Oooh, feeding time's overdue."

We follow Missy toward the stucco carport, painted to match the guacamole. Inside, I count at least a half dozen cats, curled up on themselves, snoozing in the shade provided by another in a long line of Missy's automotive hand-me-downs. It's hard to pick out all the mottled balls against the concrete. Some of them look like accessories for the oversized tires, furry wheel blocks. Their various bowls are mixed in with the cans of thinner and shellac along the garage walls. Missy is the Mother Teresa of cats.

"See that one over there . . . it belongs to Sissy, she lives down the block, an occupational therapist, on a tour of Tuscan hill towns or sometheen . . . this one's Josie's, who's an Avon Lady, can you believe it? . . . she's at Club Med, Cancun . . . an' this one goes with Terry, my haircutter, goin' through a bad d-i-v-o-r-c-e. . . . don't speak the word in front of this poor child . . . an' this mop goes with Sheila . . . shoot, wasn't she supposed to come fetch it today? . . . I hope so. She's two tons of fun. An' the world's supreme waitress! Sheila's the one who broke me in at my last dinner house."

"Now you can open a coffee shop for cats."

"A new challenging role for the divine Miss M.!" says Miss M. "I couldn't refuse them, could I?"

"Just like you couldn't refuse Sojourner."

"Oooh, but that one was really crazy!" At the word "crazy," Missy's dimples glint in unison.

"Once she lost her tubes," Dana concurs, "she lost it."

"It was too much rock 'n' roll," I diagnose.

"Too many men," says Missy.

12:56 p.m. Nothing remains unmolested by memory.

Cats and Dogs. "Here, will you hold this kitty for a moment?"

A tabby militant was thrust into Missy's arms at an anti-R.O.T.C. demonstration. The kitten hid in her overcoat's marsupial lining, frightened by the random toppling of furniture and army file cabinets. Its owners never returned, of course. The cat was theirs: just another unwanted female, natural by-product of the centuries' feline oppression, no planned parenthood, no control over their bodies in those back alleys. They named it Sojourner Truth—though this marble-eyed mistake was more like a Moses out of the bulrushes, ready to lead their exodus from New York back to California's land of Milk and Friskies. Little did Sojourner know that her cross-country ride took her toward a rendezvous with Ebenezer. But Martin and Missy had no reason to fear the superdog who'd always been the group's ultimate mirror. He would not harm collective harmony. Ayer and Annie, Eba's current feeders, were hardly anticat.

Arriving in Berkeley, Sojourner had her first heat. Martin and Missy tried to keep her indoors. She was too young for all that pain. And Big Mac? How to find a kennel suitable for six humans, one dog, one cat? Left unsupervised while they tracked down a real estate lead, Sojourner slipped out. Missy and Martin returned just in time to watch the toms taking turns atop their kitten's trembling squat. Soon enough, Sojourner grew fat and peevish, with little respect for the loud, clumsy beast with whom she had to share her nursery. Ebenezer coexisted, cold war-style. Nightly entertainment was provided by cat hissings and dog pouncings. From the pets, Big Mac learned to snap and scratch.

In the year they'd been apart, the six of them had picked up more than separate animals. Some were students, some aspiring workers. Some wanted an extended family, others insisted on a fighting unit. Ayer and Annie became the Ebenezer faction, the rest were the Sojourner. It was Annie and Martin who became spokesmen for what came to be known as the two "camps": Annie who preached, "Organize thyself," Martin who swore, "Organize anyone but"; Annie who instructed, "Be one righteous pointing finger," Martin who announced,

"Be part of a fist"; Annie who was sure they had plenty of time and trusted evolution, Martin who was convinced they had almost none and suspected compromise; Annie who argued that true change could never be forced, Martin who countered that true change always had to be forced; Annie who extolled friendship and the golden rule, Martin who invoked comradeship and obeisance before group will; Annie who held to the values of her up-by-the-bootstraps upbringing, Martin who held to the values of his don't-be-ashamed-to-ask coddling; while both failed to notice how they spoke two sides of the same message.

The other "camp" slept unconcernedly on their side of the bed on the night Sojourner sneaked into the playroom and effortlessly gave birth to a cadre of four. Dana and Darlinda stayed up with the nervous godparents and, while inspecting the litter, began a list of demands that they knew the other couples would never meet. The bickering made everyone sick, Sojourner included. She stopped nursing, abandoned her offspring. She had indeed been too immature for the task assigned. The vet diagnosed a uterine infection, fifty bucks please. The two camps temporarily united in crisis, Ayer paying the bill. But the cat wasn't his, the orphaned kittens less so. Missy and Martin had to wash them, feed them, apply drops to prevent blindness—with help from their camp, but never the other.

Only Ebenezer volunteered. He loved those kittens like his own, whimpered over them, offered tongued tenderness. The dog never tired of playing with the kittens, though he didn't seem cognizant of how little they were. When Martin or Missy implied that Ebenezer might cause any harm, Ayer branded such talk as paranoia. Sojourner sulked in a mean daze. She didn't even notice when the first kitten was found dead, shriveled and wet with Ebenezer madly licking away.

Was he trying to revive it, as Ayer deftly interpreted, or was he finishing the kill? An answer came quickly, and this time there were witnesses. In the kitchen, setting of a thousand dinnertime debates, the dog had snapped, protecting his food, as Ayer often encouraged him to do, with a "Take no shit, Eba!" A kitten's head was gone, leaving a bloody smear on student slum linoleum, four limp paws. While Missy ran to cry in the bathroom, and Annie swept up the mess right quick, Martin launched into his postmortem.

"I knew the dog couldn't be trusted."

Meaning us, said Ayer.

"Those are our animal slaves."

Everything isn't political, said Ayer.

"Murder is."

It wasn't on purpose, said Ayer.

"That's the trouble, nothing around here is on purpose."

Don't blame our camp for everything, said Ayer. Why not blame us for the Vietnam War?

"That's not Vietnamese blood on the floor," Martin eulogized on behalf of his camp. "That's our blood."

"Then we'll have to move out."

Go on, said Martin. A dream for two years, Big Mac lasted two months. Ayer was prepared with a prophecy that sounded prerehearsed.

"The collective of six will become collectives of one."

1:00 p.m. People and dogs: best not to look either directly in the eye.

Fire is munching like a goat off Missy's fig tree.

"How rude!" At least, he's got his pants back on. "What's the matter, don't you go for my dips?"

"Those are pasteurized. I'm homogenized." He looks serious.

"That's cool. I know you, Fire. You don't believe in private property, right?"

"I believe in figs. I'm gonna bag me some z's under the biblical figs."

"You do that."

He looks so comfortable that I'm tempted to join him. But I can't once two tons of fun blusters into the yard.

"Yoo-hoo, Melissa! Pick up table seven! And don't forget your peppers and salts!"

Familiar with the shortcut to the backyard, the world's waitress supremo has ambushed us. This suburban guerrilla's battle outfit is a pink chiffon muu-muu, white sandals with plastic daisies glued to the toe straps, and a flowered kerchief that covers a head full of curlers.

"Oh, girl! Why didn't you tell me you were gonna be entertainin'! Woe is me!" She's shaking like a Santa Claus in maternity dress. "I'm revealed as the lowlife I truly am!"

"Sheila!"

"Are you gonna introduce me, or do I simply look too casual?"

"These are my oldest and dearest friends from Steffens College."

"College? When did you go to college, gal? I never heard about this. Melissa's secret life."

"We call her Missy."

"And sometimes, Crash."

"Oooh! All these aliases! Come on, gal, 'fess up about your days with the C.I.A. And that Mexican abortion! . . . Or are you savin' your life story for the *Enquirer*?"

Sheila plops down strategically near the *hors d'oeuvres*. The sight of Fire makes her sit back up.

"What's that, girl? Is your snail problem getting out of hand?"

"That's Fire."

"Oh. Right. An' I must be Earth and Wind. About to pass wind. Oh, girl. I better skeedaddle before I let down my panty hose in front of these college folk."

"Stay," Missy urges. "We want you to stay, right?"

Nods all around. To our celebration, Sheila adds a missing ingredient: mirth.

"What kinda college was that you went to? A jaycee?"

"No. Just a regular liberal arts college."

"With fraternities an' all?"

"Not exactly. We were beyond fraternities."

"Sounds kinky."

"It was."

"Lots o' party hardy, right? I wish I coulda gone to college."

"We were mainly demonstrating. Taking over buildings. Fighting the cops."

"What for? Sounds like you had it made."

At the moment, in the glaring sunshine, I can't seem to find a "what for" no matter where I squint.

"You remember the sixties, no?" Missy tries. "All the longhairs?"

"The sixties. Let's see . . . that was before Scott, after Roger. That mean bastard of a teamster. I spent four years livin' in the back of his rig. Back when I could still climb into a rig. I guess I missed out on the action, didn't I?"

"You just missed some good drugs."

"Missy and drugs! That's another scoop!" But Sheila may not want to hear it all. Having polished off the onion dip, she's fidgeting and scanning the entrance to the garage. "I really ought to say *ciao-ciao-ciao* to my Ramona. Is the dear feline still kickin'?"

"Of course."

"And flea-ridden, no doubt. . . . You know, I want to tell you about your ol' friend Melissa, or Missy, or Miss Who All Ever. She's one pillar of this here community. She'll cover a shift for ya without even blinkin', drive you to the gynecologist, stir your soup for ya, board your pets an' your kids an' your cooties an' your ex-husbands . . . an', honey, I got a carport full o' those! Between you an' me," she leans across the picnic table to whisper, "Melissa here is the only one I ever saw who could cool down those hot-tempered Greeks!"

"Oh pooh!"

"No, I seen it. Your friend's got a heart as big as a Crockpot."

"That's what we always said."

"And she's some waitress. Always smilin' while she pours her warm-ups, always takin' that guff. . . . She was born to wait tables."

"Born to play ball. . . ." I echo, recalling Missy's days as the second baseman of the Steffens SDS softball team.

"Ain't that the truth! This gal over here really knows how to serve the people."

1:07 p.m. The people: I have never loved them, except as an abstraction. And the feeling's mutual, buddy.

Go Amongst the Workers and Peasants. Four attempts:

2. Ma Bell hates women. It didn't take Missy long to find out. Along with the rest of her kind, she was fitted with a headpiece that felt like a harness. Instead of giddying-up she had to recite, "Information, please. May I help you?" Every fifteen seconds, every minute, every day. She was stuck in a plastic cubicle on the ninth floor of an unadorned turret with no windows. That was always the way to spot Ma Bell's cabin: no glass and plenty of radar dishes on the roof. They were like military installations in the midst of every American city—manned by women. The supervisors were mostly female, too. They were the kind who took pleasure in turning against their own kind. Missy had to get their permission to pee and it was rarely granted. Answering Ma Bell's call came before answering nature's. If only the supes could have arranged their staff's menstruation in shifts! They initiated speedups, switched assignments without warning, and made a work force with a permanent hum in their ears sway dizzily from day to night, until they were accustomed to the windowless, seasonless world of Ma Bell.

Lunch breaks were swift in Ma Bell's canteen—just a couple of unreliable vending machines. But this was where Missy got to meet the women without their headsets. Missy didn't just ogle the tough-ass black ladies and gum-cracking Chicanas and spinsters with lifelong stiff necks. She was cantankerous enough to join their ranks, even if she wasn't always able to join their ongoing chatter about baby showers and boyfriends' choppers. She didn't dare mention the collective, not yet. This made Missy feel a trifle manipulative. But how would she even begin? She wanted more than anything to be one of the girls and explaining only got in the way.

Still, Missy was relieved when, several weeks into the job, she spotted a face from the previous night's general meeting of O.W.L. That face was hard to forget: an angry forehead exposed by sawtoothed black bangs, Asiatic cheekbones round as doorknobs, choppy terrier teeth which warned of her terrier grip on all conversation. It bore enough pancake for a clown act, lipstick cracked and colored like Japanese eggplant. It was makeup applied for the first time by a tomboy—part of a disguise that this woman clearly wanted to be found out. Even though she wore tentlike blouses over jeans, this woman was undeniably scrawny. Missy never saw her have anything for lunch but coffee and Cremora, her withering-away was overcompensated by a ferocity of enterprise. Her black eyes were always calculating; her nose was an exclamation point. And she spoke in rant, shouting at Missy, "I know you, girl! I see a sister!"

This operator didn't bother to lower her voice in the canteen. Missy wondered if she gave out the numbers of hair salons in the same harsh tone.

"You're in some collective, unaffiliated, not Lesbian, not yet. You here for the money or the kicks?" Missy wasn't sure how to answer, especially when supervisors were within earshot. "That's okay. I didn't mean to expose you, girl."

The woman had a New York rasp and kept tossing out that "girl" like someone who'd been imitating black speech all her life.

"I'm Meryl Schwartzkopf. Red and proud. You wanna join our caucus?"

So organizing was as simple as that! Nothing more was required for Missy. She was ready to join her sisters in most any enterprise, even if it included Meryl Schwartzkopf. Once Missy got used to her abrasiveness she admired what this woman had made of herself. So what if her style was borrowed from the movement's male "heavies"? Meryl was showing the way. She was so confident: there was no way to argue with that sort of leadership. But so female: she could let down when she had to, put her arms around you when she drove too hard. Missy really liked the other women who were already in the Ma Bell Hates Women caucus. They all lived in a house together. The first time Meryl described it, Missy thought she was spinning a fairy tale. A house that was all women! No men inspecting, hovering, no men dominating your ideas, dotting your i's! Mainly no men to coddle! Nothing to slow down the sisterly dance! The arrangement was intoxicating—and allowed the tenants to sleep, eat, and possibly mate with the rape and desecration of Ma Bell as their sole aim.

And it was so much more fun to have company at union meetings.

The union, it turned out, hated women too. Communication Workers of America had a communication problem. The officers were male, reelected for life. Slavic men with pork chop sideburns, they puffed cigars and overruled any motion that stood in the way of completing their agenda. Usually they had no problem because they called these sessions for Saturday night, at a union hall in one of Oakland's most foreboding spots. The fewer the rank-and-file that showed, the better. But Meryl and her housemates began plaguing the stunned leadership. They brought along their own agenda: demands for company child care, increased maternity leave, protection from sexual harassment, a medical plan that included abortion on demand. Meryl and the local prez turned the meetings into their Ping-pong matches, using Roberts' Rules of Order as the paddles. In the short term, the union officers won by chuckling with condescension, dismissing all objections. They proclaimed the female sex out of order.

From Meryl and the others, Missy hoped she could learn to be so single-minded. She was sure they could teach her to be an operator of another kind.

3. Darlinda hit the jackpot. Now she would get all the anatomy lessons she wanted. She could take a cram course in the dynamics of healing. In the emergency room of Alta Vista General, Darlinda could have her fill of disaster.

It was no surprise that she felt right at home. Like most everyone else in the place, she arrived unexpectedly. She'd begun her job search with days of deep breathing, followed by counseling at the state office of economic development. She tried to find an opening for an activist/dancer. There weren't any listings under that category. So she decided to apply the secretarial skills—sex-based as they might be—that she'd honed as a Chicago Kelly Girl. She took the qualifying exam for nurses' aides—after clearing the political correctness of the idea with the collective. Since it was possible she might end up serving one or another feeble arm of the government that they were all seeking to overthrow, she wanted to be correct on the issue. Everyone in the house seemed to think it was dandy to be "infiltrating the public sector." Darlinda vowed, before all of them, that she'd never help process any eviction notices or court summonses. She would help people. A week later, assigned to the state hospital in Alameda, she was doing just that.

The cursed system provided Darlinda with such a delightful opportunity that it took her a while to notice that she was the only one around who felt that way. She dared not admit it, but she enjoyed her new job so much that she was afraid that, when the proper time came, she might not be able to go on strike. She had to keep reminding herself that this really was a job and not a demonstration/lecture on the wonders of our biosystems. "The Spine: Our Very Own Forklift." "The Blood: Call Me Mister Clean." She was well-suited for the work, except that she moved a little too deliberately. When a patient was in critical condition, she couldn't always pause to inspect her turnout. Gripping a wheeled gurney, she still tried to be mindful of her posture. Her supervisor, she discovered, didn't appreciate runaway wheelchairs or torn intravenous bags just so Darlinda could take time for a stretch or two. Darlinda continued to sneak in a little relaxation at work when she could. She thought it was particularly important here, where no one else was relaxed. She was sure it would make her a better aide—even though she wasn't sure whether it was politically for her to try and be better.

Her duties consisted largely of filling out the necessary paperwork on the stricken. Eight hours a day holding a press conference with shock. But Darlinda was experienced at asking questions. She thought it was very important to ask about things you didn't know, and it seemed like the more she asked, the more she didn't know. Answers didn't matter, really—it was the same questions, posed over and over, that served as toeholds on her scramble through life. When it came down to it, "Do you have Blue Cross?" wasn't much different from "Is the sky blue?" Not if it was asked with the proper inquisitive spirit. Too bad Darlinda had to write down the replies, all the addresses of kin and creditors, the medical history and known allergies. She wrote it all out in her kindergarten block lettering, or, if she was really rushed, in her own sort of pictographs. A smiley face meant superficial wound, a balloon meant artificial resuscitation, a sketch of a daisy meant DOA.

Darlinda had problems keeping up with the ceaseless toll which Oakland extracted from its citizenry. There was a high price being paid for hot-wired cars, cheap wine, faulty space heaters, tumbledown stairs, lead-painted schools, high-turnover assembly jobs, drugs from basement labs, electricity, apathy. Darlinda, the farm girl, wanted to put a warning label on the big city: "Apply caution. Follow instructions for proper use." The city fried people, chewed them, mangled them, imploded them, sniped them, came at them. The city, it seemed, was nothing more than a stalled invasion, a battle that stayed in one place. Especially if you were black. Being black was like leaving the trenches without a helmet. Being black was like dodging the shrapnel in your jockey shorts. Being black, Darlinda saw, was like skipping barefoot through a mine-field.

In the emergency room, Darlinda found herself wondering about being black. She felt queasy sometimes about the fact that she was white and could always escape to her commune. She didn't want to escape, that was the odd thing. Once or twice, she caught herself daydreaming about becoming the Florence Nightingale of Oakland—though she knew such thoughts were far from correct. Occasionally, she had to admit, she was drawn to the black bodies she tended. She enjoyed stroking those vast, mysterious frames, the exotic bulk of blotched stomachs and scarred backs passing before her. Their skin felt slicker than her own; their hair was so coarse and tenacious; the smell of strange pomades and dime-store perfumes melted off them in shudders. A lot of these bodies were very muscular, it was true. Marked by labor. A lot of the men acted as if they could overpower Darlinda in an instant, with only a tiny portion of their strength, even when they were very, very wounded. But somehow, these were the only men that did not make Darlinda feel threatened. Maybe it was because they could never quite hide how much they were wounded.

They smiled, hiding nothing but the pain, revealing everything including pleasure. White people did not smile like that. Darlinda's mom and pop never smiled like that, never. It wasn't until she got around black people that Darlinda realized that she'd always felt at a disadvantage around white people. With her own kind, she was always one question back, one minute too late in discovering someone's true motives. In the emergency room, the only motive was to survive. It was just pain and absence of pain. Maybe Darlinda didn't always keep up with her paperwork, but she could keep up with that. In fact, the emergency room was the first place where Darlinda wasn't a step behind. Nature made her feel powerful. Nature was guileless, easy to track. Nature worked as inefficiently as she did.

1:11 p.m. What Marx could not have foreseen: that man, living in opposition to nature, could still manage to live in opposition to himself; that solidarity is not necessarily a byproduct of overcrowding.

Nothing very interesting ever happens out-of-doors. That's where Missy keeps pushing us.

"I've got to wake Irenka, feed her, change her, bathe her. A thrill-a-minute, huh? Why don't you walk over to the neighborhood slide?" She points through the picture window of her living room. "See that field across the way? Just follow the path through it. Look, there are horses! Go explore the country!"

Despite Missy's claim, the other side of Easy Street isn't the country. Through a gap between clapboard cabanas, we find ourselves on the first of several mounds that undulate toward the municipal reservoir several miles off. These California folds of foothill are so gradual they look shaped by a potter's hand. The high grass that covers them has turned to straw with summer, an invitation to pyromaniacs. Crouching black oaks dot the sloping expanse in assymetric balance. Over the first spur, we pass three Shetland ponies, probably grazing in this gourmet pasture for the sake of some tyke's cowpoke fantasy. We join the horses on the downhill trail toward the blue oval which dares to call itself a lake, the work of a single huge scooper. Ah nature! The ponies whinny between the straightaway roars of motorboats lugging water skiers.

Annie leads the way, less abashed in hiking boots than the swimsuit competition. The great outdoors, or what remains of it in the subdivision, makes her whirr like an Evinrude.

"I'd like my garden to look like this someday," I can just hear her telling Fire, a packless bearer this time. I can't see what she's talking about, but Annie could commune with a compost heap. "Planted with whatever makes its way there. She the blue wildflowers underneath the alfalfa? How could anything be more harmonious than that?"

"This is His garden. We are but His weeds." The Gospel according to Fire.

In that spirit, his sister warns him about the poison oak. "See the reddish tips of the leaves! They're speaking to us. If we were Indians, we'd know how to hear all the plants."

Poison oak: that would be Annie's idea of beauty. Form and function united, equally potent. The gorgeous red of warning, the sumptuous red of rash.

"I think I'm allergic to this shit." Dana sneezes, straggling behind since we got off Easy Street.

"Reunions?"

"The high grass, dude." Stopping to whip out a handkerchief, he provides us with the opportunity to fall farther behind.

"What's with you today? You're usurping my role as group grump. Are your fallen idols that distasteful?"

"Shit, Marty. Cut me some slack. You keep preaching at me like I'm straight on a beeline to the top. About to make chief executive officer."

"You're capable of it."

"Yeah, I'm also off to a mighty late jump. I got a proven track record of vacillation. Fartin' around in a principled manner."

"It's not what someone actually ends up doing that counts, it's what they wish they were doing."

"That ain't too Marxist, bro'. Everybody's got to do something to eat."

"Not us. We're postscarcity. Beyond got-to-eat."

"Speak for yourself, pudge. How much is it the paper pays you per word?"

"Not enough to make me do it."

"Nothin' was ever lofty enough to make you do anything, really. Not even politics. But I say there ain't no progress without coercion.

Worthy tasks make worthy people, son. Which is why you'll find so few of either."

"Now that sounds like the old days, only you've changed bosses."

"And you've gone solo . . ."

Go Amongst the Workers and Peasants. Four Attempts:

4. Being a paper boy has to be the most demeaning job in the world, especially when you want to be Prince Kropotkin. Especially when you're no longer a boy. Of course, Dana wasn't one for very long, and he wouldn't have been one at all if he hadn't gone and labeled himself unemployed. He was rolling along fine until then. And the job wasn't forced on him by the government either, but by the people who were trying to overthrow the government.

In California, the best Dana could be was unemployed. He concluded that after making the rounds of steel mills and industrial parks in his VW van, offering his inexperienced self to the lowest bidder. The only work he'd manufactured was showing up at the local Manpower office, waiting for salt-of-the-earth assignments along with the winos. He'd been paid with another futile routine, unlimited swigs from half-pints of Ripple, and the slogan "Manpower to the People!" Since he'd tried organizing students, youth, lumpen, the alienated and the unorganizable, he figured he'd find it easier to organize the folks most like himself. He kept looking for them. There had to be someone else like him somewhere.

That's why he put so much faith in the Council of the Unemployed. This time, there was no doubt he was one of them, was there? Like a hungry suitor, Dana copied down their phone number from a coffeehouse bulletin board. When the night for the first meeting came, he got dressed up in his best suitor's duds—which meant work clothes. The unemployed always wore work clothes, didn't they? But he was calling on the Movement, and the Movement didn't put out so fast. It never kissed on the first date. The Movement always lived in a ramshackle Victorian. The Movement rarely painted the town, but entertained at home. It cleared a space on the floor in the largest room, hoping the space would be filled with recruits; it scrounged for clean coffee cups; it shoved last month's newsletters behind the sofa. And this courtship was too parliamentary, this romance had a flavor of bondage to it.

At the Council of the Unemployed, the one with the whip was Turk. Dana could tell by Turk's teamster crew cut, his one-way shades and that button on his denim shirt which so ostentatiously displayed Josif Vissarionovich Dzhugashvili, a/k/a Uncle Joe. He knew that the only people who'd absolved the gentle Georgian of his sins were the Maoists, and that's what Dana presumed Turk to be. He also presumed that about Bill and Emily, the presumed hosts and parents of the baby he presumed to be howling in an antechamber. Now he couldn't just be unemployed, he had to be a Maoist, too. That was the problem. You walked into an unswept room, plopped down on a couch with three legs, and all of a sudden you owed your allegiance not only to this one branch of the council, and its controlling cabal, but to some board to which this group reported, and to the obscure party somewhere that sponsored the committees, which was merely a front for the sect that made the ideology, which was only a national section of one of a number of competing internationals, and that international had behind it a documented history of stands, tendencies, crises, theories, heretics, corrupt blocs, opportunistic splits and a million plotting sessions in rooms Dana hoped were somewhat more impressive than the one where he found himself. You even inherited enemies.

And before the few suitors knew what hit them, the Council was taking volunteers. In most cases, no one got around to doing what they said they would do anyhow. Leaflets were left undistributed, telephone lists undialed, books unread, signs unpainted. Except for our Dana. He was a glutton for orders. Which was how he became a paper boy. It seemed that Bill and Emily ran this route on weekends: it was their only means of feeding themselves and their out-of-order kid. Perhaps it was the only work they could get—no one ran security checks on paper boys, did they? Since the couple had to attend the national convention of their sect, someone else had to hold down the route for them. Dana knew it wasn't going to be Turk. He imagined himself wheeling merrily over hill and dale on a ten-speed, reading the funnies as he went along, slinging his parcels with hook shots onto front porches. His hand shot up.

Only paper boys weren't born, but made. After the meeting, Bill explained that Dana would have to follow them on their rounds to get the knack of it. Two weekends' work turned quickly into four. Bill and Emily made it seem longer: there was a likable element missing to them, and they greatly underestimated how much even the proletariat liked someone to like. "We're up in this new-jwah neighborhood," Bill told Dana, rhyming with bourgeois. "If they don't get their daily lies set down right where they customarily stoop for it, we're the ones who get the shit." Having seen their stately domicile, Dana didn't want to be responsible for the further staining of Bill and Emily's shitty existence. Their baby—clearly a holdover from the prerevolutionary days, now rationalized as "the seed of the future"—didn't see it that way. In the hot, melting plasticene seat of Bill and Emily's suspensionless old push-button Plymouth, the kid went nicely and warmly in his pants. This was further incentive for them to hurry through Dana's training.

Racing from block to block, parking on strategic corners, then sprinting through service entrances, Bill no longer looked the stern, Leninist helmsman. He and Emily huffed their way through a secret code of instructions by which Dana could follow the pattern of distribution and distinguish between master keys. When the time came, Dana found that the easy part. He didn't even care about getting up around four in the morning. But what about facing his coworkers? None of them were more than half his age. They all wore baseball caps. What the fuck was he supposed to say? Kill your parents, comrades! Off your gym coach! Eat the rich along with your Mars Bars!

Dana noticed that he sported the same black high-tops they did—which came in handy for sneaking through all those new jwah condominiums with their new-jwah parking garages and their Mantovani strings piped into the hallways and their Cyclops security eyes and their plastic shrubbery and their occasional Dobermans, Dana felt like a sneakered pituitary case. Or an overgrown jockey turned terrorist. If only he was! What if he got mistaken for a burglar and was shot? Would Turk give the eulogy? This wasn't the sort of edifying labor all unemployed seek, this was a prank.

No wonder the *capitalisti* had to bring in child labor. This paper boy bit wasn't a matter of whistling happily along. It was a bitch. For five hours lugging Sunday funnies fat with glossy advertising supplements up the up staircases, Dana earned the same number of dollars. When he collapsed back into the communal bed on that last, bright Sunday afternoon, there wasn't any way for Dana to feel properly accomplished or tired. At least, he saved the route for Bill and Emily, fed their kid, aided the organization—though, after that, Dana decided he wasn't really cut out to be unemployed. It was too much fucking work. He went back to Manpower and spent his mornings by the coffee urn, reading "What Is To Be Done?" and "Ripplin'" with the boys. The Council must have figured they'd gotten all they could out of this recruit, since they never called to thank him or woo him back. Or maybe they just weren't very organized.

1:20 p.m. A raise in consciousness is impossible without a raise in conscientiousness.

"Maybe there's nothing out there for either of us. Isn't that what we always presumed?"

"No worthy tasks, like I said. Just temptations." Dana's still not telling me what his latest is.

"But what about Polly? Doesn't she offer the possibility of full employment?"

"You know it. Just like your movies do for you. Otherwise, we'd both fall off the graphic."

"Go forever uncounted."

"Sounds mighty attractive, don't it?" And while we help one another over a break in a stone fence, I get to see Dana's first smile of the day. It develops so deliberately, and puts so many dabs of red vein around his deep Sephardim sockets, that it's hardly distinguishable from a wince. It's followed by a grudging nod to signal the start of another truce, our friendship's millionth cease-fire.

Scene Three (The Midnight Socialists). Two bearded young men, Dana Kropotkin and Martin Trotsky, are seated in a red booth at an Oakland coffee shop waiting for refills and staring out at the late-night boulevard traffic.

TROTSKY: "Why is this town an armed camp?"

KROPOTKIN: "Two more squad cars, one paddy wagon . . ."

TROT.: "Can't we come up with something better than this head count?"

KROP.: "Whaddya wanna do, Lev Davidovich?"

TROT.: "I dunno. Whaddya wanna do, Prince?"

KROP.: "We could pick 'em off, one by one, sport."

TROT.: "You've still got those adventurist tendencies . . ."

KROP.: "What good's a revolution if it don't let you be a bloody hero?"

TROT.: "There are times when it's heroic to wait."

KROP.: "I don't see nobody pinning us with no medals."

TROT.: "Certain sectors have got to catch up."

KROP.: "I know what you mean. Another night without the girls."

TROT.: "Women."

KROP.: "Whatever, they're outperforming us, dude."

TROT.: "They got an organization. All we got are your dumb I.W.W. meetings."

KROP.: "Hey, you wanna find cats with principles, they're gonna be old-timers."

TROT.: "But do they have to be in wheelchairs?"

KROP.: "The Wobblies tend to wobble. They need new blood."

TROT.: "They need to go the proverbial dustbin."

KROP.: "One big union was no easy haul, sport."

TROT.: "One big bed isn't any less problematic."

KROP.: "The vanguard ain't supposed to have fun."

TROT.: "What we do, we do for others."

KROP.: "And what about what we don't do?"

TROT.: "Have another refill, dude."

KROP.: "Is tomato juice a stimulant?"

TROT.: "What the fuck?"

KROP.: "I'm giving up all stimulants. Except java."

TROT.: "The most damaging of all."

KROP.: "I'd go into legal death without it."

TROT.: "Me three."

KROP.: "Too bad this is pure dishwater. There's nothing like freeze-dried."

TROT.: "You ever heard of Turkish coffee? Colombian?"

KROP.: "They ain't as good as Maxim."

TROT.: "You've flipped."

KROP.: "Look, with Maxim you got total control. Make it as strong or weak as you like. Advanced technology . . ."

TROT.: "You sound like a fucking commercial."

KROP.: "It's that standard of living. That's what everyone wants, right?"

TROT.: "Wrong. It must be because you've gone straight from the ruling class into the working class. You seem to be missing out on a few things."

KROP.: "Like what, Leon?"

TROT.: "I don't know—good taste, maybe. Style. A sense of the absurd."

KROP.: "Sense of the absurd yo' mamma!"

TROT.: "You're becoming a genuine flag-waving workerist."

KROP.: "At least I ain't no chickenshit student. Never again."

TROT.: "Me neither, son."

KROP.: "Speaking o' which, when are we gonna get to our fabled projects?"

TROT.: "The free bookstore, the free coffee shop, the people's radio station for people driving' cross-country . . ."

KROP.: "How about our own newspaper?"

TROT.: "That may have to wait until your old man has one of his ultimate headaches."

KROP.: "Until that time, I'm just lookin' for the struggle, babe. An' in this town, I don't have to look very far."

TROT.: "Another Black Maria headin' down East Fourteenth . . ."

KROP.: "So easy to pick off . . ."

TROT.: "Cut that shit out."

KROP.: "The intellectual who puts forward an insurrectionary line lives in relation to that moment when he's got to pull the trigger he keeps tellin' others to pull. He's gotta die so his ideas can live."

TROT.: "Reach for the book, it's a gun!"

KROP.: "Reach for the machine gun, it's an encyclopedia!"

TROT.: "Working masses, off your asses . . ."

KROP.: " . . . Idle classes, give off gasses! That's why I gotta get me a place on the line. With the people who got the power to turn everything on and off."

TROT.: "You want another refill?"

KROP.: "Yeah. An' remind me to leave this sweetheart a dollar tip."

TROT.: "You an' your dollar tips. Your still the millionaire's kid, dispensing charity."

KROP.: "That ain't all I'm gonna do to pay back these sweet dispensers of brew. I'm gonna write me a treatise. Three volumes. On the social function of waitresses."

TROT.: "Which is tending to the loveless."

KROP.: "It's two a.m. Do you know where your woman is?"

TROT.: "Shouldn't I wanna know?"

KROP.: "Someday soon, it might hurt to know."

TROT.: "Love hurts good."

KROP.: "Screw that. Love ain't nothing but emotional surplus value. It ain't worth a damn."

TROT.: "And what is, hero?"

KROP.: "The truth, babe, the universal. Learning to go out in style."

TROT.: "Truth is a shitty storyteller."

KROP.: "But nothing needs lies like rebellion."

TROT.: "The only eventuality I'm not prepared for is the planet staying just as it is."

KROP.: "I hear ya. At least, we got plenty of spare time to dream about another way."

TROT.: "In America, the best time to be a socialist is after midnight."

KROP.: "That's when it all comes clear."

TROT.: "In America, the only duty is clarity."

KROP.: "Can it, son. I can't take no more Pepperisms."

TROT.: "Look, three more cruisers! A whole phalanx."

KROP.: "One day, I wanna march in a fuckin' phalanx . . ."

TROT.: "You wouldn't be able to stay in step, Prince."

KROP.: "Just try me, drill sergeant. Just try me."

TROT.: "You want another cup?"

KROP.: "Naw, man. Let's roll."

1:41 p.m. The disease of conversation.

"How come I like you best when I'm starting to lose you?" The reference is to Dana's logic, but it comes out meaning something more.

"An' how come you can only stay my pal so long as I'm a loser?"

"At this point, you've got my full permission to succeed, not that you need it. You've worn me down with waiting. I'd just like to see you follow through on a fantasy. On anything. Just get it over with."

"It could be that some people have to be denied their fantasies, the way some classes have to be restrained from their historic role. Kept in line for their own good."

"Is that what the group was about for you?"

"That, an' gettin' lifted higher than we ever could on our own."

We've lost sight of Annie and Fire, ahead of us on the path that tumbles down the next dry gulley. From this side of the hill we've been tracing, there's a view across the sprawl of mini-rancheros toward the half-drained bottom of the bay. Around the angelic bay's outlines, a halo of smog. We haven't been traipsing through the wilds, only skimming across a bare patch in the carpet of metropolis. But there really is a back-forty swing up ahead. I can tell that by the recklessness of Annie's laughter. I can't get her to laugh like that anymore.

Sure enough, the path steepens and we totter until Dana and I can break our momentum against the trunk of what must be the largest tree in the county, a veritable East Coast elm. On the other side, Annie's sitting on two wooden planks, nailed together and tied with navy knots onto ropes that rise some twenty feet to the highest branch. It looks like a precarious contraption, strung together by some impulsive daddy who's long since abandoned it. But Annie's jumped right on, like her own tinkering Pa had customized the job. Fire gives her another push, and the way the swing's placed on the slope, Annie is catapulted not just up but way out.

"Aiieeee!"

"Ride 'em, cowgirl!"

"It's your turn next, Pep!"

"No way." I can hear the ropes creak with the strain. And I don't like heights. "I'll let the rest of you do the safety testing."

"This isn't testing. It's fun."

"An adolescent word. A paltry American word."

"We'll make you eat it."

Annie's off and they're all clapping. A chant turned into a howl; the three of them instant conspirators. Peer pressure is an ugly name for this. Collective responsibility sounds prettier. Or shall we call it, as our parents might, a bad influence? I have to marvel any time I'm susceptible to the least influence, bad or good.

"Pep's turn! Pep's turn!"

The hot seat awaits. I'm being pushed toward it. Nothing to do now but act brave and grip the ropes until the fulcrum exhausts itself.

"Bite the bullet, kiddo!" *Et tu*, Dana? His shove's the least expected, the most efficient. The group lifts us up where we cannot go alone. I'm up in the air with no company but myself.

1:54 p.m. What I couldn't do with an ego!

Voice-Over (Martin): She keeps reminding me that nothing is forever. Replace 'nothing' with me. Mister Nothing. But I never asked to be Mister Forever. Until we rot away, darling. She must know that I know it can't be for forever. It's a bad sign when someone keeps trying to remind you of what they know you must already know. She must know I know, even if I don't show her. I'm quite convinced, in the abstract, that two people who meet when they're seventeen don't have much chance of being together when they're seventy. Long odds and less reason. Personally, I don't expect to make it to forty. The most non-violent cat on the planet, but I always imagine going out violent. So stick with me until that last bludgeon, love. Since I can't have my forever with Missy, then I want tomorrow. Another day of safety, a reprieve. A money-back guarantee that when we kiss it isn't the last kiss. That this ain't the last arm-in-arm, last unspoken accord, last whisper in our language for two. I can speculate calmly about the melting of the polar ice caps, but when it comes to me, I cannot fathom the concept of last. I always want one more taste, one more turn at bat. I get sentimental over anything that's even hints at going irretrievable, like a pair of socks worn out at the heel. I refuse to accept the concept of a natural end. I am not a natural man. (I'm from New York!) I believe in cryogenics, life-support machines. Missy and I sure could use one. But if I said so, on the record, if I admitted that I knew, then all doubts would be legitimized. Once you get as far as saying it, it always happens. But when I see Missy, all I want is to sign another postponement pact, to make sure I'll be allowed to see her again. I'd never want to be caught clinging, but it's the only way I know how to build my up muscles. I'd never choose to be in anyone's way. When I'm like this, I'm in my own way. It's easy to get tripped up. When I'd like my footsteps to shake the earth! I want to learn how to bellow—or, at least, to send back food in a restaurant. Instead, I ended up apologizing for getting so apologetic. I angle for one more chance to say I'm sorry. It's not really that I'm endorsing forever. I'd never do that, not aloud. It's just that I'm not outfitted for never. It's the never that backs me into forever.

1:59 p.m. All I'd like, when it comes down to it, is to understand the workings of my own psyche like I understand the House Ways and Means Committee.

Who Am I? Soweto black on the run? Gdansk ship worker with his joy rationed? Paraguayan trade unionist with genitals fried? Alabama voting rights registrant framed on pot charges? Goalkeeper at Chile's National Stadium? Tokyo student trying to stop the big jets, Fijian guiding my raft between the Russian whaler and its prey, Laotian peasant taking down an ICBM with a slingshot, Nicaraguan armed with live mangoes? Slaughtered Indonesian Communist? Widow raising nine children who makes extra *tortillas* for the Farabundo Marti Liberation Front? Untouchable coolie, listless in Calcutta? Filipina child prostitute? The tribal chieftain whose holy ground is a toxic waste dump? A citizen in the town built over the burning coal field, with fire in my tulip patch, heat wherever I feel my feet firmly planted? Basque, Baluchi, Uzbek, Ayacucho? Minorities within minorities, condemned for their mere existence? Fanged Palestinian, or when it seems wretched enough, a Jew? Why is it that I know what these people need, hope, must do so much better than I know what I need, hope, must do?

Annie and Dana grab the ropes. They can see that I'm not enjoying this. They are letting me down easy. I can let go my grip.

2:04 p.m. Never let go of a good regret.

The Perfect Playmate. With Ayer and Annie gone, there was more space for frivolity and far too much seriousness in the apartment. So Darnel came up with another plan. They would turn the playroom into a guest room and take in someone deserving. Someone in genuine need. A returning prisoner—they never used the word "convict"—would be perfect. It would also insure that their new boarder wasn't a police agent. And of course, they wouldn't charge rent. Missy seconded the motion. They would let someone gather his solitary strength in his own room, while they sought theirs in a nightly lock-up.

Martin was appointed Chairman and Staff of the Housemate Search Committee. His job was made easy by the columns of classifieds at the back of the underground papers. They were free for inmates—of most any institution. They were all inmates, weren't they? "Wanted: a job, a set of wheels, a friend" . . . "Ex-con with skills of the heart to offer. If you can handle the Big Q, you can handle anything" . . . "Take a chance on a two-time loser. Willing to work for training only" . . . "Congenial home situation sought to help me put it back together and keep it there. Peace, chillun!" . . . "Haven needed for gentle spirit currently inhabiting the body of twenty-seven-year-old male" . . . "Heaven must be around the corner, 'cause I've already been to hell." Martin didn't tell the others, but he eliminated any budding prison poets, lawyers, or prophets. He looked for someone straightforward, unmartyred. He found him under a simple "share sought."

The applicant showed up promptly at eleven for his interview. His name was Oscar and he was a Chicano, though only nominally so. He spoke with just a trace of street twang and no Spanglish phrases. His hair was longish, but pulled back neatly into a bun. He had light freckled skin, a pert nose, tortoise shell glasses. He dressed like an assistant professor of economics: tweed coat with elbow patches, frayed button-down shirt, chukka boots. His manner imparted no monomania or suppressed rage. His crime, so he said, had been embezzling some money from a bank in Chico where he'd been working. But prison had been the best thing for him, because he'd had time to discover literature. Did Martin know Coleridge? Thomas de Quincey? *Siddhartha*? Baudelaire's *Spleen*? Prison libraries certainly had improved, and so had prisoners. Oscar was enrolling in a local junior college's creative writing program and needed a place for a few months, until he'd worked a bit and saved some funds so that he could go home and marry his *novia* back in Texas. No, he joked, he wasn't going to apply at a bank. Martin shook Oscar's hand right then and invited him into the house. For once, there was no need to consult the others. For the moment, he set aside his fears over the empty rooms. His only concern about this boarder was that he was a little too perfect.

2:02 p.m. The obvious enemy is never the real enemy.

"Every party needs its sacrificial lamb," Missy announces upon our return. "Only I forgot to bring home that nice, juicy leg from my restaurant! . . . My restaurant! It sounds so ridic . . . We do get the best cuts. It's worth a trip back. And you do want to see the restaurant, no?"

In a moment, we're packed, babe and all, into Missy's latest set of hot wheels. I reach around Dana, straddling the five-on-the-floor, for the dashboard radio controls. I try to tune in a blast from the Angeleno summer past, but settle for the current version of squealing unrequitedness.

"How come pop culture does such a good job with frustration?" I ask no one in particular.

"How come you frustrate me?" Enlivened by our walk, Dana slips his hand up my pants leg, groping for my crotch at a pace that suggests he does not expect to get there. "Mmmmmm. Cruising in the front seat with Marty!"

I squirm so a hip blocks his path to my lap. "Prevert!"

"Not Prevert, he's French. My name eet ees Alexander Pooshkin . . ."

"Your name it is Mayakovsky. The laureate of love unrequited."

"A love supreme." Dana chants Coltrane, leering.

"Why don't you go molest the child?"

"You're so cute when you're mad."

Missy's establishment turns out to be on the same block as McDonald's—now that's attacking the megalith head on. It shares parking with a drapery shop called Made in the Shade, a pet store called Puppies and Guppies, and a drive-through florist's stand called Get Fresh with Me! Maybe Missy should have gone for The Grecian Formula—you can't get a business license in this town without a pun. Now we see A Girl and a Greek. Painted in script lettering on a two-sided board shaped like a cowboy hat, the name seems out of a more personalized era. It's forties quaint, like the border of Seven-Up logos —and those beaming caricatures of the proprietor and proprietress in chefs' bonnets. Our very own Melissa, complete with that come-on-in grin that runs in the family, finally blown up into a cheery totem. Born to be a billboard.

"The place used to be an Arby's Roast Beef. See, the whole roof's a big Stetson. There's the brim! Real creative, huh?"

"How could we have missed it?"

"Easily. Like everyone else in town." She pulls into the driveway beside three pickups. "Oh, goody. A late lunch rush. I don't know what we'll do if we actually get successful."

"You could hire some help."

But that would take all the travail out of it, all the calculated frenzy—and without that, why would Missy bother? While we pile out, she's rattling on about putting in seven days a week since the grand opening two months back. "And Spyros put in eight!" Spyros' brother quit the merchant marine to take up k.p. duty. "We call him our pastry chef!" He's picked up an American bride along the way to serve as chief bottle-washer. "She doesn't know a thing about his other wife in Macedonia. Oh, Lordy!"

Once inside, we can see Missy's hand at work in the redecoration. Gingham tablecloths, plaid like her living room. Blue and white, with the same Cycladic colors on the curtains. Loud Mexican roosters and other doodads pasted over the rugged stone walls. She can't do much about hiding the wagon wheel set over the lunch counter, or the cattle brands carved in all the mouldings. The tables look rented for a church supper. At least, there's a chalkboard where Missy's scrawled the daily specials, with addenda. "Chicken Fried Veal. Spyros Does It Best! . . . Melissa's Health Shake. With Fresh Strawbs! . . . Patty Melt (Not Patty Hearst)."

The Great Vietnamese Food Controversy. It was too terribly female for anyone to notice. The first great rift in Oakland Women's Liberation was caused by a choice of meal preparation—all because the organization decided to cater a downtown, lunchtime rally. They would announce their formation to the beleaguered stenographers and bank tellers of Oakland, those slaves to panty hose! On the patch of downtown lawn that doubled as a municipal putting green, they would establish a feminist beachhead, staked out in pamphlet tablets. The theme would be broad: women learning to unite with women. It was the lunch part that caused disunity.

Plastering their politics right to their aprons, the Third World chefs and "people's war" ladies' auxiliary insisted that O.W.L.'s canteen put out a spread of Vietnamese food. Hardly any of them could identify the main ingredients of such a cuisine, and fewer still knew how to prepare it—but it was the principle, not the flavor, that counted. A foreign recipe was the only way to satisfy domestic appetites.

Aligned against such gastronomic adventurism were the trade unionists and Progressive Labor's handmaidens, the factory scullions, the spicy Trots. They believed that women would be lured out of the kitchen only for the sake of an indigenous, genuinely American uprising (and diet). According to this Betty Crocker caucus, too many principles spoiled the broth. Especially if it was seaweed broth. At meetings that obliterated many mealtimes, they argued that their buffet should be suited to the native palate. Hearty, proletarian eats like greens and biscuits would lure those who had to be organized, and fed. But, countered the stir-fry faction, wasn't such a strategy condescending? Didn't it deny the working class an opportunity to broaden their taste buds just as more privileged women had? To get their nutritional standards raised along with their awareness? Swallow unprocessed fiber along with the unvarnished truth? And didn't their opponents' brand of menu planning cater, literally, to the lowest common denominator instead of *haute* consciousness?

No, the chuck wagonists countered, the point was to tempt the masses in whatever manner possible, then transform them one seating at a time. Or even, to learn from them! To find sustenance in the recipe box of the people! Wouldn't Vietnamese food be an affront to that most developed of feminine arts, to a tradition of canning and baking powder creativity, admittedly enforced through rigid social roles, but practiced through hard times and despite the inroads of fast-food manipulators? And wouldn't such alien fare hold down the size of the rally? Wasn't the organization getting sidetracked with side dishes?

The debate came down to a question of suppliers. By a count of thirty-seven to twenty-nine, O.W.L. would heap out gooey green matter and rice at their rally. The majority preferred to spend their donated pennies at Oriental groceries instead of supermarket chains. They put the question of brown or white rice to a voice vote. Some shouted that whole grain was the whole idea. They were outnumbered by those who argued that a billion Chinese couldn't be wrong. They bought a ten-gallon drum of soy sauce, and, when the great day came, sloshed it over imperial rolls that looked suspiciously like pups-in-a-tent.

Whether this had anything to do with the poor turnout gave the cooks plenty to second-guess. About a hundred women shared the repast, ninety of whom had been bused in from Berkeley and were already well acquainted with the wholesome gruel of the oppressed. The leaders who'd insisted on the exotic menu, the ones who needed to move ahead at all costs and couldn't be bothered with stragglers, got the isolation that confirmed their vanguard status. They grappled with chopsticks and had no fear of being told they were doing it all wrong. They dined unaccompanied—free women would have to get used to that! They munched away without having to be bothered by too much company. Nonetheless, the speakers claimed that this rally was just a beginning. It was an *hors d'oeuvres* course before the coming feast.

2:26 p.m. Liberation: the catch is that those who cry for it the loudest need it the least.

"What do you think, guys? How do you like my piece of the rock?"

Though it's more like a ledge, everyone murmurs appreciatively. So this is Missy's latest excuse for zealotry. I've no doubt that she'll make the thing fly. Liquidity has nothing to do with location or traffic flow. Just ask Dale Carnegie. Ask Dana's investors. Ask Missy's regulars at the counter.

"Melissa! You didn't need to stir yourself! I'm handlin' the load just fine!" A buxom little waitress, with shagged platinum hair, frosted tips, glossy pink lipstick and the skimpiest of aprons over her Sergio Valente jeans, passes on her way to pick up an order.

"I can see that, Josie." The girl's smile is all braces. "I was just showing off the place to some friends."

"Whoopsie! Can I get you folks menus? Java to start? How 'bout some malteds? With real malt. No? There's a table in the corner—our best. With a view." Of six lanes and a shopping arcade called El Mercado Grande-Dandy. "Can't I interest you in some ice water?"

We shake off the oversolicitous teen. Before Missy disappears through the saloon doors into the kitchen, she whispers to me, "It's her first job! She was chucked out of tenth grade when she got knocked-up. . . . How could I say no?"

And how can Missy be the one who gets to say yes or no? Who balances the books and signs for deliveries?

"Are you folks from the Valley?" asks the young mother.

"No," Fire tells her. "We're from the high country."

"Tahoe?"

"No, we're late-era apartment dwellers."

"You mean Fremont?"

"Berkeley."

"Oh, I gotcha. You get high. So who doesn't? Oooh, don't let Melissa hear me. . . . I hear it's loony-tunes over in Berkeley."

"Loony-tunes," Fire confirms.

"You know, I never been out there."

"It's not far."

"I never been nowhere." She's the type that rarely strays beyond the town limits proscribed by family and gang and boyfriends and now baby. Boxed in by her own sexuality: there are less pleasant boxes to be in. "Have you known our Melissa very long?"

"Since eighty B.C.," Fire volunteers again. "Since the sacking of the temple."

"She's a peach," the waitress goes on, used to unusual customers. "The best. My saviour, that's what she is. Any friends of hers must be pretty sharp. Won't you at least have a slice of homemade walnut pie?"

We're too busy peeking through to the kitchen. All we see of Spyros are the pleats in the crown of his linen supply cap. Our introduction to his brother is a hairy forearm clutching a sponge that's draining grease from the rim of the aluminum grill vent. Missy emerges, unsoiled—except for the perfectly round postmilking stain that's seeped through her blouse. In her arms, two comparable packages: swaddled Irena, the hunk of lamb blanketed in butcher paper.

Before Missy rejoins us, she's got to drape her arms around a couple of delivery men on counter stools. She whispers something that makes them both bellow.

"She's still got the touch," I tell Annie, watching Missy linger at each table, exhibit her dimples to every diner, give an up-an-at-'em pat to the rookie waitress.

"Go on now, get the boss high as you can, will you?" The waitress is shooing her out. "*Hasta la huego!* And come back for chow any time!"

Fire decides that any time might as well be right now.

"Women replenish, men diminish," he observes, planting himself in a seat by the door. Or maybe his newfound appetite has to do with the waitress. "I don't eat salad. Blue cheese is made by sadness. Flesh is best. I'm on the Visigoth diet."

"He's cute, isn't he?" the waitress asks.

"Plate of flesh, side of bones, nice an' tender . . ."

"Later, my boy." Dana and I are hoisting him out of his seat, though I feel like I'm turning prison guard on one of my own kind. I know how long it can be between flirtations.

"Flesh now!" Maybe that's the slogan that we should have employed in the old days. But Fire isn't prepared for civil disobedience. "Good on ya, m'am."

Outside, he announces, "The devil won't eat at this luncheonette."

"You know," Missy wants us to know, "being a pig isn't as much fun as it looks."

Voice-Over (Missy). I don't actually not love him really. He doesn't give me anything not to love. He's so understanding all the time, it just about makes things impossible. Understanding should make things possible, huh? I used to think that, too. Before it got boring to be understood. Drag city. There have to be other kinds of understanding. It just seems like he knows everything about me before I know it myself. Especially what I'm feeling toward him, or not feeling. And he's never, never wrong. That must be the boring part. It's not that he's trying to make me some way that I'm not. But he's the one who convinces me that I don't care anymore. It's almost like he wants it that way, so he can say he told me so. I wouldn't notice all these little slights I do to him all the time, if he didn't keep pointing them out. I guess he can't help analyzing everything all the time. He's going to analyze himself out of the ballpark, my Pep. He's spending so much of the time trying to understand me that there's nothing left to him. No wonder I start doing things and feeling things like he's not here anymore. He's so good, too good. He always tries to please. He pays attention, like I'm under a microscope. He fetches like a dog, actually. He'll do anything I tell him, so what's the fun in that? I don't want to have to decide everything. Not very liberated, I admit. It's not like I've got to be bossed, nothing kinky like that. It's just that when he jumps at my commands, I get exhausted just having to watch. Except when he's waving his arms to get my attention, when I can see him, there's really nothing different about him. A soft mop of hair and the longest eyelashes. He's gentle and I don't mind the way he strokes my ass, he does that very well. He kisses my cheeks until they're rubbed to ground chuck by his mustache. I'm surprised I have any cheeks left. I'll need a skin graft if I stay with him. Once you say "if I stay with him" one time, then you can't stop saying it all the time. The first "if" is the only if you need. I'm sure a lot of women would like what he could give. I'm sure some women would. There's gotta be some women left who could take it. There are no surprises with him. In the beginning, he had all these places to take me. He showed me the big picture. Showed me me, in proper perspective. He's the one who taught me that one person can never be enough, actually. Now he can't teach himself that lesson. But hold your horses—I knew some of this before Pep. Give yourself some credit, girl. Think of Moose Meadow High. Cruising the foothills with Marcy and Conchita. I've always needed to find myself in other people. And he makes me feel like that's a deficiency. So what if I want to be surrounded sometimes? I think things should always be like a big party where everyone's whooping it up so that no one holler stands out. I want to go barefoot on rooftops in the moonlight. If I'm around women, I can do that without wondering if it's a deficiency. I don't have to be so correct all the time. I suppose we should be with women to get more disciplined, but there's a male idea of discipline and there's a female one. It's not a question anymore of work and sacrifice, we already know how to do that. Look at the daughters of Ma Bell, or the rice-pickers in Vietnam. Look at my mom, anyone's mom. When I'm with women only, then I begin to see how wildness is a kind of discipline, too. I think you have to be impulsive and you have to trust yourself if you want to make a revolution. A revolution shouldn't be like doing the dishes. More like an orgy, I suppose, but directed, and with no one clutching on to anyone. Meryl says that men need to possess women first, then the world. It's funny how we're made to think women had better find a man and hold on. But then, look how men are hanging on to women when all their women want to do is dance a little. Mercy! I don't know any women who need deep down to hang on that way. Not like Marty. I don't know if it's from being an only child or what. He's like a man in that he's basically conservative, he wants things to go on the same, very safe, but then he's not like a man in that he doesn't know how to be strong and calm. Did he at Steffens? He must have. I can't remember. I can remember when he was sure about his politics, about our mission, he was confident about that. And in bed, too, there was a zeal beyond reason. Zeal beyond reason is not bad in bed. I don't know. I shouldn't think these things about him. Not think them and be with him at the same time. Stop thinking, just do what comes next. I probably shouldn't be with him anymore. If I ever want a kid, I can use a turkey baster. That's what Meryl says. I don't know what Marty wants. It doesn't have anything to do with love anymore, huh? If you love something, you love to watch it change, too. I think he's just very, very frightened to change. Mister Revolutionary, keeping the lid on. Shut tight over me. Still, he's the best friend I ever had. He sees all this amazing stuff in me. He makes me feel like I've got miracles inside. So I owe him a little. I can't just go. I can't tell him about the women's house, not just yet. I don't really not love him exactly, not like I've got to just pick up and scram. I should try to make him understand. It's probably the hardest thing there is to understand, and the only thing that he can't get at with all his smarts. How can someone be so all-seeing and then so blind at the same time? It would be better if he didn't see what I was doing so well. It's just not worth that much to understand, huh? Not what it's cracked up to be. It's a kick, actually, to do things you can't control. It's really a kick to watch people suddenly turn irrelevant. Watch yourself, girl. I don't know if I can do this nice. Maybe I better do it quick. Then again, it may be part of my oppression to worry about doing it nice. I don't want to ruin him for life. Give him an excuse to shrivel up. I want him to stay with his politics, to stay with himself. I don't want to punish him for being all that. So I better keep trying, even if it's just now and then. I owe my Pep. I really owe him one.

2:44 p.m. Two things I can't fathom: why people don't love me, and why people love me.

Missy's unwrapping the meat when we're jolted by the doorbell. Signaling in layers of chime, the push button is being made to approximate a Javanese *gamelan*. I assume it's a Seventh-Day Adventist or another of Missy's cat boarders. Come to offer child care, homegrown squash blossoms in trade; to borrow algae-killer, a pair of support hose. What's with this subdivision? It operates more like a combination bake sale, flea market and Chinese commune. I don't recognize this sort of behavior from my Steffens sociology text. People are supposed to move along parallel tracks down Easy Street. But this one isn't easy enough that everyone doesn't need help.

"Oh, shoot! Can you get it?" Missy calls from the backyard, where she's threading onto the spit a leg of lamb modest enough for our dwindling Turkmen horde.

I get it, right in the eye. Staring back at me is the rubber-lashed peeper of a video camera. Along with braids of cable wire, epaulet of battery pack, it rests on the shoulder of an unknown cameraman. Maybe this is the modern version of the itinerant portraitist, who lugged a tripod and single-plate box. Or the world's first electronic hobo. I look for clues to his identity in his dress. But he's got on wing-tips and a pin-striped suit. Overdone lawyer mod. The only giveaways are the thickness of his shins, the bulldog squatness of his midriff.

"Video Man, he deliver!"

And there's the voice: that vibrato attesting to equally mixed parts of fear and assurance—a little kid's unabashed self-delight and undisguised plea for attention.

"Ayer?"

"Say cheese. . . . No, don't say that, it's got too much cholesterol. Say beans, Beans." Now I know it's got to be him. Beans is the tag he gave me once while filling out a bowling scoresheet. The nickname never caught on, since no one else ever found it particularly appropriate, yet Ayer kept trotting it out. And every time he said it, brimming with fondness, I felt he was telling me that I was full of beans, full of gas, stuffed with the mundane.

"How 'bout hello?"

"Not until you make a clenched fist. This is my opening shot, and I don't want to bother with an edit." Same old Ayer.

"What's the name of your film?"

"Performance number forty-one. Either that, or *Mating Habits of the Dinosaurs.*"

By this time, Annie and Dana have joined me to study the intruder.

"Yo! *Formidable!* Who needs a professional cast? . . . Keep that look of wonder. I just hope the color balance is right." Now he takes his hand off the trigger and lets slip his forty-pound mask. "Good afternoon, collectives of one."

Ayer flashes his stubby, patrician teeth. He fails utterly in an attempt to squelch a gloat. It's been seven years since we last saw each other, under far more strained circumstances. In the meantime, he's become a sort of vacuum-packed version of himself. Once he removes the trucker's cap that reads, "Winners Casino—Winnemucca," I see that his wispy hair trails to mid-shoulder blade, but the ponytail functions as a kind of afterthought. On top, he's been left with a shiny bald pate. His face is still chubby-cheeked, cherubic and tough as the emperor Nero, but so clean-shaven now as to give off the sheen of a freshly waxed apple. The Quaker Oats boy looks ready for a job interview.

"How did you hear about this event? From Herbst?"

"I have my informants, among the two camps."

At the mention of this dated terminology, he gives me a carnival barker's wink. The wink tries to draw me into his assumption that the past has been defused. We've all transcended that, haven't we?

Across the threshold, Ayer treats us to another of his trademarks. Very formally, with an undertaker's sobriety, he shakes each of our hands. Typically, he does not look squarely at any of us, not even Annie.

"It's perfect! Your turn to hold a surprise party!" Annie rewards Ayer's bluff of indifference with tenderness. She'd been able to be his lover because she never believed his invulnerability. "Or have you just run out of material?"

"Not on your sweet bippy, old girl. . . . I just wanted to give all of you a common enemy. Something to get all of you in the old spirit. Yanged out."

"Last we heard you were holed up in Nevada, spending some art grant."

"Correct. The Delacroix of the casinos. I exhibited my forty-foot-high baseball cards on the strip in Las Vegas. I staged a performance piece outside Caesar's Palace."

"Surrounded it with illegal aliens in chains?"

"Something like that. Let me tell you, it was big medicine." As usual, Ayer's toting about his swollen bag of phraseology. "But not as much as teaching figure drawin' on a sheep farm. Or film history on an Indian reservation. The tribe just ate up those John Wayne flicks."

"Then you and Pep are fighting over the same turf!" Annie observes. "Just like always!"

"Really? Is it Astroturf?" Ayer acts like he knows nothing about what I do, but his intonation is far too robust.

"Hey, dude, don't you know how to read?" Thanks, Dana.

"Oh yeah. You landed a little column someplace . . ."

"Could it be? You're kiddeen! Terrif!" Missy's finally come in from the yard and tries to give Ayer a hug.

"Whoa! Watch out for my cables, crazylegs!"

"Maybe I'll just snap your cable right off! What is all this?"

"He's making a documentary."

"It's for the *National Geographic*. An expedition to the land time forgot."

"And what land do you inhabit these days, huh?"

"The land where there's only two kinds of music. Country and western."

"Where's that?"

"The natives call it Las Vegas."

"Where the past's forgotten as the last roll of dice . . ." I tease.

"Amen!"

"Too bad the past's our only common property . . ."

"Don't start gettin' into it, boys," insists Annie, who was once our chief area of dispute.

"Say that again. Into the camera."

"Oh dear, is it going right now?" Missy asks. "At least, let me get on some eye shadow!"

"Please. Just go on with whatever you were doing."

"What were we doing, guys?"

"Cooking lamb."

"Yo! That's happening! A veritable postmodernist pagan rite! Where's the Weber?"

Missy leads him out into the yard, Annie and I trading glances. Dana, who can't resist a place on the technical crew, takes up the battery pack.

But Fire, licking his chops over the lamb, doesn't take so well to the camera.

"Get him away from me! This man robs graves!" And dropping his pants once more, he turns to let Ayer video his full Texas moon.

2:55 p.m. Tell a yogi to go fuck himself, and he'll do it.

Ayer's taken charge, announcing, "Into the living room!"

"For a group portrait by the mantel?"

"For a little performance."

"I thought we were it."

"But I can give as well as take . . . . Call it mixed media. A study in self-reflexive technology."

Enlisting Dana, he rushes out to his car and returns with a super-eight projector, which he sets atop a stand made from volume A through E of Missy's *World Book*. The rest of us do our best to darken the room. A screen is opened to full extension before the nonfunctional hearth, the couch is tilted to face the show.

"Come on, Mister Big-Time Critic. I've saved the front row for you!"

3:00 p.m. Viewer and viewed: this the primal power relation.

Umberto D. Martin always cried during the last scene. Weeks ahead, he'd circled the date of its screening and without collective permission, arranged his life to fit the revival house's calendar. For weeks now, Martin had been reminding Missy that this would be their big chance to sneak away for an old-fashioned date at the movies. For weeks, too, he'd been looking forward to a good cry.

Waiting under a marquee on which half the letters were missing, Martin had time to add up all that he still hoped to share with her. Two years wasn't long enough for her to complete the Pepper school curriculum. Missy had to learn about DeSica, and all the neo-realists; about the sort of realism that provoked speculation of the highest order. But Missy didn't care for foreign films. She found them too talky. She had no taste for speculation, being too much embroiled in life to make time for this other life Martin craved. For him, classic films defined the sort of world they'd all inhabit someday: the intensity of feelings and commitments, the acuity of sight which nearly made him blush and turn away. He didn't blame Renoir or Pasolini for causing him to delay his work on behalf of that world.

Only this showing couldn't be postponed and Missy hadn't arrived. Martin didn't panic because she was usually late, rarely caught up with herself. When he called the collective, there was no answer. She had to be on her way, so Martin bought two halvah bars and two tickets, giving an usher one of the latter for Missy, and tried to find comfortable seats up front. He shouldn't have bothered. In this renovated garage, the seats were salvaged from a wrecked DC-3 and all of them were up front. The paper walls let the cheery soundtrack of the musical in theater number two accompany the tragic lovers' tryst in theater one. Martin was eager to do a little trysting himself. Instead, he concentrated on the opening scene, which showed a parade of old-age pensioners, hobbling through the streets of Rome to demand increased payments from one of Italy's ten trillion governments. Martin had watched this scene a dozen times, he knew just how it would turn out. Not one lousy *lira* for any of them! It was tough to wallow in the poignancy of it all while craning his neck every few moments for Missy. She would have been moved, he was certain; she would have felt so many things, if he could just pin her down long enough to feel them. This was a familiar sort of strategizing to Martin, but the amount of time that he was having to do it of late was getting disproportionate. He was being stood up. Or was that just another male supremacist term?

Over his shoulder, he flinched at a familiar silhouette. Squinting, he beheld his blind date. By the way she came skipping down the aisle, Martin realized it was the wrong woman. Missy had turned into Darlinda. Good for them, they'd metamorphized into indistinguishable parts of the sisterhood! But something wasn't quite right. If Darlinda ever did slip into the body of Missy, the last place she'd steer it would be towards Martin.

"Marty! Attention, Mister Marty!" Darlinda didn't believe in whispers.

"Over here."

"I'm here in her place." She plunked herself down.

"I can see that."

"She sent me." As if that made everything all right!

"Why?"

"She felt sick. She's coming down with something, I think. You know how she's pushed herself. Missy's so right on. A meeting every night."

"But this isn't a meeting." He was making his case before the wrong court. "And she wasn't home when I called."

"That's not true. Darlinda saw her. Darlinda swears. You must have dialed another number, Marty."

"Keep it down, sweetheart!" came the protests from behind.

"I'm not your sweetheart!"

"Shall we get out of the dark?"

"No, no . . . we can't." Martin didn't understand that. He especially didn't understand it when Darlinda patted his hand.

He must have understood something because he stayed. He tried his best to ignore his new partner by immersing himself in the movie. The problem was that Darlinda didn't know how to get immersed. She hadn't yet taken a workshop on that. A movie lasted so long, and she was forced to keep her gangling dancer's body so still. So cramped. During the first reel, she gave herself four neck rubs, three sets of knee and wrist bends, and much determined neck-twisting. She shifted from lotus to powwow to fetal to astronautical positions. She couldn't read the subtitles fast enough, since she had to speak everything out. It was making her dizzy, moving back and forth from the mouths to the words, the words to the mouths. Whenever there was music, she hummed or sang along, trying to keep up with melodies she'd never heard before. During the plot's crucial moments, she shouted screenward, "Boo!" or "Awright!"—as though the story could be changed by voice vote. Culture, for Darlinda, could never be something "up there." She rebelled against this dictatorship of the artist. She had to wrest control and make everything a part of her sad self which she couldn't relinquish for even a single frame. She had no use for symbolism. She fidgeted before any mirror in which she could not see her own figure.

"Is this story true?" she kept asking.

Martin pretended he hadn't heard, though he vowed to find a more convenient moment to expound on postwar Italy and DeSica's ties to the Communist Party. With each of Darlinda's wriggles, Martin wanted to worm his way home. If Missy wasn't feeling well, he wanted to take care of her. If she was sick, she shouldn't be alone. And what if she wasn't alone? Or sick? While watching *Umberto D.*, Martin first caught himself using the word "if" in a sentence about Missy.

Each time Martin tried to get out of his seat, Darlinda pinned him down with more questions. "What happened to the color, Marty? Why doesn't the old man have Medicare? . . . Is Darlinda supposed to be disturbed? Can she help make a happy ending? Marty, what country is this again?"

Slowly, excruciatingly, the climactic humbling arrived. Could there be such a thing as a visual masochist? If so, Martin was it. He got decidedly erotic goosebumps from watching Umberto trying to kill his runty terrier dog because he could no longer feed it. Even Darlinda hushed up when the old man placed his best friend on the tracks before an onrushing train (as much as Italian trains onrush). At the last moment, of course, the old man couldn't go through with it and dashed to save the dog, shouting, "Flick! Flick!" Pronounced "Fly-ck." Martin's ears perked every time he heard that name. It was a name that stood for every creature ever beckoned to human attachment. The film ended with the old man calling, cajoling, whimpering to try and win back the trust of the one being he loved. With the dog scurrying off, leaving mankind to its evident weakness and cruelties. Now Martin was the one who wanted to shout, "Run, Flick, run!" Keep running before you're utterly betrayed. That's it, Flick. Run!

The lights rose. Martin took a deep breath and looked up at the cinema's ceiling, which had been done up by some hippie Correggio to look like a limitless, angel-studded sky. Martin couldn't make out the seraphim through his tears. Darlinda was stone dry. She cried every time she twisted her ankle, but not now. All she'd grasped about this film was her discomfort in watching it. Who was she to the Italians or they to her? She'd never met one.

Martin drove home faster than usual. At one point, Darlinda asked him to slow down, please, but he didn't. He raced up the stairs. There was an unfamiliar odor in the common room and curious sounds on the stereo. Oscar had to be home—so Missy had not been alone after all. The smell was from Oscar's corncob pipe, which he held in his jaw conscientiously. He was hogging the one armchair, doing his nightly reading from Hermann Hesse. He was dressed in a cardigan sweater and ironed jeans. His legs were crossed, his eyes on a metaphysical passage. He was listening to some early Ornette Coleman.

"Maybe you should turn the squawking down," Martin suggested. "Missy's sick, you know."

Oscar leaped for the dial.

"It's all right, Pep!" Missy called out at once. "I like Oscar's music. It's restful. A nice change."

"With this kind of rest, you'll get really sick!" he called into the bedroom.

"Don't make a fuss, Pep!"

Martin stood there, not knowing what else to do, or which room to be in. Oscar directed his gaze down toward the Mexicali Rose ashtray into which he was emptying spent tobacco.

"So what's happenin', *compadre*?" Oscar asked.

Martin never knew how to answer that question because it wasn't one.

"With me? I'm doing great. Have you ever heard of DeSica?"

"Sounds like a brand of dago red," said Oscar. "Besides, I don't dig subtitles."

Martin had the feeling that he'd soon be finding out more than he ever wanted to know about just what the boarder did and didn't dig. He slipped into the one place where Oscar was not allowed. Tonight, thank God, Missy was on their designated side of the mattress.

"Hey, Miss. . . . I'm home now." The lights were out, but he saw as he opened the sliding doors that she was still awake, propped up on one elbow and staring strangely into the dark.

"I know. I'm not delirious."

"Let me take your temp—"

"No! There's no point. I mean, I did it already. I did everything."

"Then you're not sick?"

"I can't tell exactly. Maybe fighting something back. Better just kiss me on the cheek."

"I'll kiss you all over. It's good medicine."

"Don't go wild, Pep."

"Why not? I haven't seen you in three days."

"Okay, kiss. I think I'm just pooped-out. Too much directory assistance."

"Too many nights out with the girls."

"Women. . . . But you're right. I needed some time to be alone."

"You always seem to need to be alone when you're going to do something with me. . . ."

"Maybe so. We've been apart too much. How does the working class stay close, Pep?"

"They leave messages."

"It's hard to love someone you never see."

"That's what I've been trying to tell you."

"It'll be different soon, I swear."

"You missed seeing me cry."

"Oh, Pep! I don't ever want to make you cry."

"It wasn't you, it was Umberto. The scene with the dog. I told you about it."

"That's right. Does the dog die? I can't remember."

"No, he doesn't die. His trust dies. His faith dies."

"I want to have faith."

"I know. Go to sleep now. I'll crawl in later."

"Okay. Or why don't you sleep on the other side. Just for tonight? I want to sleep forever. I don't want anything to stop me."

3:10 p.m. Missy's crime: mattresside.

Get on with your unveiling, Ayer. Don't keep me waiting. Is this a remake of Umberto featuring our own Ebenezer? Some graphic evidence of my former degradation? Could it be that he's found the only known print of "Yo-Yo"? Or will it be Ayer's first epic on the theft of a Colonel Sanders statuette from a Kentucky Fried outlet? Or an hour-long close-up, in a single take, of his big toe?

Of course, he's got to thread his film through a half dozen spools. I coax him on by clicking off the lamps. If it were up to me, I'd stuff up the cracks in the front door with spare blankets. Not to turn on the gas, but to pray for darkness.

3:12 p.m. There are a million stories in the naked audience.

Under Cover of Dark. Her comings and goings were getting regular as dreams in the night. Sometimes Missy left in a red waffle shirt, thermal and tight-fitting, white panties beneath. Sometimes she left in her terry robe, unbelted. Sometimes her Giants baseball jersey, just covering her privates. Sometimes sweatpants, a bra and sandals. She always came back nude as a filly.

Like a dreamer, Martin could merely monitor events, or blink in hopes of interrupting before these visions' full horror could unfold. How many nights passed before a morning came when they had to speak of her habitual exits? The rush to work kept Martin quiet; so did the specter of Oscar, who was sleeping in later and later and seemed to be eavesdropping even while snoring; so did Dana and Darlinda, who provided the illusion that their household went on as before. There was also the matter of Missy's right to polygamy—okay, polyandry, Martin would correct himself in his delirium—as proclaimed in Big Mac's operations manual. And what about Martin's right to principled opposition? He was only one more dreamer. Under cover of dark, liberation became emotional *carte blanche*; ideas, once unsaddled, ran out of the stable. So Martin went on pretending that he was just dreaming—though he woke up because it was so much colder on his side of the bed when Missy wasn't there, only to hear the canter of her high-arched stealth, catch her tiptoed return, black mane flowing, spy with one scratchy eye a goose-pimpled rump moving in the night.

3:13 p.m. History: the stuff that's made when all the participants are trying to look away.

Cinema is truth at twenty-four times a second, said Godard. If so, then what's a home movie? Twice the truth at half the speed, I suppose. Should I jot preliminary notes for my customary three thousand words of venom or praise? Luckily, I'm familiar with this cast and all their prior credits. It just so happens that I'm the director.

I've forgotten that I ever made this one, or how Ayer acquired the rights. The print is pre-film school. Steffens College is the real star, more enduring than any of us. The backdrop to every shot is the wide apron of the main quadrangle, immediate in its greenness. Into Missy's sepia-toned living room comes that well-drenched Oregon green, the green that gave shimmer to the campus that was our magic carpet, the green that, according to a hallucinating Dana, was touched by the finger of God, the green upon which the entire student body sprawled while loudspeakers blared the freshest Beatles' release, the green through which we ran from cops, swooped down for raids, the sort of green that you just ache to trample.

Blotting out the wide lawn is the starting lineup of the Steffens SDS softball team just before our grudge match with the Young Republicans. Each of the members of this hastily organized squad is decidedly shaggy, pimply and callow. Defenders of the cause on the varsity diamond, we look as ill-prepared for the task as we were for the larger one. But what was the cause anyhow besides joy? Play ball!

Leading off, at second base . . . it's Missy, in a cut-off Steffens sweatshirt (embossed with the college's unofficial motto, "Communism, Atheism, Free Love"), flexing her biceps at the camera, then her pearlies and girlish uppercut. Batting next, manning short, the other half of our twinkling diamond combination, Annie is in a tight miniskirt and sandals, wide grin but telltale bags under the puppet eyes from too many all-nighters. Hitting third, in center field, it's the "Say Hey" dude, Dana Pearl, in a most unusual uniform: purple Nehru jacket to his knees, peace medallion flopping at the chest, jeans slashed across both knees, bare feet. Say it ain't so, Shoeless Joe! Nonchalant as ever, he deigns to perform a few warm-up tosses. Though this game took place just a few days before he turned in his locker key for good, he acts as if he knows how to put this playground to better use than any of us. Batting clean-up, at first base, the radicals got themselves a working class ringer: unaffiliated Jack Giacomo, looking much the same as he had on the track this morning, both too hip and too broke to have made any noticeable concessions to the style of the day. Hitting fifth, in left field of course, Danny the Demon Herbst, looking ever more severe in his youth, his Jew-fro conk heading straight to the sky, though the film shows him modeling the ever-popular beret with red star implant in the center. What good would it do him on a high pop fly? Sixth and seventh, our battery, group power source: the receiver, Ayer "Buck" Wilcox, who doesn't need a chest protector due to his rolls of baby fat; the hurler, coming around from behind the lens, Martin "Beans" Pepper or is that Pepper Martin, wild horse of the Osage—seen here in wild mane and corduroys so baggy that he has to hitch them up before and after every toss of his slow-pitch scroogie—long before his premature retirement from the game. I can't say that I approve of his grooming, but I don't mind his nerviness, his air of casual affrontery. The hair may be unstyled and brittle, the granny glasses may glint with intolerance, but this fellow's far too sloppy for dogmatism. He sure doesn't look anything like me now, even less like the me I thought I was then.

"Pitch 'em high an' tight, commissar . . ."

"Give the man a hair net so he can see the plate! No wonder we got our butts kicked . . ."

"Did we?"

"Those reactionaries knew how to keep their eye on the ball . . ."

"We kept our third eye on the ball . . ."

"A shaky first inning, that's what did us in."

In response, the camera begins tilting wildly from sky to grass, a hand-held approximation of our fielding skills. A last appearance in this updated version of *Our Gang* belongs, as the genre dictates, to our moist-eyed mascot. Enter the campus's most daring mutt, our strutting indestructible husky enforcer, who played ball until his chops bled. To hell with studying: he preferred bullying more bookish hounds, sniffing marijuana roaches, and taking a leak in the aisle of the library. Just before the film trails off, there's one unfocused flash of his curly tail, a smooch toward the lens of black lips, a lunge of pointy teeth hoping to sink into a juicy softball or Young Republican.

"Ebenezer!" Missy shouts. "Ayer, where's our Ebs?"

"Dead."

The Middle Way. Wherever Ayer went, he took Ebenezer and Annie. First, they took a rented room in a fraternity house, so Ayer could perfect his all-American act. Next they went to a Meher Baba house, where Ayer joined in early morning meditation while watching Dept'y Dawg cartoons. Then to a Jews for Jesus house, where he doubled as a Gentile for Gautama. Wherever Ayer went, the checks followed. They arrived monthly, the return address a post office box in Philadelphia. He never told anyone the amount of his stipend, not even Annie. All she knew was that the post office box was a branch that held only the accounts of Ayer's family. Their very own vault. Once a year, he got stacks of printouts that listed his stock holdings. Ayer hid them at first, then realized that making them into collages and paper airplanes put him further above suspicion. Every act was a statement for him, a carefully choreographed show of refusal. After three years at the university, the only campus group that inspired his allegiance was the Jock Liberation Front. This enabled Ayer to hang out with the football team. He even took jock classes like "Sports in Sculpture"—hey, an A was an A. His favorite act of civil disobedience was shoplifting filet mignons from Safeway, shoved down his chinos. All his underpants got stained with blood, not his own. Ayer made sure his revolution was successful because it began and ended in himself.

Annie sat out the rest of the sixties in a sewing circle. For all she knew, it could have been the Gay Nineties. Working her way through Cal, she found a position at the one store in Berkeley that catered to displaced Southern ladies. College widows emeritus, they'd been coming in to buy the same crinoline dresses since the twenties, still in stock. Annie was the perfect salesgirl, with her ready smile and recipe box values. Rarely did she let on that she might be in sympathy with those "hooligans" who went on rampages around the campus. Strangely, they always spared Annie's store from their wrath. It was as if they didn't see it. It was no more there any more than the Berkeley that had been an oak-studded outpost of genteel reason. Majoring in psychology so she could learn all she ever wanted to know about Jungian archetypes, Annie found herself surrounded with rats in mazes. If she graduated, it was only because she was unable to attach herself to an alternative.

Annie watched the riots go by and watched the women's movement go by, too. She swapped covered dishes with the matrons, brought them upside-down cakes when they were housebound. She never dismissed the value of her feminine skills. Seeking the middle way, she may have been more of a feminist than those who postured or declaimed. Certainly she was more of a worker. It was just that she couldn't stay interested in the current. She was drawn to things outlasted, or at least, aged. She sought her lessons in the withered faces of yesterday's campus belles. She was fascinated by what remained behind after the fashionable ideas of the day. Annie was stuck with the permanent.

3:20 p.m. The truth in opposites: proven by the way some people become enforcers so they can break the law (bashing heads, running stoplights and such); the way some people become rebels so they can obey (party discipline, weighty consciences and such).

Smashing Monogamy. It meant having wrong done but never being able to acknowledge it as a wrong. It meant that Martin stopped speaking to Oscar. It meant inviting Missy to the zoo and hearing she had no interest in some silly, imperialist zoo only to phone the next day on a lunch break and find out from Darlinda that Missy and Oscar had gone to the zoo. It meant notes on the door asking him to please take a long walk around the block. It meant being told by his best pals that jealousy would not be tolerated, that he'd better just shut-the-fuck-up, then hearing Missy sweetly wax, "I'd love to see you smile that old smile again." It meant not being seen. It meant being baby-sat by Dana in their favorite all-night coffee shop while Missy and Oscar slept together the whole night for the first time. Worst of all, it meant returning home from work only to find another man holding court: his records on the turntable, his books on the shelf, his jokes and opinions on everyone's lips. It meant not just that Martin's reign was over, but that all his former regal pleasures were exposed in their hollowness. It meant that Martin's politics had left him defenseless. Martin's love had left him defenseless. It meant he got smashed.

3:24 p.m. Absurdity is a group project.

Ayer always did like to leave us in the dark. Now he's in no rush to restore the houselights. Maybe he hopes the poignancy of his images will increase as they linger. Maybe he's waiting for applause. In either case, we're unable to see the smoke. If there does seem to be a queer smell in the air, I chalk it up to singed egos, smoldering regrets. A more likely source is the lamp of Ayer's super-eight projector: poor overworked bulb straining to make a dusty diamond glow. Or is this faint scent of burnt trash a component in the performance piece? An experiment in smell-o-rama? It's getting more noisome, a tickle of burning leaf up the nose, accompanied by its own soundtrack: paper crinkling, a licking of flames.

"You *guys!* Irenka!"

Missy's scream trumpets a mother's rush to the nest.

Once more, emergency unites us as nothing else can. Stumbling over footstools and pretzel jars, the men follow Missy's charge—as if we can do anything but clog up the doorway to the child's room. Annie, on the other hand, pushes her way through. She knows that the source of this fire is Fire.

He's turned the baby's crib into an altar. It's been shoved into the center of the room and encircled with pint-sized torches made from Irenka's coloring books, twisted into cones and set alight on the pink linoleum floor. Fire's ceremonial handiwork looks like grade-school models of pyramids or volcanoes, innocent enough if they weren't burning. The more recently lit are aflame at the tip, while others emit final smoke signals. Set back, they seem meant to placate the babe rather than attack. It's just that some are awfully close to the gingham frills around the crib base. This impromptu font threatens to become a pyre.

"Blessed art thou, Prince of the Dark Star. Pass the Sterno, Lord of Arson. Campfire spirits, play. . . ." On his knees at the far end of the crib, the high priest's head is bowed. His expression is businesslike. He is saying his panhandler's suppertime grace. "In the name of the father, the son, the Texas Toast. Set the timing device, King of Kings. Nobody escapes. Nobody gets out of this one raw. . . ."

Missy's clutching Irenka. She checks her vital signs by rocking her as vigorously as a cocktail shaker. The baby's more startled than smoked.

"Let's not overdo the underdone, Lord. No electric blankets. No way to take cover. Take them all unto Fire. . . ."

His mumblings are getting downright oratorical, his head raises, his eyes open. But he can't see that the hook-and-ladders have arrived. He doesn't seem to hear the gasping alarms of Annie and Missy as they stomp on the flames. Is this the origin of Greek dancing? Or the flamenco? While the men watch from the hallway, these chaperones of the procreative crush all danger under their heels.

"Sizzle to the left of us, sizzle to the right. Make it extra crispy, Baby Jeeze. Activate holy laser for this little one. . . ."

Missy's getting her baby as far as she can from the holiness. Absconding with her unscathed package, she barrels through the rest of us, whispering fond secret mamma talk that's no more logical, no less voodoo-laden, than Fire's sermonette.

"Rib of Adam, charbroiled. The others don't count. Woman unto woman. The others jus' trying to steal their eternity. Nothing left to do but be gods. Die on the cross out of boredom. . . ."

Stooping to blow out the most stubborn candles as she goes, Annie's reached him. On her knees behind her brother, she envelopes Fire's saddlebag middle in her sure seamstress arms. She gives him a squeeze that's a most accepting form of restraint.

"Come on now, brother Jed. Good on ya, Mister Jedmas."

"Jedmas is no holiday. Ask Jerry Garcia. Savage arpeggios. Bombing runs. Beneath the crust, more crust. . . ."

The barbecuer is waking through gradiants of beatitude.

" . . . Everyone awakens with gunpowder on their lips. Accountable only to the Dalton Gang. Or the Pope. Shoot-out at the Jerusalem Corral. Out to Mars, back in an hour. I just turn the wheel. . . ."

"That's right, hon. You don't have to take this one on yourself, Jedediah."

"Oh Lord, I do. I got to." He is answering to his old name. He looks over his shoulder to examine the source of such urgent patience.

"How come, hon?"

"I heard it on the shortwave. Ultrapious frequency. High note on the wah-wah pedal. The last judgment activated the orders only for me."

"Why's that, brother Jed?"

"Because I've been designated. I'm responsible for this solar system. Extinguishers on every floor. . . . There's nothing on this planet that ain't my doin', either by its bein' so or my wishin' it so. All the evil in my image. If I'm His messenger, then this is my mess. Which means there ain't nothin' to make but amends. I got to save everyone from the doom."

"Nobody can do that, hon. We're all born to die, like the flowers on the hill. Even the flowers got to carry a piece of doom."

"No time for flowers at our funeral. Martians gonna sort out good from evil. Brand the right ones, like cattle. Mark 'em and burn 'em so they can be saved."

"You jus' save yourself, little brother. Come out to the couch an' I'll tickle your feet like we used to on Christmas morning. . . ."

"You don't want to do that. You don't want to touch a flame."

"We all want to hug you. We all love you, Jed."

"No one can ever love me as much as I love myself. That's why I'm responsible, just like Jesus. Only I'm leanin' to the Judas side. I swear to you, I could do harm if I didn't stay holy. I could use buckshot. I could turn everyone in. I've already done more harm than a bullet for lettin' so many go unsaved. I've spread the doom. I swear to you, Sis. I know what it feels like to kill."

Smashing Through. Martin made the sound of a new world being born. He did not need a rock or shovel this time. Nor was he choosy about the target. His fist attacked the lower pane of the window above where he slept in the big bed. He pushed through to the wrist, trying to get outside the scene of his abandonment. This demonstration, the blood he extracted was his own. This protest was aimed against his fellow protestors. The liberation he sought was their permission to feel what he felt, no matter how backward. To justify his disobedience, Martin carried no banners. He caused no property loss. He trashed only himself. And though this turned out to be the collective's most rebellious act, Martin could not take credit for it. The others made him tell the cop/landlord that this broken window was the work of neighborhood vandals. Blame it on the usual dark suspects. The glass was replaced, with no one the wiser, though anyone who bothered to look could have seen that the damage was done from the inside.

3:35 p.m. Bad enough that I won't let the wound heal, worse still that it was self-inflicted.

The women have turned the backyard into an intensive care unit. They're orbiting the pool in opposite directions, Missy with daughter, Annie with brother. The men remain inside, out of the way of the soothing.

"Not much future for a door-to-door projectionist in these parts . . ." Ayer is packing up his magic lantern.

"Nothing beats a live show," I tell him.

"No harm, no foul, *mon vieux*."

"Life imitates art."

"Only art imitates art, good buddy. . . . Life's too unoriginal."

"I thought that performance was quite original myself."

"Well, you always were a sucker for the heavy-handed approach."

"Like?" Ayer hasn't looked me in the eye once. He continues winding the electric cord around the projector. "Why don't you spill the beans for once?"

"What beans, Beans? I don't go for 'em, especially refried." Finally, after all these years, he's come out with a recrimination for my having picked up where he left off with Annie.

"Then what are you doing here?"

Ayer answers with a parable. "I'm on my way to a reunion of all the people I've known for a day. The invitations went out last night."

From the yard, we hear Fire shout, "I never get a reply! I can't remember God's mailing address!"

"Remember that dog at Steffens who'd been given too much acid in his Gravy Train and kept running into trees . . ."

"Shut up, Ayer." It's taken me a few years to tell him that.

"Big medicine!"

"Kiss my bongo drums!" I give Ayer a taste of his own former vernacular—though neither of us can take any of this too seriously.

"Touch me on the can during the dance! I haven't heard that one since Kampuchea was Cambodia!"

"I could recall why we were friends once, if you weren't so busy claiming to have forgotten."

"Never look back, that's the operative phrase. He who does is condemned to last year's *avant garde*. Or to ten years playing Keno in a powder blue leisure suit . . ."

"Ayer, you haven't got the exclusive rights to the eighties. None of us want to be antiques—"

"Glad to hear it, Beans. Because the past is definitely not happening!"

As usual, he's going to get the last word, because Fire is coming back inside. Annie holds him gingerly by one arm, a Victorian governess strolling on some seaside promenade.

"The road needs me," Fire announces soberly, the effect somewhat marred by his best redneck grin. "I'm thumbing off."

"Me three," says Ayer.

"Good on ya! Then you can take Fire back into town." Back to the outpatient clinic or kitchen or crawl space of his choice.

"Whoa Nellie!" Ayer starts to grumble about completing his performance with this player added to the cast.

"He won't cause you more than a whimper," Annie assures, then kisses her former lover on his forehead prow. Ayer is never so lovable as when he's trapped and trying to squirm out.

"Okey-dokey, *mon vieux*! Saddle up!" Now he sounds back in charge, though he's got to be reeling. "Just be sure and thank the missus for me. Tell her she'll be receiving a complimentary Avon kit!"

"How about a duplicate print of the softball follies?"

"You got it, pardner." We escort the two of them down the front steps. "Hey, it was happenin', wasn't it? Let's do lunch, shall we? But no *queso*. I'll pencil you in for the year twenty-five twenty-five. . . ."

From Missy's steps, we watch Ayer climb into his Austin-Healey roadster without bothering to open the door. Fire, sharing the backseat with the video equipment, is already rolling a joint. The two of them go out grinning, at full throttle. He's turned the corner on Easy Street before we realize that, for once, Ayer forgot to shake hands.

3:42 p.m. The most peculiar people on the planet, the true freaks, are those who are genuinely unashamed.

"My little lamb!" Missy's no longer talking about Irena. "I forgot all about it, you guys. I bet it's *totalled*."

We rush out to inspect it. The rotisserie rotates, the mesquite hasn't quit, the lamb's leg is indeed a blackened stump.

"The Reichstag fire, dude."

"The Bank of America in smoldering ruins."

"Naw. . . . I scorched 'em worse than this when I was a camp counselor. Slice on through an' you'll find loads of horseflesh."

"Quick, someone get me a serving dish!"

"I'll set the table," Annie volunteers.

"And the men can clean up."

"First, it was pick up the gun!" Dana gives us a thumbnail history of the New Left. "Then it was pick up the trash!"

"I wish my Spyros would do that." Missy doesn't have to specify which picking up.

She and I are alone for the first time. We don't look at each other, but down toward the animal remains. While I lift the spit, she tugs at the lamb with two oven mitts until it slides off.

"Ugh! Some restaurateur! I never was much of a cook, was I?"

"I didn't think there was a kitchen that could hold you."

"Boiled or burnt—those were my house specialties. I just couldn't pay attention to pots and pans."

"Or cats in the broiler."

"Oh, Pep! I'd wiped that all out! Wasn't I making red snapper for your folks?"

". . . when we began to smell burning hair."

"Poor Sojourner! Her whiskers never did grow back, huh?"

"How she hopped around our tiny studio!"

"It was a cozy place."

"A lot different from this one."

"Are you scandalized by me, Pep? Tell the truth."

"How could I be? You just did what we all wanted to do. You carried out the program and became working class."

"Complete with diapers and a balloon mortgage and a husband who puts in sixty hours a week. What a treat!"

"You don't seem to be having such a bad time."

"Are you, Pep? You know, I worry about you."

"Truly?" Missy's concern lasts until I've held the screen door open for her.

"I can't believe it! Annie, you always make everything look just right!"

In a wink, Missy's breakfast nook has become an elegant *boite*. The roast is at home in a Greek setting. Everything on the table's a matching Aegean cerulean blue: from ceramic dishes to linen napkins to centerpiece of cornflowers that's come, under wraps, from Annie's yard. Frosted blue decanters await whatever Dana can scrounge from Missy's well-stocked liquor cabinet. Setting his booty before us with a triumphant clatter, Dana's reenacting his first raid of the Judge's stash.

"I propose we get tanked."

"Pass the Mendocino Red."

"Fuck that. I'm goin' straight for the Old Tennis Shoes."

"No, guys, in my house, this is the poison of popular choice." Missy's reached to the back of the shelf for the *ouzo*.

"Let's not get out of control."

"Why the fuck not?"

"We've had enough psychodrama."

"Let's not dwell on it, you guys. Please, so mamma's stomach stops doing triple gainers."

"Jedediah needs a mess of tenderness." This is the closest Annie ever comes to that evasive procedure known as an apology. "He's like a human tuning fork. Just about anything sets him to jangling."

"It's not such a pretty sound sometimes."

"I don't think he was trying to hurt the baby. You-all can see that, can't you? He was trying just the reverse."

"Pure Hegel—right, Dan'?"

"Gimme that carver" is Dana's reply. "Fork over my manhood!"

"Fork power!" I've dredged up the slogan smeared in blood by the members of Charley Manson's collective, which we used to chant, tongue-in-cheek. Slogans I have known and loved. Dana responds with his best Bela Lugosi grimace, the blade held aloft.

"Wait. Don't forget our contributions!" Annie goes to the fridge for our three covered dishes, distributing them nicely around the bouquet. "Who wants to unveil?"

With no takers, Annie chooses hers first. Removing the heavy top of a Dutch oven, she shows off her blue-ribbon, county fair potato salad, just right for a picnic, yellow as a legal pad.

"*Merde!*" It's Dana.

"You too?" I groan.

Under an upside-down dish, Dana's variation on the spud theme is delicatessen-style, heavy on the sour cream, the shade of a starched collar. Below its foil crust, mine's marinated nicely in vinaigrette, speckled with parsley and bacon.

"I think we're discriminating against a couple of the major food groups."

"It's the ol' synchronicity!"

"The ol' fuck-up!"

"Come on now, boys. I won't let you be negative tonight. I won't." Missy rises out of her seat. "We made it through, didn't we? We're still kicking."

I join her to make the first toast. "To the spirit of the Bastille! To martyrdom, unintentional and inglorious!"

"To the boys on the loadin' dock!" Dana tries. "*Donnez-moi la* Milky Way!"

"To whole men and holy women!" Annie finishes. "To the pretty little cracks that time makes!"

Between the three potato salads and the burnt entree, there's not much to eat. We drink.

4:01 p.m. Why are these sated people thirsty?

But wait! Don't roll the camera yet. The elements in this shot are far too unintended. We ought to be drinking Beaujolais from hefty goblets, wearing sashes that bear the *tricoleur,* toasting the glory of some actual republic. We should be memorializing those who gave their lives instead of those who lost their minds. We ought to pay homage to Danton, not Abbie Hoffman! Maybe Robespierre and the boys were lucky to have been offed before they could renounce all, retire to sell insurance, write cookbooks, appear on talk shows. Here's mud in your tub, Marat! It's time for a refrain of *La Marseillaise,* or at least "Joe Hill." We've forgotten the words, though we can launch into every Marvin Gaye. Every Marvelettes. The Spiral Staircase. Whither our anthem, our call to arms? All together. "A *la lutte finale!*" Scream and shout.

4:07 p.m. Why is enough never enough?

Missy is an impresario when drunk. The Cecil B. DeMille of frenzy, the P. T. Barnum of uproar. Crazylegs has a knack for pushing the most theatrical buttons and the one she selects now is on her stereo. While the rest of us sink lower with each slosh of *ouzo,* she's rewinding some cassette to a passage that's meant to serve as a musical starting gate.

"Come on now, sleepyheads! Strut your stuff!" Missy clears space in the living room for us to do just that, kicking her coffee table aside, stopping to fling teething rings off the rug. She beckons with gestures broad enough to guide a Mack truck into her carport. When these don't bring results, she claps in time to the first thumping of zithers. "Come to Melissa! Come to mamma! Come on!"

Her music calls, too. Its lilt is monotonously persuasive. It turns the house on Easy Street into a whitewashed *taverna*, turns the four of us into our own village.

"This is my fave!" Is this Missy screeching? Or careening Crash? Or does she now speak as Melissa, wife of Spyros, daughter of Plymouth and Agamemnon? Tossing back her hair, biting down on her lower lip, she's shifted into party overdrive. "Annie, don't you want to learn the steps? . . . Stop making that face, Pep! I know you can shake it!"

But how can my time-honored impersonation of James Brown pass for Anthony Quinn? Annie is coaxing me out of the dining nook. "Let's go, *bouzouki* boy!"

Who can resist this Balkan pep rally? In the center of the wall-to-wall shag, we form a sloppy circle. Missy's arms go around Dana's waist, Dana's around Annie's shoulders, Annie's around my shoulder blades, mine around the instructress.

"Now, follow me. It's so simple, really! And so prideful. So Greek!"

The steps are suspiciously like a Hebrew school *hora*. Done in steady rotation, they make us rock in and out with a programmed stutter. We tighten our circle, then back away from the center with a bashfulness made formal.

"Just watch Melissa! It's left foot forward, right back, cross over. Then right twice, then left, cross over again . . ." She and Annie are doing it like old Macedonians. "Two-four-six-eight, Thessaloniki High is great-great-great!" Dana and I are faking along, bumping along, sometimes counterclockwise, sometimes trying to catch up, until we leave the circle's gravitational field and spin off to the intergalactic reaches of the dinette set.

Dana raises his arms, crooks the elbows, snaps both fingers in time with his measured hopping. Goaded by the tape's fevered plucking, he makes a sassy Zorba, prancing with patented, agonizing deliberation.

"What a good turnout!" Missy cried. "Too bad Darlinda can't see you! It's pure Leila Layne!"

"Don't gimme that! I never wanna hear that horseturd! . . . This is a hundred percent South Side!" The rest of us concede the point by trying to imitate his adaptation. There's head-bobbin', finger-poppin', shoe-shimmyin' all around. This is our self-induced trance-state, our homemade *hare krishna* boogaloo, our grape-squishing bacchanal, past-stomping hippity hop.

"Don't stop now, you guys! Keep it up, okay?" Missy takes three strides and escapes into her bedroom, shouting, "You won't believe what comes next!"

Before the cassette reverses she is back with a very long, very narrow lavender sash. "This belonged to Spyros' grandfather. For special occasions, Greek Easter. This is how he an' the boys use it. Watch!"

Missy falls to one knee, an eager suitor. She takes one end of the infinite kerchief and stuffs it in her mouth. Through clenched teeth and the gag, she orders, "Take hold! Somebody grab the other end!"

Dana does, with his fist, but Missy shakes him off. "In your teeth! Teeth to teeth!" Dana complies, biting down on the fabric, then dances toward a far corner until the cord between them is taut. As she kneels, Missy waves one hand, making imaginary lassos in time with the zithers. She swivels her head to keep Dana attached, no matter which way he saunters.

"Dana, you're still the smoothest!"

Next, it's Annie's turn, then mine, to orbit mouth-attached.

"Annie, you're still the steadiest!"

"Pep, you're still the nimblest!"

From my mouth to hers where she kneels, the ceremonial scarf is a steep and undulating flume, a conduit too flimsy for all the leaden memories.

4:26 p.m. In the dances we know, one must lead, one follow.

The Knee Job. Martin woke to a dawn that was no longer hopeful. An unwanted volunteer in a lost cause, he was up and alert before anyone required. No reapportionment of bedding could get him back to sleep. Though surrounded by bodies, the one he wanted beside him was no longer there.

Now he could hear her coming home from Oscar's new digs, right on cue. But she wasn't exactly racing the daylight back to Martin. She puttered about the empty apartment, made a snack in the kitchen, ran a bath, whistling all the while. Six o'clock and she was whistling! The tune was from some musical like *Kismet*, something about baubles and beads, steadfastly cheerful. Martin couldn't listen to it any longer. He had to make her stop. He had to get out of bed.

He found the common room bathed in a forgiving light. Martin had never been up early enough to see it before. He found Missy curled up in the armchair, sipping tea, changed into a striped bathrobe, with her bangs in disarray, her eyelids bluish, fucked-out.

"Pep! You're up so early!"

"So are you."

"We don't have to do the same things."

"No. We haven't been, have we?"

"It's not such a big thing. It doesn't have to get made into such a big production . . ."

"You're a big production to me."

"I'm going to take my bath."

"Wash him off you . . ."

"Don't make it worse on yourself."

"I don't know how else to make it."

"I can't help you. I've got to get in that hot water."

"Can I come with you? Can I watch? . . . I don't know what's allowed anymore."

Missy stood up then and he came closer. He thought she was about to open her arms to him, but instead she began fiddling with her split ends and shuffling toward the bathroom. Martin fell to block her. He discovered what knees are for.

"Don't end it now, Miss."

A shaft of morning sunlight lit their tableau. Martin wrapped both arms around Missy's knees, and when he heard her giggle, that only made him clutch harder. She didn't try to leave, just fidgeted with her hair and giggled. The tighter Martin held on, the less there was to grab. Missy's knees were elusive, while his were obstructive. They didn't buckle, like his wanted to do. The knees he encircled were nimble and well-oiled, and incorrigible. They were selfish—and he had the proof that he wasn't, now that he'd fallen to impale himself on those knobby knees, to rope in cowgirl calves like they were collector's items, to capture a pair of warm thighs as if warm thighs were an endangered species, to genuflect before the patron saint of his youth, begging that youth shall not stop.

4:31 p.m. Subjugation is the subject I know best. Subjugate: I want, you wish, he yearns, she craves, we need, they wait, it goes.

Missy could keep on dancing this dance forever. Dana is the first to give out, flopping onto the tartan couch.

"What's the prob, Dan'? Out of shape?"

"Outta shape yo' mamma! I can still Greek you under the table. It ain't that. It's the nicotine shakes."

"What?"

"You really don't notice shit anymore. I'm cold turkey on cigarettes."

"Good work."

"Hard work is what it is. Ass-bustin' triple overtime, like all meaningful changes. I haven't had a Marlboro since last night."

"Is that all that's put you on edge?"

"Naw, it ain't all, motherfucker."

I wish he'd just be done with it and tell me. At least, I know how to provoke Dana. It is, in the end, the best thing to know about old friends.

"Now that you've gone healthy, sport, you're finally a citizen of California!"

"Naw, man. I'll always be an Illinois hacker. I'm registered to vote in the twenty-ninth ward."

I've left the Zorba circle to recover beside the couch with my hands on my hips. For once, I'm looming over Dana.

"Then what are you quitting for?"

Before he can answer, Missy directs, "Alrighty, the jig's up. All of you onto the couch! I'll just run for my Sure Shot! Rearrange your pusses! It's documentation time!"

4:37 p.m. A document: anything purporting that reality is to be found in those acts which cannot be undone.

Substantiating Evidence. Martin discovered the photograph beside a farewell note from Oscar. The note began with an epigraph from Hemingway: "Then, too, he was sentimental, and like most sentimental people, he was both cruel and abused . . ." The rest of the message was a trifle less cryptic. "I have repaid my debt to Society, but only Missy can repay my debt to you. I hope that she does. I know you're smart enough to realize that I could have been Any Man." Or did he think of himself as Everyman? "And remember, *hombre,* there are women on every street corner."

If there were, Martin could not see them. He had never been able to look at more than one woman at a time—so what good was this surplus, this plenitude to which other men so often referred? He could only get what he needed from one place. His eyes were all on Missy—especially as she looked in this smudged Polaroid. He assumed it was taken at his rival's send-off back to Chico. He had no idea where the party took place or who took the snapshot. The snapshot told him that everyone had a grand time. Dana's arm was slung around Darlinda's shoulders, Darlinda's around Oscar, the presumed guest of honor, while Oscar had plunked his leftover limb over Missy's collarbone in finest caveman fashion. If Martin had done likewise, Missy would have called it territorial. She would not have struck so gleeful a pose.

Nothing in the expressions of Missy, Dana or Darlinda indicated that anything might have been out of the ordinary at this gathering. It looked like Oscar's head had been pasted in over his own. Now Martin knew how Trotsky must have felt. Now that it had finally happened, it wasn't such a bad feeling to have been airbrushed out of history. He felt relieved, actually. Why shouldn't the collective rearrange their membership roll? Why not eliminate certain documents from the files? Or pluck those unflattering snapshots of the scrapbook?

Martin could understand how the photo had come to be taken. What he never understood was why they kept it posted on the bulletin board for weeks after Oscar was gone.

The self-timer is ticking. Missy hurtles onto the couch and gets her arm around Dana just in time. Just one pose for old time's sake. It is just like old times: both the women snuggling close to Dana.

"That was perfect!"

"It better be, 'cause it might be the last."

"Oh, Dan'! Your deadpan is so dramatic!" Missy observes. But I recognize that combination from the last time he left and the time before that. On short notice. Without prior consultation.

"It's all mapped out, then?"

"You got it, dude." He turns to stare at me now, but I can't see a thing through the executive glasses. "You must have known the direction I was headed, eventually."

"Are you moving back for Polly's sake?"

"How about for my own sake? For some stability, man. A steady job, Chicago-style, and maybe a kid or two down the line."

This last admission explains the attempt to toss the cigarettes and brings more nuzzling on the couch from the girls. But Dana continues to make his appeal.

"You know all about what I got to prove."

So prove it, finally. Get it over with, irrevocably. Only what comes after? Is there life after proof? It's not that I don't want to make the same vault into maturity. It's just that, at the moment, I cannot stomach the sight of my "number one." I grab for the big shade off a lamp on the end table. In the most violent act of my life, I place the shade over Dana's head.

4:44 p.m. The fate of friends: no more easily altered than the fate of nations.

One Down, One to Go. Darlinda went around all morning whistling, bursting into dance, actually smiling. It was making Martin nervous.

"Has world matriarchy been declared or what?"

"It's just a decision," she told him in a reverent tone. "Decisions are so clean. In an hour, you'll know. When Dana and Missy get back. We want everyone to know at the same time."

When Dana got home from an afternoon's pointless vigil at Manpower, he confirmed what Martin was fearing.

"I'm throwin' in the work gloves, my man. . . . Look at this shit! This pair never even got worn through!"

"Wait, wait for Missy! Let's be democratic!"

"Even democracy's got its leaks," Dana countered, flashing Martin a look that suggested even he was tiring of Darlinda's officiousness. Though he'd never get his best pal to admit it aloud, Martin knew that Dana was experiencing more than one form of underemployment.

He was a good boy until the end, keeping mum while Darlinda led the four of them to their favorite blighted square of park. She headed past the all-day partying at the barbecue pits and straight for the park's three remaining oaks. She made everyone get cross-legged.

"I think you all know the occasion for this powwow." Dana started in with a politician's formality, chief for a day. "I'm cuttin' out, an' that's how its got to be, gang. There's nothin' constructive goin' on for me here."

Including his side of the bed?

"This is what it means when we say politics first," Darlinda answered Martin's unspoken question. "Everyone is free to do what they have to."

"I thought the collective meant that no one does anything without group approval," Martin challenged.

"You gonna use your veto, son? On what grounds?" Martin had no ground to stand on. "Listen. If I get back to Chitown before the summer Sears catalogue run, they'll hire me back at Connaly's. . . . An' I gotta get back inside a factory. California's just too tight a market right now. Too much white-collar fluff in this economy."

"What about your old man?"

"He ain't gonna know I'm back in town. He's got no business with me so long as I'm out in the jungle."

"The one by Sinclair Lewis? Or was it Frank Norris?"

"Man, I can almost sniff those blast furnaces!"

"And what about your loyalty to the group?"

"The group's evolvin'," Dana informed its remaining male member. "I'll just be its Midwest branch."

"It's perfect!" Darlinda screeched. One boyfriend down, one to go.

"We'll miss you so much, Dan'." Missy provided the human touch. "Let's all hug."

Sliding on their knees, they drew their Indian circle tighter, linked arms, bowed heads. The dwindling collective took a conclusive breath together, Dana's Marlboro staleness mingling with Martin's pickled sighs, Darlinda's touch o' clove, Missy's nut-flavored gasps.

It wasn't until he and Dana were left alone in the house that Martin dared break the silence. Lying on the big bed that night, he watched his pal complete his methodical packing. As if by rote, Dana stuffed his trusty duffel bag with Dr. John and Silver Apples albums, Bakunin pamphlets, obscure French journals, I.W.W. memorabilia and the shoplifted Mayakovsky *oeuvre*, his spare hobnail shit-kickers, his bandana collection, solid black T-shirts, the triple-thick wool socks that his mom bought him, that he'd never been able to wear in California. Steadily, with the confidence that came from having done it many times before, Dana fit everything into the duffel until it looked like a huge canvas slug.

"We never got to study a single one of your anarchist tracts. . . ."

"There'll be time, man. Ideas don't disappear."

"Just people."

"Temporarily, son."

"It's all gotten pretty temporary."

"I been telling you, son. You gotta go with the changes."

"Maybe in the world, but not in this room."

"Take it slow, dude. Take it feminist."

"I'm trying. I'm just not as well house-trained as you."

"You just got more woman to hang onto."

"Is that a compliment at the last minute?" It was certainly the first time Dana had even implied some dissatisfaction with Darlinda. "Or do you mean to emphasize the 'hanging on'?"

"I mean you can get through tougher challenges than this one."

"You overestimate me."

"I suppose so. A person always overestimates his number one."

"I'm still your main man?"

"There's no doubt."

"Around here, I'm gettin' mighty superfluous."

"If you feel that way, bail out. Come to Chitown. Give yourself the most revolutionary address you can have."

That had never occurred to Martin. Life without Missy still had not occurred to him.

"I have deeper ties than you do."

"Maybe so. Maybe I'm not cut out to be the red-hot lover. There are other things to be."

"Like what?"

"Like a real worker!"

With a screech, Dana finished his packing and leaped upon Martin on the big bed. He overpowered his smaller buddy, pushing him over onto his stomach. Leaning down hard, he humped one of Martin's legs.

"A real worker, ooooh! A real hunk, Marty!" Once again, Dana staged a little farce to show that his impulses, while sincere, often uncontrollable, should not be taken at face value. Before letting go his stranglehold, Dana pinned Martin's eyes with his own and whispered, "If I don't become a real worker within six months, I swear I'll shoot myself."

4:57 p.m. There is no morality in the absence of risk.

"Pep! Come back!" Bolted for the backyard, I've got Missy to come after me. "Wait a sec! I've got something to show you!"

Her arms around my middle feel swell, even if they're corraling where they once caressed. She is dragging me back through the living room, presumably so that I can apologize. I don't even want to see if the lampshade's been removed. I don't have to, because Missy is steering me toward her bedroom. Did she say she had something to show me?

"Not your body, I hope." I pretend to be drunker than I am. I allow myself to add, "I've seen it already. Coming and going, so to speak. . . ."

"Pep! I'm a married woman!" And I'm in the nuptial chamber. This has got to be it. I can tell by the queen-sized posturepedic Missy pushes me onto, by the curlicued Cost Plus wicker headboard, the clock radio and reading lamp, the *National Geographics* and diaphragm case, rounded like a turtle shell. Sprawled out, I stare up at the textured ceiling, sparkling from an overhead fixture which is so diffuse it seems neither off nor on. "You stay in here awhile. You just leave my Dana alone!"

Missy has her back to me. As she bends over, her shirt rises to show the elastic on her stretch slacks. She begins rummaging through her closet.

"You were always protecting Dana," I continue, emboldened. "Some feminist! All he had to do was bat those big eyes and you'd clutch him to your breast! But you don't have to worry, Dana can take it."

"And you can't?"

"I can, sure. At a cost that I'm continually calculating."

"I never meant to make you pay." This is the first time Missy's talked to me about the way it ended. "You didn't deserve that treatment. You were the best."

"That's what they all say, as they head out the door."

"But it isn't a contest, Pep. You know that. Sometimes the best for someone isn't the best for someone else. Sometimes I felt that how you acted then had nothing to do with me."

"I know. I don't do that anymore. I don't do anything."

"What happened way back then shouldn't stop you. . . . We were so young. We were a sparkler on the Fourth of July."

"*Mais oui*. Built to burn out."

"You don't still wish that we were together?"

"I don't wish for anything, except, maybe once and a while, to feel that sure about things again. But not about you. I don't know who you are."

"Then what's the dif?"

"The dif is that it hurt for a long time. I had no idea, before you, that people did those sorts of things to one another."

"But they do, don't they? So maybe it was good for me to show you."

"Why did you pick someone in the next room?" I still have to know. "Why him?"

Missy stands to face me, a stack of shoe boxes pressed against her chest.

"I dunno. It would have been him or someone else. I guess he made it more final. Besides, all of us can be self-destructo. You're not the only one."

"I'm glad to hear that."

"You know the reasons for all those goings-on better than anyone. You even know the reason why things don't have reasons. You once told me that's what abstract art was all about. I never forgot that."

"But what if you know that knowledge is the enemy?"

Missy's answer is a gleeful "Eureka!" She's found the right box.

"Look. This ought to make you feel terrif." She sits on her knees by the foot of the bed, at a proper distance from me. She opens the lid and scatters her treasure between us. "It's your love letters, Pep. I saved them all."

There are hundreds of them, uncategorized and unalphabetized. Most of the envelopes bulge, swollen with praise.

"I don't want to look. I'm afraid that I don't know how to feel that way about anyone or anything anymore."

"Oh, crud!"

I finger the deluge. So many unabridged volumes of worship! Before me is the only writing I've ever done that isn't criticism. Maybe, just through touching, by osmosis, I can rebuild my vocabulary of kind words. But I can't resist opening one up. I squint at some stranger's handwriting:

> "*Sweet Sister M.:*
> *You are like the revolution. The best part of me, with me everywhere I go. The reason to keep on. Except that you kiss better, and taste better, and hold me whenever I ask. . . .*"

"No, I can't read them. They're yours."

"And I'm so proud that they are. . . . You know, about once a year, I take them out and read all of them, down to every P.S. And they're such beautiful letters, so flowing, so much more perfect than anyone will ever write me again. And I start to cry. . . . Don't shake your head. I do!"

"No, it can't be. Not Miss Contentment."

"Is that the only way you can see me now?"

"I see someone who constructs her own world wherever she goes."

"I try. But you remember my moods, don't you? You remember all the ways I hated this society. It was a good hate that we shared, huh?"

"Better than love?"

"More lasting."

Missy leans across the mud slide of letters and grips both my arms at the elbow. Grips them hard. She's looking at me in a very old way.

5:17 p.m. Romanticism: now there's an ideology!

Scene Four (Estrogen): Midafternoon in the house of hormones. The shades are drawn. Chairman Mao, cosmic chin-wart and all, looks down from a poster. A young couple, Missy Estrogen and Martin Testosterone, is in bed.

TESTOSTERONE: "Is it too soon?"

ESTROGEN: "Too soon?"

TEST.: "I mean, your back door man's only been gone a few days."

EST.: "Don't start this again."

TEST.: "After the way you wrote about him in your diary . . ."

EST.: "You weren't supposed to see that!"

TEST.: "I know, but you left it open, next to the bed. I couldn't help myself."

EST.: "I've got to have privacy!"

TEST.: "I thought it's been outlawed in this house."

EST.: "Okay, I mean, space."

TEST.: "You mean secrets. Christ! I can't seem like much in the sack compared to that. . . ."

EST.: "I was just trying to sound like Anaïs Nin."

TEST.: "Hold me then."

EST.: "But we can't . . ."

TEST.: "You want to make ze music, no?"

EST.: "I do, really. For the first time since . . ."

TEST.: "*Umberto D.*"

EST.: "Come on, Pep. No lookin' back."

TEST.: "How can we go forward without doing this?"

EST.: "I want to, honest—"

TEST.: "If it's your period, I don't mind. You know that."

EST.: "No, it's something else."

TEST.: "You didn't get the clap . . ."

EST.: "No siree!"

TEST.: "What then?"

EST.: "You won't believe it!"

TEST.: "I will. That's the trouble. From you, I'll believe anything."

EST.: "I've run out of pills."

TEST.: "When? The day he left?"

EST.: "No, later. I just lost track."

TEST.: "Guess you never figured you'd be fucking ol' Marty again."

EST.: "I won't let you make me ashamed of my feelings!"

TEST.: "I know, you never figured on any of this. . . . Have you called Planned Parenthood?"

EST.: "I lost the number."

TEST.: "It's in the phone book."

EST.: "I need an appointment for a full exam. I'm getting a diaphragm. I want to know exactly what's inside me."

TEST.: "Don't put anything inside yourself on my account."

EST.: "Meaning?"

TEST.: "Fucking isn't a service."

EST.: "Of course not. Trust me."

TEST.: "Like I did when you said you were 'too busy' with O.W.L. meetings to see me, only you were really with him."

EST.: "I have my own life."

TEST.: "Is that why you stopped going to your consciousness-raising group?"

EST.: "I did get detoured a teensy bit, huh?"

TEST.: "I wonder if our drives are coming out this way, like everybody's in heat or something, because we've gotten more free, or less . . ."

EST.: "Quit thinking stuff like that."

TEST.: "Why? It gets me out of the mood."

EST.: "I'm not out of the mood."

TEST.: "Me neither. . . . Maybe I could use the ol' pullout . . ."

EST.: "It's too messy."

TEST.: "I could have my tubes tied."

EST.: "I have tubes, not you."

TEST.: "You know what I mean."

EST.: "That wouldn't help us at the moment."

TEST.: "Then let's just have a kid."

EST.: "Never, never."

TEST.: "I was just fooling."

EST.: "Never, never, never."

TEST.: "We might as well get up."

EST.: "I'll call right now and make an appointment. I promise"

TEST.: "No more promises, please."

EST.: "What's happened to us?"

TEST.: "Can you remember the way it was under the colored bulbs at Steffens?"

EST.: "On Bleecker Street . . ."

TEST.: "You were the grandest checker at Union Grand. You were my starlet."

EST.: "Are we washed up?"

TEST.: "Over the hill at twenty?"

EST.: "There's got to be more than this! There's got to!"

TEST.: "I still love you."

EST.: "Right now, when I hear a man say that, it sounds like he's got a fatal disease."

TEST.: "You mean, he said it to you also?"

EST.: "I don't remember."

TEST.: "Do you remember who this is lying next to you?"

EST.: "I wish I were a tomboy. I wish I were still little!"

TEST.: "What the world needs is sons who grow up to be mothers."

EST.: "And daughters who grow up to be fathers."

TEST.: "Combination beings."

EST.: "I've got to get out of bed."

TEST.: "It's frightening how quickly you get tired of being naked around me."

EST.: "Now stop that. Being naked around you is a snap. It's just that I've got to get ready for work."

TEST.: "Ma Bell calls."

EST.: "Pa Bell. There are no women on top. We're on our backs." (In operator voice): "Directory assistance. May I help you, please?"

TEST.: "Quit."

EST.: "That's too easy. That's how everyone runs away, and nothing gets better. But I'm off tomorrow. Let's spend the day in The City."

TEST.: "Do you mean it? No meetings?"

EST.: "No meetings."

TEST.: "We could browse at City Lights . . ."

EST.: "Go for *dim sum* in Chinatown . . ."

TEST.: "See the buffalo in Golden Gate Park."

EST.: "I can finally buy that pepper plant at Cost Plus."

TEST.: "You don't need a pepper plant. You got me. Let's kiss some more."

EST.: "You still taste Jewish."

TEST.: "Is that why you preferred him?"

EST.: "Hush up! I like the way you taste."

TEST.: "Want me to make you come?"

EST.: "No . . . I'll do you."

TEST.: "No, together."

EST.: "There's not enough time. I couldn't concentrate."

TEST.: "Is it because his tongue was thicker?"

EST.: "Not again . . ."

Stage gradually goes to dark.

5:24 p.m. All soldiers for love, and not one conscripted.

"Can we-all join you in repose?" Annie's at the door with Dana in tow. "If I don't get horizontal, I'm gonna be sick."

"Come on! Come in, Dan'! We'll all lie down together."

In Missy's big bed, we lie very still. Face up, in separate morgue drawers. Two heads to a pillow. Alternating male-female, male-female. Hardly touching except where a knee threatens a calf and elbows kiss. Annie's farthest from me: the only way to get in the sack with her is with other bodies present. Just like it was at the end with Missy. We listen to each other breathing in turns. One puts out *ouzo* exhaust and the next sniffs it. We sound like a broken calliope.

5:28 p.m. If you hang around long enough, everyone becomes beautiful.

We've always done best looking away from each other and toward some point of shared astonishment. For the moment, Missy's texturized ceiling will do. Exuding false glamor, full of indecent sparkle, this prefabricated canopy becomes our chunk of sky. Those are no longer just nubs of concrete gripping stray bits of light. In this sky, we find constellations.

"There's Orion . . . with his Gucci belt!"

"There's Ursus, the big Commie bear."

"There's a unicorn . . ."

"And a tire iron . . . what's the scientific way to say tire iron?"

"I see a caterpillar."

"And his cocoon."
"The mammary arches!"
"Oh, no!"
"A third eye."
"A paw-print."
"A powdered, illegal substance."
"A sunflower."
"A canoe, made of bark."

Still children together, we'd rather invent a universe more to our liking. Won't someone tuck us in? We take turns making up all that we want and then we take turns making the mistake of naming it.

5:32 p.m. Immaturity: more sustaining than the alternative.

Martin's Poem.

"PARCEL POST"

There is a part of town like this in every America,
where the railroad used to howl,
where trailers and semis dwarf the few sedans,
where concrete forms hold inventory,
like a truss,
and another night just means
the sun didn't get any overtime.

Here rumnoses wait
for the day off to go to Frontierland,
wait among defective parts, docks and dollies, old sacks
flatulating the industrial musk of a million dead circulars
(this poem, booked and bound, would pass through, too).

We are a generation at twenty
that can't even tie our shoelaces,
still stain our underwear daily,
don't love, feel, talk to each other barely.
And we're supposed to be the revolution?
And how can I work it all out with
Whistlin' George on my back?
The fucker.

The front door slams. Spyros is home ahead of schedule. Only ten hours gripping a spatula.

"Sweetie! My little spinach pie! We're all in here! Come say hi!"

Come say hi, Spyros, to the leisure class. You won't have to go far: they're right in your bed. He hovers in the door frame, shoulders stooped in burger-flipping position.

"Allo, everybody." We've never heard him say much more, but he's never seen anything like this. "What's all dis then goin' on?"

"We just had to lie down from the *ouzo*. You know what it does! Have some, Spyrotaki." Missy's accent makes up in fondness what it lacks in finesse. "Join the party."

"I tired." And straining to sound carefree. "I don't want party."

"Oh pooh!"

Missy's always explained her husband's shyness in terms of embarrassment over his English, but tonight, his diffidence sure looks like an immigrant's mistrust of a native world he cannot fully enter. Spyros' lack of curiosity borders on aggression. His rigid pose in the door frame suggests a new menace. The years over the grill have melted his fat off and left only sinew. His curly black hair and pork chop sideburns frame a face that tapers like a pear. It is a face that most men would call pitted and most women rugged. His teeth, when he smiles, show a lack of Yankee dental work. He's not smiling.

"Melissy, you come and talk."

"Okay, Spyrotaki. Lordy, I don't want to move!" Missy sits, pats down her hair, then slides down carefully, getting off the bed without touching the men on either side. She waves us a Mark Sennett goodbye. The we-who-are-about-to-die-salute-you sketch. In the living room, the couple commences negotiations in Greek.

Spyros' tone tells all. He has staked his claim here, amidst the patched pools and the dinner houses. He is willing to do anything to protect his foothold in this monoxide valley. If only Spyros could see that he's more American than any of us!

"Let the mail roll!" Dana commands.

"I don't think I can." It's Annie. "I'm way too dizzy."

"You better. It's time to *vamos* . . ."

From the next room, the alarm of Irena's crying goes off.

"See what you did! You disturbed baby!" Missy shouts at Spyros, like she's disciplining a tough old dog for whom she's got a soft spot.

"I don' care. Dis is my house I work for!"

That's the clincher. We're all upright by the time Missy calms the child and returns.

"Where do you think you're going?" She is perfectly cheerful. "It's just the craziest, huh? I've got two babies on my hands tonight. But you must stay!"

But who wants to?

Big Sister Is Watching Me! Big Sister says, "You must get in touch with your feelings."

Big Sister adds, "You are not allowed to feel jealous."

Big Sister commands, "Let go of your possessiveness. Learn to soothe and nurture yourself because I'm no longer interested in the job."

"But don't let me catch you taking pleasure in yourself," cautions Big She. "Quit touching yourself you-know-where."

Big Sister's credo is cribbed from Big Brother: "Freedom Is Submission. Fullfillment Is Effacement. Liberation Is for Others More Deserving."

Big Sister has brothers everywhere and lovers nowhere. The only brothers she can support are in distant lands. The only men she admires are ones she never has to meet.

Big Sister disapproves of male style, male authority, and the outmoded male concept of power. Women, Big Sister proves by example, can fill any position better than men—including dictator.

Big Sister bears a striking resemblance to Big Mamma. "Clean up your room!" becomes "Clean up your psyche!"

Big Sister crusades against *machismo,* but despises uncertainty. She doesn't want men who boss, but will take them over men who cringe. Eventually, she will take them any way she can get them.

Big Sister admonishes, "Learn to be weak!"

Big Sister demands, "How can I respect you unless you are strong?"

Big Sister hates double standards almost as much as she loves cooking schedules.

Big Sister concedes, letting down her hair, removing safety goggles, that this may be a phase she's going through, a necessary overreaction. Hooked on a newfound resoluteness, she'll admit, "It really doesn't matter what I'm resolute about."

Big Sister explains, "I'm not required to be logical, precise or consistent. That's what makes me different from what came before. That's what gives me the chance to be better than men."

Late at night, when the other sisters aren't listening, Big Sister coos, "Don't worry. There's a special place in my hierarchy for the man who sees through all of this."

Big Sister is big because big boys let her be.

Big Sister would be very angry if you said she was well-developed.

Big Sister takes confession.

Big Sister makes the trains run on time.

Big Sister is watching me. May her big blue eyes never waver.

The Last Boyfriend on Earth. The big bed had been disassembled and banished to the platform of a U-Haul trailer. Where the stripped segments once flopped, a sea of blue shag washed back in. On the walls where posters exhorted, all that was left were masking tape scars, thumbtack punctures. Other than that, their household looked disconcertingly the same as when inhabited—especially since nobody was bothering to scrub or sweep up. Without a clean-up, there were few ways to tell that the Big Mac Collective was taking a summer recess before reconstitution in combinations as yet unstated. But they had put it to a vote, and the tally went as always: three against one, the ladies versus Martin.

The third lady was Meryl Schwartzkopf, who'd become the last interloper to take possession of one of the empty rooms. From the office she termed an "O.W.L. command post," Meryl presided over the dismantling of the house. Had Missy told her that she was following Oscar's act? Probably, Meryl didn't know about the boarder at all, but she sure did her best to evict Martin. When she needed the house for meetings, which was almost every night, she'd give Martin a dollar and dispatch him to—where else?—the movies. Other than that, she would bark at him when there were dishes to be done, cartons of Tampax to be bought. If she overheard the heavy breathing of incipient petting in the resident couple's room, Meryl would pound on the door and ruin everything, exhorting Martin to "Fuck like Che!"

The slogan she now advanced was, "Amazon warriors don't need no deposit refunds." All they did was set their sleeping arrangement out on the street and bring in refreshments for a going-away bash. That evening, the site of so much male divestiture was transformed into the ultimate Don Juan daydream. The collective's farewell party might have been a bachelor's delight, had Martin identified himself with so archaic a constituency. There were "Ten girls for every guy," as the lyric went. No, fifty girls to one guy! Only these girls had sworn off guys.

For the first time, the empty rooms seemed full up with genuine communality—with women chatting earnestly, women tearing into bowls of chip 'n' dip, women smooching in corners, women swapping stale knee-slappers and laughing with a lustiness that outdid any pack of stags. Where the big bed had sprawled, the partygoers dumped their female baggage and called it child care. Finally, the padded room really was a romper! From whence had these babies sprung? Turkey basters? And these ex-Madonnas? From Darlinda's relaxation class, from the dance studios, the consciousness raisers and the Rolfing workshops, from the ranks of Ma Bell's daughters, from the Lesbian Moms, from the food conspiracies and the welfare rolls. The entire mailing list of O.W.L. must have been in attendance.

Sisters were linking up with sisters in their natural and noncompetitive way, only this time they were nurturing such connections and not retreating afterwards to the cages supervised by male keepers. They were making those "primary relationships" secondary. And secondhand Martin enjoyed witnessing this profusion of lithe sirens toting day packs, swapping new-age folk remedies, stroking each other's curls, writhing to gentle women's rock, shaking it how they wanted in sweatshirts, peasant skirts, drawstring pants and any apparel that was floppy, shapeless and conducive to moving free. These ladies didn't need to be asked to dance anymore. Like uncourted high school wallflowers, the women paired up with one another, then kicked off their slippers, jitterbugged and even ground the slow grind.

At first, Martin felt right at home, not just because this was his home, but because he was once again on the outside. This time, he could observe all he liked from behind the one-way mirror of his sex. What troubled him as the party geared up was that no one, not Missy's latest bosom buddies, not even the volunteer confessors of her many meetings, seemed to know who he was. Over and over, he was met with looks both perplexed and scathing, forcing him to blurt out, "Excuse me, I'm Martin. I live here . . ." The only exception to the genital rule that guided the list of invitees, he had to keep justifying his presence amidst the militiawomen and the operators, the vegetarian antivivisectionists and the newly unweds, the whole cast of penisless thousands. Had Missy really neglected to mention his existence? That would be her style. "Oops, I completely forgot! There's this guy who keeps turning up in my bed!" Martin no longer asked to be the center of attention. He'd dropped that expectation some months back. Or was it centuries? But didn't he serve some function, at least as an obstacle? Wasn't he worthy of note, as a problematic footnote, a hairy holdover? By midnight, Martin turned relic. He flitted about like some phantom of dominance past, the butler who no longer did it. He had to keep reminding one and all that he was not only a rightful guest, but a host. "Excuse me, I'm Martin. I live here. . . . I come with Missy. A package deal."

His little speech turned to a dirge. "Good evening, I'm Martin. . . . Please excuse me. . . . This is, or was, my house too."

He hardly saw Missy all night, and when he did, Martin wished that he hadn't. He found her chatting with a group that included Meryl and the Ma Bell caucus, which had just changed its name to "W.A.R.," the Women for Armed Revolt. Missy didn't introduce or acknowledge Martin, though she offered a quasi-friendly pinch on the hip that he took, wrongly, as encouragement to join their circle. They were discussing the summer ahead and the house they were trying to find for the fall. "Better let us know for certain soon," one of the battalion was concluding. "We gotta keep count of how many bedrooms we go after. And which sister needs sunshine, which prefers a dark cave." Martin couldn't tell who she was addressing. Then he caught Missy nudging her to stop, heard that telltale giggle, followed by another of her infamous oopses. Missy's place in the dormitory of purposely single women was all but reserved. This was the first Martin had heard of it.

He wandered off, struck but not yet bleeding. He circulated no more, lest he intrude on further deceits. Instead, he took up a strategic corner from which to watch the celebration wind down. The fewer the women, the more conspicuous his presence—even when he squatted and kept his stare on the pointy toes gripping the carpet. He didn't belong with Darlinda, who imitated a foraging squirrel beside one stereo speaker, or the Sapphic tag teams whose flirtations turned into a mock wrestling match that ended in a general distribution of refreshments. Hoisting the bowls of guacamole as they skipped around an imaginary, castrated maypole, the girls flung green goop all over the walls, spurted spice on their partners. They reveled in the obvious symbolism of this whirling avocado dervish while Martin the butler moved in to clean up. But no, they'd agreed not to clean. And no, this wasn't his mess. For one last time in this house, he felt pained and conflicted. This time, the source of conflict was his recognition that he'd been suffering through the cheapest sort of pain, making the least noble sacrifice. If this was his party, why not whoop it up? If it wasn't, why was he here? It seemed possible that he had hardly been there all along.

ENDS

5:41 p.m. The moral's obvious: live by ideas that jibe with what's in your gut. But remember—fascism, racism, jingoism, all the worst "isms" spring from that gut.

It's very awkward. Through the bedroom window, we can see Spyros, exiled to the yard. In the Technicolor dusk, he hovers like a vengeful Olympian deity—his dignity only a trifle compromised in that the chariot he rides is Irenka's wooden horse. Rocking sidesaddle, he starts another smoke, taps the black heels of his boots against the tiny stirrups. Hubby is anxious to take his ease in the house that hash browns built. We're doing our best to accommodate him. Dana and I tuck in our shirts like milkmen caught in the act. Annie's gone to the kitchen for what's left of our potato salads.

"He's such a lamb, really. My tender, succulent Spyrotaki," Missy whispers to us, before squawking through the screen door, "You brute! Let the brute wait!"

Missy's more flattered than scandalized by her Neanderthal man. His major sin is that he's disturbed the baby. Now she has to shuttle between the pink room and the yard and wherever the three of us happen to be. On its tenth replay, the *bouzouki* tape thumps in time with her caroms. Missy is back in her element, which is in a hurry and put upon and having a grand time.

I've had enough of the show for this year. I persuade Annie that she doesn't have to do all our dishes right now. Dana volunteers to fetch our swim trunks off the line. He's still my suave lieutenant, able to charm the pants off a mountain lion. Is he telling Spyros that we're hitting the wind? That we only show up once a decade? Or commiserating with the old boy by trotting out his tales of workaday derring-do? In the meantime, I feign a last cootchie-coo at Irenka.

"Don't run off, Pep. Not unless you've got a hot date!"

"Right, a real scorcher . . ."

"Then stick around. I've got *baklava*."

"I think we've outstayed our welcome."

"Not with me. Never." Nonetheless, she concentrates on rattling a teether loaded with plastic keys. The phone is ringing.

"Lord have mercy!"

Now she has to dash about some more and answer with an "Allo," which is her Greek hello. Whoever it is at the other end makes her revert at once into English, then a hushed intonation that makes it impossible for me to eavesdrop. But I know how to translate that hush. Someone else has thrown Missy's emergency switch.

5:50 p.m. No way to prepare for the unexpected, since if it wasn't you would be.

In Case of Emergency. Every time the phone rang in the E.R., Darlinda came up with a new set of questions. With each trauma case, she found it harder to stifle her rampaging curiosity. She just had to know: What was the length in centimeters of a knife wound compared to the number of capillaries torn? How did white cells respond to cold steel? Was it worse to catch a steering wheel in the forehead or a chunk of windshield in the spleen? Did either actually hurt? Or was there such a thing as a built-in, organic anesthetic? Pondering the mysteries of ectoplasm, she forgot to inquire about tetanus shots. Never mind about group insurance or sulfa drugs. Once the forms were filled out, Darlinda's questionnaire began in earnest. How could skin keep burning when there was no skin left? Did dying women still want to have babies? Were kids who swallowed rat poison still hungry for milk and cookies? Could crib death be explained by eyestrain? When junkies nodded off, were they actually sleeping? Did they have condensed eight-second dreams? Was there an "out-of-body" experience, and if so, what did the body do while it was waiting?

As they were being carted off, Darlinda called out to her black charges, "Why can't I make you clot with my touch? Or do you prefer to be touched by one of your own? Is there any value in interracial massage? Would it make you fight harder to live? And what is this life you are fighting so hard for? Is it that you want a second chance to feel whole? Where, exactly, is your center of gravity and for how long can a human being walk around without one? Is the wounded body like a river forced to flow in the wrong direction? Or is it like a dam? Like a desert?"

Death didn't reply. The main thing that bothered Darlinda about death was that it was a one-way interview. She had to marvel at how numb she could get when it was required. She wasn't sure if that was politically correct or not. It was hard to tell what was correct and what wasn't in an emergency room. No one had time to give her the answers.

5:55 p.m. Death: the only thing most of us do that's spontaneous.

Having watched Missy go through this bulletin-transmitting routine hundreds of times, I'm never certain whether the news is going to be good or bad. Her first postcall "Amazeen!" suggests nothing more serious than a scandal at La Leche League. Her second makes me think of a grease fire at the restaurant. Approaching us, she's biting her tongue. The nostrils are dilated, the eyes pixilated. She looks just like she did when the Fortuna County cops dragged her off. Intoxicated by disaster.

"Guess what, gang? Wait a minute. Get in the ottoman for this one. There's a reason Darlinda didn't make it by. That was her, just released from the hospital. Her emergency room. She got beat up last night, just a teeny bit. But the main thing is, she was raped."

"By who?" Dana, too, has gone on alert. Condition red. To hell with his cigarette-quitting vow! The first butt's already out of the pack.

"A guy from work, I think."

"On her shift?" His voice has turned deep with concern for protecting all in his clan, whether their membership's current or expired. *Pater noster*, latent Abraham—I only wish that we'd afforded him more opportunities for heroic intervention. He's so good at it.

"Nope. It happened after they got off. At her house."

"With a gun or a knife?"

"Neither, I don't think."

"Was she coherent?"

"Too . . . . Just like our darlin'."

"Any permanent injury?"

"I couldn't tell, really. You know Darlinda. She kept talking about her lower vertebrae."

"Poor, poor Darlinda . . ." says Annie.

"Not too smart Darlinda," adds Dana.

"How do you know what happened?" Annie's rising to the defense of the sisterhood and I'm not touching this debate with a ten-foot phallus.

" 'Cause I got some firsthand knowledge of the victim," Dana defends. "But all that matters now is what she needs from us."

"It would be perfect if you stopped off an' saw her on the way back. She asked me to ask you. She's not hiding or anything. Darlinda's not the kind to get ashamed. Ever. That's what saves her. She's so courageous, no? . . . But I think she needs someone to make her feel that they know she's there. I'd go, too, except for boo-boo. I wish I could go."

"We'll leave this minute," Dana assures her. "Come on, Big Mac. The reunion ain't over yet."

"Get going, you guys." Now Missy's pushing us out. "Doesn't this just prove everything we were saying all along when the things we said you couldn't escape end up happening to us eventually? Isn't it wretched?"

6:00 p.m. We were the people who were right about everything. Except that being right didn't make any difference.

The Heavy's Lament.

I asked the wind not to cross my picket line.
I went on trial with the rain as judge.
I would not let the seasons recruit on campus.
I gave Mother Nature a legal abortion.
I sabotaged photosynthesis.
I occupied God's office.
I walked out on old age.
I refused my best friend because his card expired.
I rode to the demo next to the Creature from the Black Lagoon.
I formed a united front with the devious.
I proposed being content, then tabled the motion.
I talked back to the Six O'Clock News.
I questioned words with other words.
I marched to ban excretion.
I masterminded a general strike against pain.
I was in a consciousness-raising group that met at Blimpie Base.
I jerked-off lemonade, but the frozen concentrate was cheaper.
I committed myself to song, then lost my voice.
I was so honest I forgot to be kind.
I had my guilt washed at the laundromat.
I saw the past, present and future and none of them worked.
I sat-in to block the entrance to my lover's womb.
I left home because it was a nonunion shop.

On the front steps, we form a receiving line. Dana mumbles, "Thanks for the use of your crib and your liquor cabinet."

"Same time next decade?" asks Annie.

"I better see you guys before then. Before Irenka starts to talk. Oh, God, I just know she'll be a little chatterbox!"

"Next year, then? Only we'll hold it someplace else."

"Don't you dare! I'll send Spyros off to the races, how's that?"

Missy and I hug last. Take pecks at opposite cheeks. I try to remember what she felt like when she was mine. She feels like a housewife. She smells like lamb fat.

"Merry Bastille, sister."

"What a day!" Missy is squealing as in the days of old. "Amazeen! We really did it up!"

Big Mac Will Win! The poster in their kitchen showed a peasant girl in peaked cap aiming her rusted Gatling toward the Yankee intruders in the sky. The poster said, "Vietnam will win!" About such an outcome, and many others, they were certain. The newspaper headlines confirmed their faith every day. Fidel was still ranting, Mao was still swimming, the Tupamaros still sweeping down from the hills. Zimbabwe was inexorably becoming Zimbabwe. It, too, had to win. And what about them? They didn't know which game they were playing. Oakland will win! But did they even want it to? Unable to keep score in prisoners captured and hamlets reclaimed, it was natural to feel that they'd already lost.

A Very Sorry Story. Once upon an era, there was a girl who called herself a woman, called Missy. There was a boy, who called himself a boyfriend, called Martin. There was a friend who called himself a brother, called Dana. There was a friend's brother who called himself nothing, called Art.

There was the summer recess in which they all traveled even though they were no longer students. There was the home they left to see Dana, who had once lived there, too. There was Missy's hot new Barracuda to take them everywhere. There were plans to go to New York and revisit places where, once upon a semester, Martin and Missy had been happy.

There were three hundred miles to drive before Chicago, but Darlinda was already crying. Martin couldn't figure out if she was crying because she didn't want to see Dana or because she did or because she didn't want Missy to see Dana or because she didn't want to see what was going to happen to Martin. Darlinda said it was because of the cornfields.

Then there was Chicago and Dana's tour of the Gold Coast beaches, the Lincoln Park zoo, the Fifty-Third Street hoops, the Addison Street police station, the jukebox factories, the *pulquerias* of Halsted Street, the "stoned love" gangs of Madison Street, the rib shacks and the chili dives and the underground tier known as the Emerald City and the back alley shortcuts that he weaved through under the immunity of his old man's official plates. There was the fabled Pearl crib, twenty stories above the fabled lake, where they could crash in whatever upholstered chamber they chose, since the fabled Pearls themselves were in Florida. And there was Art.

The first night there was beer and the White Sox. Missy told Martin that it was much too hot for them to fuck, even though there was air-conditioning in every room. There was a great storm that made it sound like the lightning had toppled all downtown. "Chicago's apocalyptic weather," the tour guide intoned.

The second day, at Darlinda's insistence, they went off to "play." They played hide-and-seek around Civil War generals and the Buckingham fountain. There were lots of them playing. There was Art, who was quite an athlete. He had been on the Illinois football team once, before he went off to Canada to outflank the draft. At one point, he and Missy ran off to the band shell and nobody sought them. There were all of Dana's new Chicago friends, new friends for Missy. They put her in her most Missyish state.

"She's very active, isn't she?" the friends asked Martin, the tone in their voices suggesting that he might have trouble keeping up with her.

"Yes," Martin would answer, with a tone that suggested nothing.

The second night was beer and the Cubs.

The third day was Art taking Missy for a swim, while Darlinda took Martin around the mulberry bush.

The third night was Art raiding the liquor cabinet at the crib.

The fourth day was pure Art.

The fourth night was Art taking photographs of Missy with Martin's camera without bothering to set the exposure.

Part of the fourth night, which was almost the morning of the fifth day, Art invited Missy and Martin for a walk. They walked all the way to Wrigley Field. They walked across a dozen darkened ghettoes, but Martin found it hard to be frightened with Art. He was very big—almost too big to be a Jew—and pushed things even when there was nothing to push. He was very serious and deep and hardly ever sober. He loved Missy and Martin because they were his kid brother's best friends and also because they were so lovable. Martin so wise, Missy so daring.

Art wanted them to try and sneak onto the empty ballfield. Martin stood on Art's shoulders but he still wasn't high enough to scale the bleacher wall. Martin was frightened and skinned his knee on the wall jumping off Art. He tried to pretend that it didn't hurt, but he could tell Art knew he was pretending. He didn't want Art to know he was bleeding, but that was the first thing about Martin that everyone noticed.

The sixth day Art left for Israel. He didn't want to go. But his parents were paying him to see if he was a Jew and Art couldn't turn that one down. Martin was sad to see Art leave. One of Dana's friends asked Martin if he had been jealous of Art and Missy. "Why?" he asked back, and meant it.

The morning of the seventh day in Chicago, Missy and Martin tried to play in Dana's regular Sunday morning game of Clincher, twelve-inch softball. Martin could play but Missy could not. Missy couldn't believe that there were still softball games where women were barred. She was disappointed that Dana and Martin did not challenge the rule, but merely quit the game to be with her. It was her turn to cry. She walked off by herself for an hour. She said she wanted to be alone. Usually, she hated to be alone. Martin waited for her and worried.

When Missy came back, she told him that the softball game had upset her, the unfairness of it all.

When Art got back from Israel, he told Martin that Israel reminded him of Miami Beach. He also told Martin that he had received a letter from Missy. In the letter, Missy confessed that she had not been crying because of the game of Clincher that day. Missy wrote that she had been crying because Art had left. Once upon a time, Martin would have been surprised to hear this.

The eighth day, Missy announced that she and Darlinda were canceling the rest of their proposed journey and heading straight back to the women's house in Oakland. The Movement needed them now, Missy said. When Martin heard Missy use the word "Movement," he substituted a man. Martin was not invited along. He was encouraged, forcefully, to stay behind and shack up with Dana for a while. It had all been prearranged by Dana, his pal. So that when Missy and Darlinda got into her Barracuda and Missy hit the ignition, Martin stood on the curb with Dana and Dana's friends, waving good-bye. Missy did not wave back at Martin. As they drove off, everyone wished her a good, active time.

6:07 p.m. Suffering doesn't lead to wisdom any more than ignorance leads to bliss. Suffering, like anything else, is quite habit-forming. And if it made us wise, we would all have been out of this mess long ago.

"Damn," says Dana, once in the car. I hear a tapping against his knee to confirm that he's rolled his *Wall Street Journal* up into a newsprint baton. Returning to old rites in the backseat, he's turned all those Amex quotes into a deadly weapon—just the way he used to pick up a loose table leg or tree branch and make it his walking stick, stiletto cane, piece. Brushing aside more recent allegiances, the customer rep. strips down to street-fightin' man. Itching for some action beyond puts and sells, he rides shotgun on this final rescue mission with us. "Damn Darlinda's goddamn innocence. Damn the whole grab-ass parade."

"What can you do about it?"

"Can't do nothing now, but she should have. She's the one that was always exercising such control, that was convinced people had to reach a consensus just to fuckin' breathe—"

"Aren't you pronouncing judgment before all the evidence is in?"

"Maybe so. It runs in the family. I'm ready to be the judge and jury and hangman both. Just let me at the motherfuckin' plaintiff's throat. I'll do my duty like I always did. It's just that I keep scopin' Darlinda in the lotus position, spewin' shit like 'We will now take turns talking about our destinies.' An' getting all flustered when I told her socialists don't believe in fuckin' destinies."

"Hey! Don't get revisionist on me. Weren't you and Darlinda a lesson for liberated generations as yet unborn, the embodiment of love without cost?"

"Try love without feeling. The showroom model no one ever took for a spin. I mean, it was like bein' with someone an' bein' totally alone at the same time. We never even had sex right. Not once in two years. I was so starved, I'd practically shoot off in my work clothes—while she was gobblin' iron pills and slippin' brewer's yeast into her prune juice so she could get less anemic around orgasm time."

"This must be confession time."

"You got it, priest. Absolve me if you can, 'cause I keep flashin' on my own member and all the times it did its violatin'."

Right when Dana gets most crude, he also gets most lyric.

"Why're you laughin', kids? She did give the green light for me to wield it now and again."

"So what's wrong with that?"

"So permission's the only difference between me and some maniac, right? It's all a matter of agreed operating procedures. There's one thin-ass line between *le contrat social* and homicide."

"None of us ever crossed that line. Or enough lines."

"Darlinda did. Or maybe she never noticed any fuckin' lines to cross. It was like she always had to air out that body of hers. Like it was dirty laundry or something. An' if you put the merchandise out on the sale table enough times, some kleptomaniac's bound to do his number."

"You're being so heartless," says Annie.

"Hey, I've earned it, tax-free. Gettin' heartless without the guilt—that's the sweetest reward around. An' I got it coming."

Full Frontal Politics. When it came right down to it, Darlinda preferred a rubber hose to Dana. She used the short end attached to the spigot in the bathtub. With a flexible hose, complete with notches, she could control the speed and angle of friction. Though the porcelain was cold at first, she warmed up fast once she could spread herself open properly. Once her legs straddled the rim of the tub, she got her clitoris fully unsheathed. Rubbing right on it with the nozzle, she could have one orgasm after another. She didn't have to imagine anything. She could concentrate better with no one else there. For Darlinda, orgasm was applied mechanics. Or applied rubber.

She was pleased that they were clitoral orgasms. She'd done a lot of reading up on the matter, in all the feminist journals, and she was gratified to find that the research supported her own experience. There was no such thing as a vaginal orgasm. The concept was part of a male plot, aimed at making women feel inadequate, suppressing their true sexuality, and robbing them of their very own prick. Afterwards, she liked to examine her little prick. Sometimes, she looked at herself with a hand mirror. This was an exercise suggested in *Our Bodies, Our Selves*. It was so women would know what they really looked like down there, where outside met inside. Darlinda tried to love every fold—she put down the rubber hose then—to be awed by each hair and glint of mucus, to proclaim that this crevice, this pinkness is *me*.

Men didn't have a place like that! But she liked the places that men had, too. And Darlinda would avail herself of Dana's, punctually in the late afternoon, when their days off coincided. Darlinda enjoyed the closeness of Dana's bony rubbing, his nicotine-breathed need. But she could never come. She knew it was all right, that it was quite acceptable, statistically, for her to be unable to come with a man around.

However, she liked to keep trying. In bed, as elsewhere, Darlinda made a most conscious effort.

"That feels squishy . . . touch this button . . . a little higher . . . please a little softer . . . Darlinda is numb there . . . try stroking Darlinda like a teddy bear . . . don't touch under the arm . . . make every touch count . . . maybe lick the pinkness now . . . is Darlinda like cotton candy? . . . your beard scratches, you should trim it . . . let's play footsies! . . . not like that . . . I think we should arrive at a consensus about belly buttons . . . from behind, that's for slaves . . . not Darlinda . . . don't finish . . . not yet . . . stop . . . Darlinda needs a long, long time . . . now, faster . . ."

Sex with Darlinda was a bit like haggling over a rug with an Afghan trader. Still, Dana was proud of her efforts. And her coldness was his spur, another mountain to climb. He reached the peak during those moments when she actually stopped telling him about what she was "experiencing." Darlinda liked to nibble, pound her ankles against his buttocks, or just wriggle erratically when she was underneath. Sometimes, she would jump up in the middle of everything and do a breezy dance.

Once, while celebrating, Darlinda discovered that their fleshy negotiations were being observed by three or four children, aged no more than ten, crouching on the fire escape of the adjoining apartment house. Dana sprung up, covering himself with a blanket while he reached for the shades.

"No, no!" Darlinda stopped him from pulling them down. "We mustn't make them think it's for hiding! They have to know that it's natural!"

Dana went along, in amazement and out of exhibitionism. Sure, at Steffens he'd enjoyed strutting in the buff around the dorm when all the guys were stoned, but this was serious, civil code stuff. Your basic moral transgression. Darlinda was making him stand very still, at her side. They were models of male and female, facing outward. She opened the window and began class.

"Do you want to look? It's all right to want to look." The black kids had scattered at first, but now they took up peanut gallery posts, hiding their heads between hunched-up knees while they peeked. "That's better. Settle down in your seats. We want you to look. It's good to be curious. . . . Pay attention. Now who wants to point out the difference between a boy and a girl?"

None of them pointed, or blinked.

"Now this is it here. This is called a weenie . . ." She touched the corresponding part.

"A mighty whitey!" Dana could resist, though it was quickly losing its mightiness.

"Dan'! Darlinda says that's chauvinist! And you-know-what! . . . Darlinda says this is an average-sized male penis . . ."

"Thanks, sweetheart."

". . . and here, underneath all this nice fluffy hair, is where it goes. This is how a man and woman fit together. This is the vulva. Or is it the vagina? Dana, I'm mixed up. . . . Maybe I should go get *Our Bodies, Our Selves.*"

"Don't bother. You're close enough." So was the neighborhood gang, leaning forward to see through the glare into the dark bedroom.

"Yes. Dana's right. Words aren't important. We've got to show them so they'll understand."

"Understand yo' mamma!"

"Come on, show the world." Darlinda stretched out, head at the foot of the big bed, her insides spread before the windows.

"Now? All the way? In front of the little dudes?"

"Darlinda wants them to know where they came from!"

"Not from me—" But Dana was used to carrying out Darlinda's directives, especially in bed. He wasn't used to seeing Darlinda this stimulated.

"There, quickly! Can you? It's very wet. I mean, I'm very wet. Okay, good, but sideways. Sideways so they can follow the motion!"

Dana looked over to find that they were following very well.

"Isn't it pretty, kids? And it's not just for babies. No, women's bodies aren't just for babies. They're for touching. They're for pleasure."

Dana was pleased to find this out. He had been given to believe that pleasure was the province of the rubber hose. For once, he didn't hold back. This time, he strained to complete his assignment. He could tell that, for a change, Darlinda was eager for him to finish as quickly as he could. And he figured that he better get the job over in a hurry, considering all the statutes that the two of them were breaking.

6:15 p.m. Sex is the way we imitate machines.

"At least, Darlinda's finally had the worst happen. There's no small comfort in that."

"Is that all we've got to look forward to?" Annie interrogates. "Don't you think anything can happen to us past the age of twenty but the worst?"

"I'm just charting the graph, even if it goes downhill. I take measurements of our slide, like a surveyor."

"And what do you see along the way?"

"That the sun also sets."

Not even Annie can deny that, with the baroque symptoms of a California nightfall all around. Sliding down our highway shelf, we fall toward the cup of the San Francisco Bay: its rim of coastal ranges going ceramic cold, an orange twilight clinging to the horizon like some greasy residue.

"You can't fool me, Pep. You're no pessimist. You're such a raw-boned youth!"

I take refuge from Annie's fond recriminations in the freewayscape. What makes the asphalt so hard and us so soft? Are these twelve lanes speeding us along to anywhere but more interchanges, cities that are all lanes, sixty-four across? "ONLY . . . WAY . . . FREE . . ." go the warnings stencilled on the entry ramps, and I've stayed in the habit of reading them backwards. When I first glimpsed these concrete carpets, they seemed to have been poured just for me. "O vanguard of vanguards, thou vanguard who art ever another mile down the road . . ." Every bumper gleamed with infinite possibilities, but it turned out I was spellbound by the emptiness. Emptiness is what California does best. There's so much of it around and so much more in the planning stages. Here, where internal and external highways merge, the routes that twinkle with rubberized markers lead away from accountability and the track that's most clearly demarcated is the one to be traveled alone, at high speed, with the music going. Only way free! The slanting taillights ahead form one red piece snaking its ways through the dark. The race leads nowhere, the onrushing has become us. We're just another segment of one slithery, battery-powered serpent that's venomous, short-sighted, about to pounce.

"If you're expectin' straight lines," I hear, "then don't look at where you're goin', look at where you've been."

Dumbfounded, I await Dana's further elucidation.

"Determinism ain't all that bad, dude. Even if it takes us all downhill. It's just the time bomb of history goin' off."

"Poor, abused Marxism . . ." I can't help muttering.

"Poor, abused Marty!" Annie can't help herself, either. "Maybe you two philosophers can think about gettin' me to the right turnoff. Do you-all remember where Darlinda's house is at?"

Dana answers, "Do you-all remember when this guy was my number one?"

6:29 p.m. The only thing wrong with a perfect world is that it's got to be populated with perfect beings.

One Little Bed. Dana provided Martin with a dandy place of exile: his Isle of Elba near Wrigley Field. It was a ratty one-bedroom on the first floor of a brick-court apartment compound that could have doubled as a prison exercise yard. Or a mortared monastic cell—with all the comforts of a cloister except spirituality. Dana tried to brighten the place with poster homages to Godzilla and Durutti, the Partridge Family and the Haymarket anarchists. Neither he nor the super could do anything about the window in the front room that was stuck open all winter and let the fearsome Hawk winds blow through.

Though the apartment boasted a functioning kitchen, neither of them chanced it—blame the cold, the cockroaches or their previous years of k.p. duty. Half a block away was Dana's all-time favorite greasy spoon, where the two of them went on full board. Three breakfasts a day, give or take a few banana cream pies—and all the maternal waitress warmth that flagrant overtipping could garner. From their customary table with a view, they were entertained by the nightly *son et lumière* pageant of cop cars—in a profusion Oakland could never provide—doing battle with North Side arsonists. For the other kind of sustenance, there were Chicago's blues clubs ready to remind Martin that no matter how low-down, done-in and abandoned he felt, someone else had already been and gone lower. Misery seeking company in sixteen-bars beat—that was this town's curious consolement, giving Dana another civic boast to advance. Welcome to the world's best place in which to feel bad! Martin was in no position to question the claim.

One slight consideration had been overlooked. There was only a single bedroom in the apartment, with space for a double bed. But Dana thought he'd worked out the perfect arrangement. He would do his prole duty from midnight until eight at the printing plant, wake Martin so they could share an over-easy breakfast with "da people," then sleep from ten in the morning until he was blasted awake by the evening news. Give or take a few headlines. At night, the bed was all Martin's, while by day he could retire to the outer room, bundled in spare blankets, there to ponder what to do with his life. This sleeping in shifts might have worked just fine were it not for the fact that Martin had forgotten how to sleep.

If Lake Michigan had been a giant flotation mattress, he might have slept soundly just once that winter. If only there were primers on heartache, how-tos for Martin on how-to-be-solo! What a stupid sort of sorrow, divorced at twenty when he didn't even believe in marriage! Each night, Martin shivered and shook with the *tremens* of his withdrawal from Missy. Every part of his body was in revolt: internal organs straining to simulate the seven warning signals of cancer, bowels quivering from overdosage of java and Vienna red hots, enough cramping to suggest he was having a baby. Worse still, the mind that occupied this half-Pepto-Bismol body was rightfully seeking another home. Off it flew whenever Martin lay down, on a magic carpet ride, a delirious Baghdad shuttle above Chitown in which Martin was pilot and passenger both. Floating like static on Dana's clock radio permanently dialed to a deejay known as the All-Night Blues Man, Martin became the all-night invisible superblue Superman: loop-da-looping the Loop, swooping low over the whole city at once, seeing into every kitchen where God's chillun gnawed and snacked and knifed one another, moving horizontally through cross sections of apartment sets where lives were played to crushing finales, stopping to hump the moth-tattered pillows in each master bed, stuffing each yellowing commode with his own sopping paper, each wipe carrying a message written in ink that was fadeless, sewer-proof, leaving hairs that curled on themselves around the seat but meeting no one, not even Pervis Spann's next dedication, "Miss Odessa Heartbrain, who lies sick and mournful!" Fueled by the whole monster city's misspent teamster passions, the excess steam of ten zillion immigrant trysts, Martin was kept up in the air—teeth chattering, balls knocking, arms numb from gripping his flying sheets. He grew wings, his eyes were red warning blinkers, his cabin depressurized, and he got vertigo despite being horizontal, thankful to make it back down by five a.m., Voice of the Negro time, syncopated Standard Suffering Time.

Martin's white blues were a self-fulfilling prophecy. Social contacts: none, responsibilities: none, capabilities: zippo, physical functionings: temporarily impaired. House specialties: delirium and gastro-entreaties. In the dawn, Martin drew graphs of his life, but the results were all too vividly precipitous. The charts pointed straight down, down faster than the Dow-Jones on the day the White House went up in smoke, descending to the present. And how far would this trend extrapolate? Off the paper's edge and into some fourth dimension? All Martin's decisions, taken one at a time, had been terribly moral, driven by the highest ideals. Now the involvement he'd counted on to keep him uplifted was whispering, "Take a break. Be an individual for a while." But if decency and morality had gotten him to where he was now, what was going to guide him out?

Certainly not Dana, who didn't care to hear Martin's excuses for failing to relinquish his spot in the sack. Dana stuck doggedly to his fantasies of factory insurrection, his baloney lunch pail routine and unquestioning loyalty to the brave women who'd left them both behind. "Sympathy ain't what we need, clown," he'd advise. "What we need is some action!" Since they had only that one bed in which to conduct such action, it was just as well that neither of them could locate any willing partners. Instead, they shared forays to all-night bowling alleys and corner taverns where they hoisted Old Styles, while resorting to occasional old-style male grumbling. Or they watched interminable reruns of the Untouchables, then staged their own chases down sinister Capone alleys outside their door, anything to break the monotony of their untouchability.

Until the next daybreak when Dana would come home cranky, sore and wrist-beaten from a shift's worth of Sears catalogs flying past, only to find his disconsolate, insomniac roomie just coming in for a landing. The two of them ended up grappling on their springless mattress mounted like a bier. They each tried to hog the covers in their bedroom meat freezer which stank with Dana's cigarette breath, the recycled dampness of stiffened socks and unwashed work clothes on the floor in stolen milk cartons. But there wasn't enough square footage in this bed, not for this combination. The tug o' war went on until Dana's adenoid trills and worse, the unexpected sexy softness of feet pads touching, drove Martin forever from the ice palace.

6:43 p.m. Poverty can be chosen, certainly failure often is—but one cannot choose oppression, any more than one chooses to catch a disease.

Somewhere else, they would call Darlinda's building a tenement. In Oakland, it's an eight-unit historic. Named the Bella Vista Apartments because in Oakland a "bella vista" consists of a peek over one of the few stands of palm, actually a line of straw fans trying to circulate the smoggy miasma. On a good day, you could glimpse one shore of downtown Oakland's man-made lake, actually a dumping ground for stolen weapons. From the bay windows, the tenants can also look out on a park, actually a safe zone for heroin dealers. Just down the hill, actually part of one gradual coastal mountain, there's an elementary school, actually a holding cell for juveniles, around the block from a hospital, actually a disability claim center. Darlinda has remained here longer than any of us. She thrives where nothing is what it seems.

Not far from another pioneer's villa where the baby Gertrude Stein romped, Darlinda's building sits, ghettoized but austere, at the rise in its bottle-strewn half-acre plot. With gables, turrets and cupolas in peeling gray coat, it's the sort of place for which we should have a ticket. Darlinda's Mystery House, with ghosts of old prospectors in the pantry! With attractions like the world's highest ceilings and largest hypodermics! One sitting parlor turned into three kitchenettes! The real mystery is why the original inhabitants needed so much room back then and why today's need so little.

"Who wants to go first?"

We pause at the stone gate, vined with graffiti, which opens onto a long pathway of foreboding.

"Did anyone bring a flashlight?"

"Or a spare crucifix?"

"Buck up, kids." Dana leads the way, past a couple of lurid yellow succulents, huge brittle sentries at the front steps. Glass doors twice our size creak open. The lobby is dark, but Dana manages to locate the familiar name among wooden mail cubbyholes. Where's Igor to lead us to the master? We grope up a stairway that's creaky as in any Transylvanian castle—where's Vincent Price?—and sweeping as in an antebellum set—where's Bette Davis?—onto the landing where a series of doors have been tagged with brass plates, boardinghouse-style. The hall's carpeted with dingy runners that smell of mildew and meanness.

Still trusting enough to unlock before shouting an inquiry, still unfazed by her surroundings, Darlinda opens the door before we knock. Her head cranes out, a Jill-in-the-Box.

"Look at the faces!" She motions us into the mustiness. "Faces from another time. Darlinda needs to see those."

Perhaps eccentricity is the quickest route to get indomitable. Did I really think that eight years in the emergency room could change her?

Aside from the bruise that looks like a ballpoint leaked under both eyes, she's still waxen and flaxen, the human corn husk. Her button nose has elongated some, but the smile comes easier. It no longer unfolds like some dreadful admission.

"Old friends to sit with me! Darlinda feels chirpy!" She still resorts to speaking of herself in the third person, and still walks with proper care, waddling on inner arches and holding her backbone so upright it reminds me of a stack of gambling chips. Perhaps some lingering soreness exaggerates her bowlegged gait. In mismatched socks, drawstring pants, a sweatshirt over a leotard, she reminds me of Walter Brennan.

"Will you have some knitbone tea? It's working to knit up Darlinda already."

"We can all use a gallon of that," Annie tells her.

"Good. Now where can we sit?" There's not much choice, since a blue exercise mat fills much of the L-shaped main room. "On the floor, like old times!"

Darlinda's place is an exhibit hall of that time: one giraffe-necked reading lamp attached to an orange crate; one stuffed chair, with black shawl draped over both arms to hide the wear, set for meditation beside the bay windows. Every window ledge is crowded with avocado pits in mayonnaise jars, a few of them sprouting. The window panes are steamed up, perhaps permanently, from Darlinda's concocting of herbal brews. Her kitchen resembles a homeopathic drugstore, with jars of powders and roots labeled with Darlinda's crayoned script. Held to the refrigerator door by magnets is an old Cuban silk-screen that shows two women's faces on opposite sides of one head: the one European and applying lurid lipstick, the other Vietnamese and dripping Max Factor blood. All her posters show heroic women. The various cracks in the apartment's longest wall are covered by a hanging that depicts—in *batik* yet—the first international women's day. She's even kept a classic from the big bed house, where the women were represented by expanding circles, or maybe bubbles. The one exception is a portrait of Jack London, Oakland's finest, looking sufficiently macho at the helm of his South Seas clipper. Where the great writer's maxim begins, "Man must be a fiery orb . . . ," Darlinda's crossed out the first word and scratched in "Woman." Waiting for the tea, I study her women's calendar, on which she charts her number of hours dancing, her moods, her meetings, her periods; scratches off the weeks and months without a man.

"Let Darlinda look at Dana. Dana, where's your billy goat beard? I liked to tug at it." She tries now, but comes up with air. "Dana, why didn't you call and say hello before now?"

"I ain't big on nostalgia."

"Are you happy happy in love now?"

"Near enough."

"Oh, Dan'! That's dreamy!" This hardly seems the response authorized by her posters. "Who is she?"

"Polly, from Chicago." Dana's trying to keep mum.

"The girl at the end of the shopping list," I explain.

"Not a girl. A woman, I'm sure."

I haven't been corrected like that in a long time. Nor shared a cup of the dreadful stuff that steeps in Darlinda's gravel-colored pot.

"I wish I felt strong enough to come to the party," Darlinda calls from the stove. "Was it a happy party?"

"Until Spyros showed up."

"And Ayer."

"And Fire."

"Loads of surprise guests," I tell her.

"Just like there were in the big bed," Darlinda surprises me once again. "No group is alone, really. It's good to be reminded of that, no matter how." I don't recognize this Darlinda who admits, "It's better not to be alone."

"Unless you take in boarders like Clayton or Meryl . . ."

"Those names! Darlinda had almost forgotten." Joining us on the floor, she lets out a sigh that seems to have stages and a "Brave, sad Meryl!"

When Darlinda finds someone else sad, you know it's serious. When Darlinda calls someone else brave, you know that she's in big trouble.

"What's the word on her then? Did she finally waste away to spite the male persuasion?" The moment I've asked about Meryl, I remember that Darlinda may presently harbor some spite toward the male persuasion.

"Maybe Darlinda shouldn't say. She was a sister."

"She was a witch."

I expect to be scolded for using such a time-honored sobriquet, but Darlinda answers, "That's true. That came later, Marty. I went to her coven, just for a few months. We mixed a great potion of herbs from womanly gardens. We practiced black magic. Spoke in tongues. Darlinda couldn't do that very well, but I tried. We met in Redwood Park at midnight and danced in circles under a full moon. Darlinda could do that. I'm very lunar. Meryl was the most lunar. That's must be why she became a working girl."

Here, the use of the word "girl" is apparently called for—along with an explanation.

"It was after she went underground. She found a job in a massage parlor. For fund-raising. For the Movement!"

"Our Meryl? On her back? With men?"

"I only hope my sister gets plenty of rest," Darlinda continues. "Will you rest on the bed with me?"

This Darlinda I know. She's the one who carries the ceremonial pot and cups into her bedroom and onto the nightstand that's already loaded with Chinese horse pills, Ginseng infusions, Tiger Balm, chewable Vitamin C, cotton balls, brown-tinted vials. I know the thirty-two-year-old who climbs into the world's largest water bed, getting under the covers fully clothed, then bounces a bit and giggles at the waves she's made.

"If you want, you can bring in kitchen stools." But we don't need to, this bed is so big. "If you want, you can lie down with me."

Another bed. More rest. When do we wake up?

"We can't stay very long," says Dana.

"I know."

"We just wanted—"

"I know. You wanted to help Darlinda heal. Everyone is a healer when they want to be, did you know that?"

"What needs to be healed first?"

"Darlinda isn't sure," says Darlinda. "Maybe trust."

"Do you trust us?"

"I can trust you from before, from remembering. But I don't know why you stopped visiting me, why everyone stopped. Darlinda is very good by herself, but when she doesn't see anyone for a long time, that's when bad things happen."

"Do you want to talk about it?"

"If you ask me, I can't say no."

"You don't have to talk about it."

"When you ask, Darlinda can't say no."

6:57 p.m. The inability to say no and the inability to say yes. At a certain point, is there any difference?

Voice-Over (Darlinda): Darlinda can't say no, except to capitalism. Or so she tells us. Can't say no to the hospital grievance committee. It's an honor to be needed like that. It's not right to say no when asked to be chairperson of the nurses against nuclear waste. It seemed wrong to say no to being Leila Layne's volunteer secretary. She says yes to everyone until the second she lays down at night in her water bed. Slish, slosh in the bed. If she says yes enough, gets tired enough, she can almost say no to herself.

Just can't say no, she confesses, when the random suitor approaches. She would like children now, but also to frolic with the other sex. For a long time, she's wanted men who will play. But when one asks for more than play, and they usually ask it so suddenly, Darlinda gets flustered and the word no isn't there. She wakes to find herself awash in the water bed. Sometimes she has dreams about baby showers and eligible white men. But the only white men Darlinda meets are computer programmers and auto mechanics and they're built too small. They're so small they don't even give Darlinda yeast infections. Darlinda giggles. White men don't understand, have no politics, can't play.

The black men she meets . . . well, she can hardly say no to them, either. That would be improper. Undemocratic, Darlinda. And also you-know-what, you never-say-what. Besides, most of the men at the hospital are black and she gives in to the law of averages. Darlinda probably gives in too often. She doesn't have to be a slave to the law of averages! Most of them are orderlies. Most of them have nice smiles. Most of them have big cars. Most of them are married, too. Law of averages. Darlinda thinks there should be a law against married men. But most of them know how to play and they know how to dance. They like it when Darlinda lets go at the disco, shakes her hair around and does her turnout, her porcupine, her drunken armadillo. They don't make her feel ashamed. And they have politics down to their toenails. Can't say no to that, to staying angry and being on the outside. Could she say no?

Darlinda couldn't say no to the patient admitted for a superficial knife wound, especially when he told her that some dealer was trying to force him to shoot up. He says that he doesn't do that sort of thing. That he has a religion and that religion is called self-respect. Respect your body, he says, the body is the temple of the spirit, and Darlinda agrees with that. He runs twenty miles a day, he says, like he did when he was in the Marine Corps. He cusses out the Marine Corps and Darlinda likes that, too. And when he hears, on his second day in the main ward, that Darlinda is the union rep, he tells her that he's a good union man, too. He's in the steamfitters' local, he says, but he doesn't say anything about a job. One day, he and Darlinda overhear another patient calling a janitor "boy." He and Darlinda have a very productive discussion about why white people should never call black people boys, even if the black people are under eight years of age. This patient is smart. He's quite sweet, even with the scar near his right eye. He must be healthy, too. It takes him such a short time to heal. And Darlinda is sad when he's leaving. Darlinda catches herself, because she is not supposed to be sad about patients anymore. She is supposed to say no to them, that's a rule, but when he's discharged he asks her out and she can't say no.

Who cares about the scar? What if he's a patient? He can be special, like her. And he knows how to play. He's a very good dancer and he looks better when he's in a dark suit, not hospital issue. He takes her to an all-black disco where she's never been, where Darlinda gets a lot of stares, but she's careful to move to the music when *she* wishes, that makes it all right, and she doesn't care whether they like the way she moves or not or whether they're staring because she's tall and blonde and isn't wearing a bra. The patient doesn't try to showcase her with his friends and Darlinda likes that, too. He finds a quiet table and he acts like he doesn't care what anyone else thinks. Acts special gentle with Darlinda. And she can't say no when he asks for her phone number or when he calls her on his off day and suggests she come around to his place. She's a bit fearful, she's not dumb, this Darlinda isn't dumb at all, so she makes him meet her for coffee. A neutral place. Darlinda doesn't drink coffee. Neither does the patient. This time, he drinks too much. But it goes all right. He just plays around, flirting like in the hospital and making Darlinda feel special and tells her about his family in Arkansas and how he's gonna bring them up here but it sure as shit can take a long time—he still doesn't say how he gets his money—and he even listens to Darlinda telling about her family, though he gets up and starts pacing a little. They take a walk in Fruitvale Park, have some bar-b-que and he excuses himself at eleven, doesn't even try to kiss.

Then he vanishes, like so many of them. Gone with the wind, Darlinda. He isn't a patient anymore, maybe he's not in West Oakland anymore, and if that's true, Darlinda can only be happy for him. But Darlinda isn't happy. She wants to see him, and she gets upset when she finds herself almost wishing that the next ambulance would bring him, on a stretcher, back to her. Not in critical condition, just satisfactory. Just a little bruised, maybe. Darlinda doesn't like herself for wishing this. She makes herself forget about the patient, good Darlinda, until she gets a phone call from this lawyer. The patient—she barely recognizes his name—has been arrested on suspicion of burglary and attempted rape. Darlinda flinches when she hears the last word. The lawyer says it's a matter of mistaken identity. The description of the suspect always the same for every crime in Oakland: tall black male in warm-up suit, mid-twenties, with afro. And what about a scar over the right eye? Darlinda doesn't ask about that. She is thinking about the law of averages, while the lawyer tells Darlinda that the patient has listed her as a character reference. Would she be willing to testify on his behalf? Darlinda cannot say no.

She regrets saying yes on the day she has to wear a dress and even shave her legs and wait by herself on a bench outside the courtroom. She doesn't like the lawyer. He has bad posture and keeps trying to stroke her arm. He has to touch her for as long as he talks. But he doesn't prepare her. Darlinda knows that she's going to get flustered. Darlinda doesn't like to search for words in front of all those people. After she's led to the witness stand, she's happy to see that there aren't too many men at the trial. There is a judge, though. The judge looks a bit like her father. Darlinda wonders if judges ever judge while they're drunk. She starts out by telling a part of the truth: just because he's a black man doesn't mean he has to be guilty. If that's true, then everyone's guilty. The lawyers don't let Darlinda go on talking like that. They aren't interested in all that. So she tells them another part of the truth: that he was a good patient, that he's a good union man, that he has a nice smile, that he was always respectful with her. But the prosecutor, that meanie, makes Darlinda admit that she only knew the patient for several weeks. When the prosecutor asks Darlinda if she and the defendant ever had "carnal relations," she is surprised. The lawyer didn't tell her there would be any questions like that. Darlinda is disgusted. She thinks the law is disgusting. Boo, law. Yay, Darlinda! But the prosecutor is repeating carnal relations very slowly, so that she has to say something. Darlinda says that she really doesn't know what that means. Which is partly the truth, too. She wonders if they would ask her such a thing if the man on trial wasn't a black mid-twenties male. Darlinda is crying. She doesn't know why. She starts talking very fast, the way she used to do when she was unsure of what to think. Darlinda tells them it's her own beeswax, and she tells them that men and women should love who they want, even that women should love women, and Darlinda says that maybe the judge should say who he has carnal relations with. Darlinda is excused.

Once she's alone in the hallway, she realizes that she should have answered with a simple no. That would have helped the patient more. She also realizes that she did not look at him, even though he must have been there somewhere. In a way, Darlinda is glad she didn't see him. Or smell him. Or remember the way he danced. She isn't sure if she should have helped him, so maybe what she said is for the best. It's the truth, anyway, or part of it. She decides that she doesn't want to see him, even if he's innocent, even though that's not fair. But she doesn't want the patient put in jail either, even if he's guilty. She can't say yes to the idea of jails. She wonders why he had to rape someone, when she was around. The law of averages reminds her not to think such things. Darlinda leaves before she can find out about the verdict. Right afterward, her yeast infection acts up.

A few days later, which is yesterday, the patient calls Darlinda at the hospital. He wants to thank Darlinda. He is free. He is different, too. He doesn't sound healthy to Darlinda. Maybe from jail. She doesn't know until later that it's because he's drunk. He tells her that he's celebrating. He asks her to meet him after work at a bar on East Fourteenth. She knows it's a bar where she'll be the only white person. Darlinda looks around, trying to decide, and she is the only white person at work. Besides, Darlinda can't say no. And Darlinda drives there when she gets off her shift. It's true, she's the only white person in the bar, the only one with white shoes, too. There are only two men in there at this hour. The patient is one and the other is an older man whom Darlinda thinks she recognizes as a junkie whose stomach she helped to pump out. It's hard to recognize someone from their bile. So Darlinda still doesn't say no when this older man is introduced as the patient's main pal and buys her a drink. Just a beer, Darlinda says. She doesn't say no when she gets a whiff of the two of them, smelling way above legal alcohol level, the patient looking different from before, grinning too much, and the older man so beaten down. She drinks quickly, the way they do. They seem in a hurry, but Darlinda doesn't see how a no can slow them.

When they ask her if they can get out of this funky bar and take a six-pack over to her place, Darlinda doesn't say no. She doesn't know why she doesn't. She was so careful before, when there was so much less reason to be. In the liquor store, can't say no. In her car and down the pathway, can't say no. Up the stairs, while they're so quiet, there's no no there. Fiddling with the key while they talk bad, very bad, punch each other around, she can't say no. She doesn't think they'll do anything. She doesn't see why they should do anything. That's the law of averages. She's sitting cross-legged on her exercise mat and boiling tea, but meanwhile sipping on another beer because she can't say no. The two of them won't sit down, but lean against a far wall and makes jokes she can't hear, in their different language. Then they ask her if she goes with white men, too, and she has to say yes. She tells them that white or black, it doesn't matter. So you take on anyone? That's what they ask Darlinda. She doesn't say yes to that. When they ask her how come she isn't hitched, that's not a question to be answered with yes or no. When they ask if she always wears that leotard underneath for protection, she can't say yes or no. She can't say anything. She can say yes when they ask if she's got a water bed in the next room. Sexy water bed. The older man adds, "Don't you, bitch?" Darlinda tries to explain, very calmly and without being condescending, why some people take offense at the word "bitch." Why it's no different from the word "boy." But the patient doesn't want to talk about words. "Like to make waves on the water bed, bitch?" Darlinda thinks that the patient is just showing off for the friend, maybe it's an older brother, but the patient is so different. She keeps thinking it would be like it was before if only the older one would go away, even when the patient starts to unbutton his pants. Even when the older one says that times are tough, if you want good pussy, you gotta rape it.

Then Darlinda says no. Probably not loud enough. When the patient tells her to get on the water bed, she says no. When the two of them come at her, the patient's legs very black beneath his white underpants, when they push her down and drag her across the floor then up onto the bed, pinning her down, she's lost the chance to say no. When the patient falls on her with all his weight, Darlinda tries to remind him that the body is the temple of the spirit. Darlinda wishes she'd studied karate all these years, instead of spinal erectness.

Darlinda hollers. She doesn't like the sound, and she's almost happy when the patient makes her stop. She kicks her legs against his back. Darlinda's proud of how strong and long her legs are. She's doing all right until the older man hits her. Just once, across the eyes. He just watches after that. Darlinda has trouble opening her eyes—they smart so—but she can tell that the older one is too drugged for anything except watching. She does not hate the man, she does not hate either of them, but Darlinda has to concede that she hates what they're doing. She tries to relax. She tries to let go of the tensions within her and let gravity support her, let the bed take over, like Leila Layne always says. She does deep breathing. She thinks that it helps.

The patient doesn't take very long. She can feel it when he finishes, all the spurting, because she's so dry. It hurts because she's so dry and also because of her yeast infection. She wants to give the patient an infection. Usually, her vagina's like a sponge. Darlinda thinks that women can soak up anything. Now it's like gauze. It's a covering. Darlinda hears the older one ask the other one if it's juicy. The patient says that white pussy's never as juicy as it looks. He gets up to go. He asks Darlinda if she's gonna tell, asks it real sweet like he was in the beginning. Darlinda tries to answer but nothing comes out. She can't talk unless she can see and she thinks that's quite intriguing. She wants to find out why that's true. The older one answers the question for her. He says that she ain't the kind who's gonna tell. Darlinda doesn't know how he knows. The older one doesn't want to do anything except throw his empty beer can between Darlinda's legs before she can cover up. She hears them go.

Darlinda floats on her bed until she can see. In the meantime, she does stretches. She tests her flexibility. She is pleased with her flexibility and she wants to keep from getting too sore. She knows that the years of dancing will make the soreness go away more quickly than it would with someone else. Darlinda wishes she were someone else. It's not like she thought this could only happen to someone else. Darlinda knows about solidarity. She knows it means being very aware at all times that whatever happens to anyone else can happen to you or already has happened to you, in a way, just because it's happened to them. That's better. That's true. Afterward, Darlinda is calm. She drives herself down to the emergency room where she works. She can be calm because she always knew she'd be a patient someday. That's what made Darlinda so good with the others.

In the emergency room, Darlinda thinks America is an emergency room. They are all in the emergency room together and they can take care of each other. Even if they're the ones who hurt each other to begin with. She doesn't mind that she knows all the nurses and they know what happened. They understand that things like this happen to people like them, from time to time, and Darlinda is happy that they think she is one of them. The ones who take care. That's why she doesn't talk to the police. She can't turn to them, not now, not after so many vows about self-sufficiency, after the classes she's taken and the speeches she's heard. Besides, she's heard how the police treat women like her. Especially feminist women. The police will only say that she shouldn't have testified for him, that she should have said no from the start, but everyone can't be saying no to everyone else all the time and anyway, that's not the point. The point is she didn't say yes. She didn't. From the emergency room, Darlinda goes straight to the women's center for crisis counseling and they make her feel better about not having said yes. They get it right. They try to convince her to reveal the patient's name, but they don't try too hard. They respect her. They want her to heal.

Darlinda has to heal by saying no. Doesn't the body have to say no all the time? If the body didn't say no, it would get diseases. It would have all kinds of other beings living in it. So the body has to say no, even if it's not very kind. Got to say no. Time's up for saying yes to everyone but Darlinda. Have to say no to the union, or Darlinda has no time. Say no to the emergency room, quit tending to the others. Say no to Leila Layne, unless she stops supporting free labor and starts paying her staff. Darlinda thinks this now. She isn't afraid to think it. She is thinking a lot now. She even thinks that she must do nothing, the hardest thing for Darlinda to do.

She doesn't want to quit folk dancing at the women's center. Never wants to stop doing things with women, but all her old friends are married or gay or both and she doesn't know why they don't call her or like her or aren't really friends. Darlinda needs friends, not just people who need her to do something for them. None of them were friends to her, they were sisters, and sisters stop calling when the picket line's filled, the workshop's recessed. Darlinda gets angry when she thinks of this. Darlinda tries to relax then. She remembers the black ladies in the emergency room and they relax her. They were real friends. They laughed at her jokes, not because they were funny, but because they had to go through this thing together. Darlinda doesn't want to go near the emergency room, not ever. She daydreams about going back to the farm. She is considering whether it might be correct to go back home.

To drain the water bed. Only she doesn't want to give up. She doesn't want to unlearn a thing. And what if she's pregnant now? Each time Darlinda falls asleep now, she dreams that she's pregnant. She wouldn't mind that, even if it means someone else to take care of. Something you can't say no to. Darlinda needs to dream right now. She doesn't know if she needs a baby. In principle, she wants an abortion. But Darlinda has seen too many of those. And she thinks she could have the baby back home on the farm, though she doesn't really want a baby without a husband. She can't give Oakland many more years to find her a husband. She knows it's not really a good place for that. Husbands are not what Darlinda came to Oakland to find.

Scene Five (Target Practice): PAN down the gallery of an outdoor shooting range. CAMERA PAUSES in each stand until a Woman for Armed Revolt has raised a rented weapon, barrel straight to the lens.

MERYL: "Find the center, girls. Zero in on the heart of the artichoke!"

MISSY: "I love artichokes!"

MERYL: "Always green, like the Man's money. Always lots of leaves to peel away."

DARLINDA: "And what's the heart?"

MERYL: "Violence. That's all there is to this thistle."

MISSY: "Mer, you're a poet!"

MERYL: "An' I know it! . . . But casualties are what make the verbiage ring true."

MISSY: "Just ask Kissinger, huh?"

MERYL: "A perfect choice! You get more accurate when you've got a definite target in mind. Score me one flabby, male executive rump!"

MISSY: "Mer! You're too much!"

DARLINDA: "The hardest part, for Darlinda, is afterwards. You can get sore afterwards if you hold it too tight."

MISSY: "Like something else we know!"

MERYL: "That's enough of your sass. How about some r-e-s-p-e-c-t? A pinch of democratic centralism, girl."

MISSY: "Sorry, commander."

MERYL: "We're not playing with boys anymore. Now handle your pieces like you mean it."

MISSY: "Aim at my supervisor?"

MERYL: "That's it."

MISSY: "And our dear union Prez!"

DARLINDA: "When Darlinda looks down the sight, Darlinda sees racist paramedics. Oooh, how they smirk when they bring in another black hide! All shot up!"

MERYL: "Shoot back, avenger!"

MISSY: "Bang! There goes another chief-of-staff at the Pentagon!"

DARLINDA: "Now the girls are getting inspired! Darlinda's getting happy! Aiiee!"

MERYL: "Hey, keep it down. I didn't tell you, but this range is run by Birchers!"

MISSY: "No!"

MERYL: "Who else is taking up arms?"

DARLINDA: "We are!"

MISSY: "This one's for the landlords!"

MERYL: "This one's for the meat eaters!"

DARLINDA: "This one's for the rapists!"

MISSY (lowering her barrel): "This is horrible! I just can't think of anyone else!"

DARLINDA: "I know you can. You can do it."

MISSY: "Woe is me! I'm humiliated!"

MERYL: "Come on now, visualize. Think specific. Unforgiving."

MISSY: "I know there must be someone! When I look at the bull's-eye, I just go blank!"

MERYL: "Think close to home. Turn the pain around."

MISSY (squinting back out at the target): "I just don't know if my pain is enough."

7:31 p.m. And why is it so often said that pain leads to good? Either what we call pain isn't really pain, or what we call good isn't really good.

"Darlinda feels the healing," says Darlinda, looking neither too good nor too pained. "Funny how talking is medicine, too."

Big medicine. At her story's end, I have the feeling that she may burst into self-applause. "Good girl, Darlinda!" I expect her to shout admonitions at her one and only protagonist the way she used to shout up at movie heroines, "Don't do it, girl! That's it, go the other way! Yay! Alrighty! Escape the bad guys!"

Instead, she takes a swig of tea and confesses, "Maybe if I talk about it enough, I won't have to go home."

"That's where I'm headed," Dana says. "There comes a time to make peace with your demons."

"Very good, Dana." Darlinda's clinic is open and she's the admitting clerk once again. "Does this mean the Judge is speaking to you?"

"Nope, but he sends letters. Typed out by his secretary. The personal touch."

"Then he didn't write you out of his will?"

"How the fuck do I know? But if he ever actually did it, what else would he have to threaten me with? It's like nuclear deterrence. Mutual assured destruction, for father and son."

"Don't say that, Dana."

"Hey, I'm his last hope. Since I was the only kid who had the balls to rebel, who never sucked up to him, I'm the one who earned his respect. The perverse motherfucker." Now Dana hoists himself from the edge of the soft bed. He leans against the far wall and stares down at his shoe tips. "The old man's even arranged a homecoming present. He's landed me some obscure executive vice-presidency."

I don't say a word. I don't want to further ruffle Darlinda.

"Is it helping people, Dana?" She's still loyal to the old criteria.

"Fuck no. The old man has no access to that. It's help thyself to fifty grand a year and my own Wang terminal. A private office to wang in. Shuffling investments for Technotrex."

"What do they make, Dana?"

"Money. Or something worse."

"What will you do, Dana?"

"As little as I can get away with. It's just a stepping-stone position. For making contacts in Chicago business. Maybe I'll go into politics. Become a judge myself. A Republican, even. Or something worse."

"Will that make you feel like Dana?"

"Or something worse."

Darlinda's too preoccupied for registering much surprise or continuing the line of questioning—and I can't, not in this setting. Dana looks up now and I think I spot some chagrin for having used Darlinda as a shield for his latest admission. In his eyes, I see suitcases. In mine, Dana must see stop signs that he already knows how to run.

7:37 p.m. Faces are false advertising.

Give the Drummer Some. When Dana got laid off, he also got laid. That must have been what it meant to be a real worker. A pink slip was the only kind of vacation he got. So Dana left Martin to cover his shift in their bed and hopped a flight west: Chicago-Oakland, his industrial axis, the ends of the pendulum that swung between two kinds of obligation. This time, the California clan was going through more than one divorce. It was eerie to arrive at the airport without fanfare or greeter. Missy was working graveyard at Denny's, her first waitress gig, so she couldn't be there. He didn't want Darlinda to be there—or know he was here. Dana's feelings for her were embarrassingly final. He'd written Darlinda off the way people repudiate beliefs they've tried too hard to defend. He felt like a spy sneaking back into town. But that didn't stop him.

Dana preferred public trans. anyhow. He was with the masses all the way. So what if the proletariat takes the bus which makes too many stops? If it took three transfers for him to get to the all-night java stop? Dana was on vacay, no rush. The long ride made it all the more sweet when he spotted Missy through the full-length booth windows. She was all in white, a nurse doing her rounds of refill, soothing the boys. Ah, the social function of waitresses! Missy's hair up in a bun, topped with a paper crown that looked like a used coffee filter. Her hygienic support hose couldn't mask those good legs. The pink apron only accentuated her rump. Dana had to give Martin credit: that sexist dog sure knew how to pick 'em. But that wasn't going to stop him.

Dana slid into her section feeling like another bakery driver, another pimp, another regular. Before she noticed Dana, he realized that Missy had found her calling. It was obvious—like watching Picasso make his first doodle. She looked so bloody cheerful, trotting about at four a.m. in this fluorescent oasis with its tentlike booths of orange Naugahyde. Missy wasn't born to play ball like her Say Hey Kid. Born to wait tables. Nothing could stop her.

She set down the laminated accordion of a menu before examining the customer. Then came Missy's twinkling agony of surprise—and an attempt to catch up on gossip interrupted by a rush for more orders, cradling six plates to an arm as she passed by, winking at the old-timers who were giving it to their straight-arrow gal for comporting with a bearded wildman. Could Dana stay up 'til she got off at six? Why not? Was he gonna call Darlinda? What for? Did he want to stay at the W.A.R. house? What the fuck? Dana hadn't banked on such an invitation. But if any man could penetrate their hideaway, it had to be him. It was time to cash in on all those brownie points, Dana decided. There comes a time when even nonsexists cash in. And no lady warriors could stop him.

When he got to the front door of the gynocottage, Dana was quaking in his steel-toes. He identified Meryl's beady eye in the safety peeper. She took her time looking him up and down. "It's just Dan'. He's cool, Meryl. He's too cool, right?" There was still some hesitation on the other side before the unlatching. Inside at last, Meryl led him to the broken-down couch as if she didn't know him. Since he'd seen her, she'd lost weight—though he didn't realize she had any to lose. Meryl looked like some concentration camp outpatient, an experiment on herself. She was so anorexic that even her dog wouldn't eat. She didn't stop to chat.

Dana made that couch his h.q. for the next week. He didn't have to worry about his snoring because the others were all at their assigned posts during the day, except Missy who was also sleeping it off. During house meetings, he'd take a discreet stroll, grab a meal at Chuck's Chuckburgers or Taco Pup. Missy would supplement his diet later. The meetings were supposed to be classified, but Missy admitted to Dana that they were learning to make incendiary devices. Missy wasn't sure just why. She felt like she was the only one in the house who wasn't making progress. It was tough to organize waitresses citywide, tough enough to walk the floor all night. And, she had to admit, she was sneaking out to see this really sweet black truck driver, once or twice a week. The others disapproved. Everyone said that she was a white woman taking a black man out of his community. That she was luring him away from where he was needed. Missy agreed. They were so right. But that didn't stop her.

Still, the house gave Missy a sense of purpose. And she'd made a good friend in Eve Huberman, another phone operator, once a potter and not so doctrinaire. Dana liked Eve too. She was the only one of the bunch who bothered to ask where he'd dropped in from, what he thought about the Symbionese Liberation Army, if he got high. She was a stocky Jewish kid who dressed like a sharp black lady. She was clearly in over her head, but toughing it out. And she had the widest, roundest tits Dana had ever seen. He couldn't help looking at those. He couldn't help lusting after anything that moved. That was Dana's best-kept secret. Only Martin knew, though Dana liked to make his old pal feel like he had it worse. But Dana was getting less abashed. Back in Chicago, he'd begun to see a therapist—so he could make his peace with the old man—and they'd just passed that point in the process where the Oedipal question had been delicately shoved into view. Dana shocked his shrink by admitting first off that, yeah, he wanted to fuck his mother. Why not? If he couldn't just spill it to his shrink, then what was he paying the cocksucker for? Dana had gotten so good at holding back that he knew just when to let go. The secret of his charm rested in an uncanny sense of knowing when to get unambiguous. One evening, with Eve at the other end of the couch, Dana let it rip. She wasn't his mom, but he said it anyhow. Eve, I'd like to fuck you. Thus spake Dana. Right inside the belly of the W.A.R. monster. The politburo wasn't around to stop them.

Eve, whom Missy had grouped with the Lesbians, readily agreed. No preliminaries, no passion. It was like taking a voice vote on a position paper. Dana started to imagine some positions. Now Eve proposed an amendment: Missy had to be in bed with them, too. She and Missy had already made it, didn't he know? Dana pretended to take it in stride. This was getting better by the minute: Eve would do all the work and he'd bag Missy, too. She made the invite when Missy got back from shopping. Dana lay back on the couch, looking casual but cringing inside, wondering if Missy would smack him. Instead, she pointed out matter-of-factly that neither of them were using birth control anymore. Everyone in the house had made a vow to toss away such facilitators of male sexual dominance. So it was off to the drugstore in Eve's torn-up Chevy, giggling all the way, like they were back in high school. Dana stood at the counter before some bald chemist, ordering a pint of Stolichnaya and a dozen Trojans. He was thinking big. He was off on another one of his power trips, but there was no reason to get conservative, not now, not even if the girls waiting for him happened to comprise two-sevenths of the Women for Armed Revolt. Don't stop now.

They did it in Eve's bed. This made Dana feel a little less like he was trampling on the memory of Martin. The three of them got undressed and lay there for the longest time atop the covers, bestowing compliments upon one another's parts. Missy told Dana how she admired his square fingers, bony chest. Dana told Eve all she'd ever want to know about her tits, though he had to use all these ridiculously formal words in place of tits. Eve told Missy how she loved to cup her hands around Missy's buttocks. Dana smoked a Marlboro while the two of them straddled each other. Eve was having paroxysms within thirty seconds; Missy was obliging. She winked her waitress wink at Dana. They had to wait their turn. Eve offered her chest to Dana. One gobble at it and he was having to hold back shooting off. It really felt like fucking his mother, or what he thought it would feel like. When he and Missy got down to it, he *knew* he was fucking his mother. Hadn't she and Martin always taken care of him like an orphan, coddled him through his exile? Wasn't he always fated to be the third man? Trying to hold himself back, he kept hearing the refrain of that old James Brown gut-buster, "Give the drummer some." Yeah, give the backup boys, the rhythm-makers, the stick-wielders their due. Ugh. Dana managed a real James Brown ugh. He knew that Martin would call him a dog going after the available bone. He could hear Marty advancing such an analysis. But words weren't about to stop him.

What stopped them finally was Darlinda. She called Missy to see how the collective was going. Though Darlinda was a sympathizer, and took target practice with them, she hadn't been invited into the house. Among the liberated, too, there were insiders and outsiders. Darlinda was alone, working hard, dancing hard. But Missy didn't conceal anything from her sister, though concealment was one of her specialties. She told Darlinda that Dana was there and what Dana had done. She didn't expect Darlinda to get so upset. She didn't realize Darlinda still cared. After all, it was Darlinda who'd practically pushed Dana out.

Still, it wasn't surprising: men got over these things more easily. Even good Dana, who didn't get angry when he heard Missy had snitched. He realized this was her way of terminating the experiment. The next day, Dana flew back—just in time to get recalled at the plant. And Dana knew how to tell Martin what he wanted to hear: about the paranoia, the Sapphism and the sophistry and the bomb-making, about how thoroughly he'd disowned Darlinda. He left out the part about the drummer. Dana stopped there.

7:46 p.m. Sex is mostly waiting around for sex.

The Smallest Social Unit. For the last time, Missy sent Darlinda in her place. Into the spare room of the Pearl crib, where they were all staying on that final trip to Chicago, came the volunteer mop-up squad.

"Time to play, Pep," she announced, so her sister could have time to pack up. Darlinda didn't mind that she had to tend one more wounded man. She could be magnanimous now. Soon, she'd be the only one left to tend to Missy. And go on calling Dana her boyfriend, too.

Though it was nearly midnight, Darlinda proposed a walk down to Lake Michigan. Martin knew this was some kind of ruse, but went along rather than stick around for another of Missy's surprises. It was a quick jaunt down to the nearest cement beach, pummeled with inky thrusts that seemed to be machine-generated.

"I can't see the water." Martin contemplated an accidental drowning.

"You need to get more carotene, Pep. Eat lots of rabbit food, including the stalks. Do you think you-know-what has anything to do with night-blindness?" This was Darlinda's way of admitting to the other hazards of the place. "I mean, their faces are darker. Maybe that's why we can't understand. Our optic muscles are lazy."

So was Martin and he wanted to sleep. Was this Darlinda's idea of a stall? She had taken her shoes off and was merrily swishing her toes in a tide rough enough to chew the city's battlements. She didn't seem to notice that she was the only one playing. If she fell in, he was not going after her. He could plead lack of carotene.

"Can't Marty unloosen? I think Marty needs a massage."

"In the park?"

"Upstairs."

Darlinda would savor her victory by soothing Martin's loss. So come to bed, Darlinda—with sweet dreams of carrot juice by the jug! Don't turn on the lights that would reveal the place in the bed where Missy would no longer be sleeping. Just "strip down to nothing," Nurse Darlinda ordered. "Otherwise, it doesn't work."

She stayed clothed, sat astride his buttocks and got busy. She had nice fingers. They were the least ambivalent part of her. When it came to exposed flesh, Darlinda had no hesitation, did not observe any territorial limits. Unlike Martin, she didn't give a hoot for the visual. The way it looked to Darlinda's eyes had nothing to do with the way it felt to Darlinda's fingers. She played: crinkling his spine, pinching him as though she were putting a rivet into each vertebra. This was her finest trick, leaving a trail of chills. It made Martin feel like his nervous system had gotten a dusting.

"Relaxed now?"

Darlinda reminded him that touch was democratic. It could feel good from anybody.

"Let me do you."

"Alright, I'll just take off my top."

Why the sudden modesty? After so much brazenness, this was a real invitation.

Martin figured that if he tried hard enough to ignore the look of Darlinda's mole-specked expanse, the rest would follow. Actually, her back wasn't bad. By itself, it had an exaggerated curve he couldn't help admiring. He kneeled beside her at first, but that turned everything sideways, so he climbed aboard Darlinda as she'd done to him. Martin was going for a ride on that horsey he'd watched neighing and bucking for so long. He leaned down on her hard.

"My back is stretchy tonight." Stretchy or not, he liked it. He was shocked. He was stimulated. He particularly enjoyed the way he was sitting on her, asshole to asshole. Darlinda's lesson was reinforced, the lesson of skin. Anyone could feel good, on any given day. With eyes closed, anyhow. Sex wouldn't be what he'd lack without Missy. Sex was the easiest thing to replace. Then what was making him feel so incomplete?

From birth, Martin had been taught that "the smallest social unit is two." Brecht said that and Brecht was his parents' idol—his parents who'd led him to believe that he'd never be left alone. Martin was convinced that there was no such thing as a moral or immoral man, taken all by himself. In the singular, uninfluenced and unable to influence, there was hardly a man at all. Now that he was going to be alone, how would he judge himself? And what had happened to units larger than two? What about the plan for threes and fours? One plus one equaled nothing but sorrow.

She must have felt his erection by now. Announcing the completion of his massage, Martin leaned down and swept Darlinda's burnished hair from her neck, then kissed the nape. It was a kiss of thanks, not seduction. But Darlinda didn't refuse. She turned over so she could peck him back. She kissed like a sparrow grabbing for bird food kernels, eventually finding Martin's mouth. She offered frantic little buds of kiss, bursting. Her kisses were forceful and tentative at the same time. They sounded like sugar snaps.

Martin was fully atop her. Darlinda's indented, hair-sprouting nipples, that usually made him cringe, her Formica table of a tummy felt as good to him as Missy's, as anyone's.

"We shouldn't," Darlinda informed him calmly.

"We aren't," Martin answered. Not quite yet.

Yet she asked, "Do you want Darlinda to take off her pants?"

"Yes."

How many times had they rubbed together accidently in the big bed? And recoiled from one another when Darlinda tried to snuggle up against Missy? On this one occasion, limb fit limb. Martin's hands grazed, then explored, Darlinda's concave nipples. His erection was coaxed on by the rise and fall of her breathing, the tickle on his groin from the ends of her two-tufted *mons*. Ashamed, he vowed not to enter. He didn't need to—he already knew Darlinda inside and out and they were the same. But he went on kissing her, slowing their nibbling into a slobber.

"You're helping to remind me that touch is nice." This was about as romantic as he could get.

"Darlinda's glad." She sounded vaguely aghast. "Do you want to listen to my heart?"

Martin took up her offer, pressing his head against her collarbone so that he could hide his face while he came against her leg. He shut his eyes and searched for her heart. She'd already found his.

"It's beating so fast! . . . Darlinda can feel it. Darlinda is honored . . . Your little drum thumping . . . Your heart is beating sooooooo fast!"

7:49 p.m. Hardly shocking that they got around to sleeping with one another. Or that it brought no self-improvement.

"Darlinda's sleepy-snoozy now."

"Tired of company, I'll bet."

"No, Dana. Positively no. How can Darlinda get tired of someone I see once in eight years?"

"That's more than enough."

"Not for me, Dana. I miss you." And Darlinda, used to lack of reciprocity, continues without the encouragement of a similar admission from Dana. "I miss Kickapoo Creek. I miss our apartment in Uptown, especially the winos on our front stoop. I miss Chicago thunderstorms."

"Apocalyptic, babe. Hot 'n' nasty like noplace."

"That was a summerfest."

"The sunshine of our love, babe." Dana leans down and kisses Darlinda on the forehead.

Before we're out the door, she's slipped beneath the covers, swallowed up in one gurgle by the water bed.

7:51 p.m. The point, after all, isn't to find the sturdiest lifeline, but to quit feeling as though one is drowning.

One Huge Bed. How lonesome Darlinda had looked! The last one, stranded amidst three sets of mattresses, mismatched top sheets, J. C. Penney blankets, wilted comforters, and six overburdened pillows! More room for Darlinda to canter, stretch, unlimber! Or so she'd joked. But she began engineering crises to gain attention. She burned her knee on the gas heater, stubbed her toe on a table leg, tried anything to provoke injury so that she could crawl in with Missy and Martin and demand soothing. Darlinda hurts! Darlinda needs a cuddle! She couldn't keep herself from trying to get between this couple. She couldn't stay put. Even Darlinda had to get out of the big bed to get what she needed.

7:53 p.m. In the vanguard of the Movement, no movement; in the forefront of the counterculture, no culture; at the cusp of the love generation, no love.

Voice-Over (Martin, 2). Leaving Chicago on the coldest day of the year, on a day when the whole sub-Arctic's got its window stuck open. Even the Loopster people seem to move quicker in this twenty-below, with that wind-chill numero they loved to brag about as though they could take credit for all the hardship and shiver power. Dana's brusque on good-byes and words freeze in our mouths anyhow. As usual, he takes pride in hauling my valise on his shoulders through the station and onto my bus. Good stevedore, troubadour, paramour of the long-shore! Glad to see me go, so he gets bed, blues and brawniness to himself. The duffel he carries is new. Missy took our old one and this is my first real moving man outfit. Very moving. A toilet kit and even contraception, in case of wayward encounters on the turnpike. Dig ya later, clown! Gone in his White Sox cap, a lamb off to a nonunionized slaughter. Until that time! Then Dana hurries off, bustin' his fanny to make it to the uprising that's nowhere in sight. Just lookin' for the struggle, as he would say. But he can't see me anymore.

Last call and I'm skittering about with caked mustache on frostee-creamee sidewalks, astonished by the clear moment of light winter gives, revealing every blot on my hands—old friends, I should know you better than I do! Time to climb aboard. Leaving Chitown by bus: over the skyway, the Mare's metal prosthetic arm thrusting itself out of the Southerly Side granting everybody one last over-the-shoulder look back to reset the postcard romantic mold one's supposed to cart off to less prosperous burgs, to inspire final stirring fund-raiser sentences that are actually relieved exhalations at getting out of the mills and muck at last: So long, world's busiest, world's heaviest, world's tallest, most productive, most killingest! Chicago, grid-and-coordinate brick toenail dipping itself daintily into the lake, testing the waters of self-expression! Chicago, we sing to thee and hope we hear ourselves!

If the ice caps are melting someplace, then this day will firm them up quick. I'm waiting to see a glacier rumble through this land, wiping out sales tax and other minor state-line distinctions. There's nothing prominent, tender or tolerant at this end of the Indiana Tollway, "Main Street of the Midwest." Passing land as neutral as God knows how to make it. No, I wouldn't want to eat anything grown on these farms. Sheet cold in the bus and the only people there have black faces. White people who join them are just poor trash frightened of flying, of privilege, frightened on principle. Only seat I can get is right up against the toilet, riveted crapper door banging open on the curves, bellowing out an icicled camphor smell, yellowing wicks excreting a deodorant more cloying than piss. The engine whines beneath me, complaining of schedules to be met. The passengers seem in no hurry. They sit in their overcoats like me, though mine's furrier and higher priced, and chat and laugh those loud signature laughs the way they always seem to do.

How silent America would be without these forgiving, distinctive, wise trumpeted notes of laughter! And how can they actually be getting jolly in this moving Frigidaire? There'll be one stop for hot chocolate in a foil pouch, maybe, but at least the burden of this landscape's been lifted by an early dark. Someone heads up to the fatherly man at the wheel and whatayaknow, golly gee, he tells anyone who cares to hear, I think you folks is right, the heat in this baby ain't working after all, no sir there ain't none whatsoever. No news to the backseat boys. Someone is singing to get warm, "My baby, she changed that lock on my front do', My rusty ol' key, it don't fit there no mo' . . ." I can't raise my voice to join him, but at least I know that never again will I sit back fat and fully fed assuring myself about the poor: they have what they want and what they don't have they don't know they want. I am one of them surely, I'm legit, have to be by now. And someone's opened up a "half-pint thang" of cheap gin. We can sniff it, overtaking the camphor, a scent all souring and warming us already. An old gent in a feathered fedora moving upright at seventy miles per through the night turns out to be the unguilty party with brown paper bag and he begins passing it 'round. The almost-emptied Gordon's-in-excelsis comes to me and I sip from it. I sip nervously, sloppily, masterfully, eagerly, blessedly, unrepentantly, noisily, nastily, expectantly, gratefully, puckeringly, lengthily, glancingly, elegantly, coolly, singularly, gurglingly, tonguingly, bloodily, repeatedly, peacefully, greedily, respectfully, deftly, exhaustively. So leave me here near Ypsilanti—so lonesome, so lonesome, so free at last! Isn't it swell? The crowd is my lover, and I have learned to lay with it, with the bus riders so dark and cold, cheap perfume. I can get along without anybody, without any one body. It had to be so much less complicated to just love everyone.

7:53 p.m. Miserable in the most fashionable places, fashionable in the most miserable places.

The First Woman I Ever Exploited. Martin sought the comfort of his family, but found it was no longer there. His mother had banished his father just like Missy had banished him.

Seated in a Barcelona chair beside the Saarinen dining table below the Ben Shahn lithograph in the sunken living room of the apartment on Riverside Drive, his mother soliloquized, "It's not going to be easy getting used to an empty bed after thirty years. There's no meaning in life unless it's shared."

She was telling him? Never had two people wanted less to be on their own, had two people made such a religion of attachment—and never had two people so lacked the adaptability to make it possible. Now mother and son were stuck together, alone. They became partners in a solitude neither believed was of their own choosing.

"I tell you, men are monstrous! Remember Brecht? 'Why be a man when you can be success?' "

Martin remembered, but he wasn't sure where that left him. His mother apparently considered him the sole male exception, not because she'd noticed how many of her traits he'd inherited but because she'd never seen him realistically. He had been the most gifted little boy in the world, and only occasionally an ogre who sided with his father on such crucial questions as whether or not the lamb roast was dry. From his mother, he'd learned to idealize and to cringe at the prospect of being idealized. He knew little about the emotional compromises in between. Maybe that was why Martin had been urging his mother to walk out the door. He'd been her ally ever since he'd first realized that other mommies and daddies didn't wrangle that way. After all the years of raging against Doctor Pepper's inaccessibility and know-it-all-ism, Mrs. Pepper was finally taking the big step. Martin found himself more proud of his mother in flight than he'd ever been when she was trying to be the perfect wife. By encouraging her independence, he encouraged his own. But wasn't that what he'd tried with Missy? And did he really want his mother to go quite so far?

"Our generation has so much to learn from women like Missy," Mrs. Pepper suggested over a breakfast of bagels and lox. "I want to thank you, my darling, for bringing such a courageous, such a conscientious girl into all our lives."

At the moment, Martin wasn't sure it had been that good an idea.

"You know what Missy did?" Martin nodded. He knew, but his mother didn't. If he told her now about the ways her favorite feminist had chosen to escape her favorite son, Mrs. Pepper probably would have labeled it disinformation. "Missy sent back that gorgeous dress your father bought her at Saks. She wrote that she didn't feel she ought to keep it. That women shouldn't let themselves be bought off! And she's so right! That dress was another piece of your old man's foolishness. It wasn't appropriate for Missy, not a young person's style at all. He should have saved his gesture for someone a little older."

Martin knew who she meant. All Mrs. Pepper wanted was for Doctor Pepper to say "yes" to her. For America to say "yes," just once in a while. Martin's mother had long blamed Martin's father for all the things that she had not become. Especially, she felt, he had not properly encouraged her to remain an actress. The unspoken accusation was that, instead, he had forced her to give birth to Martin—another charge which Martin greeted with some ambivalence. Still, to him, and undoubtedly to his father, Mrs. Pepper remained the fiery, redheaded agitprop ingenue who first took the stage of the Empire Burlesque House to harangue the audience about the evils of capitalism—only to be yanked off with the proverbial hook. And she had remained part of the theatre through her casting agency, saw the world through theatrical eyes that made all her battles curtain-risers. She was a sworn enemy of Broadway's commercialism. Each day, she jousted over the telephone with all manner of hacks, *poseurs*, phonies, mutilators of the true art. She had a telephone voice the way some people had a stage voice—husky, emotive, perfectly enunciated—and Martin knew that when he heard that voice, his mother was being true to herself and her mission. Though she liked to jab at Doctor Pepper for failing to earn enough to take them to Europe each summer, she herself scorned big money, chose a proud failure. Now that the two of them were thrown together, Martin began to find out how exhausting failure could be.

Their first evenings together, she brought out an old scrapbook that Martin had never seen. In her husband's absence, she'd been organizing these archives to soothe herself. Mrs. Pepper worked like she could have alphabetized the world out of its misery. Now she showed Martin a prophetic snapshot of his father at sixteen, a curly-haired poet in the family used car lot, holding a "For Sale" sign in one hand and a red flag in the other.

"Your father was so committed then, so adventurous! To think of what he's become! What we've become!"

"Please, Mom . . ."

Martin got his mother to put her pictures away and tried to cheer her with outings to the theatre. Films were out of the question, since she cried at every one even under ordinary conditions. She was the one who'd introduced him to the purgative wonders of *Umberto D.!* But nothing troubled Martin's mother more than a poor production. She seemed to take them as a personal affront. Yet she doggedly supported struggling basement repertory companies where Yale drama majors overemoted their way through Strindberg and Wedekind.

"Why be a tragedy when you can be a farce?" Martin was his mother's favorite critic. In the aftermath of all that had happened, he feared that she might be the only woman who would ever find him man enough. And this fear turned to terror when, introducing Martin to the director on one of her obligatory dressing room visits, Mrs. Pepper mispoke, "I'd like you to meet my husband . . ."

Martin began to wish that his father would return to take up the job—and quit sulking at the Kinsey Institute. Martin booked a ticket back to California—but not before his mother could stage a farewell party. The guests turned out to be two actresses. They were some years older than Martin, but just within his range of fascination. For the sake of their profession and their budgets, his mother's two clients were elegantly flightly, fashionably scrawny. They had watery brown eyes and spoke in breathy stage whispers, as theatrical people did. They touched Martin gently on the forearm to let him know they were listening. Like most everyone else associated with his mother, the actresses were too good to be anything but failures. As far as Martin was concerned, they were successful as women.

The four of them ate Swedish meatballs on the Saarinen table. During and after the meal, they talked with great sincerity about almost nothing. When Martin spoke, his mother cleared the way for his words, practically announcing him. She prompted him to show off his knowledge of various European capitals, with inquiries about hotels "we" had stayed at, museums "we" had savored—as if they had been the couple doing the touring, and his father had been twelve years old. Ordinarily, Martin cringed when his mother did this, but he found it pointless to evade the actresses' attentions when they were so easy to get. Practicing their emotional range, from light amusement all the way to innocent awe, the two women conspired with Mrs. Pepper to spoil Martin. He knew that he was getting preferential treatment because he had a penis—but it had been so long since he had that he took it.

It wasn't until his mother instructed Martin to escort the actresses to a taxi that he realized she was trying to make a match. In spite of everything, Mrs. Pepper's fervent desire was to see Martin settled happily into the niche from which she'd so long been trying to escape. She often spoke of "the woman you're going to marry," usually after admonitions aimed at making him develop more hygienic habits. Apparently, that woman now had to be a feminist, and, in her daydreams, Mrs. Pepper made no provisions for her son's supposed resemblance to his mysogynist father. Nothing got in the way of her romanticism. But did Mrs. Pepper want her son to love women to prove he loved her? And what did she expect him to do with two at a time? In her living room?

Usually, Martin had no trouble resisting his mother's introductions. Now he was in a weakened condition. Waltzing step for step down the block, Martin couldn't help wrapping his arm around both women's waists. He drooped his head onto their shoulders in turn, and they returned the gesture. By the time he reached West End Avenue, he was in love. Only after he'd put them in a cab and called out for their phone numbers, did their giggles tell Martin that, like his mother, they might only be acting. He couldn't decide whether to boo or applaud.

7:57 p.m. But then, the women's movement was not made for men.

No one speaks until we're in a better neighborhood.

"That was a bell-ringer, Pep. An exhale for the ages."

"Sighing is one of my few innate talents."

"It comes easy when so much happens in a day."

"So much deteriorates."

"He's hopeless," Annie tells Dana.

"He's got too much invested in being the keeper of group purity," Dana answers from the back.

"I quit, then. I've sure done a shitty job."

"Sit on it and swivel."

"I'd rather do that than sit in some boardroom."

"Can't you just appreciate Dana for what he *is* and not for what he does?" Annie asks.

"I guess I'm one of that dying breed which doesn't admit a difference."

"A breed that's dying for good reason."

Maybe so, but I've got to make one last stab. "Don't take that job."

"Gimme something better to do," Dana answers timidly.

"Make it yourself."

"How? I got no abiding passion, like you got for the movies. Unless it's for digging up first editions of French historical screeds. I got no calling, except to serve."

"Then serve some good cause."

"I would, if the cause had a personnel office, a training program, a set of company rules, a dental plan."

"I'm relieved to hear that."

"Gimme some credit, sport. Recognize that I'm just as stubborn as you are."

"Just as perverse. I'll buy that."

"And so much more, head! Don't you realize that you're a hard act to follow? You taught me to accept nothing less than the abolition of Western civ., progress, linear time. Everything else is so fucking reformist that it makes me want to quit before I've even begun trying."

"Is that a compliment?"

"Marty, don't let that isolation of yours get retroactive. Don't rub yourself out of the old photographs. It's like you don't really think anyone's listenin', for all the words you churn out. Man, I used to take every sentence to heart."

"So why did I fall off your pedestal?"

"You didn't fall off, Missy tore you down. You got hurt once in your life, the same way a billion guys get hurt, except you've refused to recover."

"All men are not created equal."

"Bull-pucky. In some arenas, when aesthetic questions are on the line, you're one of the most sure-footed cats on the planet."

"It's odd. I've always been enough of a man in the eyes of other men. Plenty enough. But with women . . ."

"You're always blamin' everything on those penisless ones. . . ."

"And you're defending them, you guilty-ass motherfucker. Big Sister is still watching you!"

"An' she's still right. I won't let you suck me into an us against them."

"Don't worry. It looks like I never will."

While Annie waits for us, I cling to his torso, my forehead poked by rib ends.

"So long, Gypsy."

8:01 p.m. Superb at good-byes and hellos, spectacular in transit.

Dana's Poem

"AWAITING TRIAL"

O miserable Fortuna night!
How is it you do not 'low me sleep?
Too dark, I know
quiet save the sound
of lovers turning close by my head

Nowhere to go
No peace for me
No late shift waitress smile
Instead I crouch low on cowboy sidewalk
Maneuvering to catch the glow of a street lamp
The soft pain of tears out of sight
A soft hand miles from my cheek

On the steps of justice we cry out
to be heard by those we fear most
The sea of brown shirts surrounds us quickly
The shiny bracelets subdue us and the
iron grate between me and the enemy screams

Imprisoned
by the air we sought to breathe
the life we tried to lead
Away we went round
flaming corners
Then more colors brown all of them alive
all of us dead in their hands

This time it's for real
And this time there will be no answer
even from my own heart

Yes, Pep, we lost this one
the first big game in our series
I know because the pig
is grunting my name again
Tell me
which trip will end
in the naked room
of blinding light and billy club and my blood?

Case History. Mr. Dana P., henceforth referred to as "Patient," is a twenty-three-year-old white male presently residing alone in a Chicago courtyard apartment. Patient is a potentially attractive young man who appeared at his first appointment dressed in purple flared trousers, a torn blue T-shirt, a leather jacket with decal advertising a well-known hamburger emporium on the back, work boots and a headband that seemed to be a used belt. He chain-smoked through his first session, and all since. Patient was well-oriented in time and place, sensorium was clear.

Presenting Problem: Patient has begun therapy at the behest and funding of his parents. Though they expressed concern over the patient's failure to complete college, his arrest record, antisocial attitudes as well as general maladjustment, the parents' offer to pay for therapy was readily accepted by patient and appears to signal an attempt at rapprochement. Patient has expressed open apprehension at the prospect of being "shrunk," but admits an eagerness to make peace with himself and parents, boost self-confidence and social standing. Patient is weighing a return to college track courses and the postponed solidification of personality structure. Patient has joked that he's going along with therapy so he will not be written out of his father's will. He may have come here to forge his own—an inference which caused patient's amusement to cease.

Childhood: Patient's troubles began early, as if there were a better time to start. Third of five siblings, second of two sons upon whom an authoritarian father placed excessive demands. Patient was offered a conditional love based upon the completion of ritualized tasks of homage to the "old man." From the father, Patient learned the three P's of the anal triad: punctuality, parsimoniousness and punctiliousness—subsequently referred to, in the patient's terminology, as "my rut." During first session, patient described his father's note-taking, use of the dictated form letter in personal correspondence, his compulsive repainting of white walls as soon as he notices the slightest scuff marks. Patient's mother is an attractive, aloof figure with potential for seductiveness, were it not for her full support of her husband's caustic, disciplinarian approach. Overpowered in psychic strength by an infallible father and mother and bullying older brother, the patient found himself, to cite one of his favorite songs, "on the outside looking in." Internalizing the aggressor was his only solution. His frequent reference to resisting the Vietnam War is mere classic analytic resistance. All conditions presently afflicting the patient can be traced to this centrally frustrating constellation.

Who else but a person with an overwhelming sense of genital inferiority would consciously throw away a ruling-class future to "get his rocks off," as patient phrases it, working next to immense phallic machinery alongside the impulse-ridden, Id-ic elements of society? It is only since he has begun working that patient has been able to break his adolescent habit of carrying a large stick by his side at all times. At twenty-three, he reverts to childlike, attention-grabbing behavior in the presence of any parental figures and admits that he squelches the impulse to address everyone over the age of forty as "Sir."

What sort of cathexes could have created a character disorder in which a man identifies, from the earliest age, with the same menacing blacks and minority group rowdies who beat him up regularly when he was a child? Or make a man carry the same bologna sandwiches on onion roll to work for months? Or refuse, for the sake of an exaggerated masculine facade, to button his coat even on the most frigid of Chicago mornings? An undeniable element of masochism—undisguised by the rubric of "radical politics"—streaks Mr. P.'s confusion over object, aim and choice. Hostility to analysis has been a problem—though patient has stated that "this is the place where I get to let it all hang out." Like an infant delighting in the discovery of his own sexuality, patient is eager to let any authority figure have a gander at what he's got hanging. He has admitted to taking pleasure in "whipping it out" before friends and comrades. In the well-known reaction formation to his anal tendencies, Mr. P. has overcompensated *in extremis* with his rebellious attitudes and exhibitionist streaks.

Vita Sexualis: Patient recently reported that a female acquaintance called him "my sexy worker." However, this only frightened the patient out of her bed, reflecting the ambivalence which has thus far charged his relations with the opposite sex. With a pride reinforced by his so-called utopian beliefs, Dana P. admits that he has never been "in love" or felt a passion which has overridden his conscious control. Since patient feels he can never win his mother, he seeks aloof female companions who reinforce the feeling that he is somehow unworthy of genuine affection.

In keeping with this desire for frustration, patient has a tendency to seek out love objects whom he has little chance of obtaining. For some years, he has harbored fantasies over a best friend's companion and former "commune mate." (At one time, all three of them slept in the same bed!) Since returning to Chicago, he has become fixated on turning a wraith of a Polish-American checkout girl into his "A. & P. princess." (Patient admits that he never met a waitress he did not want to indoctrinate or impregnate—or both.) He refers to his latest interest as "the girl at the end of the shopping list." Once or twice, he has followed her, from several cars behind, on her drive home after work. But he has yet to make his approach. The attraction suggests that Mr. P.'s father-identified need to rescue, protect and take on responsibility for some frailer creature may finally be coming to the fore. The appeal of the cashier may also be a manifestation of the unconscious connection between sexual gratification and feces (in nickel rolls).

Summary: Mr. P.'s skull is loaded with goodies. Unfortunately, he practices a monolithic dream censorship, militantly blocking the uprising from within his unconscious. Mr. P.'s house divided cannot stand—in order to unite his warring parts, the triumph of the stronger compulsions is assured. Psychotherapy, in this case, must needs be the graveyard of defiance.

Somatic Symptomology: Migraine headaches most often caused by phobia concerning headaches.

Required Medication: Placebos (Buffered).

Recommended Therapeutic Approach: Antiauthoritarian. Patient needs to believe he is making his own choices and coming to his own analysis. Without external threats, Dana P. should become exhausted with his posturings and strut his way back into the fold. Patient wants to walk straight into his own traps—otherwise, why would he have set them out?

Diagnosis: 326.4 (Transient situational personality disturbance; obsessive-compulsive features).

8:08 p.m. The accommodation we dreaded was to ourselves.

"So we all became like our parents, while proclaiming how differently we were going to turn out."

"Spare me," says Annie, driving homeward.

"But don't you think Dana's a goner? Can you just accept anything?"

"In acceptance, there's wisdom." Yet I seem to be the one living thing that Annie cannot bring herself to accept. That's how I know she cares.

"And what about making judgments, intervening. How about change?"

"If change is so important to you, Pep, how come you've been the one who's changed the least?"

Now that she's dared me, now that we're rounding the last corner onto Annie's street, I've got to speak up. I've got to tell someone.

"I'm just a late bloomer. There's always a chance I'll become a published author one of these days."

Annie brakes. Her car bears a bumper sticker that reads, "I Brake for Lawyers." It should say, "I Brake for Epiphanies."

"Pep! Did you hear?"

"Not yet."

"I had a feeling, this morning, that a big yes may be on its way."

"You're the second person who's said that. How come?"

" 'Cause it was the first time in months that you didn't go on about your insomnia over the damn thing. . . . But why didn't you say a word about your book all day?"

I don't have to answer that one, because I know Annie will.

"Can't admit that you're after some recognition, too? I bet that would have undermined your purity."

"Annie, I was afraid none of them would give a shit. You're the only one I can count on to give me the proper level of applause."

"Come on, hon. I'm just the only one with whom you've got nothing to prove. . . . You know, Pep, real soon you're gonna thank the rest of us for growing away from your rigid idea of how we should be. Because so long as you stick around this group, you'll never be able to admit that you've grown up, too. But you have. We all know it. You're the only one who doesn't. You don't realize just how little we do for you. It's fantastic. You should celebrate, Pep. You don't need anyone but yourself anymore."

"That's to celebrate?"

I catch myself asking this question with a rhetorical inflection that belongs to some wary immigrant, some sorrowful Jew, some dogged street-corner Socialist. Why the sudden appearance of such an accent? It is making a last stand. It is not my own voice.

8:11 p.m. No one begins their own life until they've lost everything.

The Empty Rooms (2). Martin did not find his voice until there were no more slogans to shout. Upon his return to Oakland, he was hardly his own man, but he was no longer aspiring to be anyone else. He was neither vanguard nor rear guard; not an outside agitator, just agitated. He was ready to be what came most easily: a loner.

But even loners need silverware. They have to fold their sheets and take their vitamins. They have to purchase an indestructible rubber plant or two—the leaves fell off, Martin discovered, when placed too near the hot stove. Most of our leading nonconformists, including Martin, require furniture. Lamps, he discovered, need something to clamp on; chairs were invented for a reason; toast in the broiler is an approximate affair; and grievances, however collectible, didn't look as good on the mantel as miniature ships in a bottle. A few pots and pans inherited from communal households made up his trousseau, the Movement's dowry. Now Martin was going to have to be husband and wife both—and for so many years. It must have been because he had so much to learn.

His first classroom was a vast space on the third floor of a green-shingled monstrosity called The Casa Verde. This building shared a downtown block with two body shops, an auto glass center, a longshoreman's hall. Martin's view of this picturesque region was marred by an entanglement of electric lines and capacitators at window level, earning his hardwood expanse the nickname of High-Voltage Ranch. The one lesson he should have learned already was that he ought not to have rented an apartment—no matter how much of a bargain—with so much space to be filled. He should have known all about the high-voltage danger of spare rooms.

Into that room came Missy, the main person that he hoped to avoid. Actually, it had not been so difficult for him to see her. He didn't find her so sensual in waitress's polyester pinks. He had far less patience for her flightiness now that he'd given up the challenge of being her pilot. When she came crying for his help, he took silent satisfaction in a host of "I-told-you-so's." He knew Missy couldn't hack the boot camp regimen of the Women for Armed Revolt. Of course, she'd been severely reprimanded for "accidentally" leaving the rifles in the trunk of a loaner car from her father. Martin wasn't surprised that she was expelled from the house for the crime of "flagrant heterosexuality." He could have told her, if only she'd asked: to get away from a man, she needed a man. To stay away from men in general, she needed a man in specific. To be the woman that she was supposed to be without men, she could not be without a man.

He could not have told her that her latest flame would be a black speed freak who helped himself to Missy's tip money and cars but failed to give Missy a ride to an abortion. Martin wouldn't have predicted that she would now try to hang on to this worst of candidates for almost as long as Martin had hung on to her. Moose and Mina Monroe had finally forced her to move her belongings out of his rattrap and into the back of their pickup. Now she was in full flight from the fellow, who missed his free transportation something terrible. So what better place to hide out than with the one man she'd tried so hard to escape? She used Martin's empty room just to sleep between odd shifts—and soon enough, not even that. She quickly started up with a short-order cook named Spyros. Compared to the men she'd been around lately, he seemed so gentle and considerate. So solid—and yet undemanding.

Around him, she felt attached and yet free to spin her mania. It was love at first sight over a steaming plate of fries!

Missy was soon followed by Ayer, who needed emergency lodgings now that he and Annie were separating. Unable to show his wounds, especially around Martin, Ayer filled the spare room with bluster. He lined all four walls of his room with butcher paper, then provided crayons for any and all visitors to contribute to an ongoing mural. Ayer drew cattle for the High-Voltage Ranch. They were longhorns, wearing baseball caps. To find materials for his sculpture, Ayer made expeditions into the depths of Martin's refrigerator. His homage to the sour side of romance was fashioned from the festering lemons that Martin deposited on every shelf.

Through all the forced jollity, there was a tension between the two outcast prophets of the group. One of their first mornings together, Ayer laughed too heartily at Martin's burnt toast breakfast and blew a mouthful of hot coffee in his host's face—accidentally *à la* Missy. Their rivalry found more vigorous expression on the basketball court. They played in nearby Chinatown, the only playground where they were considered tall. But most of the time, unable to scrounge up Oriental point-guard challengers, they went one-on-one, shirt against skin, never admitted to another game being played out. On the court, Ayer usually won—but often because Martin felt himself letting up. He still deferred to what he saw as Ayer's greater need to come out on top. He convinced himself that winning didn't count, so he could retain the loser's privilege to grouse and nurture resentment. Annoyed at Ayer for throwing an elbow on a rebound or leaning out a knee to stop a drive, Martin was merely forestalling the moment when he would start playing dirty, too.

Annie was certainly encouraging him. One night, after she'd fortified Martin's manhood with collard greens, pepper steak and three bottles of Lone Star, they'd slithered down onto Annie's Tibetan rug and scratched a long-term and jointly held itch. And though it felt better than they'd expected, they both assured one another afterwards that it was no big thing. It couldn't possibly last more than a week or two. But continuing behind the back of Martin's new roomie turned their affair into a big thing. When Martin finally felt obliged to tell Ayer that he'd taken up with Annie, it was much bigger than just crying "foul."

This schism, Ayer had no speeches ready. No dire predictions—except a vow that Annie would never get custody of Ebenezer again. He moved his crayons out in a huff, leaving the room free for Martin's purposes once again. So that no one else could ever take advantage of his vacancy, Martin filled his empty room with a desk and a typewriter and his growing library of cinema books. Now that he'd acted on behalf of his own satisfactions, he could begin to forgive all those he'd seen do the same. He did not have to be the one to lose anymore.

8:14 p.m. Success: doing unto others what never should have been done in the first place.

Celebrate. It's a word I find hard to hear. Celebrate yourself, Annie's chanting.

That's not easy in Oakland. After our day in the pseudopastoral, the place looks ready for a communal hosing down. This city must be under some terrible stress, since even the sidewalks are cracking up. The pavement's gone ragged as a madman's logic. Sooty exhaust gathers around window frames, giving a worried outline to the staid sea captains' houses. Annie's block, which usually looks pleasant enough, is giving me claustrophobia. Everything in sight is of a piece, no less so than a Kurosawa re-creation of old Kyoto: all the eaves droop, all the empty lots menace, all the electric wires lead the eye toward more tangle.

At a final stoplight, Annie and I watch three sisters in white knee socks form a chorus line on the corner. They are showing one another the latest boogaloo variations, while licking sno-cones purchased at Jawool Brothers' Arab grocery. I see that the windows of the market have been replaced with plywood sheeting. But too late—since last month, one of the Jawools had been blown away in a nickel-and-dime robbery. Falafel and malt liquor, praise be to Allah!

We pull up alongside the picket fence that protects Annie's garden. The fence looks to be the only piece of carpentry for blocks around that's level. A piece of work, like Annie. With what tortured reluctance had she put up this barrier between her one-woman Ecotopia and the local toughs, pranksters, vagrants, lunatics, mutts! In the dark, from where we idle, she peers out to see if her fence has done its job for another day.

"The sunflowers survived!" she proclaims, as if the reprieve's undeserved.

"*Vive le peuple!*" I answer, recalling what's been wrought by the guillotines of this neighborhood's anonymous terror.

"They've made it through, just like us!"

Annie doesn't take the most humdrum of miracles for granted—nor recoil from quotidian perils. I recognize how hard she's fought to go on treating her casually wanton neighbors as "just plain folks," not as threats. I want to tell her how much I admire her ability to go on, placidly, single-handedly, with the business of community improvement. Refusing to yield to fear or to relinquish her gentle curiosity for everything in her vicinity—that's something to celebrate, in my book. And I realize now how much this curiosity, bordering on familial affection, is born of the acceptance for which Annie thumps. As she hitches up the parking brake, I want to tell her that I accept her, annoying tolerance and all. I want Annie to know that, in my own way, I too am fighting the battle to keep myself from becoming insular, shrunken.

"What are you up to now?" Just as today's party is ending, I begin to appreciate the guests.

"Oh, there's this silly ol' deal I've got to attend—"

"Really? A social event? With penisless ones? Can you get me through the door?"

"No, Pep. I wish I could, but this event's for women only."

An imaginary door has shut in my face. It's the door to the house where I always outstay my welcome.

"Is it some kind of consciousness group?"

"Oh, Pep! I can just tell what you're seizing on, but it's nothing like that at all!"

"Is it your coven? . . . Some moon goddess rite?"

"I only wish. It's this get-together at the house of the chief designer of Cupcakes. She calls it a hen party. I'm embarrassed to tell you, Pep, but all these women show up to swap clothes. They trade off last month's outfits. They give each other advice or their best colors. They take turns modeling in front of the mirror!"

8:17 p.m. Is this what's become of yesterday's neo-Amazons? This hen's nest the final abode for those spirited gals who were going to get themselves unshackled forever from biologically determined roles? Could it be that I'm actually pining for the feminists of old, with their dark panty hose hiding unshaven legs? Have they all reversed gears? Did they do it too late in the game? Where can I find those prime genetic candidates for bearing the best in all of us? And if I did stumble on one, how would I feel my way through all the fashionable layers they model? Would I find flesh beneath, or prickles? Or only more designer sadness? Women, women, all around . . . but they're rummaging in thrift stores for the perfect earrings, huffing away in leotards, arm wrestling one another, furthering careers while cuddling the babies of their cleaning ladies, collecting baskets, churning out Grand Marnier truffles, they have fallen into the mirror. In short, where are the women?

I know where I can find one, if I have to. But first, take one last shot at Annie.

"Come on, kiddo. It's a Saturday night, you know. We can go on a real Saturday night date, like we never have. Got a paper? I'll check what's playing at the drive-ins."

"No, Pep. No more dates. No drive-in."

Yet she's in no hurry to get out. Reaching back for her dishware and leftover salad, Annie tells me, "I've got an announcement, too."

"Swell. You've always got to stage your surprise parties. Only I'll bet this one won't come as any surprise to me."

"It might. I just got accepted into an apprenticeship program for textile making in Japan. It's for a year. You learn everything: from spinning silk to making dyes from natural sources, designing your own motifs. Every step from planting cotton in the earth to slipping the kimono on your back. It's a terrific opportunity."

"And do you get to be a geisha, too?"

"Bug off, Pep."

"No, it's very admirable. Taking the transoceanic plunge."

"We've all got to do it. You especially. You've got to quit hiding behind the group and dive into the world."

"Does that mean I'm officially on my own?"

"We're all on our own. That's the predicament, hon."

"Then I guess there's no more 'reassessment' of our relationship."

"No more."

"It's just like Missy's polyandry. Another fancy word for good-bye."

Annie gets out abruptly. I come around the hood to reclaim the driver's seat. She meets me halfway, mustering the last in her series of exasperated looks.

"You'll see it different real soon. Beginnings are hard. It's been a day full of beginnings. A day of gifts."

Only Annie could see it that way. "You know, you're getting to be a real crackpot."

"Am I?" Annie grins like she's just won an Oscar. She throws her arms around me, so that her covered dish stabs me in the kidney. We hug a hug that should last all the way to Japan.

8:20 p.m. What this country needs is a few good arranged marriages.

The Jewish Stud. That's what Annie called Martin. At least, he seemed to recall that she murmured it once. She must have in those first weeks, atop her armchair, on the floor, out at the beach by Half Moon Bay, or flopping into the enlarged pantry that was Annie's bedroom, big enough for a mattress and a Moghul erotic print. Stuck up at eye level over one pillow, the print showed some rajah and his water-bearing girl trying out one of those contortionist side-entries. Martin and Annie followed their lead, trying it every way they could, Annie often turning classic compliant maharani, her ankles chafing the back of Martin's neck.

What was the harm of yielding to this long-postponed whim? They became spendthrifts with the whim, using it up fast as they could because this recombinant combination was too preposterous to last. After all, hadn't they been the spokesmen for Big Mac's two "camps"? A working illustration of the unity of opposites—it was no different when they made love. And weren't they doing this just to get back at Ayer? If so, they needed to forget about him as often as they could. Sometimes, they needed to forget three or four times a day. Or some days, just once—but a perfectly modulated once, in the missionary with the pads of his feet pressing the pads of hers in symmetric squirm as they timed their contractions to the millisecond.

Pale shoulders wobbling slightly off the bone, small pubic tuft pressed down by tight jeans, wide peach nipples: who knows what will work until it works? Annie didn't mind modeling black stockings, backless silk dress and Martin spread her out before a fireplace and they wished they could have been more original but allowed themselves to be unoriginal sinners, satisfied copycats. With Annie, it was easy to get satisfied. With her, he always made it from observer to performer and then did an encore. Was it because there were no expectations? Because they renewed their contract week by week? Because Ayer's Hamletian specter lurked? Annie told Martin that she'd never felt like that with anyone before. No even Ayer? Not even. He felt even for what Oscar had done to him. The revenge of the Jewish Stud. Never mind that Frenchman do it *de rigeur*, Latinos do it with *salsa*, aborigines do it outback! Always choose the chosen people, since they've grave doubts about why they've been chosen and will keep trying longer and harder to please.

Never so good, Annie said. But six months later she was flirting with every hillbilly barfly. Because they were only a rebound, she said. Because, Annie said, never say love. Say renewal of contract. Six months later, Martin was taking his Hebrew best to the parlors.

8:23 p.m. All the pretense, all the posturing—so we can pounce on each others' genitals like bears.

On this summer evening, I'm sniffing my way toward the edge of the garden. No more jasmine or honeysuckle. I have a nose for other scents: evaporating ethyl, oxidizing scrap metal, the stench of city dumps, the reek of landfill, industry's cheap aftershave, *eau de* exhaust. I don't want to be one of the upstanding landscapers. I want no part of pruning and watering my patch of consciousness. Let me trample on a few weeds for a change. Maybe I'll become a sunflower slayer.

This is how I begin what Annie calls my "adventures." If only she could see how dreary they are! Nothing's more predictable than compulsion. Despite outward appearances, there's no element of risk or discovery to it. Though my car takes me a million miles from what usually drives me, this is a short and familiar route I'm on. This habitual movie of mine—like the kind you can see for a quarter a turn, the kind critics never review—is spliced into one loop. From urge to urge, with the same landmarks rotating past: darkened warehouses of installment-plan sofa beds, lo-ball poker parlors, rib shacks that resemble Texas roadhouses, haunted Chinese luncheonettes with Mom 'n' Pop swabbing up, iridescent gas stations deserted as Antarctic way stations, liquor store oases and then, the adult bookstores with plywood facades, the peep shows beckoning with yellow blinking bulbs. Down the side streets, under the piss-yellow anticrime lights a smattering of street hustlers sauntering on cork heels. These scrounging creatures of want are signposts of the approaching parlors.

It is a revelation every time: I, too, am a creature of want. But the point of my search isn't to actually find what I want so much as to be reassured, through one ghastly episode after another, that this can't be the place where I'm going to find it. Has whoring always been such a feat of illogic? I am here to taste the worst and then admire myself for the fact that I remain unquenched.

8:30 p.m. The major consolation of life in urban areas is that, no matter how peculiar your urges, there are thousands to share them.

Only in this heady realm of transparent pretense can everything be as it seems. All these storefront flights of fancy! On the left, there's Adam and Eve's, an Eden housed in a trailer manned by flat-chested tarot card dealers; on the right, Kon Tiki, where gap-toothed African Amazons wander about in grass skirts; next to Wandering Viking, a Mafia-run labyrinth of mirror rooms; and Xanadu Palace, its harem stocked with recent flunk-outs from beautician college. My preferred hangout of late is at the next corner—Dream Girls Studio and Health Spa. It's hardly a spa, hardly healthy. And why do they call these places studios? I never saw any artists inside, just space-age Toulouse-Lautrecs like me, wallowing in cut-rate eroticism, lingering in a world where sex has been quantified, defused of mystery.

I park two or three spaces discreetly removed from the pink facade of a former Japanese steam bath that's now bordered in neon, emitting a color much like overkneaded flesh. The Dream Girls' management has tacked up black vinyl sheeting behind the windows, beaded curtains to be drawn back seductively, exposing a walnut veneer door (complete with peephole and brass knocker) that gives the establishment an air of easily approachable exclusivity. A low-lit "waiting room" awaits: fat maharaja pillows floating on a sea of foam rubber divans, table lamps with marble vases shaped into nudes, swaths of Indian muslin pinned to the ceiling and ballooning out like sultans' trousers. But I'm never fooled by the dime-store theatricality. This is just a doctor's office gone naughty. But there are no forms to fill out, no need to recite symptoms. Ordinarily, I prefer the sort of medicine practiced here.

A car with a rattle, a heart with a rattle. Where I come from, you can't fix either without laying out plenty of cash. The Fiat's idling, and so am I. Can I book Federico for "leading an idle life"? The car's so much better at it than me. A small sign keeps flashing with large promise,

"Dream Girls! Always on Duty! We Rub U Rite!" But the message is blurring out, my windshield is getting steamed over. It's starting to look like a teen couple's parked here. My indecision is more strenuous. Trying to escape choices, it feels like I've merely set up a more difficult one. Why is it so much harder tonight to make that last turn toward the hidden customers' entrance? How come it looks more than ever like a dead end?

8:40 p.m. Fear of acquiring a social disease. Is there any other kind of disease?

The Local. "See what you like, Daddy?"

He never could get used to that name, nor to this moment of choosing. He always got shamefaced at the last moment about assessing the available flesh. He couldn't just reach for one or another package of body parts, showcased in see-through variants down a mile-long sofa like they were boxes of cereal on a supermarket shelf. Should he push the button for twitching pill popper or lobotomized big mamma? Root beer or lemon and lime? "How about it, El Hairy Chesto? Ready for El Good Time?"

Getting up from her place, this Creole in snakeskin slacks towered over him. But she wielded more than a physical advantage: she knew he was anxious to have his mind made.

"What's the matter, El Big Boy? You ain't shy, are you?" She cracked her chewing gum. Her face looked laminated. "You want my Shake 'N' Bake? My Quick 'N' Thick? My Long 'N' Wrong? You look like you can afford it, baby, with that fancy white coat. El Fauntleroy."

She had him pegged all right, but before he could say yea or nay, he was startled by a girl who emerged through the rippling curtain of bangles that led to the stalls. She wore a red polka-dot dress that just covered the tops of her wide, squeezable thighs. Her plump legs ended in tiny feet that slid into matching open-toed, pumps. Her face was chubby, but kind; the skin was unprotected by pancake. Even her weariness was inviting. The decision was made for him. He wrested his arm away from El Giant and strode across the waiting room.

"What's your fancy?" his choice asked. Her voice was thin but solemn.

"Half-and-half." It was just a formality. The real bargaining went on inside.

"I got a break coming," she told him. "I just finished with a customer."

He held his ground beside her.

"You want that one?" the night manager shouted from behind a Formica desk. "You don't like the others?"

"No."

"Wait then," the manager told him. "By the time you pay up, she'll be all rested."

She didn't look like she'd ever be rested, but he went for his wallet. He didn't mind prolonging the wait. He'd been doing this long enough to know the wait was the best part. And he didn't care if he got his money's worth. The point of a visit here was to make your money seem worthless. You paid for the privilege of being reminded that you were someone who had to pay. If there were times when you got something that could not be paid for, you tried not to tell anyone—not even yourself.

The masseuse returned to lead him into the parlor's lotion-smeared labyrinth of cabanas, saunas, homemade orgone boxes, "fantasy rooms." He could never figure out the floor plan, or how the parlors' traffic flow was organized. There weren't any numbers on the doors. But his choice kept him marching until she could push him gently into the assigned cubicle.

He was reminded once more of the doctor's. The slab on which he'd be "cured" always had a fresh, sterile sheet on it, though this one dispensed with those kinky pelvic stirrups. Instead of tongue depressors and swabs, he saw rows of body creams. Only one item had been borrowed from the examining room: vaseline. Petroleum jelly went everywhere, lubricating the sickest squeezes, easing the most unlikely dockings. Vaseline was the primal grease. It had clearly been present at the creation of life.

Luckily, his cubicle had been painted a very unscientific pink, and the temperature was kept nice and tropical. It was a ready-made cardboard womb: inside, it was all too easy to undress. He figured that the customers had to undress themselves, then wait for their girl's reappearance. He wondered what she did in the meantime. Haggle with the manager? Adjust contraceptive gear? Wet down her insides? The first few times, he stripped down as far as his underwear, in case some stranger burst in. By now, he knew that they were all strangers. When his choice returned, she found him comfortably naked on the edge of the table, counting belly hairs.

"Lie down," she commanded. They always tried to make him lie down before he wanted to lie down.

"I'll wait. I want to watch you."

"Suit yourself, Romeo." The first round was easily won. "What's your name?"

He told her and she said hers was Candy.

"I'll bet that's not your real name."

"How did you know?" Her question was serious, and unanswerable.

She stepped out of her dress, but kept on her coarse white panties. On the hip was sewn the word "Tuesday." Actually, it was Thursday. She kept on her walking shoes. Her breasts were bigger than he had suspected, with flat, bloodless nipples. She was a formidable woman, Germanic to the neck.

"They make us take different names, who knows why. I wish I'd chosen Shoshona. I wish I was a Kyoko. My real name's Sydney."

"That's a nice name." He was shocked that she had told it to him.

"Is it? I always got teased for it, my whole life. . . . Go on, lie down now. Don't look at me that way."

"Why not?" He reached out to put his arms around her, but she rebuffed him.

"After the massage . . ."

He yielded, lying on his chest. Sidney, or Candy, sprinkled talcum on him and began rubbing it around his back in tiresome circles. She wasn't much of a masseuse, but that wasn't news to him. He knew that this was but a brief respite between rounds of negotiations. While she stood over his neck, he lifted his limp arm off the edge of the table and put his hand on her thigh. All was quiet. Then he reached under her panties. It felt softer. He swirled his fingers in her hairs.

"Turn over," she said. But she looked just as bored now that she could see his obvious interest. Of course, she'd seen it before. At our most intimate, there was only anonymity, uniformity, identicality! Such standard equipment! Still, his hand went on working on her without interference and she even announced, without prompting, "Hold on a sec. I'll take this off."

She had large white hips to match her thighs and a light, gentle incision across her padded groin, probably the result of a cesarean. She'd tried to hide it with several tattoos of meandering butterflies. She had stretch marks, too, but they looked like playful scratches left by some animal with which she'd grappled. Her pubic hair was all in one twist and light brown. "Nice pubes," he'd wanted to tell her. Instead, he said, "You're beautiful."

He found it so much easier to say such things when he was paying for it. When he was being touched. When he meant it. He particularly liked the way her breasts looked from below, pulled his way by gravity.

"Get off it, I'm fat! I gotta drop some of this soon or I'll get canned."

"I thought maybe this was your first day."

"My first day, plus a million years!"

"Where would you go if you left?"

"I know a bar I could work out of."

"Why don't you do something else?"

None of them answered that one. She was finished applying powder. Quite a bit too late, she pulled his hand away from her, then leaned against the wall of the cubicle. The walls never went to the ceiling, in case a masseuse got in trouble and had to cry out. They had to whisper their bargaining or the manager would hear. If a girl talked too loud, you knew she wasn't going to give you much of a discount.

"Now, what'll it be?" Sidney asked nice and soft. "You can't go on touching me forever, you know."

"Why not?"

"You're a funny one." She tilted her head at him, and looked at him, really looked, with her wading-pool eyes. "You know why not."

It was almost like she was trying to remind him where they were. But that was his charm: to be here and be able to pretend that he wasn't. In here, he could get so much more charming, more conniving, more bold than he was anywhere else.

"What do you charge?"

"Ten for a local, twenty for a french."

"I don't like either of those."

"You *are* a funny one. What do you like? You want me to hit you with a belt?"

"I like to kiss . . ."

Kisses were the hardest thing to get. There was an interdiction against them in this and all other health spas. Strangely, the more ordinary acts were the most elevated. Kisses weren't just unsanitary, they were sacred. They were reserved for family, and most of these women had left theirs.

"Are you stoned or something?"

"No, I'm lonely."

Sidney tilted her head in a curious, affectionate way.

"Most men who come here . . . they know what they want. They tell me what to do and I do it. But this kissing . . ."

"If I just wanted to come, I could do it at home. I could do it all by myself, couldn't I?"

"I don't know. Could you?" Remarkably, she was blushing. They laughed together.

"I really like you," he told her.

"I'll bet you say that to all of them," she answered in a role reversal, making him realize the roles had indeed reversed. He didn't say that to all of them because most of them weren't worth hustling. He wasn't usually the hustler. Now he wanted to hustle her unashamedly, full-out, like he could nowhere else.

"You're not so bad either," she told him, hoisting herself onto the table beside him. "You're not like some of those wrinkled old geezers I get."

"I bet *you* say that to all of them." They were two naked people, waiting on a bench for a bus. Until he tried to pull her down.

"Wait, I don't do that." Again, the parlors turned the normal into the perverse. Oral sex was ultimate sex, and the missionary position had been outlawed.

"I'm too small in there," she stuttered. "From my baby. It hurts too much."

"Looks like you're in the wrong line of work then." He wasn't being cruel, he was calling her bluff.

"It costs more than you got," she whispered, while he kissed her neck and ears and shoulders, white even in this meat-case pink.

"I have what you want," he said, trying to get at her lips.

"I can't kiss, I told ya. I got a strep throat. You don't want to get sick, do you?"

"From you, I do." And he knew just what he was doing. His lips were on hers. She opened up at once and they tongued each other like crazy.

"Lie back down, please!" she was begging. He'd never gotten a parlor girl to kiss him before.

"Not unless you lie with me." He was reaching between her legs.

"I shouldn't, honest . . . my boyfriend, he's one of the managers . . ." He hoped, for her sake, that it wasn't the one on duty. "He can always tell when I've been balling . . . He doesn't like me to ball . . ."

"He'll never know."

"Oh yeah?"

"He sounds like a shitty boyfriend anyway," he gambled.

The gamble worked. He had asked Sidney to give him something better than he'd come here for and she was flattered by the request. On the outside, he would have been more honest—and felt more dishonest. In here, with the head start of having paid for it, his trickery could even win him the truth. He reached inside and discovered her secret. Fount of all pleasures, lure to disasters, end that brings beginnings, coveted dark hole! If he had a cunt, he'd be more careful with it.

"You're sopping wet." She was coming down onto the hard pallet with him. He mounted her. He fell on her broad shoulders, letting himself be buried against the enormity of her warmth. Get it up like Guevara! Lay it on like Lumumba! Screw like Sandino! Hump like Uncle Ho!

"Go on. You got me now. I'll have to charge you next time, you know that. But we can practice. Everything good takes practice. Just tell the night manager you got a local. He's been trying to get in my box for months. You sure are a funny one. Or maybe it's the moon in Cancer. Did you know that's where it was? I guess I'm a funny one, too. I got this problem. This thing for men. I figure someone's got to have my problem. Right, kiddo? Will you come around again?"

He knew that he would not come around again, and that she did not really want him to. He knew that she would never leave her boyfriend, and that he did not really want her to. The lack of possibilities held them tighter in their embrace.

8:40 p.m. The highest form of sex is understanding.

Involuntarily as I got here, I'm turning back. Nothing works more slowly than redemption, except a traffic light. At this hour, they regulate a few stray dogs that pant in teams down the center dividers and fewer unleashed members of the urban pack. Some wild hound! Just give me my own four plasterboard walls, festooned with my movie posters, my running toilet waterfall, my distinctive collection of English mustards rattling against the Frigidaire door! Suddenly, I'm aching to surround myself with all that defines me—until, if I'm lucky, it all accrues to my inner being, congeals around me like I'm a Popsicle stick. I want to sit forever at the center of the passions that demand the best of me. I need to get pinned down by my own centrifugal force.

8:50 p.m. In all of us lurks a good citizen.

And hitting the radio push buttons in search of melodies to power me there, I'm transported to a sunnier stretch of highway and no longer alone but riding with Big Mac, turning left, ever leftward in our utopian limousine, making a pit stop to unwrap dialectical tidbits or more likely potato salad, relishing those few moments when it was good, before the candles burned down and the guitar strings popped, then heading for our place at the barricades, fighting valiantly but refusing to wear name tags, then snuggling up with the whole yellow pink brown global commune in that big bed we cannot help sharing.

8:54 p.m. Give Ayer credit. We did all become "collectives of one."

Jump Cuts.

1. Flame by flame, the Fire goes out. No one understands why he moves back to Texas. How will he ever fit in? Who'll feed him? Then comes word that, gasp, he's taken an apartment. Just a roof to put his sleeping bag under, but next, it can't really be true, is a job. Front-end work. He's pretty good with his hands, if he just shows up regular and he has to show up to make payments on his first bike. Step by step, he's born again into what he was all along: a good old boy, in the goodest sense of the term. Good old boys could still sport untrimmed beards and skullcaps, they could even rant about the Lord once in a while. America's true mystics can be found in saloons, and underneath Ford transmissions. They're sure-thumbed, steely-eyed, droll. The only ones who really believe life is but a veil of jukebox tears. It doesn't bother them none that this one has a gift for preaching. They humor Fire's yen for sermonizing. They let him write homilies for friends' weddings. Hallmark cards with a twist. Finally, comes word of a steady girlfriend to share motorcycle jaunts into bayou country, with plenty of picnickin', Cajun-style. Fire's renowned for this crayfish etoofay—only his name's Jed again. Someone who pays his rent and wears wing-tips. Somebody

you wouldn't mind hanging by at the end of the bar. And Jedmas only comes once a year.

2. Her first night on the *tatami*, huddled against the Nagoya cold, Annie is visited by her dream sage. She feels like she's come to some final clearing. Christmas ornaments and caramel corn hang from dead branches sprouting from the maypoles of light. At the treetops, where stars of Jesus should sparkle, there are Stetsons. The folds in each hat wink like the Buddha eyes of her great-granddaddy. That's when a woman comes, looking for her son in the snowstorm, and helps Annie into the hut of woven bark where the Indian woman lives. She is just like Annie recalls her: young/old, mother/daughter, priestess/guide, Indian/Chinese, homemaker/nomad. She does not have to speak because she is light. Annie listens for a long time. She lets her eyes get lost in the woven walls. She counts three beads on the Indian's necklace, three blackened corn kernels. Three layers of robe, moccasins with three toes. Her guide opens a flap in the circle that's different from the one where she'd entered and points Annie out. Down a path, through a big front lawn, to a ramshackle Victorian, very cozy, like the place she grew up in. On the front porch, there are black cleaning ladies up on ladders, painting shutters, tidying up. They all smile like they knew Annie was coming and one of them says, "It's mighty cheap to buy on this street." Annie tiptoes through the house, dropping coins to mark her trail. Upstairs there's one big room with nothing in it but a poster bed, Confederate flags flying from each post. When she looks to see what colors the sheets might be, the bed fills with dirt. The Indian woman reveals her true voice for the first time and tells Annie to lie in it. When she does, she is lying in the backyard, which is untended and weedy. "Perfect!" Annie thinks. "So much for me to work on!" And she gets out of the bed so she can plant things. Push people into the good dirt. Jed falls in backwards, laughing. Martin goes willingly, too, but he keeps asking which tribe the Indian woman comes from. Ayer turns into a frog and leaps in. Missy dives headfirst, alongside the black cleaning ladies. Sitting Bull sits on top. Everyone sings gospel. In one of her palms, Annie finds the three black kernels. After covering everyone, she sows these seeds at once, making a hole for each with a nail. They come up in three shoots. She goes to fetch water from three faucets. Annie wakes up about then, in the middle of a freezing night, on the other side of the world. But she's lying in the rich compost of the past. Where nothing's wasted—not betrayal, not even frostbite. It is cheap to buy on this street. All they have to do is follow the path. Trust each other. Weave a sturdy fabric from their dreams. Dreams are what keeps us warm until we all get where we have to go.

3. Missy's restaurant keeps expanding until it's not Missy's anymore. Isn't that the American dream? To put yourself out of business. Off the map and into the backyard. Some people do their best work off the map. Spyros' Grecian Salad Dressing gets bottled, available at your local supermarket. He and the Missus spend summers in his native Macedonian village, where Melissa recruits just as many girlfriends and babysitters. Irena wins the local beauty pageant back in the subdivision, which is now not only incorporated but has its own cultural center: the Valley Players Theater Company, the Doodlers Art Gallery, plus a branch of Neiman-Marcus. She goes on to be Miss California, 2001. By then, the swimsuit flesh strut has been replaced with an *aikido* exhibition. Three falls to a contestant, with no undergarments allowed. The talent show features log-splitting, tractor-driving, jack-hammering. Irena sends in a video of her rock band, Acropolis. For an encore, she does bench presses with her dimples. She wins a two-week vacation at the Sea of Tranquillity Ramada Inn (American Moon Zone) and a scholarship to veterinary college in Leningrad and marries three dentists (at the same time) and visits her mom at her retirement cabin to exchange gossip. Every Saturday night, Missy drops in on the old restaurant, just to prove that the grinning lady up on the billboard really was somebody once.

8:56 p.m. I'm sorry, Carlos Marx. All history isn't the history of class struggle. History is the struggle between the people who make do no matter what and the people who can't stand it no matter what.

The Big Q (2). Their history stopped when they stopped seeing the prisoners. Martin knew it, but kept quiet in the back seat, while the women up front chatted on about cosmic massage and Ken-Po karate. Riding back from that last peek inside San Quentin, watching the gentle bay waters lapping against the prison gates, he figured they would stop because their bleeding hearts had bled all they could, or because they decided this wasn't their real constituency, or because they could no longer stomach something they could do so little about, or because they felt like they'd already taken a census of every last cage. They couldn't stop looking at the places they lived, so they would fight things out there. They couldn't stop breathing or eating, so they would concentrate on improving the quality of what they breathed and ate. Some obstinate types would even claim they couldn't stop thinking and might set about upgrading the content what they were allowed to think. A few zealots for humanity would go so far as to insist they couldn't stop loving and breeding, and would devise better ways to get those jobs done. But if they watched their t.v. screens with selectivity, chose their company with consummate care, they could avoid looking at those damn jails, and the hordes in them. They would act in their own self-interest now, like everyone else. That was more honest. Less abstract. Expunged of guilt. But Martin couldn't convince himself that it was really in his self-interest to forget about that singular threat to everyone which kept some men sitting and stewing and unseen. Arriving home, he found it was still morning and the day already done.

8:57 p.m. Home is where the heartache is.

Home again, home again, jiggity-jog. Leap from the car, sprint upstairs, race to get inside the protective custody of my Pit! One advantage to entering this darkened apartment is that there's not much to trip over, no room to fall flat on my face. The main comfort here is plenty of wall hemming me in, as insurance against wooze or swoon. I've found the switch that floods the whole place in light, though the single bulb's blunted by a red rice paper ball. Call me a one-bulb man—modern equivalent of the one-horse town—a one-room man, a one-frying pan man, a one-woman man (latent), one-track man. If, as my neighbor claimed so many hours ago, I've become famous within a twenty-block radius, then I've come home to famous socks strewn across the floor, famous stained underwear in the hamper, famous cobwebs, famous stenches, famous ants gorging on famous crumbs, famous stains, all my own, in a famously vacant bed.

8:59 p.m. The stunning possibility that everyone else may be concealing just as much anguish.

Hello, Bertolucci posters. Raimu glowering in the Fanny trilogy. Where's Jean-Luc? When he sees the red light district glow through the window, he'll be back for a feeding. Tonight, I don't have to open my window —the hole in it's unrepaired. Is the breeze through the breakage what gives me the feeling that someone's been here? That's the trouble with my social life. So much of it happens when I'm not around. Burglars, handymen, paper boys—guests like these don't need to be hosted. I check to see if the cat's left me a lizard cross section on the floor as calling card. I see no scattered robin down, either. This time, the clue that someone's paid a visit in my absence is the bathroom door. It's shut—now what reason would I ever have to do that? Will I find some disrobed gremlin in there?

No such luck. I'm peeing before I glimpse the note. Written on the back of a hardware store invoice, held down with masking tape, it's hardly distinguishable from the enamel atop the tank. Why couldn't the interloper have shoved his missive under the frame of my sink mirror, the way it's done by those coiffed women in perfume commercials. No high-gloss lip-print on this one, no thank-yous for a memorable night beside me and my cologne. It's a memo straight from the heart of Lorenzo Sunshine, who's fixed the interminable dripping in my toilet. Never mind that it's taken him two months to effect a couple of twists of my flusher float, as he's been rather busy with his third-floor Taj Mahal for the beauteous Princess Penny. The landlord informs me of more; he continues to press his limits, this invader who views his legal title as a search warrant. He could not help noticing, in the course of his intricate repairs, the deplorable condition of my kitty litter box. In his view, the kitty litter box is a public health hazard. Underlined: *public health hazard*. It could get the whole building condemned. If I do not show immediate improvement, I will have to get rid of my cat. He will be back in a week to "scope out the situation"—hopefully when I'm at home, though Lorenzo makes no such pledge.

I look down at the offending box under the sink. Actually, Jean-Luc barely uses it. Earthy Breton, anti-formalist, he prefers to leave his mark amidst real backyard dirt, not in this synthesized stuff from *le* supermarket. It's true that I haven't removed the kernels he's deposited here for quite some time. Why should I? They're so dessicated, they give off no smell. They're practically fossils. And there's about as many as there are raisins in a carton of Raisin Bran. I plead guilty to the charge that some of the litter has spilled over the side and down the gaps in Lorenzo's cruddy linoleum. A few inconsequential sand drifts, unavoidable geologic by-products of the ceaseless Pacific winds! As for a threat to health, it seems to me that if anyone is going to catch something from this, it would be me. But *il duce* of renovation is just looking out for my own good. Never mind that my lease specifies that I can keep one long-haired tabby. Name of Jean-Luc. Presently a health hazard.

9:02 p.m. One could die from this.

Living in this Pit is a health hazard. The deprivation is actual, the sense of living each day running uphill—that's as real as any microbe. Have researchers isolated the one that causes isolation? Why can't I be immune to the infectious invasions of people like Lorenzo? Or simply run upstairs and dump Johnny Cat down his ponytail? I really ought to do something—other than initiating stomach cramps. It's time to move out, that's all I can think. But isn't that just what Lorenzo's after? People like him have the rest of us coming and going. Taking advantage of our good taste, they get to grab all they want because they know we won't think it's worth defending. This squabbling is "beneath us"—until we find that everything beneath, below and around has been parceled off and taken away. Why make a fuss just to stay in a pit? The cause at hand rarely seems worthy of my best effort, the fight before me is never the right fight.

9:04 p.m. America doesn't need gulags, death squads, rubber truncheons. America has loneliness.

The Loneliness Mobilization. The line of march formed like the world's biggest party, with feigned disinterest and forced nonchalance, the shuffling of feet across imaginary doormats, a fretful migration toward some imaginary refreshment spread, mumbled excuses about the lack of a printed invitation. At this affair, everyone was a crasher. All of us or none of us! They assembled in downtown streets no less abandoned than they were. They kept coming until the mob was thick enough to hide in and the dusk deep enough to be called a Saturday night.

Veteran politicos had questioned staging a demonstration at such a time, but this organizing committee knew its "prime sector." The people they were trying to bring out were the very ones who'd do anything to avoid being caught by themselves on this most doleful moment in the week. The behavioral pattern of this target group was well documented; it was the inability to change that behavior which united them.

The sponsoring coalition remained confident, despite the skepticism which greeted their press conference some months back. A demonstration without demands? This could hardly be called news. A rally as a do-it-yourself workshop? A single television station reported the event as an item of "human interest." Activists and social scientists alike sounded the rallying cry, "Let's get the neurosis out of the body politic!" Who, they asked, wouldn't wish to add their voice to this great disharmonious whine? Who could resist this rolling confession?

By eight o'clock on that Saturday night, the committee had its answer, R.S.V.P. The party had become a bash. The official marshals, identified by their bluer-than-thou armbands, could no longer host this mixer. They ran out of all the first aid they carried: handkerchiefs (for weeping, not tear gas), party hats (in place of helmets), kazoos and one-liners. Yet the march continued to form out of nowhere, a wave of resentment, spawned by neglect. Unfurling their banners were the Lonely Clerical Workers, the Lonely Gays, the Lonely Seniors, the Lonely Disabled, the Lonely Veterans of Foreign Affairs; also the Rejected Rank-and-File, Despondents Anonymous, Art Ache, the League for Self-Pity, the Moaners Alliance, Incompatibles International, Youth Against War and Blind Dates, the Defensives' Defense Committee, the Anti-Social Socialists, Rights for Willing Victims, Daughters of the Pathetic, Center for the Incommunicado, Kvetch Brigade. These official delegations dragged their feet in unison, shrugged their shoulders to a drumbeat. They took to the boulevards shyly—as if a million people in one place could be shy.

At the front of this terrible procession, an honorary wallflower and her court rode atop a float whose theme was "Waiting to be Asked." The float was fashioned in soup-for-one cans and displayed a heroic frieze of women reading gothics by their night-lights. Behind came smaller tableaux, bearing messages like "All We Need is Like," "Brother, Can You Spare a Hug?" "Lower the Minimum Rage." Someone carried a hand-lettered placard, "Hypochondriacs Are People, too!" An all-Lesbian fife and drum corps skipped their rendition of "Bread and Roses" and went straight into "Sometimes I Feel Like a Motherless Child." A militant fringe known as the Netherpeople took up the dirge, "What do we want? Joy! When do we want it? Shortly!"

Police presence was light, meant to corral the stragglers, the saddest of the sad. Bag ladies and drifters were swept along. It was no consolation that there were so many of them. No one seemed in any hurry because nobody knew where they were going. They had no city hall to petition, no corporate offices to blockade. Their confrontation was with everything, aimed against no one. When, at last, they came to a wide city park that looked like a scratchy army blanket, everyone sprawled on it as if it were their picnic spread. Tables awaited them, displaying nostrums from various pamphleteers of the soul, from Wilhelm Reich to the Brothers Grimm and Quotations from Chairman Kafka, the Joy of Insomnia, road maps to delirium, the Anorexics' Cookbook, the Autistic Coloring Book. The authorized mobilization T-shirt was available, in small, medium or forever shrinking, deep gray or the ever-popular bluest blue, bearing the official slogan of the day, "Sulk Power!" Buttons proliferated, particularly the kind that popped off shirts, and lonely bachelors got theirs sewn back on for free. Food stands offered humble pie, gruel, sweet and sour whatever.

Everyone realized this was a *bona fide* demonstration when the generator shorted and the sound system went on the fritz. Feedback whistled through the speakers like an urgent homing call. After a delay, the rally opened with some obligatory folk tunes. "Guantanamera" was replaced by "Oh, How I Hate to See That Evening Sun Go Down." The introductory remarks were properly tiresome, getting everyone into a proper funk. A maiden in red flannel shirt offered a tirade on the antilonely bias of the media. She demanded equal time in advertisements for frowners; she insisted on full employment in the fashion industry for the deformed. She knew there was a class action suit somewhere in all of this. An ecologist linked the despair of urban life to the despair of the last horn-toed moose, the preservation of wilderness to the preservation of wildness, asking, "Have you ever seen a repressed dolphin?" A heckler rushed the stage, begging for shock treatment. A Nobel Prize-winning physicist raised the slogan, "No Atoms! No Atomization!" A Gestalt therapist in flowing kaftan called depression "the final solution" in social engineering and depressives "the ultimate peons." Instead of applauding, the demonstrators sighed. What got their approval was the starless night that cloaked their forlorn glances. When candles were lit, the leprous crowd cringed. This was no quaint candlelight vigil; it was a pause in lives that were vigils.

What a relief to be done with the keynote address! The fellow who delivered it was far too well-groomed and self-possessed to really be one of them. He even dared suggest why they shouldn't feel alone. "We are the people next door—and the people next door to them! We are a majority of misery! Vulnerablility is our weapon! We don't know what we want, and that makes us the force that we are!" Then came a nondenominational benediction, followed by the usual appeals. "This isn't a one-shot affair . . . we're going back to our communities . . . knock on every door . . . build a consensus around the issues we've raised . . . create an ongoing movement . . . win the war, not just the battle."

At this point, many of the participants were seen slinking away. Knock on every door? How about one? Build a consensus? They couldn't even build a relationship. They had not come to serve the myth that being alone was somehow good for people. They were not heartier for their isolation, they were further weakened. One night's play-acting couldn't change that. A demonstration, after all, is not the solution to a problem, but its expression.

As the rally dispersed, a splinter faction of the Netherpeople tried to provoke a riot. They linked trembling arms and charged the nearest facade, which happened to be the Swedish consulate. When the police drove them away with hoses, the militants battled back, ineffectually, with their tears. Drenched by the spray, they chanted, "We are loved, we are loved . . ." But few joined them. They knew easier ways to get attention. Or they had lost the taste for attention.

The party ended long before it had to. Those who'd arrived uninvited had to be sure they weren't the last ones there at the end. Who wanted to be caught lolling by the pretzel bowl when the lights came on and the stereo was shut off? Everyone left in a pack in order to make it less noticeable that they were going as they came, unaccompanied.

When the one million got home, they saw nothing had changed. The love seats were hardening from lack of use, the bathroom held the singular odor of its sole attended body, the sheets were soaked with the scent of a highly particularized anguish. The same bright posters and family portraits were tastefully hung, a gallery that never opened, over the divan no nude would ever lounge on, beside pillows dying to be crushed, next to closets of the heart that were cluttered with dry-cleaning hangers to a point of impassability. Some day, the millions vowed, a crowd will gather where it's really needed. The next march will tramp right through here.

9:06 p.m. "I've got mine"—nothing more horrifying than this phrase. But without getting mine, how will I ever know thine?

Tearing the note off the top of my tank in disgust, I find there's an envelope underneath. Sealed, stamped, official. Lorenzo Sunshine has been considerate for a change and brought me the day's mail. The paper is textured and the return address makes me flinch. This is the one I've been waiting for. I test its weight before ripping away. Not much inside, not much hope for me. But I should know, from vast experience, that excuses are what make for long-windedness, that a yes never needs embellishment.

> *"Mister Pepper—or should I call you Doctor Pepper?*
> *Okay! 'Films Against Their Audience' is rueful stuff, erudite, and of course I don't have to tell you that it isn't just about the movies. How do you manage to range so far and stay so funny? This will serve as quite a departure for our list. And my superiors are well aware of exploiting your local following. Let's do it. Will phone next week with an embarrassingly low offer on an advance.*
> *Looking forward to working with you on this project. Cinematically yours, etc. . . ."*

My first reaction is to get very resolute. This news is not going to make me do anything different. (Why not?) It is not going to make me act different. (I could sure use a change.) It is not going to make me feel different. (If only it would!)

9:08 p.m. Taking moments, surreptitiously, to admit that we enjoy being alive. They feel like splashes of water on the neck.

Happy endings aren't supposed to take place in the bathroom. According to my soon-to-be published collection, they aren't supposed to happen at all. No, this moment is pure Hollywood—and how can I savor it when I've so long railed at Hollywood as the enemy? When it comes to reaping rewards, I've always managed to write myself out of the script. The system's unjust—and the proof is that it does not bestow just desserts. How, then, can I savor the sweetness of this one?

Slumping onto my couch, the best I can do is start posing for that portrait in sagacity on the back jacket. How much smarter I've become in the last five minutes! How much more gracefully I've aged! But I have to stage this day's second set of festivities on my own.

Of course! There's always a late show at the cinematheque. Why didn't I think of it earlier? Probably because I assumed Big Mac would still be in plenary powwow. I should have known: we never lasted as long as projected. Now where is that screening schedule? In the bottom drawer of my overflowing desk, I've stashed all the cinematheque calendars for all the years I've lived in California. The circles I make around the films that I want to see are the only continuous log of my cerebral expeditions. Maybe I should think of my circles like the ones on Darlinda's feminoid poster. Sometimes the circles look like the opening to tunnels, a way in. Sometimes they look like patches. Sometimes they look like rings of worry. Sometimes they make me feel whole. On the schedule, I scan a life measured in movies made or missed.

Unfolded to three times the size of my bulletin board, the current listing has defeated the strength of a common thumbtack. Burst free, it's slipped under my *futon*. I dredge it out from a reef of dust. I speed-read past the previous week's tribute to Raoul Walsh. And tonight—can it be?—there's a star under the date and a banner in italics:

> "*Join us for Bastille Day!* A French banquet in the museum cafe followed by a restored thirty-five-millimeter print of René Clair's charming souvenir, *Le Quatorze Juillet*. Called 'the most Parisian film ever made.' First West Coast screening in a decade. Black-and-white, 1938."

Parfait! I am not alone. You never are once you've learned to appropriate other people's forms of expression, other people's tragedies. Culture—that's the most dependable entrée to the party. So what if the invitation is hardly personal?

Scene Six (On the Ideology of Happy Endings). This was the title Martin gave to the first course he volunteered to teach—at the coercion of that self-appointed principal, Dan Herbst. He stood before a movable chalkboard, a fold-out screen to his left, a projector on telephone books at the back, in a room strewn with Lincoln Logs and toy trucks. By day, this was a child care center; by night, it served as the headquarters for the newly founded East Bay Center for Radical Reeducation. A half dozen students in folding chairs awaited a lecture, unaware that this was the beginning of their teacher's reeducation.

TEACHER (voice quivering): "I never thought I'd be on this side of the classroom. Please, don't think of me as your professor, but as your usher. Each week, we'll watch a film together and try to do some thinking about it out loud. Tonight's feature is the quintessential expression of American small-town values, *It's a Wonderful Life*. Directed by Frank Capra in 1946. Now who brought the popcorn?"

STUDENT NO. 1: "Popcorn ain't no better for us than this Grade-B tripe."

TEACHER: "You make a cogent point. But all popular culture reflects the prevailing ideology of its period—particularly the movies, that great reflector. It is my hypothesis that the dynamism of Hollywood makes up for the lack of dynamism in most of our lives. The triumph of Hollywood is the triumph of enforced optimism. And the moguls of Hollywood are the great storytellers because the American story has never quite begun. . . . But I'm no expert. I don't believe in the cult of expertise any more than I believe in happy endings. Let's hear what you think!"

STUDENT NO. 2: "The spectacle is the show, man. We pay to see ourselves written out of the story. The higher the ticket price, the more we honor those who bring home to us our irrelevance."

STUDENT NO. 3: "I don't get your objection. Don't you think the working class has earned a few hours of hopefulness at the end of an unfullfilling week? Who are you to gainsay one of their few pleasures?"

STUDENT NO. 4: "I don't know much about movies, but I know what I like."

STUDENT NO. 5: "Don't they have happy endings in the Soviet Union, buster?"

TEACHER: "Any society that must believe in happy endings is a society recklessly at odds with nature. There are no happy endings in nature, only tragedies deferred."

STUDENT NO. 5: "Not in the Soviet Union!"

TEACHER: "Happy endings imply a society of just rewards. If you work hard enough, you'll marry Jean Harlow. I'm sure you can come up with other examples—"

STUDENT NO. 3: "Yeah. Happy endings are the Atomic Energy Commission telling us they'll keep us protected from underground plutonium for ten thousand years—"

STUDENT NO. 4: "Wasn't the Third Reich going to last that long?"

STUDENT NO. 2: "Happy endings do not take into account layoffs, underemployment, low wages, racist foremen, industrial accidents, claptrap housing, the fuzz—"

STUDENT NO. 3: "Or daughters with Down's syndrome, child abuse, incest, the high divorce rate—"

STUDENT NO. 4: "Jimmy Stewart could never be a wife-beater."

STUDENT NO. 2: "No one would march off to war unless they believed in happy endings."

STUDENT NO. 4: "A faith in positive outcomes is the seed of everything terrible."

STUDENT NO. 5: "Not in the Soviet Union!"

TEACHER: "Remember, the movies create a world that's been made to be photographed. That's only one step removed from a world made to be lived in."

STUDENT NO. 2: "Are you implying that the closest thing we have to Nirvana is a studio set?"

STUDENT NO. 5: "Not in the Soviet Union!"

STUDENT NO. 3: "I still don't get it. Surely, people have the right to their illusions. And they create their own all the time, without the aid of M-G-M."

STUDENT NO. 2: "Hey, man, the narrative form's an escapist scam."

STUDENT NO. 3: "And don't all classes crave an occasional escape?"

STUDENT NO. 5: "Not in the Soviet Union!"

Now Martin knew how his professors must have felt. The teacher raced toward the projector. He flipped the switch.

9:12 p.m. Once, they talked this way about books.

I've got just enough time to make the show. Two strides get me down the hallway to the Pit's only closet. From its placement and size, it's meant for overcoat and umbrella only, but I've managed to shove in my full complement of tennies and parkas and back issues of *Monthly Review*. On a hook, always at the ready, is my white linen jacket. Dare I rummage for matching pants? No, don't go all the way, don't get too splendid. Stick to blue jeans and leave the panama on the shelf. There's no need to complete this Halloween disguise. I just have to get a tad ostentatious to make up for a profession that's a tad superfluous. I step into my booth-sized changing room and *voilà*, Supercritic!

Only when fully outfitted do I remember about freshening up. At the sink, I reach under my jacket, through the middle buttons of my shirt, to dab soapy water under my arms, a kind of perfunctory bird bath that splashes mostly into the disputed litter box. This is followed by a weakling once-over with toothbrush and a futile attempt to pat down hair that, like an unruly son, has been going its own way since puberty. The best strategy is to make spinning moves in the scalp with my fingertips to encourage fashionable curls. Then comes one slice of the scissors on each side of my mustache—an act of optimism, just in case some lady sitting next to me, any lady, should ever wish to get past the walrus impersonation and onto my lips.

Double optimism: I scrounge behind the mirror for a special elixir in my cabinet. According to the label, this precious stuff is guaranteed to contain the natural olfactory triggers that cause females to come sniffing. Pure testosterone, I suppose, plus a gallon of ambergris! I've yet to notice this hormonal cologne having the slightest effect, but I nonetheless dab it behind both ears. More optimism: sweep the crumbs from my *futon*, should any random encounter find its finish there. Multiple optimism: spread out my pristine Hindu magic carpet. Red, lavender, ocher: those colors sing out like my new resolve.

I'm all set, except for my notebook. By reflex, I pluck a pocket-sized spiral-bound off my desk. How many times have I sat in the cinematheque, jotting notes and pretending to work because I was there by myself? How often did I come up with a cogent comment that just begged to be written down so I wouldn't be caught staring at the cheerleaders auditing Introduction to the Documentary? The notebook always goes on my lap, covering the parts that are the real culprits. I can't celebrate properly with a ruled pad. I must find something more responsive. Letting the notebook fall from my hand, I remember the obvious candidate. How could I have forgotten her for a moment? But will she be insulted by a last-minute proposal? If necessary, I can always pretend that I've come to tell her about the latest skirmish in the landlord wars. I can leave the conversation at that, unless she notices my linen jacket or picks up my over-the-counter mating scent.

9:16 p.m. Please, the cry goes up, take me as I am! But please, pretty please, don't leave me that way!

Must I go through with this? It's obvious how we make commitments to others—a matter of public record. What interests me is how we honor commitments to ourselves. Changing into my best sport shirt, a commitment. Coming up with matching socks, a commitment. The contract I've just signed isn't with Daphne Woo. The strongest binding agreements are enforced from within. The greatest pressure on a man is to complete himself.

I hop downstairs so jauntily, a veritable Fred Astaire. At Daphne's door, I give myself and her a last reprieve. One more movement in her direction, one ordinary gesture, and I'll be past the point of no return. With one knock—her bell, like mine, is nonfunctional—I'll start up the exhausting cycle of presentation and concealment, dependency and flight. The whole bloody charade! With a sound that isn't sure it wants to be heard, I'll announce that I want something from this particular someone. Knock, knock, who's there? Euripides. Euripides who? Euripides pants an' I kill you. You rippa dis ego an' . . .

Calm down, son. Name thy dread and banish it. How badly can this turn out? For starters, the lady on whom I'm so unexpectedly calling may appear with her sinewy arms draped around some beefy beau—probably a lead guitarist in a slashed muscle shirt, black chinos and nose ring. Maybe he'll hold a leash attached to Daphne's spiked leather collar. No, please, not Daphne! While I'm hoping that no man's ever trampled on her womanly dignity, I'm positively praying that she won't be home to give me the chance. What I fear most of all is that Daphne will turn out to be much as I see her: intriguing and intrigued, spunky and willing, all too qualified. Worst of all, after the women I've forced myself upon, hung around, glommed onto, after the alabaster coldness on which I've planted kisses, the indifference that only seemed to prime me, she may offer a galling accessibility, an unforced tenderness and obnoxious tendency to like me just fine. This can't possibly lead anywhere. But I hold my ground, actually a doormat. Knock, knock. I hope I'm not interrupting, intruding, affecting, appealing. Who's there? No one really. Knock, knock. I don't want so much really, just everything. Who's there? Just me really. My heart is bludgeoning down the door to my chest. My hand is a blind man's cane tapping for Daphne.

THE WRONG REAL

10:16 p.m. Meanwhile, back at the cinematheque . . .

"Everything a mix-up."

Or so Daphne posits in the dark. Her name is Daphne, right? Not Marcelline or Arlette, like that limpid-eyed frog ingenue up on the screen, not last year's one-night cameo or last decade's vamp. Glance away from the screen to make sure: yes, a Daphne is still a Daphne, unspooked and immune to the dark's transmogrifications, whispering, "All mix-up now. No way to be winding back."

Only Daphne isn't talking about my film within a filmgoer. Someone's pulled the rug out from under our reverie, run a visual shell game. Now you see the most Parisian movie ever made, now you don't. Poof! An edit leapfrogs centuries and continents. What's become of the earthy cabbie steering the soused millionaire about Monmartre's bumpy quaintness? Or the couples strolling in their shopworn finest? Our projectionist giveth, and taketh away. In one frame, *joie de vivre's* been outlawed. *Th-th-th-that's all folks!* Cut to: establishing shot, a phalanx of marauding Samurai, moving in formation through fortress gates toward zen pillage with ponytails dangling, armored calves flashing.

Voilà! Movie magic! Ready-made montage! There may be cobblestones in both pictures, providing plenty of shadowy contrast, but the zinc bars have been replaced by rice paper inns, the church spires by pagodas, the closed, painted sky of a studio Paris clogged with chimneys has been outdone by a lightening dawn south of Kyoto, ominous in its preindustrial breadth. The moaning accordions of an open-air quadrille give way to the plucking of *koto* strings in time with knocking of shields. Yes, Daphne, someone's fallen down on their *mixage*. See! Discontinuity reigns! Gawk! Image kayos image! Shudder! The Mercator projection hacked to bits and respliced!

Nothing brings me in for a quicker landing, unless it's the tearing of sprockets or an improper insertion of black leader. How dare they do this to me? I'm not ready to come back, back to reality. Interesting that reality is never referred to as that which carries us forward! While this mistaken shadow play grinds on, I turn my gaze away—only to find another Oriental apparition hovering close. The eyes are glinting beneath Daphne's hereditary mask, the folds of lid and delicate eyebrows arch skyward, the Mongol cheeks stretch with glee. This woman warrior's got a black belt in ironies. "I love the mix-up! Technical deficiencies, no?"

"Difficulties."

"Whatever, I love! Whole planet becomes Japanese!"

"It's the second reel of the wrong movie." And I am indeed back, the expert once more. "Some bozo must have put the wrong label on the wrong can."

"Who saying it's wrong?"

"The cinematheque schedule." But who can read it in the dark?

"Then you don't want surprise?"

"Not here, not now. I've already had enough for one day."

If I risk the darkness, it's so I can grope for the obvious. Contrary to popular belief, this critic craves the consolation of predictability. My highest rating—four Pepper shakers!—goes to those who are best at telling me what I already know, what all of us ought to know about ourselves by now. Never mind revelation, I want confirmation. Gimme a lifetime supply of those infinite befores, those boisterous durings, and those clearly demarcated afters!

"I think best art all surprise. Surprise and accident—that can be the greatest."

Okay, kiddo. Sure thing. But if cinema is mass dreaming, as has been claimed, then nothing in dreams can be called accidental. There are no mistakes in the movies, just jump cuts that don't meet our demands for linearity. It's real life that's full of rights and wrongs—surely not these altered moonbeams, never anything you love. That's why the critic needn't ponder what he does or doesn't like, but what it means to like at all. Labeling good and bad is the easy part. Don't bother with what works or doesn't work, stick to determining what is the work of all art! No film can be as "wrong" as its audience and the best films may even be against their audience—as a soon-to-be-published treatise suggests. The critic's task is to go beyond criticism and prolong the dream.

There's no reason that the dreamers can't wake refreshed and enlightened, poised to attack. My only objection to the organized sleep of entertainment is that everyone has to get up eventually. The major complaint I have about most films is that they have to end. This cinematheque crowd must feel likewise, since they continue to be transfixed. They carry on staring screenward in the hopes that if they stare long enough, the second reel of Kurosawa will just as suddenly revert to the third reel of René Clair. No one protests, or even titters. Nobody begins the insistent convict thumping that's usually prompted by the loss of sound or focus. Holding to our seats, all we want is to go on believing! Whether the projected titles say, "July 14, 1938" or "Paris" or "Once upon a very sad time . . ." they could just as well read, "Peace declared" or "Misery outlawed" or "Welcome to the future." As this audience goes on sitting, accepting the latest nonsensical turn of events, it is telling itself: if only we can sit long enough, we can make anything come true!

The passive position has been given a bad name. In culture, as in politics, it's far more instructive to get screwed than do the screwing—and far less depleting over the long haul. The main difficulty with getting used to being prone comes when you feel the need to rise up. The pitfall of this addiction to darkness is that it gets tougher and tougher to reemerge into the light.

Now there's no choice: the Samurai are stopped in one blurred lunge, the houselights come on at full glare. It's shock treatment for a room of catatonics. I feel sunstruck, like old stock indiscriminately exposed. We're all exposed now, in mid-gawk, at mid-movie. The curtained exits screech open. This is worse than *coitus interruptus. Cinema interdictus*, maybe.

"All finish?" Daphne has no trouble readjusting to the glare. She merely reaches under her seat for her straw hat and pulls down the brim. "Very short date."

"I'm sorry." A first sign of romantic intentions: this incessant need to apologize.

"Okay, be sorry. All your fault they show movie in half-and-half."

"Could be a bad omen."

"Oh, no! Please! You the one who is Chinese."

"How?"

"Always looking for signs from heaven. That no good. Maybe short date is best for starting."

"If you say so. But what are we starting?"

"Bad boy!" Up-to-date Daphne is delightfully easy to scandalize. "You not supposed to ask such question!"

The museum audience is forming a few of their own. If anyone can assuage these thwarted patrons of the arcane, it's the cinematheque director—appearing right on cue. He slips through a chink in the funereal draping like a Marx Brother escaping from one scene of mischief only to find himself in another. I recognize him as the director because, as they say, "we move in the same circles." An apt image, since a circle is invariably bent in on itself. I'd met him before he'd begun his rise, while he was still a volunteer dispatcher, working on the museum loading dock while writing a doctoral tome on the use of indirect lighting in *The Cabinet of Doctor Caligari*. Nowadays, he's identified as a charter member of Coppola's Zoetrope gang—at least, he makes sure to be seen at their garlic-drenched haunts. He gets his name in George Lucas credits for unspecified technical consultation. He's been known to beat Steven Spielberg at Parcheesi.

Hardly fazed, Cassavetes cool, the director fumbles under the podium for a microphone. From this podium, through that mike, I've heard the mumblings and bluster, the apologia and incoherent theoretical obsessions of a parade of genuine directors. Professional eyes should be spared having to be mouths: Nicholas Ray, with imposing eyepatch, the trademark of so many Deadeye Dicks who see only through viewfinders and moviolas, boasting drunkenly about the lasting existential impact of *Johnny Guitar*; Satyajit Ray, insisting that every great shot is but an amalgam of foresight and cloud formations (Daphne would have liked that); and Godard, maestro of the arresting non sequitur, hiding behind shades and coy dialectic. Only he could have tackled the q. and a. from groupies and grad students about tonight's Gallic-Nipponese epic.

"And can you tell us, sir, how you raised the capital?" (Giving blood.) "And how far did you come in over budget? (Not as far over as you were in Vietnam.) "Is there a symbolic determinism attached to the fact that the soundtrack suddenly switched into Japanese?" (An image, sayeth Godard, is nothing dangerous. It is a postulation about the world. If you don't approve, please rearrange. Better yet, close your eyes!) "Was it tough getting actors to handle the switch? What do you think of actors, anyhow? Should a director let them think for themselves? And who are your greatest influences? And why haven't you made a picture in technicolor? What was your final shooting ratio?"

This director knows that he won't have to face any such barrage. He blows into the mike to make sure it's on.

"Looks like the museum's outdone itself tonight. Uncovered the legendary bilingual René Clair. A truly international coproduction . . ." He pauses for chuckles that don't come. "It's one of those shipping snafus that come our way from time to time. Mislabeling on the distributor's end. The last reel was probably sent to Alaska . . ."

Still, the audience won't grant him a titter. Like me, they are powerfully stunned.

"The cinematheque policy in such cases is twofold. You can accept a refund, along with our apologies . . . or you can select any substitute from the permanent print library. Our archives are at your disposal!"

From the front row, an audible gasp.

"So what'll it be?" The director wants to know, like a waiter who stands with pencil cocked before his diners have opened their menus. "A show of hands, please. Your money back or the film of your choice."

And why not just grant us an hour more of darkness, with the roof opened to the sky?

"Anything you like! Every major American and European feature you can name!" He would make a good carnival barker if he wasn't so blasé. "Come on now, people. I'm talking infinite choice. Name your poison, the lesser of evils. I'm talking unlimited access. Your basic kid in your basic candy shop. I'm talking free will!"

He's talking participatory democracy. He's talking "control over the decisions that affect our lives." Like Tom Hayden did in the Port Huron Statement. He's talking power to the audience. He's talking councils of the soviets. He's talking mutual aid. But why bother talking that way before such unrepentant grandstanders? Who among us wants to seize power when we've paid for the privilege of being overpowered? What audience really prefers to clap hands and sing along? Do we have to reveal what we want? Must we go through the interminable wrangling and compromise and, most frightening of all, the coming to actually *like* one another that must accompany anything truly democratic?

Up and down the aisles, craning their necks, everyone's waiting for someone else to take the lead. Somebody with a megaphone, or a divine mandate. A movie *Führer*, a Cecil B. DeMille. The programming director in the sky. Why do I get the feeling they're all looking at me? It doesn't help to be widely known as a walking Warner Brothers retrospective. I catch several editors oozing my way. But they should know I don't volunteer my opinions for nothing! The oversexed Madame Butterfly and the underaged Little Bo Peep are sneaking knowing glances at me. Save your faith for someone more forceful, ladies. Maybe, in place of an alternate feature, we could stage a live drama: the trial of Martin Pepper, charged in the indiscriminate spilling of seed, assault with a deadly ambivalence. And quit prompting, Daphne! Don't nudge me with your elbow like that.

"Famous young critic!"

My mouth is stuffed with choices. There's a riot inside my catalogue head. So many goodies to grab! So much perplexing freedom! Any movie I want! But how do I know what I want except when presented with what I don't want?

"I think you're desiring to make them show a millions of things."

"Too many to utter." I am desiring to show Daphne a millions of things.

"Can't be so. Speak one favorite film. You giving me clue."

"Never."

"Is it double bill?"

"Triple bill, quadruple bill . . ."

How about a film to fit a mood, to coordinate with a favorite couch, to match scuffed shoes or bleary eyes? That's how Daphne might do it—a world determined by compositional shadings, in which the one untransgressable rule is to avoid clash. It would probably be better than any world we've come up with so far. Do I want a film to uplift me or a film that sinks me further? It's only for ninety minutes or so, unless I choose a Visconti or a Syberberg. Keep reminding yourself: it's only a movie! Yet the memory's racing, the computer's stuck on search and programmed to be thorough. I've become lost in my own archives. Shall I start under "e" for endearing? Then it's *Pather Panchali, Red Beard, The Last Laugh, Grand Illusion, Zazie Dans le Metro.* Under "a" for anticapitalist: *Memories of Underdevelopment, Generale Della Rovere, The General Died at Dawn, Invisible Stripes* (with George Raft and his bedroom eyes), *Two or Three Things I Know About Her, Un Chien Andalou, Battle of Algiers.* Under "m" for miscellaneous, always the largest bin in the unconscious, there's always *M, The Conformist, Phantom India, I'm All Right Jack, Pepe* (I cry every time Pepe gets separated from his horse), *Out of the Past, Double Indemnity.* Is it any surprise that I favor films with flashbacks?

And don't forget, since I never do, a little more "p" for pathos: *Nights of Cabiria, Tokyo Story, The Bicycle Thief, The Baker's Wife, City Lights, Il Posto, It's A Wonderful Life.* Why not that life? I'll swap ecotopia for the picket fences of Normalville any day. I'll trade all my consciousness to become earnest Jimmy, recipient of Donna Reed's soft-focus devotion. No Berkeley woman would dare beam up at a man that way without feeling she'd lost a part of herself—and so we're all losing parts of ourselves, sworn off beaming, given up the attempt to gaze upon what's best in one another.

Yes, of course! My suggestion's *Umberto D.* It's got to be the film of betrayal! A perfect warning on a first date. The story of a master who loved his dog so much that he had to place him on the railroad tracks. "Flick, Flick! Come back, Flick!" I am he, the discarded mutt. "Flick, *vieni qui!*" That little dog must be my heart, in flight from human fickleness. But isn't every true heart a dependent heart? Show me, Flick! How does the story end? Will we do anything to assuage our masters? Can every cur forgive and forget? And must I take another screening?

The director is waiting, the audience is waiting, my date is waiting.

"Hey, you!"

"I'm right here."

"No, mister. Where you go?"

"Fled into too many possibilities."

"Too many turn out same as too few."

"Don't I know!" A first whiff of love: this tendency to be overcome with unworthiness. "I just can't decide, okay?"

"Silly boy! You take it too serious."

Now, for the first time, she takes those sure, sculpted fingers of hers and strokes my wrist where it's draped over our joint armrest. Her touch feels wondrously cool, also elephantine tough, and the perfect reward for my having invited it throughout the show with a slouch toward her side. Yet I flinch and wrench myself free.

I have a hunch about what follows this maternal number, these comforting tweaks. Next, comes the kiss. And kisses, I'm told, lead to the harder stuff.

Withdrawing my skin from hers, I'm all the way back to reality. Another reason I don't want to be there is that I already know how this little subplot of ours is going to turn out. My crescendo of self-recrimination is predictable as a Grade-B Guy Kibbee potboiler.

"You make too many meanings." Daphne retreats as I have.

"Isn't that what art is about?"

"Art and life different."

How can someone be both so naïve and so wise? I ought to hug her, claim her, bottle her for personal use. But if I can get a Woo, then why not a Wong? If it's this simple to bag a China doll, why not hold out for a half-Thai, an eighth-Serbo-Korean? If a Daphne, why not a Cleopatra? A Rosita? A Lakshmikrishna? Why bed down go down hunker down settle down sack down run down this one as opposed to any and all other ones? Since I've gotten used to not having them, they always look better when I can't. The ass is always greener, as they say. So keep your options open, kid, your heart closed. Anyone who'll have me so readily is someone who can obviously be had. Too many does end up as too few. I've lost the knack of grabbing my fortune wheel by its spokes and slowing it to one particular stop.

"Last chance, gang." The cinematheque director is tired of shifting his weight from one *huarache* to another and tapping the mike against his hip. He's never had to wait this long for the party talk to develop. "It doesn't matter to me if it doesn't matter to you. Class is excused."

The back rows are already standing, sprung from their rarified dilemma. I don't feel in such a hurry. I would still second almost any motion, but wait for others to make it. But they are reaching for leather coats, down vests, satiny Oakland A's jackets. And I can't open my mouth.

The subject of my story may be activism, but its theme is passivity. Ten years since anything made me leap to attention, and I can't get out of my seat. Ten years of watching other people lock loins, ten years watching other people emote, ten years watching other people act and declaim, ten years watching other people shot, rescued, triumphant, terrorized, ten years of watching other people's tales brought neatly to conclusion. Maybe I never want to stand up, just lean back and watch adulthood pass. Leave self-assuredness and grit to the Samurai, or John Ford's cowpokes. It's just too hard for me to move at the moment—maybe because I know that it means beginning all over again. Carrying out my own missions! On my own power, at last! Instead, I'm having a power failure.

Daphne remains by my side, looking baffled and fiddling with her straw brim. She must figure I'm waiting for the aisles to unclog. Poor thing, she's never seen anyone glued to their cushion. She can't guess that I'm shooting for a Guiness Book of Records entry: most years, viewing not doing. Most lives led, vicariously. Most regrets in a twenty-four-hour period. Most hours lolled away without ventilation. Still groping for darkness, I'm not prepared to stumble out onto mortality's buckled sidewalks, trying to recall where I parked my car, wondering where I parked my life. I certainly can't face the perfumed garden beyond. This bountiful garden! It's here you'll find the most deprived people on earth. And I am one of them.

Look how they scurry: rats fleeing a sinking museum! Under the circumstances, this audience ought to use the emergency exits. Man the lifeboats! Okay, woman them! Out file the pigtailed therapists and the imitation Georgia O'Keefes, the cinephiles in suspenders, the Francophiles in fishnet sweaters, the Free Speechers turned mute, the amateur and professional cranks, the Peeping Toms of class struggle, the aisles of bodies briefly met and more briefly caressed. Heads bowed, their silence suggests they've been overwhelmed by some epic work, rather than humbled by their own imaginative collapse.

"Up!" Miss Daphne commands, but I pretend not to hear. I'm too sapped by this day. Finally, wondrously, I'm exhausted with the past. The statute of limitations has run out along with my energies. Could this be what passes for the wisdom of maturity? I don't really care to know what's wrong with me now, just so long as it's not what was wrong with me then. Hardly absolved, I'm merely fatigued with this life lived askance: one eye on the silver screen, one on the bomb. Sick of knowing too much to think I can make a difference, knowing too little to really do it. I am actually tired enough to climb into bed where I can climb into those dreams of mine where I am trying to climb out of the audience and into the movie. "Lights, camera, unction!" I am tired of watching. Maybe I'll become a short-order cook. I am tired of offering the "minority opinion." I am tired of opinions. I am tired.

And still, after all the banner-waving, head-scratching and palaver, never to have turned a single spade of earth!

"Quitters! Parasites!" Echoed from the darkened galleries, someone is shouting my thoughts aloud. "Running dogs! Careerist lackeys!"

A snarl this recondite can only belong to Dan Herbst. I'd forgotten all about him, but he hasn't forgotten about us. Caught napping by our premature expulsion, he's had to rush back—from a cozy *café latte*, no doubt—and resume his pestering. No need for him to leaflet the same crowd twice, but someone's obviously explained to him what just happened to our late show. Damn it, terrible Herbst. Where were you? Trotskyists are just like corner cops—never there when you need them. Inside the hall, he could have staged a most effective "intervention." He might have harangued us all he liked about war and fascism and the manipulation of the mass media, then made points as the only fellow around who knew what he wanted to screen—assuming there are any movies pure enough to make his sect's approved play list.

I can hear him start up a slow clapping. To his own beat, Herbst reaches back for a ditty we used to chant in the corridors and lecture halls of Steffens: "Working masses, off your asses!

Idle classes give off gasses!

Working masses, off your asses!

Idle classes give off—"

Involuntarily, I'm mumbling along, "Idle classes give off gasses. Working masses, off your . . ."

I can take up the chorus, if Herbst and his ilk don't hear me. I'll do my bit, when I'm certain it's not mandatory. I still know how to show solidarity, just so long as I'm in a separate room.

"Working masses . . . idle classes . . ." Herbst and I are no longer in the same key. What was it he warned me on the way in? "There are no individual solutions." I've known that from the moment I became an individual.

"You okay?" The cinematheque is empty but for Daphne and me. "I just checking."

"No, I'm not okay. Maybe I should just leave you alone."

"Not possible, unless you stand up first."

"It's better this way."

"Better you're giving me a ride home." The startling properties of the logical.

"Of course, I'll take you home. I'll even give you a tour of the Pit."

"That can be nice . . .Then after, you run away."

She stands over me and drapes herself in the coat that's one swath of black felt. Asking, "Where you go when you run?"

"To visit The Dream Girls."

"Is it better there?"

"No."

"Is it because we neighbors?"

"No."

"Is it because I too young?"

"No."

"It is because I artist?"

"No way."

"Because I not pure white?"

"Never."

"Because I woman?"

"I hope not."

"Because I go too fast?"

"Maybe."

"Because you can tell I am liking?"

"Just give me a chance to finish the movie . . ."

"Okay, I give."

". . . try me on for size one more night . . ."

"Okay, I try."

". . . and count me in when it comes to the rent strike. Or any other kind of strike . . ."

"I count."

"You see, this old boy isn't really that old, doesn't know how to do for himself, be for himself . . ."

"I see."

And hoisting me up, Daphne tells me what no one ever has before.

"If you run away, maybe I run after. . . . Maybe I catch you."

She undoes her monk's robe and wraps me inside.

10:31 p.m. Thus chastened, thus tried and true, yet somehow untried, fundamentally untrue, Martin Pepper began the long, slow descent into happiness.